The Twins

Praise for *The Twins*

'This excellent novel spans the entire twentieth century. De Loo interleaves the twins' story with that of two countries locked in bloody conflict. A moving read about humanity's darkest hour' – Sebastian Shakespeare, Paperback Choice, *Evening Standard*

'A huge success . . . a memorable and moving tale' – *Sunday Telegraph*

'Pleasantly elegant . . . de Loo poignantly details the closeness of their early childhood, that way in which twins can seem a single unit' – *Daily Telegraph*

'Best-selling Dutch novelist Tessa de Loo's real achievement is to personalize this still unassimilated period of history' – Amanda Hopkinson, *Independent*

'The tensions and rivalries between the sisters make for an acute and compassionate exploration of individual actions against a background of political upheaval and war. Throughout the novel recurs the question of whether old enemies can become friends, and de Loo's approach to history is made more impressive by her deceptively simple prose' – Louise Harrison, *Literary Review*

'The novel that has impressed me most this year' – Joan Smith, Books of the Year, *Independent*

'That rare thing, an intelligent historical blockbuster' – *Ham & High*

'A beautifully written novel. *The Twins* has already sold over a million copies – a much deserved success for an outstanding novel' – *Oxford Times*

'A flat-out masterpiece: exhilarating and unforgettable' – *Kirkus Reviews*

'A novel of considerable substance – one that is historically acute and richly imaginative' – *Publishers Weekly*

'All-seeing, it is brimming with scenes that are moving and sometimes disturbing' – *Der Spiegel*

'A fascinating and wonderfully complex story of memory and loss, woven with the captivating detail of historical truth' – Richard Zimler, author of *The Last Kabbalist of Lisbon*

'Outstanding. Women of this gallantry exist in every country but it is a rarity to find them so truly and vividly transmitted' – Nicolas Freeling, author of *Some Day Tomorrow*

Tessa de Loo

The Twins

Translated from the Dutch by

Ruth Levitt

ARCADIA BOOKS

LONDON

Arcadia Books Ltd
15–16 Nassau Street
London W1W 7AB

www.arcadiabooks.co.uk

First published in Great Britain 2000 (four impressions)
This B format edition published 2001 (fourth impression August 2001)
Originally published by Uitgeverij De Arbeiderspers, Amsterdam, 1993
Copyright © Tessa de Loo 1993
English translation copyright © Ruth Levitt 2000

ISBN 1–900850–56–7

Typeset in Monotype Ehrhardt by Discript, London WC2N 4BN
Printed in the United Kingdom by Bookmarque Ltd, Croydon, Surrey

Acknowledgements
Arcadia Books Ltd acknowledges the financial support of the Foundation for the Production and
Translation of Dutch Literature and of the Arts Council of England

The following quotations are reprinted by permission of their respective publishers:

Karl Marx, *Capital*, translated from the third German edition of *Das Kapital* by Samuel Moore and
Edward Aveling and edited by Frederick Engels, Swan Sonnenschein & Co. Ltd, 1896.

Friedrich Rückert: 'Kindertotenlieder' in *Penguin Book of Lieder*, translated by S.S. Prawer, 1964.

Goethe's *Faust*, Part II, Act V translated by Louis MacNeice, Faber & Faber, 1951.

Arcadia Books distributors are as follows:

in the UK and elsewhere in Europe:
Turnaround Publishers Services
Unit 3, Olympia Trading Estate
Coburg Road
London N22 6TZ

in the USA and Canada:
Consortium Book Sales and Distribution, Inc.
1045 Westgate Drive
St Paul, MN 55114–1065

in Australia:
Tower Books
PO Box 213
Brookvale, NSW 2100

in New Zealand:
Addenda
Box 78224
Grey Lynn
Auckland

in South Africa:
Peter Hyde Associates (Pty) Ltd
PO Box 2856
Cape Town 8000

For my mother and Maria Hesse

❧

Die Welt ist weit, die Welt ist schön,
wer weiss ob wir uns wiedersehen.

The world is wide, the world is beautiful,
who knows if we shall see each other again.

The translator warmly thanks
Rosemary Mitchell-Schuitevoerder and Jake Schuitevoerder
for their generous help.

Contents

Part 1

Interbellum

I

'Goodness me, what is this, a morgue?'

Lotte Goudriaan woke with a start from a pleasant doze, a light lethargy: to be old and yet not to feel your body. Through her eyelashes she followed the rotund figure, naked like herself under a dressing-gown of innocuous pale blue, closing the door noisily behind her. With evident distaste the woman waddled into the dim rest-room, between two rows of empty beds, up to the one where Lotte was lying – her body an old, long-drawn-out history of ill health between pristine sheets. Instinctively she slid deeper into the bed. The language the woman had made her inappropriate remark in was German. German! What was a German looking for here, in Spa, where every square, every public garden, had a monument with lists of the fallen of two world wars carved in stone? Her own country was swarming with health resorts. Why Spa? Lotte closed her eyes and tried to think the woman away by forcing herself to listen to the cooing of the doves that gathered, out of sight behind white ruffled silk blinds, on the eaves and in the courtyards of the Thermal Institute. But the German's every movement was a provocation in sound. Quite audibly she pulled back the sheets on a bed directly opposite Lotte's. She stretched herself out on it, yawned and sighed pointedly; even when she finally lay still and seemed to surrender to the prescribed quiet, the silence she produced was painful on the ears. Lotte swallowed. A feeling of tension was crawling up from her stomach to her throat, a mental queasiness that had also come over her the previous day when she sat, up to her chin, in a peat bath.

While she had succumbed to the heat of the sour peat that relaxed her stiff joints, an old nursery rhyme, hummed in an

3

elderly woman's unsteady mezzo, floated into the bathroom through a crack in the door. This song, that for the first time in seventy years, from a neighbouring bathroom, penetrated her awareness, released a mixture of vague anxieties and irritation in her – feelings an aged patient in a peat bath at forty degrees Celsius ought to guard against. A heart attack was lurking in the brown sludge, between the lumps, granules and half-decayed twigs that drifted about. All of a sudden she could not bear the heat any more. Laboriously she heaved herself up until she was standing shakily in the metal bath-tub, her body covered in a film of liquid chocolate that evened out all irregularities. As though I were already dead and buried, she thought. When she realized that her state would give the woman who was soon coming to rinse her down a foolish, alarming impression, she sagged slowly at the knees, back into the sludge, holding tightly with both hands onto the edge of the bath. At that very moment the song stopped as abruptly as it had started, as though it were no more than the flicker of a memory presumed lost.

The German could not tolerate being in bed for long. After a few minutes she shuffled across the worn parquet floor again, towards a table with two bottles of mineral water beside a stack of plastic beakers. Lotte followed her actions intently, despite herself, as though she had to keep on her guard.

'Excusez-moi madame...' With a slight inflection, in ponderous school French, the woman turned unexpectedly to Lotte. 'C'est permis ... for us ... to drink this water?'

The story that follows probably would not have happened if Lotte had also replied in French. But on a reckless impulse she said, 'Yes, das Wasser können Sie trinken.'

'Ach so!' The woman forgot the water, retraced her steps to Lotte's bed, exclaiming delightedly, 'You're German!'

'No, yes, no...' Lotte stammered. But she had already lit the fuse: crackling softly, the woman was coming towards her. Everything about her was broad, round and curved, an elderly

4

Walküre who would not go away. She stood at the foot of Lotte's bed, casting a shadow over it. She looked candidly at her, 'Where are you from, if I might ask?' Lotte tried to retract her impulsiveness, 'From Holland.' 'But your German is faultless!' the woman insisted, spreading her plump hands. 'From Cologne originally,' Lotte conceded, in the flat tone of a forced admission. 'Cologne! But that's where I'm from too!'

Cologne, Köln. As the name of the city continued to resonate in the rest-room that had never known anything other than absolute silence inside its walls, it occurred to Lotte for a moment that Cologne was a cursed city, somewhere you were better off not to have come from, a city totally annihilated to punish the arrogance of a people.

The door opened. A preoccupied, middle-aged man shambled in; he selected a bed and slid noiselessly between the sheets. In the dim light only his death mask remained vaguely visible. Everything was as it had been again, except for the German. She leaned over and whispered, 'I'll wait for you in the lobby.'

Lotte stayed behind, the victim of confusion and irritation. That sounded like an order: I'll wait for you! She decided to disobey it. But the longer she lay there the more restless she became. The pushy German had somehow succeeded in depriving her of her hard-won calm. There was no escaping her: there was only one door out of the rest-room and it opened onto the lobby.

Finally she got out of bed brusquely, slid into her slippers, tied her belt tightly round her middle and walked to the door, resolved to shake the woman off as quickly as possible. Entering the lobby, which was bathed in light, was like setting foot inside a temple dedicated to the goddess of health. The floor, laid diagonally with large tiles of broken white marble, together with an open atrium that gave an uninterrupted view of the balustrade on the first floor, created an illusion of expansiveness. This was reinforced by a ceiling painting of a fondant-coloured Venus driving out of the sea in a shell, ringed by plump cherubim. And there was the constant sound of running water, created by two grey-brown veined marble fountains on either side of the lobby, flanked by robust Greek pillars. A glittering spout emerged from a gilded female head, like a protruding tongue dribbling a thin trickle of water. The one fountain, discoloured brown from the iron-bearing water, which in better days the rich aristocracy of Europe had sought as a cure for their anaemia, was directly connected to the Source de la Reine; the other to the Source Marie-Henriette, a spring from which flowed velvet-soft water that drove all toxins out of the body.

In this sanctuary of eternal youth the elderly German had appropriated an antique chair for herself. Turning the pages of a magazine, sipping a glass of spring water, she was waiting for Lotte who approached her reluctantly, with the excuse, 'I'm sorry, I'm pressed for time.' The woman squeezed herself out of the austerely carved Empire-style chair. A pained expression skimmed over her face. 'Listen, listen,' she said, 'you're from Cologne. So I must just ask you what street you lived in.' Lotte sought support from one of the pillars, the ridges pressed through the towelling into her back. 'I don't remember that any more. I was six when they sent me to Holland.' 'Six,' the woman repeated excitedly, 'six!' 'All I remember,' said Lotte hesitantly, 'is that we lived in a casino ... or in a building that had once been a casino.'

'It can't be true! It can't be true!' The German's voice broke, she brought her hands to her head and pushed her fingertips into her temples. 'It can't be true!' Her bellowing filled the empty space irreverently, it echoed off the marble floor, rose up to disturb the peaceful scene on the ceiling. She stared at Lotte with wide eyes. Full of horror? Of joy? Had she gone mad? She opened her arms, came right up to Lotte and hugged her. 'Lottchen,' she moaned, 'don't you understand? Don't you understand?' Lotte, crushed between the pillar and the German's body, was overcome by dizziness. She felt an intense desire to escape from this preposterous intimacy, to go up in steam, to evaporate. But she was caught between her origins and her selective memory, which had long ago entered into a hostile alliance. 'You ... Meine Liebe,' the woman said in her ear, 'I am Anna, the very same!'

❦

The magic lantern of the early twentieth century leaves a lot to the imagination. The gap between the projection of one slide and another has to be filled in by the observers themselves. They are shown a *Jugendstil* bay overlooking the street, on a first floor. Two noses press flat against the window, two pairs of eyes anxiously scrutinize the passers-by down below. From above, all women look the same: hats on their pinned-up hair, long fitted coats with small buttons, lace-up boots. But only one of them is clutching a small shiny aluminium cash box under her arm. At the end of each day they see her on the opposite side: she shuts the double doors of Hope behind her and crosses the street with the day's takings in the cash box. As soon as she comes home the girls lose interest in the cash box; they cling on to their mother who first has to undo a million buttons before she can lift them onto her lap. Very exceptionally they are allowed to go to the shop with her; its name tells the passer-by that it is a socialist co-operative. Their mother, enthroned like a queen behind the high, brown cash desk, fetches a chocolate marshmallow out of a cardboard box for them; she is the linchpin of all money transactions. Since she has been at the cash desk takings have doubled. She is intelligent, hard-working and trustworthy. She is also ill, but no one knows that yet. The illness is slowly taking hold of her even though on the outside she continues to look like a plump, blonde Westphalian.

Another slide is placed in the projector – carefully – they have to be kept in proper sequence. The girls only go inside one particular room in the house with their father. Its permanent twilight is saturated with a bittersweet smell. Their mother is lying in an oak bedstead beneath a malevolent engraving of black rocks and spindly spruces, a stranger with sunken cheeks and blue shadows under her eyes. They recoil from the despairing, resigned smile that appears on her face as they approach. Their father, who gently

7

pushes them towards the bedstead each time, is himself one day lying on an improvised bed in the living-room. He instructs them to be as quiet as mice because he is ill and must sleep. Dejected, they sit next to each other on the sofa in the bay with their chins on the window sill and look down below – in spite of the woman beneath the rocky landscape, expecting the cash box to appear, to put an end to the strained silence. It is gradually growing dark. They have no sense of time; for them its passing is the same as the failure of the cash box to appear. Then the bell goes, hesitantly. They rush to the door. Anna always has to be the first, driven instinctively since birth; she stands on tiptoe and slides the bolt open. 'Aunt Käthe, Aunt Käthe,' she clings to her, 'have you come to fetch us?' 'Have you come to fetch us?' Lotte echoes.

The next slide suggests the projector is going to saddle us with a maudlin tale. On the sofa there is a rectangular coffin and Anna and Lotte are sitting on top of it, with their backs to a room full of unfamiliar relatives. Thanks to the coffin they can put their feet on the window sill. They have discovered that they can drown out the wailing and muttering by tapping the soles of their shoes against the window – the eerie black polished shoes that Aunt Käthe got for them – at the same time they are kicking out this incomprehensible hold-up in their existence and trying to restore everything back to normal again. Initially those present are inclined to be tolerant – after all, there are no rules of conduct for three-year-olds who have lost their mother – but when the tapping persists and the girls remain deaf to friendly warnings, forbearance turns into annoyance. Doesn't the foot tapping have something about it of the primitive drum-roll that, according to the illustrated magazines, accompanies the bushmen in Africa on the last journey of their deaths? A modicum of Christian piety might reasonably be expected of the children in these circumstances. They are ordered off the coffin but they refuse stubbornly, lashing out at the hands of those who want to lift them up from it. Only when the undertaker's bearers arrive in their sinister outfits and begin to haul the coffin away do they allow themselves be taken in hand by Aunt Käthe. After that they behave in an exemplary manner, apart from a small incident in the long procession that shuffles behind the bier beneath an unseemly warm spring sun. In the nick of time Aunt Käthe realizes that they should take off their black woollen coats that their mother in bed had sewn, specially for this occasion. Underestimating the resilience of her body, she must have miscalculated the season.

The principal absentee from the funeral is in hospital. Every evening at half-past seven Aunt Käthe positions herself opposite one of the walls at the side, holding hands with each child. Then a face appears in one of the many windows, just clear enough to convince Anna and Lotte that he has not been swallowed up into nothingness in the same treacherous way their mother was. They wave and he waves back with a large white hand that passes back and forth in front of his face as though he wants to wipe himself out. Afterwards they go to sleep reassured. He comes home one day, thinner and drawn. When they climb up to hug him he puts them back on the ground with an embarrassed, melancholy laugh. 'I mustn't kiss you,' he says weakly, 'otherwise you'll also become sick.'

The slides acquire a more cheerful character. He resumes his occupation as the manager of a socialist institute, located in the former casino, which serves workers who want to liberate themselves from their ignorance. 'Knowledge is power' it says in gothic letters above the library entrance. There is hardly any demarcation line between their home on the first floor and the rest of the building. Anna and Lotte, growing up by a happy turn of fate just like the caretaker's children in this proletarian palace of culture, play tag in the wide marble corridors, hide behind sturdy pillars and in the wings of the stage, play leapfrog in the immense circular hall, where their shrieks rise up to a high stained-glass window that coats them with carmine red and peacock blue when the sun shines through it. Lotte has discovered the acoustic; she stands directly beneath the highest point in the arched ceiling, throws her head back and sings the Cologne slow-tram song. Anna, by nature too restless to be able to stand still, and urged on by the boy from next door, uses a satin-upholstered Biedermeier couch as a trampoline until the springs begin to squeak and, dizzy from jumping, she falls, grazing her mouth on the mahogany arm rest. The couch is in the foyer, which still shows off its worldly *fin-de-siècle* luxury. Above a richly ornamented refreshment bar with copper taps chandeliers hang from a gilded, flaking ceiling. Dozens of stained mirrors hang round about and still reflect the compulsive gambling in the eyes of the former moneyed élite and their parasites, as well as a girl's face turning red with a bleeding lip. Her father has strictly forbidden access to this room. Contrite, she rushes to his office. With her wounded upper lip, she is at the mercy of his enquiring gaze. 'What happened?' he asks, his index finger under her chin. On the spur of the moment she invents a lie. Spontaneously she creates a different situation, so readily available to her that it already seems instantly more plausible than the truth. While she was playing in the garden, she confesses with downcast eyes, she fell against the edge of the wooden table on the grass. After he has staunched the blood quite equably, he takes her to the garden with him. 'So,' he says, 'let's see how it happened.' The treachery of the lie now dawns on her: the garden table is so high that a girl of her stature would have to fall straight down from the sky in order to be able to strike her upper lip on its edge. 'Ach soooo...' says her father in a melodious tone – a melody that makes her suspicious. Between thumb and forefinger he pinches a piece of skin on her bare upper arm and it gives her a pins and needles feeling. It is the only punishment she still remembers years later, a punishment that condemns her, all her life, to a stubborn preference for the truth.

But her wildness does not submit to being reined in so easily. Soon after that she breaks her elbow in a romp on the marble stairs in the hall. She rants and raves like a hysterical countess who has gambled away all her possessions, backed up by Lotte, whose capacity to feel pain and panic extends symbiotically to her sister's body. A plaster cast is fitted and the arm is hung in a sling. When Anna comes out of hospital thus adorned, Lotte bursts into tears again. No one knows whether it is from solidarity or jealousy. She only calms down when her own left arm is hung in an imitation sling improvised with a tea towel.

Now a Christmas slide. From the moment Aunt Käthe took pity on the children she never left them. Their father married her quietly, to avoid being forced to be separated from them after he was discharged from hospital because no medical intervention could alter the clinical picture of his prognosis: a man with an infectious disease that could only be influenced by time, for good or ill, was regarded as not suited to bringing up children. To Anna and Lotte it goes without saying. Aunt Käthe is there as usual and is decorating a snow-clad tree in the room; all the branches bend under an anarchy of witches, Father Christmases, chimney sweeps, snowmen, dwarves and angels. The pungent smell of evergreen branches mixed with resin gives them a foretaste of the natural world that begins where Cologne ends. Their father's youngest brother, Heinrich, a bony youth of seventeen, has come from his village on the edge of the Teutoburger Wald to celebrate the festival of the tree with them. He too has brought natural aromas into the house: hay and pig manure, spiced with a dash of rising damp. His image as a young, jovial uncle smashes to smithereens when, out of petulance, he garbles the words of the Christmas carols they are singing. His brother joins in with him, grinning. Suddenly they are competing with each other to find meaningless rhymes. 'Don't, don't,' Anna screams, horrified, hammering on her father's chest, 'the carol doesn't go like that!' But the men laugh at her for her orthodoxy and surpass themselves in inventiveness. Anna sings in a trembling voice in a vain attempt to get the proper version to triumph, then runs despairingly into the kitchen, where Aunt Käthe is slicing bread. 'They are ruining the Christmas carol,' she cries, 'Daddy and Uncle Heini!' Aunt Käthe enters the room like a goddess of vengeance. 'What have you done to that child?' Anna is picked up and calmed, handkerchiefs, a glass of water. 'It was only a little joke,' soothes her father, 'the Christmas child was born nineteen hundred and twenty-one years ago, now that's a good reason to be happy.' He sits her on his knee and straightens the large bow on her head, which had become crooked in the consternation. 'I'll teach you a proper song,' he says, 'listen.' In a hoarse voice, now and then interrupted by the cough, he sings the melancholy song: 'Two Grenadiers marched to France, They had been caught in Russia . . .'

The magic lantern projects a stage; the scenery is a forest of tall tree trunks. The theatre director is in search of a short actress; she must not be more than a metre tall. 'Listen, Herr Bamberg,' he says, 'I'm looking for a girl who can take the part of a poor child who has got lost in the wood. Now I'm thinking of one of your daughters . . .' 'Which of the two did you have in mind?' 'Who is the eldest?' 'They're the same age.' 'Ah, twins . . . curious . . .' 'Which did you have in mind?' the father repeats. 'Well, I had thought . . . the one with the darker hair. The blonde one seems to me too plump to play a starving child.' 'But she would never dry . . .' He fingers his moustache proudly. 'She is . . . remarkable, in that respect.' Mindful of the exhortation above the library door, he usually dedicates his free evenings to classical writers and poets. In between times, as a playful experiment, he has taught her a poem. 'Our Anna,' he explains, 'has the memory of a parrot. She can recite Schiller's "The Song of the Bell" without missing a line.' 'Good,' the director capitulates, 'you're the father, you can judge better than I.'

'I don't approve,' demurs Aunt Käthe, 'the child is still too young for such a performance.' But there is no gainsaying this father's ambition. So there the aunt sits on the day of the performance with Lotte and the father beaming in the front row, flanked by her seven sisters. In the wings, the wardrobe mistress hides

Anna's dress under a grey, worm-eaten winter coat and ties her white hair ribbon loosely to the belt. Without suspecting that it is a dress rehearsal for reality, that she is going to interpret this role for ten years without an audience, without applause, Anna presents such a believable, pitiful child on the stage that tears prick the step-aunts' eyes. After two men in hunting suits have carried her off between them out of the imaginary forest, she peeps inquisitively into the hall from the wings. The audience, no more than a collection of heads, does not interest her. She sees but one face in the semi-darkness, raised up towards the stage – that of the smallest person in the hall, insignificant and nondescript between the adults. Anna stares at her, overcome by an unfamiliar, terrifying sensation. Through the play and her role in it, Lotte and she for the first time exist as two individuals separate from each other. Each with a particular point of view – Lotte from the hall, herself from the stage. This awareness of separation, of unwanted duality, suddenly upsets her so she storms diagonally across the stage, through the two lovers' reconciliation scene – the unbuttoned pauper's coat flaps round her and the belt with her hair ribbon slips backwards and onto the floor. Aunt Käthe's youngest sister cries excitedly in Cologne dialect, 'Ach, look at that little one!' A roar of laughter breaks out in the hall. There is applause as though it is the director's stroke of genius. Unperturbed, Anna jumps down from the stage. She goes straight over to Lotte and only calms down when she has wormed herself in next to her on the same seat.

The projector, like a moonbeam, illuminates a bed with pale blue sheets. Beneath them Anna and Lotte fall asleep at night, their limbs firmly intertwined like mating octopuses. Without their noticing, the night tactfully unties this knot so that by morning each wakes up on one side of the bed, their backs adjacent.

The magic lantern has access everywhere – it shows us a classroom. It is as though we can hear the scratching of the dip pens. Anna's passionate temperament does not lend itself to calligraphy.

Whereas Lotte appropriates the alphabet with a steady hand, under Anna's regime the letters will not obey. After school Anna sits next to her father in the office and scratches letters on her slate, which he keeps wiping off saying, 'Once again, no good,' until she comes up to his standards. From time to time he goes over to spit into a blue bottle that is then closed tight so that the angry spirits can't escape. Afterwards, as a reward for her efforts, she is allowed to help with the cash. She deals tattered inflation notes into piles of ten with swift fingers – the balance runs into billions – until a fiery rash on her fingertips brings this pastime to a close.

Every Monday morning before lessons begin, the teacher pierces the pupils with her gaze and asks in an insinuating tone, 'Which one of you was not in church yesterday?' Silence prevails, nobody stirs, until Anna raises her finger. 'Me.' Immediately Lotte's higher, brighter voice follows, 'Me too.' 'Then you are the devil's children,' decrees the mistress knowingly. The sisters see their excommunication reflected in the other children's eyes. 'But you are still far too young,' their father protests when they inform him of the traditional duty to attend children's mass on Sunday mornings, 'you wouldn't understand a word of it.' They have never seen either him or Aunt Käthe go inside a church. Each Sunday they implore him; they can no longer bear the annihilating look of the teacher nor their classmates' teasing. Finally he puts his mug of beaten egg down on the table and rests his hands on their shoulders. 'Tomorrow,' he promises, 'I'll go to school with you.'

But when they are on the way, one on each side, it seems more as though they have to protect their father, so feverish and fragile does he look in his black coat that sways roomily about his thin figure. Leaning heavily on his stick, he has to pause every ten steps to breathe. The tap of the stick on the cobbles echoes behind him – a chain of echoes that prevents him from falling. They go inside the school building; he gestures to them to wait for him in the corridor and knocks on the classroom door. The mistress, thoroughly unsettled by the unusual interruption, invites him in with forced courtesy. Leaning side by side against the wall, Anna and Lotte fix their gazes on the door and listen. Suddenly their father's hoarse voice lashes out above the mistress's, which is struggling to maintain its self-control. 'How dare you! To children who are weaker than you!' Anna and Lotte look at each other dumbfounded. They straighten their backs; they no longer need to lean against the wall. A delightful, against-the-grain strength flows through them. Proud, triumphant, self-assured – they cannot put a name to it but it is there. Thanks to him.

The door swings open. 'Come in,' he says, suppressing his coughing. Anna crosses the threshold first, quickly followed by Lotte. They stand by the blackboard. The mistress is not on the floor in small pieces. Yet it looks as though her spine has snapped in several places. She grips her desk, with bowed head and sagging shoulders. The pupils, motionless on the benches, look up shyly and respectfully at their father, whose handling of the stage management is faultless. 'Right,' he pushes Anna and Lotte gently towards the teacher, 'and now apologize to my daughters, and that goes for the whole class.' The mistress eyes them obliquely. Her gaze immediately slides away again, as though it has come into contact with something unclean. 'I am sorry,' she says without feeling, 'for what I said to you. It won't happen again.' A silence falls. What now? Could anything be added to the mistress's humiliation? 'And now I'm taking them home with me,' they hear their father's voice above them, 'but they will be here again tomorrow. If I get to hear of anything like this ever again I shall be back.'

Fortunately the mistress kept the promise that had been exacted from her, because he would not have been able to carry out his threat. He is already much less able to cope with the trench warfare raging in his lungs. A new slide: stretched out on the sofa like a romantic poet, he deals with his administrative work, wheezing. In between he receives friends, who carefully hide their concern behind cheery chatter – his promising daughters in checked dresses with white starched collars are a welcome distraction with their poems and songs. That Lotte's song is interrupted as many as three times by a dry cough alarms no one, except Aunt Käthe. Experience having taught her to be suspicious, she has Lotte examined by the family doctor. For several minutes he taps her thin chest, simultaneously bringing the stethoscope and his moustache close to her pale skin. He asks her to cough, which she does very easily as though she has practised the cough like a song. 'I'm not happy about it,' he murmurs behind her, 'I hear a weak sound in the right lung.' Lotte stands in front of an anatomical dummy and fingers the pink heart with a slight shiver. With a bottle of cough syrup and an appointment for X-rays, he lets them go.

It is not only the father's declining days we see in the dusky gold-yellow slide but also the family's, in this ensemble. From the casino the same influence emanates as when gambling was still going on there: all or nothing, to the death. It was a building one entered full of expectations and left ruined, an alchemical trick whose secret recipe was kept within the four walls of the sanctuary. With his long, thin index finger he beckons his daughters over to him. Breathing heavily, he sits on the edge of the sofa. 'Listen,' he says slowly, as though speaking with a thick tongue, 'how long do you think I've got to live?' Anna and Lotte frown – this is a sum of astronomical numbers. 'Twenty years!' Anna bets. 'Thirty!' Lotte adds a little extra. 'So, that's what you think,' he says indulgently. He looks at them, his mouth open, with feverish, glancing eyes, as though he wants to say something else, but then he is overcome by a rasping coughing fit and drives them away with a fluttering hand.

A few days later, as soon as they come back from school, they are led to the bedroom by Aunt Käthe. A smell of red cabbage with apples and cinnamon hangs in the house. The company in a circle round their father's bed contrasts unpleasantly with this spicy-sweet smell. Uncle Heinrich, a crumpled cap in his hands crossed in front of his belly, stares at his sleeping brother with a farmer's distrust. Is this such a special spectacle that they all must stand there and watch? Aunt Käthe pushes Anna and Lotte towards the bed. 'Johann,' she says, bringing her mouth close to his ear, 'here are the children.' When he discovers his daughters, his eyes begin to shine as though he is surreptitiously amused by the ridiculous play-acting around his bed. He will get up immediately, Lotte thinks, and send them all home. But then his mood collapses. His gaze goes agitatedly from one to the other. He raises his perspiring head – from his secret inner world he seems to want to say something to them that cannot be delayed. 'Anneliese...' he utters. Immediately the head falls back onto the pillow and he sinks away again. On the sunken cheeks there is the dark bloom of stubble. 'Why does he say Anneliese to us?' asks Anna offended. 'He's thinking of your mother,' says Aunt Käthe.

After the meal, one of the seven sisters takes them away from the celebration that is not really a celebration. They are put into an unfamiliar bed, a raft on a strange ocean that they can only prevent from sinking by hugging each other fervently and lying without budging exactly in the middle of the bed. In the night, they dream that Aunt Käthe wakes them up and kisses them with a wet face, but when they do wake in the morning she is nowhere to be seen. Seven pairs of hands get Anna and Lotte out of bed and lift them onto a chair, to make it easier to dress them. 'Your father,' remarks one of the seven, pulling on an underslip, 'died in the night.' At first the communication does not produce any reaction, but during the laborious lacing-up of the boots Anna sighs, 'Then he won't have to cough any more.' 'And won't have any more pain in his chest,' Lotte backs her up.

The last slide shows the farewell. The funeral is invisible, as is the constant dreadful 'curtseying' that is expected of the girls on this occasion. Also invisible are the rows, Aunt Käthe's tears, her threat of legal action, and the packed suitcases. The last Lotte sees of Anna: she is standing half-way down the staircase in the hall, surrounded by members of the family who have come from afar. To one side, already cast off, stands Aunt Käthe, the traces of futile lamentations on her face. Anna is full of self-confidence, in her mourning dress, with a large black bow like a crow settled in her blonde hair. Next to her stands the uncle who made fun of the Christmas carols; on the other side an aunt with a bust of intriguing dimensions, on which a golden cross rests, glittering. Several unclear figures without distinctive features complete the row. Behind Anna, his bony hands on her shoulders as though he has already appropriated her, stands a stiff old man in a worsted suit with a ragged moustache and a rampant growth of tufts of withered grass sticking out of his ears. The last Anna sees of Lotte: she is already by the door, right under the stained-glass window. Only from her face can you tell it is her; the rest is thickly wrapped up as though she is going on a polar expedition. Next to her is a stylish old lady leaning on an umbrella, with thin leather gloves loose between her fingers and an elegant hat with a veil. All day she has addressed the old man, whose hands press heavily on Anna's shoulders, in a superior, teasing tone of voice as 'Lieber Bulli'.

Neither Anna nor Lotte are worried. They do not throw themselves into each other's arms, they do not cry, they do not say goodbye in any way whatsoever – how could they do that, they have no notion of the phenomenon of distance in space and time. The only one who makes the slightest gesture towards the fitting pathos of farewell is Aunt Käthe, who dashes across the hall at the last moment and in a torrent of tears presses Lotte to her breast.

2

'J'ai retrouvée ma sœur, madame!' Anna accosted a passing spa guest who shrank back horrified. Lotte recognized with distaste the impetuosity and clamorousness of long, long ago.

'It's unbelievable.' Anna grasped her by her shoulders and stroked her arms. 'Let me look at you.'

Every muscle in Lotte's body braced itself. To have to be inspected now as well! That familiarity provoked her repugnance – she was somehow being sucked in and lacked the strength to resist that pull. But to have been born virtually simultaneously from the same mother seventy-four years ago was not something she could walk away from, however sophisticated the mechanism of repression she had developed over half a century. Two shrewd, light blue eyes were looking her over curiously and somewhat ironically.

'You've turned into a real lady,' Anna decreed. 'Still so slim and with that pinned-up hair . . . sehr schön, I must say.'

Lotte regarded Anna's opulent form and short hair with reserve; it suggested something youthful and self-willed about her.

'I never managed that,' said Anna with a laugh that resounded with self-deprecation as well as pride. She squeezed Lotte's arm, brought her face close, a shining, determined look in her eye. 'And you have Daddy's nose, wunderbar!'

'How . . . did you come to be here?' Cornered, Lotte deflected her. Thank God, Anna let go of her.

'I've got arthritis. The body's entire locomotion system is worn out, you see.' She pointed to her knees, her hips. 'Someone told me about the peat baths at Spa – it's not far from Cologne. And you?'

Lotte hesitated, anticipating that what she was going to say would please her sister. 'Arthritis too,' she mumbled.

'It must be a family complaint!' Anna cried enthusiastically. 'Listen, let's go and sit somewhere. I can't stand up for so long.'

There was nothing to be done. Something inevitable had commenced; resistance was of no avail.

'Meine Schwester, just imagine it!' Anna rejoiced, half-way along the corridor. An old man dozing on a bench by the wall jolted upright, his bony hands clasping his stick.

Carrying cups of coffee from a machine, they went into the lounge dominated by a bold painting of a young woman in the company of a swan. By the time Lotte was comfortably seated and had drunk a few mouthfuls of coffee she was regaining some of her former equanimity.

'Who would have thought we'd ever see each other again...?' Anna shook her head. 'And in such an extraordinary spot too ... that must have a deeper meaning.'

Lotte squeezed the plastic beaker. She did not believe in deeper meanings, only in dumb coincidence – and it had considerably embarrassed her.

'Are the peat baths doing you any good?' Anna did not know where to start.

'I've only been here three days,' Lotte vacillated. 'The only effect so far is a leaden tiredness.'

'That's the toxins coming out.' Anna assumed an annoyingly professional tone. Suddenly she bounced up. 'Do you still remember our bath-tub in Cologne? With lion's feet? In the kitchen?'

Lotte frowned. Another bath came to her mind. She gazed outside contemplatively, where a wintry sun gave the buildings a naked look. 'Every Saturday evening my father washed us one by one in a wash-tub.'

'Your father?'

'My Dutch father.' Lotte smiled uneasily.

'What was he like? ... I mean, what sort of people? ... As a child I imagined all kinds of...' Anna groped in the air with her hands. 'Because I knew absolutely nothing, I made it up in my own fashion ... I dreamed of calling on you ... You have no idea how hard it was not to hear anything from you ... Everyone behaved as though you didn't exist ... So, anyway, what kind of people were they ... ?'

Lotte pursed her lips. A dubious attraction emanated from the idea of raking up old memories. They were lying deeply stashed away in a corner of her memory, under a thick layer of dust and cobwebs. Wasn't it better to let them be than to go poking about there? Yet they were a part of herself; there was something tempting about bringing them to life. In such improbable surroundings as the Thermal Institute, going after them at Anna's request. Challenged by the absurdity, even the immorality of it she half-closed her eyes and began to murmur softly to herself.

❦

On Saturday evenings he scrubbed his four daughters clean in a wash-tub filled with warm soapsuds, growling 'Sit still!' while his wife was taking advantage of late shopping hours. The ritual was rounded off with a glass of warm milk; he whistled as he brought it to the boil. Four nighties, eight naked feet – sipping as slowly as possible to spin out the time. After he had accepted four goodnight kisses he resolutely sent them to bed. In summer the scenario worked differently. Then a group of older girls from the village gathered on the overgrown football pitch in front of the house to do rhythmic gymnastics in the mist rising from the grass. The silhouette of a delivery van was outlined against the red sky, churning up clouds of dust along the sandy path as it approached at speed. It came to a halt at the entrance to the field, the back door was opened, and then the miracle was performed that took Lotte's breath away every Saturday evening: muscular arms hauled a piano out and placed it in a strategic position in the field amid buttercups and sorrel. Then a young man in an off-white summer suit sat down at the piano and launched classical melodies at marching pace into the evening sky.

The girls from the gymnastics club kicked their legs high and bent far backwards; they stood on their toes with their arms stretched over their heads as though they had landed on the ground all together with invisible parachutes. All to the pianist's inexorable quadruple time. Mies, Maria, Jet and Lotte, still warm from the bath, observed the spectacle from the edge of the fence until they saw their mother looming up in the distance, erect on her Gazelle bicycle, its handlebars seeming to sag under the weight of bulging shopping bags.

No bath for Anna. Soon after her arrival at the ancestral farm on the Lippe, it turned out that baths were regarded there as an exceptional, generally mistrusted activity. Immediately after the journey her grandfather sank into his usual chair, resting his clog socks on the edge of the cast-iron stove – an acrid smell of mould filled the small cluttered living-room – he was to die without his pale chest ever having been defiled by a piece of soap. 'I want a bath,' Anna whined. Mollified by the stubbornness with which the niece stuck to her principles, Aunt Liesl put a large kettle of water on the fire and filled a wash-tub on the flagstone floor. Thus was the tone set for a long-lasting habit, which Anna maintained single-handedly after Aunt Liesl had left the house. Years later, when she began to lock the door for the process, Uncle Heinrich rattled the handle and called with a titillated laugh, 'You must be absolutely filthy if you have to make such a fuss.'

The village children were thoroughly suspicious of her town manners and cultured accent. They pinned a note to the back of her coat: Go away! She was outstanding at school – her classmates observed her *tours de force* with a mixture of fear and envy, and shunned her company. She was gradually realizing that to be dead meant that someone would always be absent from now on and could not be brought back, even by your fervent longing that he would make short work of your tormentors with his powerful demeanour. According to this definition Lotte was dead too. Anna kept hammering away about her return, circling around her grand-father until he uttered viciously, 'Don't be so impatient! If she doesn't recover properly she'll die too. Is that what you want by any chance?' Desperately she turned to Aunt Liesl, who was spinning and sang in a thin high voice, 'Ich weiss nicht what's supposed to happen...' Her sagging bosom rocked in time to the wheel's movement. Above her head hung a print that the family had received as a gift during the war when a son had been killed in action. 'There is no greater love than to lay down your life for your country' was written in decorative letters beneath a dying soldier and an angel who held out to him the palm of victory. Anna slunk off outside in the vague hope that Uncle Heinrich could shed some light on the question. But he was sitting on the WC in the back garden, in a wooden hut painted dark green, tall and narrow, and lopsided because of an underground branch in the Lippe. The door had a heart shape sawn out of it; it stood wide open. He was sitting sprawled out, involved in conversation with a neighbour, who was engaged in the same activity on the other side of a field of mangel-wurzels, also with the door open. The tête-à-tête concerned the shooting match and girls – Anna did not hazard this rifle range.

She trudged despondently to the river, crossed the bridge and stood with shoulders drooped in front of a shrine to the Virgin, in the shadow of an overhanging elderberry. Someone had put a bunch of dark red peonies at the base of the statue. The mother was looking down devotedly on her child, a mysterious, hidden intimacy suggesting that all curious stares were excluded. Anna had the impulse to upset this introspection and to damage the pious face. Instead of that she tugged the flowers out of the vase, ran on to the bridge with them and threw them into the Lippe with an angry toss of the wrist. She looked at them as they floated slowly away towards Holland. One peony behaved deviantly: after circling wildly in an eddy it was sucked into the depths. Anna stared enviously at the spot where the flower had disappeared. To vanish from one moment to the next, she wanted that for herself too – to join her beloved absent ones. There was a stiff breeze carrying the smell of damp grass and straw. She did not resist as it took hold of her and raised her up, her clothes flapping. It went aloft, in a deafening rustle, straight into the cloudless sky. Far down beneath her she saw her grandfather's farm, half hidden beneath the crown of a lime tree. She saw the fields, the grassy alluvial sand banks where cattle grazed, the school, the church, the Landolinus chapel – the whole settlement on both sides of the Lippe, which tried to transcend its insignificance through desperate contortions, its inhabitants inflating the village's status with fabrications about Widukind who, with his Saxon hordes, had offered bloody resistance to the king of the Frankish empire there. Anna, hovering far above it, had nothing to do with it.

Lotte lay in the garden in a pine summerhouse that was set on a rotating axle so that it could be turned towards the sun or away from it as preferred. Stretched out in bed she turned with the weather – her narrow face on a white lace-trimmed pillow. Her Dutch mother drew a kitchen chair up to the bed and taught her Dutch; she also gave her a book of fairy-tales by the Brothers Grimm, with romantic illustrations. In German, 'So that you don't forget your mother tongue,' she said. She herself looked as though she had stepped out of the book of fairy-tales. She was tall, erect and proud; she laughed easily – her teeth were as white as the doves that flew to and fro to the dovecot at the edge of the wood. Everything about her shone: her complexion, her blue eyes, her long brown hair held in place by a few strategically placed tortoiseshell combs. An abundance of the joys of living poured forth over everyone who came within her orbit. But the most fairy-tale thing about her was her unfeminine strength. If she saw her husband lugging a sack of coal she rushed over to him to take the burden lovingly off him – she carried it to the fireplace as though it were a bag of feathers.

Lotte soon realized that she had ended up in a related branch of the family: those of the long noses. The head of the line looked strikingly like her own father. The same acute melancholy gaze, the

thin arched nose, the dark hair combed back with the same moustache. In fact he was a first cousin of her father and had passed his
genetic characteristics onto his daughters undiluted; a similar
proud and sensitive organ of smell was already developing in them,
via the round children's nose. Years later, when it had become dangerous to have such a long nose in the middle of your face, this
simple biological fact would almost cost one of them her life.

Depending on the position of the sun, Lotte was always able to
see another part of the universe from her lodge. There was the
wood, on the other side of a wide ditch that bordered the garden
on two sides. A group of conifers formed a natural gate by the
dovecot, a dark niche that drew her gaze to it – across a mossy
bridge straight into the twilight between the trees. From another
sightline she saw the orchards and kitchen garden where the pump-
kins expanded so fast that Lotte thought she could hear them
groaning from their growing pains, having become susceptible to
fairy-tales in which apples and bread rolls could speak. Then there
was the view of the house and a sturdy octagonal crenellated water-
tower – all in masonry with decorative arches in green glazed brick
over the windows and doors. One day she saw her Dutch father
climbing up there to hoist a large flag. Her breath caught when she
saw the diminutive figure at the top beside a flag that flapped in
the wind like a loose sail – was it not the fate of fathers suddenly to
be blown away out of the world?

At night she slept inside the house in a separate room. Then
the nighttime landscape unfolded: never-beheld hills and rocks, fir
trees and alpine meadows, mountain streams. Her grandfather was
hovering above them on the tails of his mourning coat; Anna was
hanging from his claws, screaming silently. Lotte dashed over hills,
up high, down low, to escape from the shadow he was casting over
her. The ground was rolling away beneath her, she was stumbling
over cobbles – she woke up screaming and coughing. She was lifted
up and put into another bed, where she slept in the crook of her
Dutch mother's arm without further upset.

'Then why did they rush off with us, like thieves in the night,' Lotte asked herself, 'straight after the funeral?'

Anna laughed wrily. 'Because it was a disaster. With the useful bonus of an extra labourer on the farm. It was a village of conservative, Catholic farmers – that's what it was like then. Father fled from that milieu when he was nineteen. He went to Cologne and became a socialist. That short-sighted old man had never been able to stomach it, verstehst du. And then, as soon as the son who had defected was dead, he came to rescue us from that hotbed of heathendom and socialism. A hit-and-run operation, to prevent Aunt Käthe keeping us.'

Lotte had a light-headed feeling. It was unbelievable that this grotesque family history concerned her too. All of a sudden, just like that, the wax was being broken on a bitter mystery that she had sealed down an infinitely long time ago: shhh, don't think about it any more, it never happened.

'But...' she objected weakly, 'why did he ... me ... let me go to Holland then?' It seemed as though she was hearing only the echo of her own voice, or someone else was speaking on her behalf.

Leaning forward Anna laid a plump hand on Lotte's. 'It didn't suit him that you were ill. A healthy child was a good investment, but a sick child ... Doctors, medicines, a sanatorium, a funeral: that could only cost money. It suited him that his sister Elisabeth offered to take you – although he entirely disapproved of her and was deeply suspicious of her fashionable mourning outfit. Her son, she said, lived not far from Amsterdam in a dry, wooded region, which was therapeutic for TB sufferers; there was even a sanatorium in the district. Na ja, you know all that much better than I do. This aunt herself had escaped from life on the farm in the previous century – imagine it, about a hundred years ago – to go to Holland as a maid servant and to marry there. I heard all that from Aunt Liesl, years after the war. Grandfather never showed the slightest interest in you any more, not even after you were cured. A cat that was sickly in its youth never grew into a healthy strong animal, was his attitude.'

'I wonder,' Lotte forced a smile, 'if he would have let me go if he had known that I had been entrusted to a Stalinist who brought me up on torrents of abuse against the Pope and the Church.'

'Mein Gott, really?' Bewildered, Anna shook her head. 'What an irony ... because I would not have survived for long without that same Church.'

⁂

Bread and hobnails, sausage and safety-pins, nothing was unthinkable in the richly stocked shop and adjoining café where Anna read out her shopping list in a clear voice. 'Do you want to earn ten pfennigs, child?' lisped the woman behind the counter; the missing front tooth did not restrain her from smiling with a grocer's cunning. Anna nodded. 'Then come and read to my mother twice a week.' The mother, blind from cataracts, sat in a back room by the window, crumpled up in a worn-out tub chair. On the table in front of her were the mystical reflections of Catharina van Emmerik. Each session of reading aloud had to close with the old woman's favourite passage: the one concerning the flagellation of Jesus before the crucifixion. The saint of Emmerik sketched the various stages of the flagellation without reticence: first he was whipped for a while with an ordinary whip, then a new, well-equipped soldier took the former's place, with a split whip, and as his strength diminished he in turn was replaced by a soldier with a flagellum, the barbs of which penetrated deeply into the skin. At each blow the woman hit the arm of the chair with her bony fingers, her mouth uttered moans that were somewhere between shrieks of pain and encouragement. Anna also reached a climax every time: the fusing together of her compassion for Jesus and her rage at the Roman soldiers and the actual instigators, the Jews. After she had closed the book with trembling fingers, the feeling of indignation slowly ebbed away. 'Come over here...' the old woman beckoned. Reluctantly Anna approached her chair. The old fingers that had drummed rhythmically on the armrest just before, groped at her plump limbs. Coolly Anna noted the signs of decay – liver spots on the white face, bags under the pale staring eyes, thin hair where the scalp shone through. 'Ach, stroke me on my head . . .' said the woman softly, squeezing Anna's hand. Anna did not obey. 'Bitte, bitte, stroke my head . . .' Was this part of the reading aloud, like an encore? Eventually she did what she had been asked, quickly and mechanically. 'Our Anna prays for money,' Uncle Heinrich chuckled to everyone who would hear him, 'till she foams at the mouth.'

Anna did not ignore the flagellation of Jesus, who had gradually been taking the place of her father. Each Sunday she sat between her grandfather and her aunt in the Catholic church that dated back to the mass conversions of the Germanic peoples. Looking round, her eyes had soon discovered a bas-relief depicting the event on one of the whitewashed walls. One day Alois Jacobsmeyer, the pastor, who was reciting his breviary in a side chapel, saw her walking down the aisle with a wooden stool in her hand. Intently, she turned to the right, towards a series of age-old bas-reliefs depicting the crucifixion of Christ. She climbed onto the stool and began to give Jesus's tormentors a tremendous beating with her fists. 'So!' resounded vengefully through the church. 'So!' Worried, scratching his head, Jacobsmeyer asked himself whether the relief would be able to withstand such iconoclasm.

3

The get-together was threatening to take on a slightly more caustic character. Lotte had been uncomfortably nettled by the scene in the church as Anna, not without tenderness, described it. Suddenly a razor-sharp, hideous feeling flamed up in her that had lain smouldering all that time.

'And in that way the Church gave all of you a nice little alibi for murdering six million people,' she said. Red blotches were appearing on her cheeks.

'Exactly,' said Anna, 'that's it exactly! That's why I am telling you, so that you'll understand that its foundations were already matured when we were young.'

'I do not believe,' Lotte slowly rose from her chair, 'I need to understand. First, all of you people set fire to the world and on top of that you want us to go deeply into your motives.'

'You people? You are talking about your own people.'

'I have nothing to do with that people,' Lotte cried, full of abhorrence. Urging herself to be calm, she permitted herself to continue condescendingly, 'I am Dutch, in heart and soul.'

Did any compassion seep into the glance Anna cast her? 'Meine Liebe,' she said soothingly, 'for six years we sat on the same father's lap, you on one knee, me on the other. You can't actually rub that out just like that. Just look at us now, old and naked beneath our bathrobes, in our plastic slippers. Old and a bit wiser, I hope. Let's not accuse one another, but celebrate our reunion. I suggest we get dressed and go to a pâtisserie in the street named after Queen Astrid. They have ...' she kissed her fingertips, 'delicious cakes there.'

Lotte's rage ebbed away. She nodded, ashamed that she had let go like that. Together they walked along the imposing passage to the lockers. Together – what a word.

A quarter of an hour later they descended the steps of the monumental bathhouse, involuntarily holding on to each other because it was snowing and the steps were slippery.

It was not far. They went inside a nondescript shop, walked through to the back, past a display cabinet of delicacies gratifying to the eyes, to a refurbished living-room where elderly ladies in fur hats were succumbing in complete silence to the matriarchal rite of coffee and cakes. A wagon wheel lamp fitting hung from the ceiling and cast flattering light onto the clientèle; on the walls paintings of imaginary landscapes in gaudy colours confirmed the atmosphere of reassuring kitsch.

They ordered 'merveilleux', an artful variant on a mouthful of air, held together with meringue, whipped cream and flaked almonds.

'Now I understand whom I heard singing yesterday.' The piece of meringue that Lotte was bringing to her mouth came to a pensive standstill midway.

'Who?'

'Yesterday, in one of the peat baths, someone was singing the Cologne slow-tram song.'

Anna laughed. 'I am guilty of bathroom coloratura if I think no one can hear. But ... originally you were the one who liked singing.'

Lotte frowned. Round about them was the sound of civilized chatter; the shop bell went now and then and a snowy customer came inside. 'I only went on to sing properly,' she corrected her sister, 'after I had fallen through the ice.'

❦

Lotte was standing on the frosty grass at the side of the ditch. Her sisters were gliding by, swaying on Friesian wooden skates, making a long chain with the gardener's daughters from a neighbouring property and an attached Brabant cousin who was staying there. The cousin's mother also appeared on the ice, a sturdy woman in a brown felt hat with a weather vane of duck feathers that indicated the wind's direction. She distributed sea-green and red striped peppermints to the children from a large cone. 'Just going to visit your Mum for a minute,' she said, holding on to Lotte's hand, 'want to come with me, lass?' She took a run-up and slithered screaming exuberantly over the ditch, dragging Lotte along with her in her pleasures on the ice. Thus they pelted and slid towards the house, the woman chatting non-stop in an incomprehensible dialect. They reached a dark green, half-submerged rowing boat that marked the start of the danger zone where the tower drained overflow water into the ditch; the children had been warned about this. 'No further, no further!' called Lotte, but the Brabant woman was chattering on as mechanically as the little wind-up locomotive at home that permitted no one to divert it from its idiosyncratic route between the table legs.

As the ice began to crack Lotte instinctively pulled herself free. She was not frightened. The firmness beneath her feet disappeared and the crystal floor opened to admit her into the territory of a sweet, premature death, ornamented with ferns and algae that moved together in a stream of air bubbles. The ice conscientiously closed over her head. As the variety of forms slowly coalesced in light green, turquoise and silver, she thought with regret of the miniature sewing box that she had been carrying since Christmas in a pocket of her underslip . . . Shame too about her new red pullover and the new-born baby. Like links in a chain her Dutch mother, her father, her sisters were strung out one after the other – a long way behind them came Anna, vaguely visible in a burst of filtered light. No more, she thought. No more aniseed rusks.

A dying scream rose out of the Brabant woman, alerting the skating children. They scurried over to the woman; she was standing in the water up to her heavy breasts, rigid with terror. Not another sound came out of her wide open mouth. The hat was still straight on her head; only the feather moved. 'Lotte . . . where is

Lotte?' cried Jet, the youngest, shrilly. She got her skates off, ran home and returned at a gallop with her mother, who slid over the ice on her front to the unfortunate woman whose lower body had already drowned. With her hands under the woman's armpits she tried to drag the heavy body out of the water. But the petrified colossus would not move, stuck firmly in the mud. The gardener's wife came running over, screaming. She observed the rescue from the bank, in no state to do anything, pulling hairs out of her head. Because of her wailing eventually her husband appeared; he had been a military hospital orderly before changing over to cultivating oleanders and orange trees. He stamped on the ice from the bank and, by fragmenting the ice, cleared a path to the drowning one. At that moment Jet's high-pitched voice pierced through the freezing air. 'Mister, mister ... Lotte's here ... Lotte, my sister's here!' With a trembling finger she pointed to a spot in the ice where a triangle of Lotte's imitation fur coat was shimmering through the ice. The gardener cast an expert glance at his sister-in-law, left her upright where she was and dived beneath the ice. An eternity later he returned to the world of the living with Lotte's dripping body. 'Stop,' he said, spitting water, to her mother, who was still tugging at his sister-in-law's body ever more desperately but had not managed to rescue more than a packet of sticky sweets, 'she's been dead a long time.' With his free hand he pointed to a trickle of blood dripping from the left corner of her mouth.

One glance at Lotte's slack body was enough for everyone to abandon hope. But the gardener, who had not hauled her out of the Lethe for nothing, refused to give in. She was laid naked on the dining-table. It was reckoned that her sojourn beneath the ice had lasted for half an hour. He tried mouth to mouth resuscitation, slapping her body all over, and rubbing her with a towel her mother had warmed on the stove. He persisted desperately until a growling sound signalled the start of breathing. Thus was Lotte slowly rubbed and slapped back to life, through the stubborn perseverance of someone whose actual speciality was keeping plants and trees alive.

She only properly regained consciousness in her mother's bed, ringed by interested parties who came to inspect the medical miracle. She was not surprised. Years ago Aunt Käthe had taken over caring for her, then someone unfamiliar took her by the hand to Holland, and now a total stranger had taken her to the world on the other side of the ice. What else could she be but sanguine about a pattern that kept repeating itself with almost aesthetically well-founded insistence?

Downstairs the other drowned one was now lying on the table. They had placed her hat on her belly with her hands over it, so that it looked as if she was reporting bashfully at the gates of heaven. 'It's my fault she's dead,' cried the gardener's wife, rocking tormentedly back and forth on a kitchen chair. 'God has punished me! I saw Lotte lying there all that time and I said nothing. I thought: if I tell, you'll let go of my sister and she'll drown.' Lotte's mother corrected her, 'Don't deceive yourself. Your sister's heart gave out because she had just had a hot meal, your husband said, and Lotte was saved because she hadn't eaten yet.' 'And I had cooked such tasty chicken livers with sauerkraut and fried bacon,' lamented the other. 'That couldn't kill a person, surely . . .'

Back at school, the girl who had drowned was allowed to sit by the stove. She was her old self again except for one small flaw: her speech had not entirely thawed. She stammered so badly that her privileged position by the stove was nullified because she was passed over when it was her turn to speak in class. It took too long for her to express herself. A little monster sat between her thoughts and their utterance, pulling back the syllables just before they left her mouth. A superhuman effort was required to speak aloud through this opposing force, her head was put under great pressure, her heart went wild, her paralysed tongue twisted out powerlessly. A cruel censor was standing at the entrance and let almost nothing through.

Her mother discovered that she did not stutter when she sang with the others. Her clear voice could be heard above everything, she knew all the verses and effortlessly improvised a second part without stumbling over a word. The sandy path beside the football pitch led on to an avenue lined by beech trees that passed through a district of old villas to the radio station's studios. Lotte's mother cycled there on her Gazelle and persuaded the conductor of the children's choir, which sang on the radio each week, to give Lotte a chance. The fact that she was the smallest was amply compensated for by her voice, which lost none of its purity even in the strait-jacket of a simple nursery rhyme. Each week the conductor selected someone to make their début singing a solo song of their choice. Lotte was placed on an orange box to reach the microphone. The artificial situation did not trouble her; the diffuse anxiety about stuttering that always lay dozing on the threshold of her uncon-scious – one eye open, one eye closed – disappeared instantly as soon as she started her song. Focusing on the conductor, whose grey mane waved in time with his baton, she broadcast 'In Holland there is a house', her favourite song, into living-rooms without a hitch. A couple of days later a picture postcard was delivered for her. 'You have a lovely voice,' was written in ornate handwriting. 'I hope your parents take pains with it.'

❦❦

'Ach ja,' Lotte sighed, 'the conductor was deported in the war. He was Jewish.'

There was an uncomfortable silence. How can there ever be talk of forgetting, Lotte asked herself, looking furtively at Anna. You have to be vigilant, with every representative of this people.

'I don't really know if it is wise,' she hesitated, 'to be sitting here with you eating cakes and behaving as though nothing was the matter.'

Anna sprang up. 'Who says we have to behave as though nothing is the matter? I was brought up in a culture you detest. You escaped from it just in time. Let me tell you now how your life would have turned out if you had stayed. Let me . . .'

'We know that past history of yours,' Lotte interrupted her wearily. 'The insult of Versailles. The depression.'

Anna shook her head. 'Let me tell you something about the place the Jews occupied in our lives, in my life, before the war. In the countryside. We'll order another cup of coffee. Listen.'

<hr />

It took years for the grandfather to die. He hardly came out from behind the stove – only in a warm draught did his bones stop rattling against each other. He hobbled outside once more on an oppressively hot day and stationed himself on a small bench in front of the house. Anna went to sit next to him. A black barouche came driving by; an old woman in widow's clothes was sitting on the box – wisps of grey hair clung to her sweaty face. She turned out to be a sister of his who lived six kilometres further on, on a large farm. They had not seen each other in twenty years. 'But Trude, what are you doing here?' his voice cracked. 'Well, if you won't visit me,' she snapped, baring three solitary teeth, 'then I will have to come to you.'

Uncle Heinrich, who preferred reading to milking cows, just like his dead brother, carried the full burden of the destitute farm on his shoulders. Above the stable doors of the Saxon half-timbered house built in 1779 it said: 'Grant, O greatest God – what thou commands from us – we will dutifully accomplish this – in the utmost devotion.' A prophetic motto, with the emphasis on 'dutifully'. While Aunt Liesl hurried back and forth between housekeeping, chickens and kitchen garden, Uncle Heinrich had the greatest difficulty allocating his attention between the seduction of the printed word and fifty pigs, four cows with calves, a cart-horse, fifty acres of their own land and twelve rented.

Even when doing business he scarcely put aside his reading matter. When the cattle dealer, Papa Rosenbaum, turned up, having scented that a cow was for sale, Uncle Heinrich would sit dourly in the kitchen with a book and continue reading during the traditional game of bid and counter-bid. 'What do you want for it?' Papa Rosenbaum clapped his fat hands together. His hat was set back on his head as though he were a Chicago gangster. On his square chest hung an antique watch-chain. 'Six hundred,' Uncle Heinrich mumbled without looking up. 'Six hundred? I'm sorry, Bamberg, but that's laughable! I'm laughing my head off!' He burst out in an epic laugh; Uncle Heinrich was just becoming engrossed in an intriguing passage; Anna made herself invisible in a corner of the kitchen. When he had stopped laughing, Rosenbaum made a case about the price of cattle in the context of the wretched economic condition that the country found itself in. Where was that leading? He could offer four hundred, not a penny more. Uncle Heinrich did not flinch. 'Four hundred and fifty.' Nothing. 'Do you want to ruin me! I really can't do business like that.' Papa Rosenbaum stalked out of the kitchen and closed the door behind him with a bang. The tail of his coat had stuck in the door, obliging him to open it again to jerk it out. Hissing, he pulled his coat back. Then they could hear him pacing up and down in the yard, complaining loudly. 'I'll go bankrupt! My family will starve!' He got into his Wanderer and started the engine, got out, came inside again. 'My soul, my poor soul is dying!' The whole arsenal of threats and self-pity bounced off the invisible wall surrounding the impassive reader. After the ritual had been repeated three times, Rosenbaum took his watch out of his waistcoat pocket. 'I've been at it for an hour already, that's how my business is going down the drain. Very well, you get your six hundred.' Later, after she had witnessed this ceremony many more times, Anna understood that the outcome of the cattle trading had been settled by the antagonists beforehand and that it was done for both their amusement.

A class photo was taken. Among fifty-four children's heads, Anna's was ninth from the left in the third row. She was looking straight into the camera, still wearing a black dress with a loose, drooping black bow on her head. Though the other children were standing close together there was a space around Anna as though they were instinctively afraid that homesickness might be infectious. Yet she had survived the village children's ostracism and, thanks to her inborn fearlessness, had won her classmates' trust. When she grew out of the mourning dress she received a collarless garment of indestructible dove grey material made with room to grow. The number of permanent tasks imposed upon her on the farm rose in proportion to the centimetres she gained in height. There was one day of holiday in the year: the expedition to Wewelsburg, a medieval castle not far from the village. The hay carts were decorated with birch bark and coloured paper and pulled by cart-horses, and everyone fought for a place on the cart of Lampen-Heini, a rich farmer who had swift, light horses. On the way they forgot everyday life, which was becoming increasingly meagre, and exuberantly sang walking songs.

They had a whole lot to forget. The millions of unemployed in the towns, for example, who had no money to buy anything, so the farm butter, potatoes and pork kept being sent back. Because of the rent, artificial fertilizers and taxes they could not afford, they could only dream of a pair of new shoes or a skein of wool to mend stockings. There was a state of emergency in the Ruhr area. The unemployed were being sent out to the countryside to work for the farmers in return for bed and board. The children came next, the church doled them out to every willing farmer's wife. The mysterious arrival of the pale, listless children and the almost metaphysical mediating role of the church so moved the imaginations of Anna and her friends that they invented a game: 'The Ruhr children arrive'. With a stick they drew an imaginary village in the compressed earth, with a church and the farms scattered around. They took it in turns to play mother. She fetched a Ruhr child from the church, walked through the village with it and brought it into a house they had designed. What happened after that did not bother them – it was about accepting a poor child; it touched their awakening maternal instinct. Anna played passionately, identifying with the displaced children, until the game became unexpectedly real in the person of Nettchen, who was brought home by Aunt Liesl.

This was a Ruhr child in flesh and blood. She came into the house with Aunt Liesl, spindly and grimy and in worn-out shoes. Two long brown plaits were pinned on top of her head; there were scabs on her lips which she could not leave alone. She laughed mysteriously at everything they said to her but said nothing in reply. Initially they imagined that Nettchen could not speak, but eventually, once she opened up falteringly, it appeared that she simply did not have many thoughts. She could not keep up at school. She came home with corrected homework – underneath on the slate the teacher had written: 'Dear Anna, aren't you ashamed to let Nettchen go to school with such exercises? Is there no time for you to help her?' Anna could not ignore this challenge. Evening after evening she dedicated herself with iron discipline to the renovation of Nettchen's neglected intellect. She was baffled that her efforts bore no fruit at all. Nettchen's mysterious laugh at every question she persisted in answering incorrectly drove Anna to despair. 'Why give yourself all that trouble?' Uncle Heinrich said laconically. 'Isn't Nettchen much better off as she is than you or I?'

Nettchen was certainly interested in love. The handsomest of all the boys living on the banks of the Lippe for miles around was in love with Aunt Liesl. Each Sunday Leon Rosenbaum came to the farm with a bunch of flowers. Their impossible love hastened to an untimely end on a rusty garden bench overlooking a bed of young cabbages. They were mute about what they had to say to each other. Instead they held each other's hand and mumbled generalities that instantly evaporated. Anna and Nettchen lay behind the gooseberry bushes, expecting greater boldness. Sometimes Leon gave Aunt Liesl a chaste kiss. Her bosom rose and fell languorously, the golden cross heaved with it and Nettchen pinched Anna's arm.

During the Friday liturgy Anna grasped a vague sense of the connection between the half-heartedness of the advances and the ending of the ever-recurring passage 'Flectamus genua' uttered in kneeling position: 'Let us pray for the Church, the Pope, the bishops, the government, the sick, travellers, the shipwrecked...' No single category was missed out, not even the Jews. When it came to their turn, at the very end, the faithful rose as one to their feet from their kneeling position – after all, the Jews had knelt mockingly before Jesus with the words: 'King of the Jews!' The prayer was rounded off: 'May our Lord God lift the veil from their hearts so that they too acknowledge our Lord Jesus Christ.'

When Leon realized that all his efforts were foundering on the golden cross, he ceased his visits. Aunt Liesl relapsed into dull taciturnity. For weeks she seemed to do her work blindly, until she made a decision that was more fitting to a threepenny opera: she took herself off into a Carmelite nunnery. On her departure she clasped Anna passionately to her and kissed her tenderly on the forehead. Nervously she fished a curled photograph of Leon out of the black handbag that she would have to relinquish at the convent gate and pushed it into Anna's hand.

Her departure fired the starting shot for a series of radical changes. Nettchen was returned to the church. The grandfather, whose all-seeing eye had maintained symbolic control to his final days, exchanged his earthly existence for immortality. He was buried in a snowy churchyard next to his wife, who had departed fifteen years earlier.

Back on the farm Uncle Heinrich rested a hand on Anna's shoulder. 'So, Anna, now there's only the two of us and the stock. And you and I are no farmers at all. Come, let's get down to work.' The heroic acceptance of this lot reminded Anna of her father, who had reconciled himself to his illness in the same way. In an empty gesture she clutched him by his funeral coat. When he dies too, she thought, I'll really be alone.

4

'I wrote you dozens of letters,' Lotte sighed. 'I lay in my garden house and wrote. My mother had bought special writing paper for me with violets in the top left corner. All my letters ended with, "Dear Anna, Why don't you write back? When will we see each other again?"'

'They must have intercepted all those letters and thrown them away – after they had read them out of their farmers' curiosity. And there I was thinking you had forgotten me.'

Their eyes strayed to the other tables. Both were silent. Here they sat, almost seventy years later, and they still felt taken in and deceived; they did not know what they ought to do with these feelings. Had the lives of all these ladies here, with their silk blouses, their gold earrings, their carefully painted lips, also gone awry through such misunderstandings? Anna began to laugh sarcastically.

'Why are you laughing?' said Lotte suspiciously.

'Because my indignation has lost nothing of its strength, after all these years.' Anna drummed her fingers on the table. She remembered she had decided one day that Lotte had died from the illness she was meant to have recovered from in Holland. Nobody had thought to send her an announcement of the death. Perhaps her grandfather had indeed received it, but kept quiet about it so as not to upset her. She had made Lotte dead like that because a dead Lotte was more bearable than one who had simply forgotten her. Moreover, dying ran in the family.

'It's like a book,' said Lotte. Time was rustling past her. Still she could hear her mother, talking about Anna and saying compassionately, 'The poor child, landing up with such barbarians.' This description, which she had taken over gratuitously from her German mother-in-law, made Anna's fate became more and more puzzling. Was Anna herself a barbarian too now? Didn't barbarians have any writing paper? She invented all sorts of excuses for Anna in this way, in order not to have to live with the thought that Anna was simply not allowing her to hear from her at all.

❦

Between Uncle Heinrich and the delicate, blonde daughter of a gentleman farmer, strict unwritten laws stood in the way that were best expressed as statistics: the quantity of livestock, the number of servants, acres of land. With Martha Höhnekop, who was her opposite in every way, he was trying to rid himself of his chosen one. He met Martha at the shooting match. In mutiny against the terror of rank and position, and capital, he had allowed his eyes to fall on someone who had nothing to lose. She was the eldest of a family of fourteen children. Her father ran a café that everyone with a dash of self-respect avoided. But Uncle Heinrich was drunk and Martha Höhnekop available.

One day she walked into Anna's life. With big, rough strides that contrasted coarsely with the cream-coloured lace on her wedding dress, she entered the stuffy living-room, threw her bouquet of roses and phlox onto the table and dropped, puffed out, into grandfather's chair. She could breathe again: the town hall, the church, the celebration meal – it exhausted her to try to be civilized and charming. Anna observed her closely. A sturdy woman with a large, flat face, narrow lips and broad jawbones; above were her eyes, crooked, mysterious, unfathomable, sunken. Her shiny black hair was pinned up; the rose that had been stuck there that morning and had stayed in place the whole day now slid out slowly. Her cheeks looked unnaturally red. Anna thought that was because of the wedding, but later on it seemed that the blush in her cheeks had been tattooed, as though she were suffering from a permanent excitement that could find no outlet. 'Send that child to bed,' she said to Uncle Heinrich, waving her hand at Anna. 'We've only just got married and yet we've such a big girl already,' replied the bridegroom with a false laugh. 'Not many could imitate us.' But the bride, who had had enough of Anna's candid, staring gaze, did not see what there was to laugh about.

The one thing about Martha Höhnekop that worked was her womb: a child was born every year. Beyond that she did not make the grade at all. When she got up at nine o'clock, yawning and scratching her head, Uncle Heinrich's day was already four hours old. From then on, she knew how, in her pigheaded manner, to give the impression that she was kept busy by the housekeeping, but in fact, with her gross body like an elemental force, she swaggered about the small dwelling without lifting a finger. Much work would have been left undone had an outlawed eleven-year-old girl not gone round seeing to it. A girl who actually belonged to no one although she ate with them and slept under the same roof. The one who is lazy has to be clever. Aunt Martha understood that an indispensable labourer had fallen into her lap in the form of this so-called niece.

With every baby that was born, a part of the child in Anna shrivelled up and the beast of burden increased in size in its place. Seven days of her week began with milking the cows – the churns had to be standing by the road by six o'clock. Then she had to feed the pigs, horses, cows, calves and chickens, pump drinking water for them, clean out the cowshed and cook the pigfeed, rub down the cows. This chain of activities was called morning work, the pendant of which was evening work. It began all over again in the afternoons at four o'clock – after school. If the pendants had been figurines on the mantelpiece, they would have shown two slaves sagging at the knees with their backs bent – the clock ticking inexorably between them.

The existence she had been dreaming of, that of a grammar school pupil, was becoming progressively more tenuous. In that dream her life was still proceeding according to the original plan, in which her father set high demands on her intellect – which fitted in badly between the cows and pigs. Two teachers and a pastor had naïvely come to the house to persuade Uncle Heinrich to permit her to go to the grammar school. But their hymn of praise to her talents was cast aside by that single primitive argument, 'No, we need her on the farm.'

He was never to surface from the shock of his impulsive marriage. Apart from being an escape, his lightning raid had perhaps also been a juvenile attempt to repair the fragmented family life. That he had brought a much greater woe on himself as a result was clear. He armed himself against his disillusion by throwing himself into his work with grim doggedness. He acquired the harsh, fixed expression of a farmer who already knows early on that, however hard he drives himself into the ground, his fate is immutable, so out of pure masochism he adds a little extra to it. If Anna had not been there, his little companion in misfortune and sorrow, then he would have had to do battle with the primal force calling herself his wife, in order to get her to work too – a battle in which the loser would have been certain from the outset.

High mass on Sundays freed the house from Aunt Martha's presence for a few hours. This offered Papa Rosenbaum's youngest son the opportunity to take Anna by surprise one hot summer's day. She had just put the potatoes and carrots in the soup simmering with a piece of bacon. All of a sudden, through the steam, she saw a boy standing in the doorway. He took a few steps into the kitchen. She recognized Daniel Rosenbaum, who had sat near her in class. 'I'm going swimming in the Lippe,' he said casually. 'Can I undress here?' Anna looked at him absent-mindedly. 'I suppose so,' she said, vaguely pointing, 'you can use that room there.' Swimming in the river, she thought with surprise, nobody ever does that. She did not know anyone who could swim. Peering at the bubbles and swirls on the surface of the simmering soup, she saw before her the life-threatening whirlpools of the Lippe. When she heard a sound behind her she turned round automatically. The young Rosenbaum was standing naked on the doormat, his erect member was swathed in a beam of sunlight that was entering through the window. He stared at her with defiant seriousness. The cooking spoon fell out of her hand. Independent of his thin boy's body standing out there darkly, the thing with the eye at the top seemed to be aiming straight for her, like a rising cobra poised on the point of attack. She did not know anything like it existed, she refused it, she would have nothing to do with it and fled from the kitchen, past the salute that had been brought to her, outside, to hide behind the privet hedge. She was trembling. In the far distance the severe spire of the Landolinus church was sticking up above the trees. That was pointing upwards too. She stooped to pick a bundle of grass, and pulled the blades apart one by one. How was it possible that, while high mass was being celebrated there, here something like this could manifest itself – that both could exist in the same world?

Jesus had said, 'Be perfect, as Our Father in heaven is perfect.' Anna tried to keep this commandment scrupulously although her efforts were put to the test severely on All Souls' day. All prayers for the salvation of the souls of the dead were heard on this day in November. Those who had the opportunity to do so went to church six times to make the most of the chance. But the prayers were not only for dead loved ones. The greatest sacrifice was a prayer on behalf of the godless, 'Do something good for the sinner too.' She had already prayed for her father, for her mother, grand-father and for Lotte too, to be on the safe side. For whom else can I pray now, she brooded, what is the very greatest penance I should do? Then the naked Rosenbaum appeared unbidden before her, on the doormat, swathed in a sunbeam. In a flash the sacrifice being demanded of her was clear: why shouldn't she pray for one – arbi-trary – dead Jew?

❦

Lotte sipped a glass of Grand Marnier that accompanied the third cup of coffee. 'It could just as well have been a non-Jewish boy.'

'Of course! I am only telling you to show you how ambivalent my attitude towards the Jews was and how that was fed by the church. Now comes the worst.' Anna tossed back the final dregs. 'At some point they had disappeared: there were no more Jews in our village. No Rosenbaum came to buy cattle any more; a Christian cattle dealer took his place, without ceremony. Yet I never asked: where has the Rosenbaum family gone? Never, you understand. Nobody ever asked anything, not even my uncle.'

'What did happen to that family?'

'I don't know! It's true when people say "we did not know". But why didn't we know? Because it didn't interest us at all! I reproach myself, now, that I didn't ask: where have they gone?'

Lotte had been getting hot, she was feeling dizzy. Anna's self-reproach sounded hollow in her ears – what could you do with it? All the fur hats around them had disappeared. The lights in the wagon wheel were still on, but at half strength. 'I believe they want us to be on our way,' she mumbled.

Anna stood up to pay, Lotte would not hear of it. But Anna beat her to it. She had already paid when Lotte was still searching for the lost sleeve of her coat. The Germans were too quick for everybody, with their strong Deutschmarks.

They had just been roaming about in the 1930s; now they stepped outside into a white, timeless world – the compelling silence that now prevailed created the presentiment of a great void. Anna took Lotte's arm. Under the impression that their ways would part here, they stopped by the Lanciers monument in the Place Royale – a heroic rider marching to war wearing a helmet of snow.

'Until tomorrow.' Anna looked at Lotte solemnly and kissed her on both cheeks.

'Until tomorrow . . .' said Lotte weakly.

'Who would have thought it . . .' said Anna again.

Then they both crossed the road in the same direction.

'Where are you heading?' Anna asked.

'To my hotel.'

'Me too!'

They both turned out to be staying at hotels on the other side of the railway line. 'That can't just be chance,' Anna laughed, holding onto Lotte's arm again. Thus they walked on, the snow crunching pleasantly under their feet. On the railway bridge they stopped to look out over the snow-covered roofs.

'Just think,' mused Anna, 'of all the famous celebrities who have come here to take the cure over the centuries. Even Tsar Peter the Great.'

'The town still has something distinguished about it,' Lotte endorsed, brushing a strip of snow off the balustrade with a gloved finger. She loved the atmosphere of aristocratic *élan* and faded glory emanating from the buildings below. The nineteenth century was still tangibly present and evoked a longing for a more harmonious and better organized way of living that had been lost for ever. At the Thermal Baths, whenever anyone on the staff held out a hand to her to help her out of the bath and into a ready warmed bathrobe, she deluded herself that she was a dowager or a marchioness who had brought her own lady's maid with her.

They shuffled on, from one lamppost to the next, from one pool of light to the next, until they were standing in front of a villa with two round towers. 'I'm there,' said Lotte. The building of white fondant sprinkled with icing sugar created an unreal, dreamy impression. This day, with all the implausibilities that had occurred, had been dreamed, and Anna beside her was not real.

'A palace,' Anna assessed soberly. 'I am lodging further on, it's altogether rather simpler.'

Lotte sensed the criticism but was not inclined to explain that a sober family hotel was hiding behind the de luxe façade. 'I wish you ... a pleasant evening,' she stammered.

'I can hardly wait until tomorrow,' Anna sighed, pulling her firmly to her.

It took a long time for Lotte to fall asleep. A pain-free position was difficult to find. And whether she lay on her side or her back, she continued to replay the meeting and the unburdenings that had ensued. An amalgam of conflicting emotions hindered a blind submission to sleep. How shall I tell my children, was her last thought as she dropped off, towards morning.

5

Full of sombre forebodings, Lotte woke. The hotel room appeared strange and hostile to her; the snow-covered branches through the window evoked no poetic sentiments. Everything was painful. This body was evoking aversion in her, not only because she could feel it with every movement but because its origin could not be denied. A Dutch person, in a German body. In Belgium. She would have liked to have made off silently, but the cure was a gift from her children, so how could she take flight from her own birthday present? Allowing herself to be led astray by Anna was a form of disloyalty: the pain in her limbs was a warning that she had already gone too far. Those first years of life that Anna referred to – what did they really represent in a human life? They had been put into the world together, half-way through the First World War, while there had been wholesale death not even a hundred kilometres away. There was something improper about being born at such a moment, and twins at that. A curse must lie upon them. Great estrangement deservedly existed between them, it needed to remain so. Perhaps an impersonal historical guilt lay upon them and in the course of their lives, independently of one another, they had had to repay an amount of misfortune brought about by circumstances.

As Lotte was waiting in the basement for the preparation of her peat bath, Anna appeared in the doorway. There was already something familiar about her – hopefully this was not the precursor of some sort of family feeling! Anna slid next to her on the white bench.

'How did you sleep, meine Liebe?'

'All right,' said Lotte superciliously.

'I slept wonderfully.' Anna massaged her thighs.

A woman in a white overall beckoned to Lotte. Anna grasped her by her shoulder. 'There's a lovely café next door, Relais de la Poste, let's meet there. This afternoon!'

Nodding vaguely, Lotte glided into the bathroom. How was it possible: once again Anna succeeded in taking her by surprise, presenting a *fait accompli*!

In the Relais de la Poste time had stood still since the beginning of the thirties. Dark brown wooden chairs, white table-cloths beneath plate glass, copper lamps with glass bulbs, everything originated from that period. The owner had seen no reason to change anything to the post-war fancies for steel, plastic or pseudo-rustic. It was quiet there, a few regulars chatting softly at the buffet. Passers-by with turned-up collars walked through the snow where, across the street, the walls of the Thermal Institute contrasted grubbily. The woman behind the bar recommended a regional drink to the ladies, to warm them up: Ratafia de Pommes. This apple liqueur infiltrated Lotte's resistance to the meeting with a sour-sweet refinement. After the second glass she spotted a primitive radio in a dark corner, with a lovely wooden case. Delighted, she walked over to it and let her fingers slide lovingly over the polished wood. 'Look at this,' she called. 'That crazy father of mine had one like it too!'

❧❧

The purchase of a gramophone from the firm Grammophon and Polyphon in Amsterdam brought a cause of quarrels and sleeplessness to the home, apart from a source of pleasure. Hours of musical gastronomy had preceded the definitive choice. Lotte's father listened with eyes closed to Caruso's divine voice; his 'Hosannah' and 'Paliaccio' almost caused Polyphon's luxurious auditorium in Leidsestraat to come apart at the seams. The turntable lay beneath a flap in the top of the new piece of furniture. It acquired a prominent position in the living-room; from then on the house was permeated with the symphonies of Schubert and Beethoven, with the voice of the famous tenor Jacques Urlus – who sang 'Murmelndes Lüftchen' – but also with the serene voice of Aaltje Noordewier in Bach's Passions. He played the new machine until deep into the night; it enabled his love of music and for the very newest achievements of electrical technology to enter into a perfect symbiosis. His wife kept him company to the very end of his nightly sessions since she had discovered that in his intoxicated state he forgot to put out the lamps and stoves before going to bed. He liked it loud. The children were developing sleep problems through the excess of heavenly sounds. They dozed over their arithmetic books at school; Lotte could hear the melting songs of *Orfeo* in surging waves right through reading lessons.

Polyphon's warehouse contained a stock of four thousand five hundred different gramophone records. Lotte's mother was regularly surprised by a representative from the firm holding a bill under her nose. A quarrel about money then flared up through the music in the evenings. 'I've already paid it.' 'You haven't paid it. They were at the door again. That's no way to behave.' Jet and Lotte slid out of bed and sat on the top stair, their arms round each other's shoulders. What had merely sounded like a threat from the bedroom grew into danger out here. The music continued mercilessly, their parents' anger raised above it. Sometimes an object hit the floor with a bang. Eventually they descended the stairs crying, and entered the scene of battle in bare feet, preparing themselves for the very worst. 'We had a bad dream,' was their alibi. Lotte held on tightly to the sleeve of Jet's night-dress. An instant ceasefire was declared. Their father went to the miraculous object to put another record on; their mother hugged them guiltily to her bosom.

Their father's hunger for new music was, however, surpassed by his addiction to sound machines. Soon the reproduction of the gramophone no longer satisfied his demands. The Concertgebouw in Amsterdam was his standard; that was how it had to sound in the living-room too. He installed all kinds of experimental advances in his workshop, amid a chaos of transformers, distributors, switchboards, loudspeakers and earth electrodes – the tips of his moustache were singed from the soldering. He already had a series of successful attempts as a radio builder to his name; his home-made Chrystalphone surpassed those from the Edison works. He introduced so many ingenious alterations to the gramophone that the original machine could hardly be recognized any more. When an Ultraphone was unexpectedly launched on the market, he adapted it immediately. This machine, which delighted even the most reserved of critics, had two sound arms and two needles at its disposal, so that the sound was transmitted twice with a short pause in between – a stereo effect ahead of its time. The gramophone with the human voice, wrote the press. Lotte's father took this as a personal declaration of war. Once more he stationed himself in his workshop; he did not rest until he had built a unit with two conical loudspeakers. Not only did the sound come from different sides, as in the concert hall, but he was the front-runner in the race to conquer surface noise. The two polished beech cases that dominated the room brought him a fame that extended beyond the rivers Maas and Waal. Engineers from the light bulb industry drove north in a company car to hear the acoustic phenomenon with their own ears. Sound technicians from the broadcasting company, musicians, hobbyists, vague acquaintances followed – evening after evening new interested parties enjoyed the brilliant sound reproduction and the ever expanding record collection. The instigator of all these technical and musical *tours de force*, completely autodidactic in the world of sound, found himself in a permanent state of spiritual inebriation as a result of the overdose of interest and recognition. He put his records on the turntable with just as much vanity as a violinist tucks his violin under his chin. His moustache, once again restored to its former glory, shone as never before.

As a result of these exciting evenings, the local community's power and water supply was at risk. These were his responsibility –

a job he had attained through years of self-tuition about electrical theory. He was sleeping late in the mornings. Because there was no one else to do it, on dark winter mornings his wife got out of bed, where she had spent no more than four hours, putting a housecoat over her night-dress, to turn on the pressure pumps in the ice-cold water-tower. Sometimes it got too much for her. 'You think only of yourself,' she flung at his head when he eventually stumbled downstairs, his eyes still thick with sleep, 'when it suits you. Egoist. Salon socialist.' He protested weakly, looking in vain for arguments with which to defend himself. She, driven to despair by the sudden irresponsibility he hid behind, punched him. The children saw him stagger; they fled over the bridge into the wood to build a hut as an alternative to the parental home. The building activities were drawn out as long as possible in the hope that the war would have subsided when they crossed the bridge in the reverse direction. Hours later, hungry and agitated, they walked gingerly back to the house. From the wood they could already see their parents sitting on the garden bench under the climbing pear tree, arms wound around each other and blissful smiles on their lips – equilibrium had been restored.

The children did their homework in the back room; the gramophone was silent whenever their father was out on a tour of inspection. A company Harley Davidson took him round the outskirts of the district. He raced along majestic avenues in his long leather coat, leggings on his calves, his eyes protected by huge goggles, the flaps of his cap fluttering against his head like the wings of a drunken bird. When he got home and had taken off his rig, he took a volume of the collected works of Marx or Lenin from the bookshelf and flopped into an armchair with it.

Suddenly the sliding doors would open. 'What are you doing?' he said sternly. 'Homework.' 'Which subject?' 'Dutch history.' 'Close those books, you can learn much more from this. Listen: "... Wherever a part of society possesses the monopoly of the means of production, the labourer, free or not free, must add to the working time necessary for his own maintenance and extra working time in order to produce the means of subsistence for the owner of the means of production, whether this proprietor be the Athenian perfect gentleman, Etruscan theocrat, civis Romanus, Norman Baron, American slave owner, Wallachian Boyard, modern land-lord or capitalist."' He cast a meaningful glance at them over the cover of *Das Kapital*, decorated with floral stems. 'Understand, the worker labours by the sweat of his brow so that the rich can dedicate themselves entirely to doing nothing. That's how the world works. Get that into your heads.' And he continued his lecture, which could last for hours when he got into his stride, until they were released by their mother, who would assign them imaginary tasks. When they complained about having to weed the kitchen garden he rubbed their noses in the fate of people of their age from the previous century. 'At two, three, four o'clock in the morning children of nine to ten years were dragged out of their unhealthy dormitory towns and forced to work for their mere subsistence until ten, eleven, twelve at night, while their limbs wasted away, their bodies bent, their features dulled and their human countenances stiffened into expressionless masks, just one glimpse of which was terrifying.'

He treated guests with more subtlety. First he tempted them with heavenly music. When he had entirely hooked them and their souls were enfeebled by emotion, he turned the volume knob low and, as though in spontaneous inspiration, opened a book which just happened to be lying ready there all the while. Some politely managed to do a bunk in time, others got into strenuous disputes that lasted deep into the night. He only really provoked genuine resistance when, in the early hours, with the imposing loudspeakers in the background as proof of his resourceful intellect, he made known his opposition to the monarchy. Spurred on by the gin, they were prepared to go a long way with him in his arguments about historical materialism; they were even prepared to turn a blind eye to his philippics against Christendom, but as soon as the royal family was mentioned he was stepping over a boundary: this was implacably opposed. His music, alcohol and powers of persuasion were no match for their love of the House of Orange. He did his best to conceal his contempt, stroking his moustache with a pointed index finger. One of the guests became so addicted to the debates that he came back to philosophize every Saturday evening until the bottom of the gin bottle showed: Professor Koning, lecturer in colonial history at the University of Amsterdam. Lotte's father, who had a child-like, unsocialist respect for authority in the province of learning, was very proud of this friendship, which went so far that the professor bought a thatched house on the other side of the wood.

On the Queen's birthday, her father refused to hang the flag on the water-tower. But a prominent member of the provincial council, who lived in the neighbourhood and took a stroll in the wood every day, reported his negligence. 'Come on,' said his wife the following year, 'hang out the flag, otherwise we'll get into trouble.' 'Preposterous,' he protested, 'to hang out the flag for a perfectly ordinary woman.' 'You're talking about the Queen.' She looked like a queen herself, in her cream-coloured shantung dress, proud, charming and unrelenting. The children supported her, and had decorated their bicycles with conifer branches and orange lanterns: 'Everyone hangs out the flag, Dad.' He sniffed: the masses! 'If you won't do it I will.' His wife marched off with large strides; he followed behind angrily. At the door of the water-tower he grabbed her and turned her round. He went in, jaws clenched.

An inspector came to the school to compile a register of the pupils. He stood in front of the class with a list: they had to stand up one by one and say their names. In a flat, routine voice he added: 'And what does your father do?' They answered without faltering. Lotte owned to the surname of her Dutch parents absent-mindedly: Rockanje. But she stared at him open-mouthed without saying anything when it came to her father's profession. 'Lotte,' said the mistress affably, 'you do know what your father does?' It took a great effort of strength to emit the words: 'I d-don't yet k-know.' Her head was ready to burst. Did she have to list everything her father did? Where ought she to begin? The inspector bypassed this hitch in the machinery and continued his checking with a neutral expression. Suddenly Lotte had an inspiration. She raised her finger, 'I k-know it now.' 'Well,' said the mistress and inspector in unison, 'what is your father then?' 'Tower watchman for the Queen!' she cried without stuttering.

❧

'If grandfather had known that you had gone straight into a Communist nest . . .' cried Anna with hilarity. 'What a joke!'

'But my mother was against it. "Don't think," she said to him, "that the workers will be more humane if they seize power." She would sometimes pull him down petulantly from his pink cloud when he wouldn't leave off his glorification of Marx and kept harping on righteously about money and work. "Try to live like that yourself, dear. Only fine words come out of your mouth."'

An old man came in, stamping his boots, snow on his bushy eyebrows. His watery blue eyes timidly assessed the clientèle. He left a track of melting snow behind him on the way to the counter. Lotte had red blotches on her cheeks from the Ratafia de Pommes. Anna's eyes were shining. Lotte's old-fashioned, precise German sounded like music to her ears, interspersed now and then with a Cologne word that had gone out of fashion long ago.

'That Schicki-Micki type,' she said, 'who fetched you from Cologne, what kind of a person was she?'

Lotte stared outside the window. 'I went to stay with her in Amsterdam from time to time. If you looked from the living-room into the mirror by the window you could see the Albert Cuyp market. In the mornings, we went to the market together while Grandpa went to the barber to be shaved. First she bought meat and vegetables. But her real aim was to touch the things on a stall full of beads, buttons, velvets, laces, silks. There she stood, endlessly dreaming; everything passed through her hands. After deliberating for a long time she bought something minuscule, a pair of mother-of-pearl buttons or something. She was still so elegant. "Look," she said once, "this is what I was like when I was young." She pulled her sagging skin taut with the tips of her fingers. I was shocked. I didn't recognize her like that. "Can't I go to see Anna?" I asked her one day. "Ach du, Schätzchen, you have no idea how stubborn and narrow-minded our family is. We have absolutely no contact with them. Later, when you're grown up, you can look for Anna on your own account. Then the two of you together won't give a damn about that whole tribe."'

Anna laughed. 'A photograph of her hung above grandfather's chair when he was still alive – as a young girl in a white dress, her face shaded by a straw hat. Ein wunderschönes picture. That photo would be a hundred years old now. Think of it, Lotte, a hundred years! The world has never changed as radically as it has in the last hundred years. No wonder you and I are a bit confused. Let's drink something more!'

The layers of time were grating over each. Before the war, after the war, the depression years, a century ago . . . diverse landscapes that Anna was hurtling through tipsily, as though in a runaway train. One moment she was in a steam train and wisps of smoke were drifting past the window, the next moment she was sitting on bright green leatherette in a modern express train. Figures from the past were standing in the stations they whizzed past. They did not wave but looked at the phantom express with screwed-up eyes and frowns. The station in Berlin was on fire, the platforms were full of smoke and dust. Where did this journey end? At the edge of time? It left her cold. She clinked her glass against Lotte's and toasted her health.

'I also asked her . . .' said Lotte.

'Who?'

'Grandma . . . Aunt Elisabeth . . . I asked her: Did you know my father when he was young? I mean: my real father. "Your father," she said, "was a nice, intelligent boy, the revolutionary of the family. I was very taken with him. That's why I was at his funeral and you are here now, du Kleine. Ach ja, sensitive types die young and those Schweinehunde grow ancient – that is how the world is..."' Lotte added tenderly, 'Grandma loved swear-words.'

'If only such a fairy godmother had appeared for me at that time,' said Anna not without bitterness, 'I would have been spared a lot of suffering.'

❦

Thirty-five marks per month orphan's allowance was paid for Anna. That was a lot of money – yet Aunt Martha carried on as though she were a parasite, a blood sucker who had clamped onto the young family with two suckers. She projected onto Anna the chronic displeasure that she had brought into the marriage with her as a dowry; Anna was broken in spirit and numb from the work, and defenceless against her deviousness. Whenever Anna looked in Uncle Heinrich's cracked shaving mirror, she said scornfully, 'Why look in the mirror? You're going to die anyway. Your father had tuberculosis, your mother breast cancer, you'll get one of the two as well. Don't fancy your chances.' Anna, who had read many fairy-tales, recognized in her the cliché of the wicked stepmother, but the justice that always triumphed in the stories was a long time coming in reality. 'Why do you need a new dress? Why should you drink milk? You are going to die anyway.'

Now that all worldly needs were being strangled at birth and ridiculed, the old longing to disappear for ever seeped into her again. But to die, how did you do that? If you got a disease, it happened by itself. Intentionally instigating the change from being-there to not-being-there was more difficult. Uncertainty drove her to the church – time stolen from the pigs and cows that had to be caught up later. By praying as faultlessly as possible she hoped for a miraculous admission to heaven. But God, her second inaccessible father, did not make the effort to descend to the modest Landolinus church. At the very most He allowed Alois Jacobsmeyer to appear out of the semi-darkness; he had had a soft spot for Anna since she had given the Romans what for. He was the one who had implored her uncle: 'Send her to the grammar school! There isn't a better pupil in the village. We'll pay for it all.' Anna seized his soutane and authoritatively asked him to give her a means of disappearing from the world that would not cause inconvenience. Shocked, he whispered: 'Don't do anything stupid! God has only given you this one life, it is all you have. He wants you to live it until it ends naturally. Have patience, you will be free when you are twenty-one.' But twenty-one was unbearably far off. 'I'll never keep going,' she said angrily. 'Yes you will.' He took her head in his hands and rocked it gently to and fro. 'You must!'

Not long after that, her body seemed to have made a decision, weakened by the daily battle of attrition and the frugal food. She caught a cold that would not clear up. Jacobsmeyer urged her to go to the doctor but Aunt Martha waved his advice aside – that sort of cold would wear off by itself. Then he thought up a trick to combat the cough without being accused of interfering in other people's business. He wandered over to the farm after mass. Anna was in the cowshed when Aunt Martha stuck her head round the corner, her cheekbones red with suppressed anger. 'The pastor is here for you.' Jacobsmeyer was sitting in the kitchen with a gurgling baby on his lap. He drew a narrow brown bottle out of his soutane. 'It can't go on any longer,' he said to Anna. 'You cough all the way through the mass, I can't understand my own words.' With a combination of triumph and indignation Aunt Martha cried: 'That one there? But she has no manners, we know that already!' 'I have brought a medicine for her with me,' Jacobsmeyer continued imperturbably. 'Frau Bamberg, will you see to it that she takes it regularly?' Aunt Martha nodded, taken by surprise. 'And if her clothes are wet from sweat,' he went on, 'she must change, so that she doesn't catch a new cold.' 'Oh yes,' scoffed Aunt Martha, 'then she'd have to go into the field to hang her shirt up on the willows and wait naked until it was dry. The men here would certainly appreciate that.' He admonished her, piqued because he had unwittingly nurtured her banal fantasy: 'You ought to buy her some extra shirts, Frau Bamberg.' He stood up with dignity and passed the baby to her. 'You must think about this little one of yours but also of Anna ... they are all God's children.' He turned round at the door: 'And she must drink a lot of milk, with cream.' 'If he pays for it himself,' snarled Aunt Martha when the door had closed behind him.

'And?' enquired Jacobsmeyer. Anna looked at the floor, leaning on one of the pillars in the nave. 'Aunt Martha has given me one of her worn-out old shirts. But I am not allowed to drink milk, that has to go for sale.' 'God forgive me,' he sighed; 'when you centri-fuge milk, Anna, put your mouth under the spout now and then. But do look round regularly, otherwise she'll see what's going on.'

Uncle Heinrich erected between himself and his wife a screen of work activities, card games with villagers, newspapers and library books, which were read by Anna too in stolen quarters of an hour. He did not object, except when she wanted to read *All Quiet on the Western Front*. He forbade it not because of the war horrors but because of an indecent scene, which she was quite unable to discover when she nevertheless read the book in secret, because she lacked the antennae for that sort of wavelength. The fate of four nineteen-year-old boys in the trench warfare of 1914–18 strength-ened her in the belief that a man's life was not valued. The life of a soldier was something like a candle in front of the statue of Mary – when it had burnt down a new one was put in the holder.

They discussed the books they had read – in the mornings while Aunt Martha was still in bed, in the afternoons when she was having a nap and in the evenings when she was in bed again. Although the conversations were fleeting, fitted in as they went along, they created a secret bond between two who were like-minded, the last descendants of one family, against the ominous background of the wife upstairs who was still a stranger to them both. Only much later on did Anna understand that her aunt must have felt this alliance, through the walls – perhaps in her morbid suspicion she had even seen an unspoken love in it. Her aunt bided her time until a chance arose to drive a wedge between them. Bernd Möller unintentionally became her tool.

Anna went to find him in his workshop to enquire whether the problem with the haycart's axle had been fixed yet. He did not look up from the threshing cart he was repairing; she had to repeat her question before an intelligible reply came from his mouth. No, he had not yet got round to it. A newspaper was open on his workbench, among the nuts and bolts. Anna bent inquisitively over the columns, avid for anything that appeared in print. Quiet returned to the workshop except for the prosaic sounds of repair work. 'Are you still here?' said Bernd Möller, surprised. 'What are you doing?' 'Reading.' 'What are you reading?' Anna turned back to the front page. 'The *Völkischer Beobachter*.' 'That's not for you, all politics.' Anna folded open the paper and held it up to his nose. 'Who is this?' With a black fingernail, under which chicken and pig muck had collected, she pointed to the portrait of a man with a clenched fist and a provoked, irate look, who was screaming inaudibly, a flag with black spiders' legs in a white circle in the background. 'Adolf Hitler,' said Bernd Möller, wiping his nose on his sleeve. She turned up her nose. 'It looks as though he wants to go and fight.' 'That is what he wants.' The mechanic put his spanner on the floor and slowly stood up from his crouch. 'For me, for you, for all of us. Against unemployment and poverty.'

He forgot all about the job he had been engrossed in just before and went to sit on the workbench to explain to her what plans the man in the photograph had for the German people. Long-awaited work, a new order – even for the ordinary man who was driving himself into the ground every day for a plate of pea soup. Look, here it was in writing. Bernd Möller had an aura of optimism about him. Someone had appeared on the horizon who was preparing great changes, who was going to put an end to the poverty and chaos in the country. Stirred by his enthusiasm, Anna had the feeling that something might then improve for her too – even if it were perhaps only something small. A long-awaited father figure who would take up the cudgels for her and who would break through the chains of drudgery, fatigue and hunger. She looked intently at the photograph. What he was giving expression to and what had initially aroused her distaste was, on further inspection, precisely what she felt beneath the veneer of slavish obedience: rage and mutiny.

That evening she said to her uncle in a conspiratorial tone, 'There's someone who is going to put an end to poverty.' He was sitting in the chair his father had died in; she was on the sofa beneath the soldier killed in action. 'That's good news,' he said, looking ironically at her over his book, 'how do you make that out?' 'It's in the *Völkischer Beobachter*. Adolf Hitler has said . . .' 'What?' he cried. The book slid out of his hands. 'That fool? You don't know what you're saying. Only dumb, desperate people trail after that ridiculous figure. Who did you learn that nonsense from?' 'From Bernd Möller,' she said, offended and confused. 'Oh, I get it, that's his way of rebelling. The *Völkischer Beobachter*! You don't read that! No one here reads that paper. Every right-thinking person, every right-minded Catholic votes for the Centre Party. Pius X's encyclical describes exactly how poverty can be overcome from the Christian point of view. Listen, girl – this Hitler with his bragging wants just one thing: war.' He bent over to pick up his book and looked at her as though he were listening acutely for something. 'I won't have you associating with Bernd Möller, understand that.'

But Anna could not allow herself to give up this ray of hope so easily. The following day she scurried over to the workshop. Bernd Möller shook his head at her uncle's reaction. 'I'll explain to you exactly why he said that – so that you don't look shocked at me any longer with your lovely blue eyes. I can't stand that.' He smiled. 'You simply have to let them talk, those brave farmers, those obedient Catholics. They don't know any better. They are just animals who have lived in a cage for too long: if you throw the door open they simply stay in there. If we had to wait until the Centre Party settled our problems we'd all starve.' His self-confidence aroused trust. She needed to believe in a chance of change, there was no alternative. And Bernd Möller kept this belief alive with cheerful hymns. She did her work at a faster pace purely to be able to steal over to his workshop in between times and talk with him, or to watch him while he fiddled inside the motor of a farm machine. They did not only talk politics. The pitfalls of everyday life, the attitude that you should take towards it, the books Anna had been reading, her cough – no subject was taboo in the intimacy of the old, draughty shed, as she sat with one buttock on the open news-paper and the other on the scored wood of the workbench.

'Although you're only sixteen, you're an exceptional girl,' said Bernd. He heaped praise on her; in his eyes she was a little, philo-sophical Virgin with a big heart that was beating for all the outcasts and unfortunates in the world. The new Germany would get off the ground more easily if there were more such young women. She had a great future before her, he assured her, squeezing her hands with their split and broken nails in his fists smeared with engine oil. Over time that future increasingly took on the form of a house he was going to build for her. A rustic, old-fashioned house with a gabled roof, shutters, a Bavarian veranda along the full width of the façade and a massive oak door, which he would push open to carry her across the threshold when she was eighteen. Anna allowed these fantasies to glance off her indifferently. Marriage she had never thought about; merely the idea of it was ridiculous to her. Whenever he conjured up these dream pictures to her she looked intently at the floor strewn with tools and machine parts – apparently this was a sacrifice that had to be made now and then for friendship.

When the rye was being harvested she had no time for these interludes. A little boy from the village pushed a letter into her hand: 'This evening at half-past eight behind the Lady Chapel by the bridge.' It was already twilight by that time and it smelled intoxicatingly of damp hay. She did not recognize him at first. He crossed the bridge in a brown uniform that was rather a tight fit and he had a parting in his hair. There was an officious expression on his face that did not become him. He grasped her by her wrists. 'Your house is going to be built, Anna! An architect in Paderborn has done a design. It's waiting for you, you must approve the drawing!' She gazed at him impassively. All of a sudden she no longer knew what she had been seeking at the Lady Chapel with a wild stranger who was badgering her about a house that ought to remain a fantasy instead of turning up on paper and, even worse, being built stone by stone on this sandy ground with which she had no affinity. Aroused by his own excitement, he threw his muscular mechanic's arms around her, demanding the impossible of his sleeves. She heard the threads snap and over his shoulder saw the neighbour passing by with a young goat on a rope. Ashamed, she hid her face in his chest; he took it for affection and increased the pressure of his arms. When he eventually let her go she dashed across the bridge towards the farm, stumbling over her own feet as though she had narrowly escaped from a great danger.

The neighbour did not neglect her citizen's duty and the next day reported Anna's wooing to Aunt Martha, who understood instantly that this was what she had been waiting for all that time. Concealing her triumph behind an exemplary display of moral indignation, she disclosed the report of the rendezvous to her husband, embellishing it with shocking details that unerringly hit him below the belt. Anna, still suspecting nothing, was fetching water for the pigs. When she turned round, Uncle Heinrich was standing on the threshold. Although he was not heavily built, he looked as though he filled the whole doorway. Why was something so threatening emanating from him? The figure, cramped by suppressed tension, approached her and came within a metre of her. She felt suddenly that an unknown misunderstanding was festering between them, which had to be resolved as quickly as possible.

'What would your father say?' he began, with a gruesomely

controlled voice, 'if he caught you with that womanizer, that agitator? Eh? Would you have dared if he had still been alive?' Anna stiffened, she could see the whole chain of cause and effect in one second. 'Would you have dared?' he repeated, lending force to his question with a slap on her face. 'Well?' As she brought a hand up to her cheek in disbelief he hit her on the other cheek. She turned away and ducked to escape his hands; this evasive reflex only provoked his frenzy further. His fists landed wherever he could reach her. When she fell over on the slippery ground he pulled her up by her hair and punched her in the stomach. The rage he dealt out to her was greater than himself and greater than the cause. It was concentrated from all his resentment against a world in which he was powerless, but also from all the like-mindedness between Anna and him, and their solidarity – perhaps even his defencelessness against the young woman she herself was without having any inkling of it. All that impenetrable, murky motivation: Anna had not the slightest suspicion of it – for her all that existed were the blows and punches, and the cries he uttered, as though he was suffering more than she in the thrashing. At one moment one side of the cowshed flashed by, next the other again, and the pigs' snouts moving on either side like amazed witnesses. She lost all sense of time until, beneath the raised arm with which she was protecting her head, she saw Aunt Martha positioned on the threshhold in order to enjoy the full measure of the punishment. Her appearance brought Uncle Heinrich out of his fury. He stopped abruptly, looking down at Anna with surprise, glassily. Without deigning to look at his wife, he pushed her aside and disappeared outside.

Anna got up laboriously – a searing pain dragged through her whole body. Aunt Martha was a pompous black blob outlined against the daylight behind her. 'What must the neighbours think?' she growled. 'You've made a hell of a noise.' 'What noise?' moaned Anna. Who had yelled with each blow? Not her, she had clamped her lips tight. The record had to be set straight, even in the midst of chaos. Collecting the last of her strength, she crawled towards her aunt, her broken nails reaching for the skin of the weak, naked arms. The woman who was so large and looked so strong, crossed her arms anxiously across her breasts; the deep-set eyes above the wide cheekbones sunk even further into their sockets. She fled backwards out of the cowshed; Anna stumbled after her and fell over on the grass splaying out her arms.

No more clatter of weapons, but absolute silence. Guiltily Uncle Heinrich put food and drink on the floor by her bed; like a wild animal she only touched the plates when he had gone. For the first days she lay on her stomach because the pain in her back was so bad, then she exchanged the monotonous panorama of woodgrain and knots in the floor for that of the wall, and turned half on her side, because the contractions and stabbing pains in her belly were now drowning out all other forms of pain. It was becoming worse instead of diminishing. An unbearable paradox; she could not endure it any more and yet she was enduring it. With each wave of pain she lapsed into a soft wail that penetrated to the kitchen down the chimney hung with hams and sausages. Eventually Uncle Heinrich stumbled upstairs to ask her what could be done to put an end to the moaning. In a rasping voice Anna complained of stabbing in her belly. That frightened him, the reproductive organs were sacred: Go forth and multiply. What had never been considered necessary for her cough was to happen now: an appointment was made with a doctor. She had to promise her aunt dutifully to keep quiet about the injuries and bruises. New tortures were announced. The law required an adult woman to be present as a chaperon at an internal examination. Lying on her black and blue back, beneath Aunt Martha's vulture glare, Anna felt his cool rubber finger penetrate a region she had not suspected of existing until then. A piercing pain split her down the middle. 'It's a bit uncomfortable,' said the voice of her benefactor. Uncomfortable! Had he ever been cleaved in half? Dull tears slid down her cheeks without her permission, a triumph she did not concede to her aunt. 'Come, come,' said the doctor, 'we're not making a drama of it. Your womb is twisted, I'm trying to get it back in position.'

The pain subsided. Aunt Martha's lust for power was stronger than ever before, as though she had been present at an initiation ritual that henceforth gave her new power over Anna. During mass, behind the stocky straight back of her aunt, she crumpled a letter for Jacobsmeyer into the hand of an old school friend, containing a simple but urgent message: 'Help! Anna.' During the Gregorian hymns her eyes strayed involuntarily to the bas-relief where Jesus was being flogged. Her breath caught. She quickly directed her gaze up to the vaulted roof decorated with tendrils, where the singing voices joined the echo of the prayers. The note reached the pastor wonderfully fast; he called her as she was leaving the church. She rolled up the sleeves of her Sunday dress and said, 'My back also looks like my arms.' Although Jacobsmeyer was, from his profession, on familiar terms with violence in the Bible and with the Christian idea that suffering was the shortest route to God, he was put off his stride when confronted by it in reality. He lifted his glasses from his nose, put them back and raised them again before he laid a trembling hand on her head.

6

'Non . . . je ne regrette rien . . .'

'Ha!' Anna cried. Startled roughly out of his reverie, the old man at the bar blinked his watery eyes; there was a puddle of melted snow under his bar stool. 'Ha! Je ne regrette rien . . . the queen of love never has regrets. When she had one foot in the grave she took a young lover – her musical heir, her nightingale who sang like a crow . . .' She laughed mockingly. 'Little Sparrow, picked out of the gutter . . . I was also a little sparrow in the gutter – now I'm an old woman teased by memories. An old woman who'll have another.' She snapped her fingers towards the bar.

'Ach ja,' Lotte said quietly, in an attempt to neutralize Anna's emotionality, 'the older you become the more you live in the past. You forget things that happened yesterday.'

Anna raised her eyebrows at this clichéd remark. But to Lotte it was the practical and ever successful opening for a lament about old age, a conversational ploy for keeping the discussion in safe waters. Full glasses were set before them, with a smile from the proprietress. Perhaps she had been on the wrong side in the war, as had many Belgians? It was difficult for her to imagine Anna, that well-fed, quick-witted woman sitting opposite her, as an ill-treated, sickly girl of sixteen in her Sunday dress, gagged by her step-aunt, who had been allocated so many bad attributes that it was a caricature. Wasn't Anna exaggerating? Had time distorted her memories? She was instantly ashamed of her persistent scepticism. Barbarians, her mother had said. She could really see why now. It was all so extreme. Lotte regarded malicious, violent behaviour as a sickness, to be cordoned off safely and kept at a distance. In that light she diagnosed Aunt Martha as dangerously mentally

67

deranged – no wonder Uncle Heinrich slowly went mad under her influence.

'That aunt of yours was a pathological case.' She took a reckless sip.

Anna laughed drily. 'Not necessarily. She was merely a woman who was good for nothing. There are people like that. According to Christian morality they are evil, according to psychiatry they are sick. What difference does it make when you're the victim of it? But let's have something more cheerful. About you.'

Lotte did not miss the insinuation: compared with Anna's youth, hers was, in Anna's eyes, a model of freedom from trouble. Of the two of them, Anna was the one entitled to sympathy. Although ostensibly she spoke with distance and irony about the past, in ways she was making a subtle call for compassion. The compassion that had always been withheld from her and was now expected from her sister – no, demanded. But that role did not appeal to her.

'About your singing,' Anna coaxed, 'your lovely voice.'

'God, I'm hot,' said Lotte. She stood up lopsidedly to take her jacket off. Fumbling with sleeves – cracks had appeared in the co-ordination of her movements as a result of the apple liqueur. There were two possibilities: to give Anna what she requested or to remain silent. The latter felt hard to her; she enjoyed talking about it. Who was still interested in it? Not her children. And if she kept quiet about it it would all be lost, as though it had never happened.

❧

Singing gradually elbowed out the stuttering: the pleasure of sing-ing was greater than the anxiety preceding the first letter. Her body grew and her voice grew with it – actually her voice was always rather older than herself. When she was accepted into a famous teenage choir, only her voice properly belonged there. The choir was directed by Catharina Metz, a dark, melancholy woman with a fluffy moustache that she sometimes shaved off but more often left, from indifference – the delicate hairs trembled with her vibrato. There were still yellowed newspaper cuttings about her singing career, which had come to an abrupt end with her father's illness. They never got to see the mysterious invalid; he lived his abstract existence in a wing of the house overgrown with virginia creeper and wisteria, and it only manifested itself in the dark rings under his daughter's eyes. Sometimes she suddenly stopped the rehearsal with a raised finger to listen with concentration to something that was inaudible to the pupils. She guided them with a gentle hand via unfamiliar French and Italian composers into the territory of the great classics.

Whenever the choir performed for the radio, Lotte's mother urged everyone to be in place in a circle round the Chrystalphone, in an improvised amphitheatre of kitchen chairs. On one Sunday morning Lotte's voice came into the living-room unexpectedly, separate from the choir, in a Bach cantata. Uncertain of the result she came home – she could not hear her own voice in the studio. There a celebration was in progress: alcohol was on the table. Her mother hugged her, moved, and presented her with a bouquet of flowers that tickled her nostrils. She had a sneezing fit. 'Mind your voice!' cried Mies sarcastically; she liked to be the centre of attention herself. Her father was looking feverishly in his record collection for that particular cantata – his way of indicating his appreciation. Lotte fell into an armchair, bewildered, and pensively spooned down a brimming glass of advocaat that Marie had held out to her with a respectful laugh. It gave her a scandalously pleasurable feeling that she was earning success with something that she herself enjoyed to the roots of her hair (the reward was already there in the singing itself). Two days later she received a perfumed letter: 'Your timbre is unique, it is a rare gift. I will still remember your voice in twenty years, and that is something others would give everything for.' Catharina Metz recognized the sender as a notoriously severe music critic. Blushing, Lotte packed the letter in the suitcase she had come with from Germany. Along with her mourning dress and Anna's embroidered handkerchief that had been in one of the pockets, here she kept the sewing case that had drowned with her and a newspaper cutting about Amelita Galli-Curci. Later she moved the letter to a drawer in her dressing-table where a scent of violets still lingered after sixty years.

She had first heard Amelita Galli-Curci in a duet with Caruso. It was a hot afternoon in September; she was walking home through the wood after school with Jet. The water-tower shimmered through the trees when suddenly she stopped. Like a force of nature, a voice was coming from an open window which was so enchanting that Lotte was all ears – a gigantic, immobile ear. Jet pulled impatiently on her sleeve and then walked on, shrugging her shoulders. Lotte wanted to delay as long as possible the banal moment of coming home and discovering that the voice emanated from a groove in an ebony disc. So she stood there with eyes closed until the last sounds had died away between the tree trunks.

The queen of coloratura singing, Galli-Curci, married to a marquis from the foot of the boot of Italy, scored triumphs in the United States immediately after the First World War 'as a lyric soprano of unusual beauty, pure and crystal clear from low A-flat to high C', according to *Opera World* of the day. In the cutting that Lotte kept, there was a photograph of a majestic, dark-haired woman who defied the camera with a raised chin – a Rembrandt-esque hat on her head at an angle, a shawl with large flowers and birds draped over her shoulders, and two showy rings on her right hand, which rested militarily on her breast, just above the heart. A Napoleonic stance. Thus inspired, Lotte slipped into the water-tower, ignoring the strict prohibition – long hair or ribbons could get caught in one of the machines. She positioned herself – chin up, hand on chest, directed her gaze upwards and brought about a change of scenery: the metal stairs no longer led to a reservoir filled with sand, gravel and coals, but spiralled endlessly upwards on their own axis, into a firmament full of stars – they might also have been theatre lights. As yet unhampered by excessive self-criticism, she sang 'Caro Nome' or 'Veranno a te' in her own Italian version as she had managed to learn it from the record. Her voice filled the whole tower from the low A-flat to the high E, ascending the stairs to where the steps became fainter and fainter, in a never-ending Escherian revolving. Her chest expanded. Drunk from the melody and the sound of her own voice, she floated away to another phase in her life – the reservoir arched high above her, a stained-glass window separated the light into coloured fragments, somewhere behind her the sound reverberated through the marble corridors of a labyrinthine building. It was an indefinable feeling that nevertheless half penetrated her consciousness and was immediately forgotten, as soon as she stopped singing.

A walnut piano of obscure East European make was acquired so that she could accompany herself. The money for it and the lessons was scraped together by her mother, to her father's bloodthirsty delight: now it was his turn to make a row about irresponsible expenditure. He readily over-indulged himself in the idolatry of such famous figures as Marx and Stalin, Beethoven and Caruso, but he could not imagine that something exceptional, for which sacrifices had to be made, could be developing within reach in his own surroundings, where the trivialities made him bad tempered increasingly often.

The piano brought a tuner to the house every three months. He was long and thin with a gypsy's bird-of-prey nose. His black curly hair was shaved on the sides but stuck up on top so that from a distance he looked as though he had a beret on his head. He always wore the same close-fitting black suit that elicited all kinds of speculations. Was it a wedding outfit from before the war, the dress coat of an undertaker, a morning coat with the tails cut off, or a theatrical costume worn by the devil or death? Below his tight trousers he wore modern American shoes which he kept in impeccable condition. He was a man of contrasts. The leanness of his body was compensated for by the visible dimensions of his genitalia, which, because of the shortage of space, he gave air in his right trouser leg, or on another occasion in his left. The whispering modesty of his voice was cancelled out by the honky-tonk sounds he elicited from the piano. The sisters fled to the kitchen, united in their aversion to his thing, but also amazed that his face remained so neutral in the presence of that which made itself so evident below his belt. They were commissioned to take him coffee, but no one dared. They clung to each other, giggling. Eventually Lotte took the cup in – he was her tuner. He accepted it with a smile, unaware of the consternation he was arousing with his controversial body. After his visit the cup was washed up with extra soap.

He was also a serviceable amateur photographer. Lotte's mother persuaded him to take a family portrait on the occasion of Eefje's birth. She had invited him on a Sunday afternoon in May; above the white garden bench that was selected to be the central ornament, a swallow's nest hung beneath the roof gable – the parental couple were doing overtime flying back and forth. Nervous activity prevailed before the photographer's arrival; up to the last moment dresses were being adjusted and straightened. Lotte's father refused to put on another suit. He was not planning to pose, he said; only the Tsar and Tsarina had themselves commemorated *en famille*. 'What have I got to do with that man?' he added scornfully. 'You don't have to do anything with that man,' said his wife, 'he's coming here to take photographs, I shall offer him a cup of coffee convivially and you will present a cigar.' But he was in the mood for sabotage, enjoying the power tossed into his lap by the occasion.

He was nowhere to be found when the photographer arrived lugging a heavy telescopic camera and stand. Irresistible in a dress with poppies on a cream background, Lotte's mother steered him into the garden. Her offspring trickled outside while he was positioning himself and his equipment where she indicated, directly opposite the bench. Mies, who worked in a milliner's business, wore a cognac-coloured suit with an inverted bird's nest of raffia on her head. Marie wanted to establish for posterity that she was the ugly duckling of the family; she had on a high-necked grey dress and refused to remove her glasses for the photograph. Jet and Lotte walked about stiffly, like fallen angels, in white organdie dresses with flounces and ruches. Koen, still a baby when Lotte had fallen through the ice, refused to wear long trousers to hide the grazes on his knees.

At the photographer's request, their mother, with the new-born in her arms, seated herself in the middle of the bench and, in the interests of the composition, she was flanked by the organdie dresses. The others stood behind, a climbing rose pricking them in the back. 'Lovely . . .' he murmured, studying the tableau vivant in his lens, 'er . . . isn't sir to be part of it?' 'Sir is in a bad mood,' said Lotte's mother, 'so we don't want him in the photograph.' 'Could there be a little smile perhaps?' They did their best to forget the big spoilsport and troublemaker and stared straight at the camera; the young swallows piped, a light breeze wafted the scent of lilacs, the photographer bent behind his magic box – the whole situation could have been agreeable if that lacuna had not existed there in the middle behind the bench, a missing figure who let his hands rest on their mother's shoulders. The photographer implored them to laugh. Forced attempts – only Mies smiled attractively, like a film star, eyeing the lens with a sensuous expression; Koen was scratching open the scabs on his knees.

At that moment Beethoven's Ninth began through the open window, booming and massive. The volume was turned up as far as the loudspeakers could manage. The photographer held his temples in his hands and shut his eyes pathetically. I cannot concentrate like this, he gestured. For the first time Lotte experienced a piercing, sweet-poisonous emotion that she could not yet define as hate. She looked over the photographer's head to the tops of the conifers that were moving gently in the breeze and wished furiously that her thoughts had the power to kill. 'Laugh!' cried their mother, prodding and pinching them, 'laugh chaps!' She showed her radiant smile, all teeth bared (didn't she want to tear him to pieces?). Her eyes joined in too, she was beside herself with plea-sure. 'We've got one more child,' she shouted above the Scherzo, 'a big, stubborn child, in there.' She gestured towards the window with her head, laughing sideways. A cloud passed in front of the sun, the photographer raised his long black arm to the sky and pushed it away. He held his breath and pushed the shutter in.

Lotte's father did not always opt out. He put up fierce resistance when she was sent to a Christian school because the state schools were not accepting any more pupils. He looked at his wife with utter disgust as though she had enrolled Lotte at an institution for the mentally handicapped. 'You'll see,' she said laconically, 'that in her case religious stuff will go in one ear and out the other.' She was proved right, though not in the way she meant.

The Bible had the appeal of the forbidden. Just as some girls sneaked into a bioscope with painted lips to watch an adult film breathlessly, Lotte was secretly thrilled by the Bible, which cer-tainly also carried the 'over eighteen' label, with all that death and killing, adultery and fornication it poured over the innocent reader. What tame reading matter her father's favourite book was in com-parison. Diligently she studied the stories of blood and miracles. Attempts to exchange ideas with her classmates ran straight into a wall of indifference. They had absolutely no thoughts about it; they were brought up on religion like a daily dose of cod liver oil. Similarly with the minister's daughter, with whom she shared her bench, the Bible was not a subject for contemplation but a duty, a soporific aspect of Sundays – weekly imprisonment in the gloomy confirmation classroom next door to the church. Their blind, unin-terested acceptance of it as a ragbag of stories, presented as 'what actually happened', shocked her. With her outstanding marks in biblical history, she was the only one taking religion seriously!

The director of the school, a man with a face etched from ice by a razor-sharp pen, spied at the pane in the door as the pupils ended their lessons with a prayer, and saw that one of them was looking out of the window waiting resignedly for the ritual to end.

He hurried into the classroom and with pursed lips said to the religious instruction teacher: 'She must stay behind.' A bony finger was pointed at her. The chosen one or the doomed? The class emptied. 'You were not praying,' declared the director. 'No sir.' 'How is it that you do not pray?' 'Sir, I never pray.' 'You never pray?' The narrow top lip was raised in an involuntary biting movement. 'No.' 'And what about at home?' 'They don't pray there either.' 'Then do you never go to church?' 'No, I never go to church.' The religious instruction teacher stroked his apostolic beard in amazement. 'But how did you end up at this school then?' 'There was no place anywhere else. My mother enrolled me. She wasn't asked whether I was a Christian.' The director stared at her with a suspicious frown, as though she were withholding from him the principal point at issue. It was clear that she was guilty of something, though he could not decide what it was. 'But you get the highest marks in the class in religious instruction,' exclaimed her teacher. 'I am hearing it all for the first time,' said Lotte; 'I have been listening very carefully.' 'And what do you make of it?' he asked, suddenly curious. 'I assume you have perceived that it is all profound truth,' said the director, supporting him. Lotte swallowed. She cast him a nervous glance – if she told him the truth that had been burning on the tip of her tongue all these months, he would expel her from the school immediately. 'Devil's children!' echoed a voice from an immense distance. 'Devil's children!' An apparition she vaguely recognized urged her on. Something black, something flapping about, the mournful tapping of a stick . . . It was no more than a diffuse feeling. 'No,' she said, suddenly seizing courage. 'Why not?' asked the director sharply. She looked over his bony shoulder to the outside, where shining black branches moved to and fro against a dark grey sky. 'It doesn't make sense,' she said. 'According to the story of creation, God is almighty and He is love. Then how is it possible that He has let the devil loose among the people . . . if He can do everything?' 'That is . . . a mystery of faith,' stammered her teacher. What a bromide! She looked from one to the other, overcome with contempt and pity at their bound-less naïvety. 'Adam and Eve lived in Paradise and ate from that for-bidden fruit...' She sighed. 'I think of it as Snow White.' The teacher took his glasses from his nose, fished a handkerchief out of his jacket pocket with thumb and forefinger and began to clean them thoroughly. The director's pronounced Adam's apple went up and down, he emitted a dry, cynical laugh. 'You cannot prove these things,' he announced, 'you must simply believe them.' Lotte scratched the back of her head. Her skull itched all over, she understood that it would be impolite, at this moment, to scratch vigorously all over with the nails of both hands. 'At one time you believed in Santa Claus,' she mumbled, 'but then one day no more.' Oh dear, she was on cracking ice, she had already gone too far. All she could do was walk boldly onwards, continuously shift-ing her weight. The director looked at her as though he wanted to tear her heathen's tongue out of her mouth. 'She doesn't under-stand at all,' sounded the deep voice of the religious instruction teacher, which gave a warm, bronzy dimension to the Bible stories. He put his glasses on and looked laconically at the director, who let his hands drop, the right one clenched into a fist; it was pointed at Lotte with the index finger sticking out like the barrel of a pistol. 'You are obliged to obey the rules of this school. Think it over. from now on you will pray with the others as normal.' He turned his high, crooked back on her with its drooping shoulders. Stooped beneath three centuries of Calvinism, he walked out of the class-room with something sharp in his step, as though he had got right on his side with this command.

※

'And...' Anna asked, her arm linked in Lotte's, 'did you pray with them from then on?'

They had left the café, whose interior harmonized perfectly with the period that was haunting them, and were walking step by step through the snow. It had already grown dark again. Nineteenth-century façades rose up on either side – balconies, towers, bays, *œils-de-bœuf*, dormer windows. In the shop window of a neighbourhood stationer's, between calendars, desk diaries and dip pens, was a book in which the Russian President set out his vision for the future; a dog was cautiously lifting its paws as it embarked on an untrodden piece of snow; the trees of the Athenée Royale stood motionless in their spot; the Christmas decorations were still twinkling in a greengrocer's.

'Of course not,' Lotte said, out of breath. The street was continuing to mount, and the alcohol too; it made her dizzy. They rested on the railway bridge. A red signal burned in the distance in the snow, a white spire stood out sharply in the dark sky. 'The director took every opportunity to thwart me. One day...' she giggled, 'I was wearing a dress with a V-neck. He stopped me in the corridor. "Now then, you must ask your mother for another dress you can wear. This one really is too naked."' A wave of Ratafia de Pommes ascended; she swallowed and began to laugh again. 'One time I rode to school on my father's bicycle. I got off in the playground and put it in the bicycle rack. As I turned round I almost bumped right into the director. "Don't do that ever again," he cried, "here, in public, in full view of everyone, getting off a man's bicycle! Shame on you!" I looked at him baffled. What did he mean, I asked myself, why does it bother him?'

Their laughter sounded drily over the cotton wool snow. They plodded onwards. When they reached Lotte's hotel, Anna invited herself for dinner. Presently they were seated opposite each other beneath a salmon pink ceiling with white ornamental borders and crystal chandeliers. At the next table was a young woman who was taking a postnatal rehabilitation treatment at the Thermal Institute. They agreed they would be better off ordering a carafe of water than a carafe of wine. For hors-d'œuvre they had *crudités* with Ardennes ham and strips of smoked pork; they cut the fat off the ham and left the smoked pork. The mother of the new-born folded her hands and closed her eyes before picking up her knife and fork.

'Wouldn't you like to ... to ...' Lotte whispered with an ironic laugh in the woman's direction, 'I mean ... before the meal ...'

'Me? Say grace before the meal?' Anna draped the salmon pink napkin on her lap. 'Understand me correctly, I do still believe, in my own way, but I renounced the institution of the Church long ago. Yet I have not forgotten what the Church did for me, then. Don't underestimate how far Church and society were caught up in one another. Those were quite different times – quite different.'

Jacobsmeyer summoned help from the child welfare agency. They sent a social worker to the farm. Aunt Martha started on about Anna, who was eavesdropping behind the door. All that time her poor aunt had been harbouring a viper: the child did not want to be good for anything, she associated with older men – she was a whore, young as she was. To Anna's amazement, the social worker encouraged her aunt uncritically in her philippic. Her last hope was flying away. The woman had come to help Aunt Martha, not her. When she had finished letting off steam, the woman said calmly, 'Now I'd like to talk to the child alone.' Anna fled back to the kitchen. With a satisfied laugh around her mouth, Aunt Martha came to fetch her. Anna went into the living-room fatalistically – Aunt Martha went outside, confident of her case. The social worker closed the door behind Anna, stood there with her back against it, opened her arms and said, 'Trust me, I will help you.'

Beneath her gaze, which was signalling that she could see through Aunt Martha, Anna's resistance melted. She understood that someone was throwing her a lifeline, someone for whom a nod was as good as a wink. A representative from another world who was objective and reasonable and perhaps (she hesitated) also more loving. Outside, she saw her aunt picking pears, right under the window, in the hope of catching something of the tirade that would be meted out to the young cuckoo. Anna relaxed. Was her serfdom really over? Would she no longer be at the mercy of the capriciousness and mistrust of a mentally deranged pear-picker?

She was plucked out of the house as she was, in her farming kit. She had a nourishing meal at Jacobsmeyer's. He gave her his blessing and money for clothes and waved to her as she rode in a car for the first time in her life out of the village on the Lippe. Up and down hills, through forests that flamed yellow and orange, until a village appeared, its houses ascending high up the slope, to come as close as possible to the ambit of the church towering over everything, and a half-timbered castle with dozens of tiny windows and slate roofs. Leaning against the church was a convent of the Poor Clares. A nun in a black habit hurried through the gate to meet them with open arms.

Compresses of crushed comfrey on the blue bruises, ointment on the cuts in her hands, age-old Franciscan calm, carefully conserved within the thick walls, foaming milk in large mugs, the unselfish devotion of the nuns, who fluttered along the lofty corridors like black butterflies. From her bed she could see the castle of Baron von Zitsewitz – a name from a fairy-tale, like the Marquis of Carabas. She had literally come straight into the lap of the mother church, together with a group of fellow sufferers, chosen ones, emergencies. They were silent about their pasts, as though by tacit agreement. From the nuns they learned the skills with which they would cope in the world later on: sewing, cooking, looking after children and even serving at table. There was a room specially for them where people from outside came to eat at lunchtime, well-fed guinea pigs (Mittagstischgäste), who consumed their experiments with relish.

That even greater preparations were being made beyond the convent wall did not get through to them. There was no radio, no newspaper, only a gramophone with a stock of fashionable popular songs, to which they danced with the younger nuns – beneath the disapproving gaze of a cardinal in purple formal robes whose portrait hung over the fireplace. The tango 'Was machst du mit dem Knie, lieber Hans' made Anna most breathless; she circled across the dance floor at a wild pace, her stockings sagging, her partner's habit clutched against her calves. It was the top hit in the convent until one day Anna listened carefully to the words and discovered that Hans was using the tango as an alibi to drive his knee like a wedge between the thighs of his partner on each upbeat. She warned Sister Clementine, who was swirling round in the arms of a sturdily built orphan girl, a blissful smile on her lips as though she were in the arms of her heavenly bridegroom. The record was put on again; still breathing hard, the nun listened to the words with her eyes closed. She swayed her head gently in time. Blushes slowly appeared on her cheeks, her mouth dropped open. The last sounds left a hideous silence behind. With raised head, Sister Clementine walked to the gramophone and lifted the record off the turntable with two outstretched fingers. Following Hans's example she raised her knee. Without scruple she brought the record down on it and broke it in two.

Anna's stained honour had been avenged, but she soon discovered that far greater humiliations threatened it. One of the Mittagstischgäste was a forester, a middle-aged man, with a jagged purple scar precisely in the middle of his bald head, as though a drunken surgeon had undertaken an unsuccessful attempt at lobotomy. Whenever anyone's eyes fell on it he declared casually that it had been a piece of shrapnel during a night-time patrol. Anna served him with scrupulous respect, *All Quiet on the Western Front* still in the back of her mind. That pleased him; familiarity would have offended him. One day with an authoritative nod he beckoned her over. He seized her by one wrist. 'And . . .' his eyes shone suggestively, 'have the nuns let their hair grow?' 'What do you mean?' With vicarious shame Anna thought of Sister Clementine's cropped head that she had once seen, moved by its vulnerable nakedness. 'Because soon, when the convents are shut down, they'll all have to get out of their habits,' he said with a greasy laugh. 'Then we'll really see what they've got for legs!' Her wrist was released. Her serving tray with full dishes was trembling in her hands; she crashed it down on one of the tables to be rid of it and ran blindly out of the dining-room without bothering about the other guests. Her pulse was throbbing at her temples, the clumping of her feet resounded through the lofty corridors. She knocked sharply on Mother Superior's door. Once inside she forgot all the rules of politeness and, out of breath, blurted out the self-evident expectation that the filthy Mittagstischgast would immediately be dragged out by his pigs ears from behind his piled-up plate, through the corridor of the convent and deposited on the granite pavement, after which the bang of the closing door would resound in his ears for days to come.

'Gently, shhh, quiet now...!' The abbess raised her hands beseechingly: 'What exactly did he say?' 'That all the sisters must take off their habits because the convents are being closed. How can he say such a thing?' panted Anna. Mother Superior walked softly to the door, which Anna had left open, and shut it carefully. 'Let us pray,' she said, turning round. 'How did he get that idea?' Anna insisted stubbornly. The abbess sighed. 'That doesn't concern us, it is all politics. They have all chosen that Antichrist together – he wants to close the convents and churches. Let us pray that it will never happen.' 'Antichrist?' Anna stammered. The forester acquired horns on either side of his scar. Mother Superior put an arm round her shoulders. 'Adolf Hitler,' she said gently.

A short circuit in Anna's head. A photograph, Bernd Möller, Uncle Heinrich, whizzed past each other, contradictory, evil. The champion of the poor and the unemployed turned out to be a destroyer of churches and convents. Her uncle was still being proved right – but did that justify the assault? How could she have been so mistaken? She was ashamed – at the same time she felt contempt for this titanic idealist's arrogance: how could he do anything to Christendom, or the Church, which had already held out for nineteen centuries? God would intercede personally, she was sure. That's why Mother Superior said 'Let us pray'. A strong faith; no attacker would be a match for it. The abbess went to the window and looked outside, a halo of yellow lime leaves around her wimple. 'What we have discussed here,' she said calmly, 'stays within the four walls of my room. Never talk about it with the others, you will get yourself into trouble.' Anna nodded, although she was not afraid of anyone.

The first month of the year 1933 was almost over when Anna looked down below out of a window on the first floor, and saw a gigantic flag flying where two roads crossed at the centre of the village. She recognized the spiders' legs with the points bent to the right; they rotated before your eyes if you looked at them for long. She hurried irreverently down the broad oak stairs, her footsteps rattling through the staircase. 'A flag!' she cried, storming into the refectory where two nuns were laying plates on the table with the precision of draughts pieces. 'They have hung out that flag, in the middle of the village, and no one is taking it down!' Mother Superior came in because of the racket, a soothing expression on her face. 'If I were a boy,' Anna raised her hands, 'it wouldn't be up there any more!' 'But you are a girl,' the abbess reminded her, 'so behave like one.' 'But that flag...' Anna spluttered, pointing through the walls at the thing that taunted the sky. Mother Superior shook her head. 'Anna you lack moderation. There are two possibilities for you: either you will become something formidable or you will end up in the gutter, there is nothing in between.' 'But the Nazarene said...' she stammered, gasping for breath, '... "because thou art lukewarm, and neither cold nor hot, I will spew thee out of my mouth"...' The abbess laughed indulgently. 'Ach Anna, we could take that flag down, but what it stands for ... we are powerless against that. Hitler became Chancellor of the Reich today.'

Annoyed, Anna ran outside. The word 'powerless' coming from the mouth of the Mother Superior was an insult addressed to the Almighty. The gate of the convent closed behind her with a crash. The road led straight down to the crossroads. She stopped beneath the flagpole. She threw her head back. It was no more than a piece of cloth. If it rained it would get wet, in the wind it would flap. There wasn't much left of the provocative character she had seen from the window on the first floor. From close up, as an object, it rated disappointing. She turned round in order to see the convent better for once. But it paled into insignificance, together with the church, the naked treetops, the January greyness of walls and roofs, in comparison with the red–white–black decoration on the spires of the fairy-tale castle. Von Zitsewitz had also hung out the flag.

7

'They were so good to me...' Anna took her leave from the nuns. Her education in the convent had been completed, the tuberculous cold treated, she had gained fifteen kilos, a layer of hard skin had grown over her inner injuries. It gave her an unprecedented self-assurance to have been brought back from absolute rock bottom. She returned home, down from the mountain to the river. She would not allow herself to be taken advantage of again. Uncle Heinrich – joy at her return gleamed through his reticence. Aunt Martha – her jealousy at Anna's rosy appearance, the frustration that she was alive at all, gleamed through her forced self-control. But she kept quiet: the eyes of the world (pastor, child welfare) were directed at her from now on.

During Anna's voluntary exile a change had crept into the village. Ever since farmers' sons with their own horses had been able to enlist in Hitler's élite corps, the Reiter SA, its image had risen to staggering heights. Moreover, he had upgraded the farming classes to the honorary first rank of providers in the Third Reich, the pivot on which society turned, the Reichsnährstand. Former school comrades, brothers and lovers of Anna's former friends – almost everyone joined the SA. No longer did anyone say: you don't do a thing like that. Only in the Catholic Congregation of Virgins, to which she had belonged since her confirmation at fourteen, were there some girls who shared Anna's distaste. The leader of the congregation, Frau Thiele, a teacher in whose class they had all been, had hastily set up a singing group, a dance group and a theatre group, to prevent her pupils going over to the Nazi youth organization, the Bund Deutscher Mädel, BDM, which had beaten her to it. Nevertheless her days as leader were numbered. A decree obliged her to join the National Socialist teachers' union. A subsequent decree forbade members of this union from being active in church organizations.

Jacobsmeyer took Anna to one side after mass. 'Listen Anna,' he looked at her conspiratorially, 'this time I want to ask something of you. Will you replace Frau Thiele as leader of the congregation?' 'I?' Anna's voice caught. 'I'm just eighteen, they won't take me seriously!' 'Shhh,' he calmed her, 'I haven't finished yet. At the same time you and a group of trustworthy girls will join the BDM.' Anna's mouth dropped open. He unfolded his plan, smiling slightly. To infiltrate the girls' section of the Hitler Youth, to bring him reports of everything that went on there and, finally, with God's help, to undermine the local section from within. 'You can do it Anna. I've known you a long time.' Anna stared at him with bewilderment. This representative of God, so trusted and reliable in the incense-scented robe in which he had just conducted the mass, would shrink from nothing! It filled her with pride that he had selected her for this mission. At last she could do something instead of remaining stuck in the fatalism that Mother Superior had preached. 'Will you do it or won't you?' Jacobsmeyer asked.

One Sunday she sang and danced for the Catholic Church, the next for the Hitler Youth – in a dark blue skirt with white blouse and brown jacket, the neckscarf through a ring-shaped toggle of plaited leather links. Jacobsmeyer was well rewarded. They received political training and learned how to write press reports. Anna was praised for her ability with the pen. Uncle Heinrich looked the other way, having been put in the picture by Jacobsmeyer. One sunny day in April the headmaster, who remembered Anna as an exceptional pupil, cycled out to the farm. 'I've brought you something.' He took a thin book out of his briefcase. 'Will you learn this by heart? The fact of the matter is a big celebration is being organized on the first of May: a play is being staged.' Anna wiped her muddy hands on her overall and leafed through it quickly. Uncle Heinrich came over suspiciously. 'The

Kreisleiter, the political chief of the district, is looking for a Germania ...' The teacher picked nervously at the lock on his case. 'she has to be sturdily built and blonde.' 'Why our Anna of all people?' said Uncle Heinrich; 'There are plenty more blonde girls in the village'. 'Because she's the only one who speaks decent German and can recite poetry.' 'Yes, that she can,' boomed Uncle Heinrich, 'but listen here ... Germania! That's really going too far!' 'We've got no one else,' the headmaster pleaded. 'I am a public servant. I have a family. I must see that it happens.'

There were rehearsals all month long. At the dress rehearsal Anna wore an elaborate wig of long blonde curls. With a straight face she had to recite the most melodramatic verses that ever flowed from a German pen. A soldier from the war with a bloody bandage round his head lay at her feet; he had to be visible from the back of the hall. Anna positioned herself facing an imaginary horizon, 'All around I see distress in German provinces, no rays of hope, no sunlight ... poor, unhappy Germania, all her sons are dying here ... the people are laid low there ...' The only acting talent required of the soldier was to be dead in a convincing manner, but the artery in his neck ignored the stage directions and pulsed so firmly that Anna burst out laughing half-way through the elegy. Shaking all over – the curls joining in subversively – Germania stumbled from the stage, her hand over her mouth, as though she might pass out at any moment. 'What's going on now,' shouted the director, at the end of his tether because it was forbidden to fail. 'I can't go on,' Anna hiccuped from the wings, 'if I've got to be serious! In God's name put a bandage round his neck too ...'

But on the first of May, Germania did not desert her role for a moment. She acted with so much dedication that she convinced herself too, not just her audience. Afterwards the Kreisleiter opened the ball. Without giving her a chance to change, he invited her to dance with an authoritative nod of the head. They waltzed over the empty dance floor, her chin on his epaulette, the goddess costume billowing out, the curls describing a circle round her head. Around them, boys in uniform and girls with garlands in their hair watched in admiration. The Kreisleiter was dancing with her! She was the tangible symbol of something they believed in, unsuspecting that the symbol in question had sneaked inside from an enemy camp. The triumph went to her head. The Kreisleiter held on to her firmly, as though from then on he would energetically take good care of the sorrowful Germania's fate. Anna felt herself submitting to temptation, allowing herself to be led with her eyes closed, and thoroughly enjoying her new status. Her former one, that of the poor maltreated orphan, was now quite hopelessly outdated. After the celebration she floated home on a pink cloud with golden edges. Uncle Heinrich tore the cloud to shreds with his scepticism. 'That's how they get young people to do their dirty work,' he said disdainfully, 'the seducers. Now even you see how they do it.'

The district section of the BDM sent a young woman with expertly pinned-up hair to the village to introduce morning gymnastics to the local section. From then on they had to gather on the square by the church at the crack of dawn, she announced, not to start the day with Our Father, but to hoist the flag, sing the national hymn and the Horst Wessel song. After that they would do morning gymnastics for a healthy and supple body, pushing up, swinging round, bending the knees, arms raised, bending over. She lectured them in a high-pitched urban accent. The charitable farmers' daughters observed her silently and full of inner resistance. How could they combine all these rituals with their work on the farm, which had already begun while it was still dark? Anna's eyes narrowed. When the woman had finished she stepped forwards out of the circle. 'I invite you,' she said, 'to start the gymnastics with me at five in the morning on the farm. You can pump water, feed the chickens and fifty pigs, give the calves water, and during the milking you can raise your arms up high and bend your knees, while the animals are content beside you.' The circle burst into relieved laughter. The leader laughed along with them, shocked; she rearranged something in her hairdo and hastily disappeared. Nearby yet unseen, Jacobsmeyer recorded her first success. There was no more mention of morning gymnastics.

In the autumn Hitler called the farmers together at Bückeberg near Hamelen to celebrate the harvest festival. Uncle Heinrich went along, curious despite himself. After he got back he fell into a gruesome week-long silence. Trustworthy people had become scarce in the village; the only person he could ultimately disclose his news to was Anna. Millions of farmers from the whole country had flocked together on that day, he recounted. In Lower Saxony, the Teutonic heartland full of holy oaks where the spirit of Widukind roamed about, they had waited on both sides of the road where the march would take place. Uncle Heinrich stood among them. He had read *Mein Kampf*, he knew that the author wanted to put its contents into practice word for word, he knew who would be coming past on parade. But what did happen was beyond his wildest fantasies. The Führer's appearance, perfectly stage-managed from beginning to end by carefully chosen artists, exceeded those of Nero, Augustus and Caesar put together. The crowds began to cheer, songs flowed through the ranks, a frenzied passion caught hold of the masses, red-white-black banners fluttered against a purple sky. Unanimous adoration went out to the single magical figure in whose hands the fate of the whole nation lay. Uncle Heinrich fought against the pull of the seduction as though he had fallen straight into a whirlpool in the Lippe. Gasping for breath, he wrested himself free from the gigantic, heaving, clamouring body and fled. 'They will follow him blindly,' he predicted, 'this Pied Piper of Hamelen. To the abyss.'

The Pied Piper's lust for power was tangible everywhere; not even the Archbishop of Paderborn was spared. He was arranging a pilgrimage to a shrine to the Virgin Mary on a Sunday; the BDM promptly organized a gathering on the same Sunday. 'Fine,' said the archbishop, 'then we'll arrange the pilgrimage for the following Sunday.' The BDM followed his example. The Archbishop was not dismayed, and once more rearranged the event, his footsteps again followed by the BDM. Eventually the pilgrimage was postponed indefinitely. Anna's patience was exhausted. 'Why are you doing that?' she asked at the next opportunity, 'sabotaging the pilgrimage?' 'What do you mean?' the leader of the BDM looked at her inanely. 'We're not doing anything.' Anna said severely, 'We are Catholics, we really do want to go there.' The others nodded in agreement. The leader shrugged her shoulders. 'I know nothing about it.' 'You're lying! You've thwarted the Archbishop of Paderborn intentionally. You are an underhand mob. I don't go along with it. I am a Catholic first and only after that a member of the BDM.' The leader's mock innocence was driving Anna into a blind rage. 'You're lying!' She pushed her chair back – the feet slid across the floor – and walked up to the woman, who hid her uncertainty behind a sheepish smile. 'I'll have nothing to do with someone who lies,' cried Anna, 'goodbye.' She went out without the Hitler salute, the door closed behind her with a bang. All chairs were immediately pushed back, the entire complement of the local section of the BDM stood up and left the room; the leader remained, her hands raised in astonishment, deserted. Jacobsmeyer's assignment had been completed: the BDM had disbanded itself in this village.

Anna was just cleaning the pig shed, putting straw down, taking the muck out, when a large black Mercedes drove into the yard, a small flag with a swastika on the bonnet. Who have we here, she thought, walking into the yard inquisitively. A sturdy woman got out, in a uniform richly decorated with badges. A real high-up, Anna could see, a Gauführerin. The driver stayed inside the car and stared glassily ahead. After a haughty glance at the farming things, and looking past Anna, the woman stuck her arm out towards Uncle Heinrich. 'Heil Hitler. I am looking for Anna Bamberg.' Uncle Heinrich looked at her with weary suspicion and said nothing. Crossly, as though she had accidentally addressed a deaf mute, she turned to Anna. 'Heil Hitler. Are you Anna

Bamberg?' 'Yes.' Anna's figure was assessed from on high, from head to toe – her muddy overall, her unpainted clogs. 'Are you the one who excelled at writing press reports?' she asked sceptically. 'Yes,' Anna wiped her nose on her sleeve, 'did you by any chance think I couldn't read or write because I clean out the pig shed?' The woman ignored her remark. The way her body had been crammed into the uniform was almost pathetic – the tension of the compressed flesh transferred itself to her fixed, controlled expression. She had come to call Anna to order: how could Anna break up the BDM just like that? 'Just like that?' said Anna. 'You are liars, that's what, just like that. I will have nothing more to do with it. Leave me in peace, I've got work to do.' She turned, picked up her muck cart and called over her shoulder: 'The Reichsnährstand is the first rank in the Third Reich.' She heard the Mercedes door slam sharply behind her.

⁂

'Ça vous a plu?' asked the waitress, bending towards them with a smile.

'Non, non, je ne veux plus,' Lotte said hurriedly.

Anna began to laugh. 'She was asking if you liked it.'

Yes, of course Lotte liked it. She blushed. What in heaven's name had she eaten? She had been chewing and swallowing automatically, absorbed by Anna's account. The enemy image that she had been fostering for years was coming increasingly under review. Everything was upside down – the alcohol had not yet worn off, the plentiful meal was taking a toll, inviolable certainties were crumbling. Two pairs of eyes looked at her expectantly – what dessert would she like? A list of sweets was rattled off, she could not understand another word of French. Coffee, she just wanted coffee.

'So you see,' Anna was indefatigably picking up the thread again, 'how Hitler caused a furore among us in the village. I'll tell you something else. A couple of years ago on a trip, by chance I went back to the Wewelsburg, you know, where we used to go for picnics with farm carts. In the war Himmler selected that castle to establish a cultural centre for the Third Reich. He had a tower built of gigantic dimensions, of diabolical beauty, a symbol of power. They could do that, the Nazis. More than four hundred people died in the construction of that monument. The cemetery where they are buried was obliterated later on. The irony is that people flock there now from all over the world – everyone is over-awed by its beauty. Himmler's scheme still works, that's the grue-some thing. They should paint that tower bright red; they should paint the Jews' martyrdom on it.'

Lotte looked around startled. Anna was becoming louder as she got more excited. The last sentences resounded provocatively through the sedate, salmon pink space. She gave Anna hand signals to turn the volume down a little.

Anna took the hint. 'Oh well,' she continued more softly, 'since the political relationships have changed they have set up a little war museum there. I looked around it a bit. There were all sorts of things on display. Right away I discovered two ballot papers from our village, neatly framed. One from 30 January when Hitler came to power and one from March in the same year on the occasion of a constitutional amendment that empowered him to make regulations, thus bypassing the parliament. My heart stood still. Uncle Heinrich seems to have been badly mistaken – at that time he thought there were only a few idiots in the village with National Socialist sympathies. From those papers it was evident that on 30 January one-quarter of our fellow villagers had already voted for Hitler; two months later it was already two-thirds. The farmers, the baker, the greengrocer, Uncle Heinrich's card-playing chums – suddenly they appeared in a different light. I was shocked, after all those years. It was lurking there all that time but he didn't know it.'

She rested her hand on Lotte's and looked at her with concern. 'Sometimes I worry that it is repeating itself. That ridiculous "One Nation" clamour for reunification, the rising nationalism. I never thought people would still be susceptible to that idiocy, in a Europe where you can fly from Cologne to Paris in an hour, to Rome in two hours. It bothers me. I don't want to be a Cassandra, but...'

'It's different for us,' Lotte interrupted her.

'The Dutch, yes ... damned spice traders!' Anna retorted. 'You have a different attitude towards foreigners because you were involved in world trade from early on. But the Germans – have you ever really thought about what kind of people we are? The ordinary man was never anything, never possessed anything. He never had any possibility of a decent existence. And if by chance he ever did have something, then there would be a war and everything of his would be lost again. And so it goes on, for ages.'

'But where did the Prussians get their pride from then?' Lotte forced herself to stay alert through the tiredness.

'If you've got nothing and are nobody you need something else to be proud of. That's what Hitler cleverly took advantage of. The little man acquired a function, got a rank, a title: block warden, group leader, provincial commander. In that way they could command, they could act out their assertiveness.'

The coffee arrived. Lotte was relieved. She raised the cup eagerly to her lips. Anna observed her wrily. 'The Dutch and their cup of coffee. Their lives and happiness have depended on it ever since they shipped the first coffee beans from the colonies.'

Lotte counter-attacked. 'Did you never have the slightest sympathy for Hitler again?'

'Sympathy? Meine Liebe! I found him loathsome. That general's voice: "Vórrr Vierrrzehn Jáhrrren! Die Schande von Verrrsáilles!" I felt nothing for him. I was an obedient child of the Catholic Church and believed what the pastor said to me because he was good to me. Very simple. Yet many obedient Catholics eventually allowed themselves to be tempted. Goebbels, who himself was brought up by the Jesuits, craftily introduced the traditional Catholic values that lay deeply embedded in people into

Nazi propaganda. The purity, the chastity of the German people, was glorified. The German man didn't meddle with sex, except when he had chosen a wife: a proper German woman, of course, who didn't smoke, didn't drink, didn't make herself up and had no illegitimate children. They married and had twelve children whom they donated to the Führer. Those ideals were hammered into them.'

Lotte sighed, staring at her empty cup.

'Why do you sigh?' Anna asked.

'It's all too much for me right now, Anna.'

Anna opened her mouth and closed it again. She realized that she preferred doing the talking, that she wanted to explain everything, everything, endlessly setting out the justifications. About the fate of the populations in the areas they had occupied, of which the Germans meanwhile had been fully informed. But they were obliged to keep quiet about what they themselves had experienced during twelve years of tyranny: for what reasons did the aggressor have to complain – had he not brought it on himself?

She controlled herself. 'If I blather on too much you must tell me to call a halt, Lotte. Father did that too, long ago, do you remember? He stuck his fingers in his ears and cried: "Quiet, Anna. Please be quiet!"'

Lotte did not remember it at all. Every time she tried to bring her original father to mind, the screen of her Dutch father slid over his image precisely because of the outward likeness – dominant, indelible. The coffee was beginning to work, she was reviving again. But Anna would have to restrain her facility for once. Enough politics, now it was her turn.

8

They were sitting on the raked gravel, the scent of a dark red climbing rose became more profound in the summer evening heat. Lotte was staring at the edge of the wood that was becoming progressively blacker. Her mother was swaying gently in time with Bruch's Violin Concerto in G, which lost none of its strength as it emerged through the open window. Opposite them sat two music lovers who came to admire the sound reproduction. Sammy Goldschmidt, flautist in the Radio Philharmonic Orchestra, listened with his eyes closed; Ernst Goudriaan, a student violin-maker from Utrecht, rested his chin on the tips of his fingers. The host himself was operating the equipment, out of sight behind the scenes. After the concert was over he came outside to refill his glass and to decline their praises with charming modesty. At that instant a nightingale began to sing in the wood, which had now turned into an impenetrable immensity.

'He means to compete with Bruch,' suggested Ernst Goudriaan. They listened with amazement to the mysterious solo song – a clear nocturnal jubilation, not intended for an imagined audience but purely for its own enjoyment. Lotte's father sat on the edge of his chair, struck by the record playing on a perfect machine in the depths of the wood. He knocked back two glasses of mature gin one after the other and shook his head: exceptional, what a sound! The following evening he stole into the wood like a thief, lugging his recording equipment, to find a strategic position, but the nightingale cancelled the performance. Much patience was dedicated to this. Evening after evening he hunted for its voice with stubborn perseverance until one night the miracle was repeated right over his head and he could secure it on a lacquer disc for ever. He went to the radio station with this hunting trophy. 'We have a surprise for the listener': the broadcast was interrupted in order to transmit the nightingale, almost live, into the ether.

Why doesn't he record my voice? thought Lotte. The more meticulously her mother followed her performances – she never failed to turn up whenever the choir was appearing somewhere, instantly recognizable among a thousand strange heads by the squirrel-coloured glow in her chignon – the more absent-minded he became when she sang on the radio. To everyone's great irritation he would begin to twiddle the knobs distractedly, as though there was something interfering with the sound reproduction. Could he not bear it that he was not the only one in the family who brought music into the house? Or was it because she had not inherited that musicality from him? Her own father was sometimes vaguely visible in the form of an imprecise longing, as though she was looking at him through a clouded pane. She wanted to clean the condensation off the glass in order to see him as he had been, to smash the cocoon of silence, to hear his voice as it had sounded. All those years he had slumbered in her – now his utter absence was infiltrating her, a negative, a total nothing. It was different with Anna. Lotte remembered her chiefly in a busy succession of movements, swift feet on a stone floor, jumping up and down, a powerful voice, a plump body that joined up precisely with her own in the middle of an enormous mattress. Anna. An illegal thought, a secret feeling. Not only did a border separate her from Anna, not only the distance, but above all the time period that had lengthened meanwhile, and opaque family relationships.

But Anna was alive. Even if it was via Bram Frinkel, eight years old, who had come to the Netherlands from Berlin half-way through the school year. Koen brought him home after school – football did not trouble itself with language barriers. Lotte got chatting to him in his own language; the words presented themselves as though they had never been out of use. For him she was an enclave of his home country – and he for her. Airily he told her why his parents had left it: there was no room for Jews in Germany any more. His father, a violinist, could pursue his profession in the Netherlands. Lotte taught him to say Dutch tongue twisters, he grimaced at the impossible 'g' sound and the meticulous 'ij'. Koen reacted to his sister's fluent German with surprise and distaste. He played alone with the ball a few metres away, offended, during her private chats with Bram.

Something happened that no one had thought possible. Lotte's mother, the radiant, the indestructible, caught an ailment that could not be dismissed with a reassuring diagnosis as flu or a cold. The first symptom was that she drove her husband out of the bedroom. From then on he slept on an improvised bed in his workshop, in a smell of solder and blown fuses, and during the day he moved about the house in a grim state – his worst moods of the past paled in comparison with this. From her bed by the three-bayed window with the view onto the rhododendrons, the meadow, the ditch and the edge of the wood, straight through the floor the children heard a torrent of enraged accusations directed at their father. The family doctor climbed the stairs with bowed head. It looked as though even he was threatening to succumb beneath the forces that were let loose on him on the first floor. Leaning on the dining-table defeated, her daughters speculated on the nature of the strange illness, not suspecting that they would get to the bottom of what was possessing their mother only after all the taboos had been gradually lifted years later.

The disease had begun with mistrust of her husband, who came home ever later from his trips to Amsterdam. One evening she had followed him with a friend – heavily made-up, dressed in fashionable coats with turned-up collars and Pola Negri hats. They spoke to him in disguised voices in Amsterdam slang. He did not recognize them beneath the street lamp in the shade of their hats. When, like a regular, he indicated his readiness to go along with their advances, they had linked their arms tightly and run off in shock and left him there puzzled. The next phase of the disease was brought home with him from the capital city and passed on to her. This was the most tangible symptom, which the doctor could combat with injections. Afterwards she lapsed into a state of great moroseness, which was followed by eruptions of rage – seen in retrospect it was the phase that preceded the cure, a cure that she herself would adopt in an unorthodox way.

Of all these things her daughters had not the slightest notion as they deliberated at the dining-table like foolish geese. They had been equipped with a minimum of sexual information, which could be summed up in their mother's breezy motto: nature must be left to its own devices. But that nature, which drove her back into the arms of the great troublemaker again after each row, aroused their fundamental suspicion. The idea of being stuck with such a man as their father for their whole lives was such a hundred per cent safe contraceptive that none of them 'had ever been kissed'. Not even Mies, with her close-fitting suits and her wide, greedy mouth. It was simultaneously tangled up with the fact that their mother seemed unconsciously to rebel against this fate imposed by nature, by allowing her daughters to read social conscience literature. About desperate servant girls who got pregnant by the master of the house, about mothers of twelve children in damp basements who had to defend themselves evening after evening from the roving hands of their drunken spouses, about black female slaves abused by those who had bought them for a few pieces of silver. Women out of Emile Zola, Dostoevsky, Harriet Beecher Stowe. If that was the 'full life' where nature was left to its own devices, for the time being her daughters wanted nothing to do with it, as they sat there round the table. So they bowed their heads timidly during the outbursts of rage that came from upstairs like a thunderstorm, which they too were powerless against.

Suddenly it went quiet up above. Without further explanation their mother got up, dressed herself carefully and left the house in silence with an absent-minded expression on her face. She was stared after by her bewildered daughters, who watched her disappear in the drizzle on her Gazelle in her familiar upright posture. That afternoon a painting one and a half metres wide was delivered, an impressionist representation of the marshlands their mother had a soft spot for: heavy, threatening clouds in a silver sky, reflected in a ripple-free lake edged by reeds and weeping willows. Shortly afterwards, she who had bought it from a very promising painter, and would have to bleed financially for it at home, returned – completely cured, her cheeks flushed with revenge. It was given a prominent place in the living-room, above her husband's sound system, and in silent competition with it. In safer times he certainly would have started a war on account of her extravagant purchase. Now, with badly faked enthusiasm, he seized the chance to make the unexpected cure permanent. Less than a year later an afterthought was born – Bart – the outcome of the restored peace.

From the inscrutability of all those emotions Lotte sought compensation in music. There was structure in it: the way the notes were arranged, carried by the beat, each fulfilling its function in the great totality, arousing the spirit by the artful ensemble. After the matriculation examinations were over she applied herself with redoubled industry to studying singing and to harmony theory lessons. An annoying factor was that her piano was in the same room as the gramophone. A symbolic arrangement: while she was practising, her father would come in and quite innocently put a record on or take a book out of the bookcase, gesturing to her to be quiet because he wanted to concentrate. She sat paralysed at the piano, cold sweat running down her back. She could no longer breathe when she was in the same room as him – he used up all the oxygen. She closed her eyes and submitted to his show of strength. Onto her eyelids she projected an Arcadian world in which the whole family, to the accompaniment of a nightingale's song, was walking in sober black behind his coffin.

On the day that her youngest sister was four, it looked as though her dream picture was actually going to come true. On his way home from work in the afternoon, her father would collect an order at the confectioner's shop. As his Harley was being repaired, he had asked for a lift home from a colleague who was just as enthusiastic a motor cyclist as he was. He left the shop with a cake box in his right hand and a bag of butter biscuits in his left. He got on carefully behind his colleague. In the interests of the cake they approached the junction they had to cross at a snail's pace. From the left at top speed, bent low over the handlebars, came a man on a motor bike, who only realized that he had to give way by the time Lotte's father was lying motionless on the ground in a strangely contorted position, his head on the edge of the kerb between a bag of crumbled biscuits and a crushed cake box, a trickle of blood coming out of the corner of his mouth.

He came round in the ambulance. 'Where are you taking me?' he enquired suspiciously. 'To the hospital.' 'No, no,' he protested, sitting up, 'I want you to take me home. There is no better nurse than my own wife.' His wishes were respected. He was carried inside on a stretcher. 'Mind your head,' he warned at a bend in the stairs, 'it's very low here.' His wife opened the bedroom door with a trembling hand. While the family doctor was ringing the doorbell downstairs they put him carefully to bed. He thanked them politely as they left, but when the doctor was examining him and asked under what circumstances the accident had happened, he mumbled in surprise: 'An accident? Was there an accident' 'You have had an accident,' said the doctor solemnly, 'they brought you home just now.' 'Who? Me?' He frowned wearily. 'Where is my wife?' 'She is standing here next to me.'

While the children waited tensely downstairs beneath coloured festoons, and the cake stand remained ostentatiously empty in the centre of the table, the doctor hesitantly diagnosed serious concussion and broken ribs. To be certain, he called in a specialist whose cool suggestion of a serious fracture at the base of the skull brought a threat into the house that was to extinguish all signs of life for six months. 'Wait,' he said, 'we cannot do anything but wait.' Marie and Jet took the festoons down in the unspoken conviction that every minute they remained hanging up would work to their father's detriment. Eefje picked listlessly at her new doll in a corner of the denuded room.

Their father had to lie flat. Grey, motionless, with eyes closed, he lay in the darkened room that smelled of disinfectants and eau-de-Cologne – as though he were already lying in state. For sure he was not dead, but nor was this life. Day and night his wife moistened his forehead, temples and wrists with a wet facecloth and manoeuvred teaspoonfuls of lukewarm water between his cracked lips. His breath rasped past his broken ribs; now and then he moaned from the murky no man's land where he was floating on the silver wings of morphine. The youngest children were taken to a sister of their mother: absolute quiet was a condition of his recovery. Everything in the house was performed with velvet fingers – they tiptoed, they whispered, they shrank from the sound of their own breath. With this radical absence of sound and the emphatic silencing of Beethoven and Bach, of sopranos and baritones, altos and basses, it seemed as though they were all unintentionally bringing death into the house, creating an atmosphere in which it could prosper. They could hear it rustling behind closed doors.

When it was Lotte's turn to take over the watch and she was looking at the stubble adorning the sunken cheeks like mould, she had the sneaking anxiety that the strength of her powers of imagination had landed him in this condition. She regretted the vengeful fantasies he had provoked in her. Had there really been covert angry intent in his behaviour or had it been his usual, familiar egoism? She fervently hoped he would survive, otherwise from then on she would have to practise strict censorship over her thoughts. More than that, the picture of her own father as he had awaited death, surrounded by members of the family, radiated through her sense of guilt. All those years she had successfully stashed it away, but it came up again as a result of the striking likeness, together with the alienating, anxiety-producing feeling that it had caused. In this way the watch was a continually recurring form of self-torment because it evoked this gamut of feelings every time.

After a few hours she was relieved again by her mother, who kept watch like a sphinx for the rest of the twenty-four hours. Sometimes she leaned over him to check with her ear that he was still breathing. 'You will not slip away from me,' she whispered, 'my old rascal.' She did not neglect herself. Regularly she changed her dress so that, on the rare occasions he opened his eyes, he would find an attractive woman by his bed. Through a chink in the curtains she saw the sun come up and go down, she saw the mist over the meadow, she heard the cooing of the wood pigeons. At night she saw the stars; she could not put a light on to read a book – perhaps that was her greatest sacrifice.

Yet even with her stubborn presence, she could not prevent him getting double pneumonia with pleurisy after three weeks. The doctor was a bad actor: it was obviously difficult for him to conceal that he might pass away at any moment. He arranged for a night nurse, who treated the peaks of the fever with cold compresses. At night the patient's delirium was the only sound in the house. The nurse attached bags of ice cubes to his head. 'No,' he protested, shooting upright out of his dream with staring eyes; he flailed them away with spastic arm movements: 'I don't want that crown! I don't want to be king of England, I won't, I won't!' The nurse grabbed the bags from the pillow and pushed him back with gentle insistence. 'You must stay lying flat,' she exhorted him. 'I don't want that crown,' he whined, 'I want Miss Simpson!' Rebelliously he sank back into his deep feverish sleep.

When the crisis had abated, he opened his eyes and in chastened calm saw the strange woman's face wreathed in a shock of stiff hair that stood on end. She looked back fiercely beneath her bristly eyebrows – her normal facial expression which was not meant to convey anything in particular. 'You look strikingly like Beethoven,' he said with amazement. 'You are very observant,' she admitted, 'in fact he was a relation.' They were just about to heave a sigh of relief when a blood clot in his leg reintroduced the possibility of dying. The doctor became entangled in conflicting treatments: the patient had to sit up on account of the thrombosis, while it was vital that he stayed lying flat for the skull fracture.

Because visits to the patient had been forbidden, the house had been cut off from the world, an island, with the poor, afflicted body at its centre. To escape from this vacuum, this interruption of the usual vitality, Lotte strolled in the garden and ended up at the back in the orchard. She stroked her hand over the peeling paint of the TB house, she picked off a piece of moss, broke a twig from the walnut tree whose robust crown embodied the fourteen intervening years. The swivel mechanism of the house had rusted completely so that the open side pointed permanently to the east. The east. She sat down on the rickety kitchen chair and imagined an unfamiliar Anna in the year 1936. Not in a clearly defined physical form, but as an accumulation of energy, lit up, vital; Anna was alive. She was full of remorse and shame for having thought so little about her for so long, as though Anna had become a lost cause. She tried to put herself in the place of the child with a lung infection who had lain here looking about her in fevered amazement. What she had been too young, too sick, too dependent for then, now seemed ridiculously simple: get on a train back to Cologne. She fantasized about seeing it again – just thinking about Anna was already a mild antidote to her father's continuing flirtation with death.

On Sunday he suddenly became short of breath. Like a fish on dry land he gasped for air with a gaping mouth. His wife propped him up against the pillows, gave him water, unbuttoned his pyjama jacket – he clutched at his heart. The doctor was alerted. An unfamiliar locum doctor gave him a large injection straight into his heart. 'A last rescue bid,' he whispered, putting the syringe away in his bag, 'prepare yourself for the worst, madam.' Hours of waiting. It was a miracle that her resilience had not yet been exhausted after all those months. The question Will he pull through or won't he? so permeated the atmosphere in the house that Lotte walked in the wood because she feared that an involuntary thought escaping the censor at such close quarters might be fatal to him at the critical moment. By the evening his breathing was regular. He took a drink of water and asked his wife to put Mozart's *Requiem* on downstairs, full volume with all the doors open. She let the needle descend onto the record with a trembling hand. Melancholy sounds floated up the stairs. Jet burst into tears. 'Be happy,' said her mother, 'that you aren't hearing the music at his funeral, but that he can enjoy it himself now.'

After this apotheosis the healing process slowly got going: he returned to life in style. Bit by bit he was allowed visits. 'But what's happened to Hans Koning?' he complained, still translucent with weakness. 'He's sure to come,' his wife pacified him. 'But does he really know what's going on?' 'Of course.' But the professor did not get in touch at all. As dependable as the weekly visits with which he had honoured the house before the accident had been, so was his absence now obstinate. Lotte's mother telephoned. He turned up on the doorstep with a dejected face, in polite response to her summons. He stumped upstairs, bumped his head at the turn in the stairs, and stood embarrassed at the end of the bed without shaking the patient's hand. 'How are you?' he enquired, coughing drily behind the enormous fleshy hand with which he was used to waving objections away. The patient did not conceal his joy. The mere presence of his bosom friend and fellow spirit brought more colour to his cheeks than all the other visitors put together. 'I'm lying here but...' he sighed, 'would you believe that I crave an old-fashioned Saturday evening...' Hans Koning looked at him tensely. 'Listen, my dear fellow, I'm no good in sick-rooms...' To demonstrate this he looked around him tormentedly as though he were trying in vain to survive in a poisonous atmosphere. 'I mean it, I simply cannot stand it for a minute!' 'But...' the patient sputtered in disbelief. The professor proceeded towards the door. 'Give me a signal when you are your old self again,' he turned round holding the doorknob. 'Get well soon.'

Faithful to his allergy, he did not show up again during the months of slow recovery. The patient had to struggle with bouts of depression. Why was his best friend staying away, just now when he had a crying need for his company to sharpen his splintered mind again, to stimulate his fantasies, so that he could repossess the viewpoints of his former opinions with bravura? The professor's absence was a personal defeat. 'What do I matter to anyone actually?' he asked himself, propped up against the pillows. 'I am nobody. What have I achieved? Nothing. I haven't any standing in the world. Why didn't I simply die?' His wife hastened to convince him of his excellence, enlarging expansively on his merits, spiriting away his unpleasant characteristics. She sincerely believed it, so fervently did she hope that he would become his old self again. His resistance to so many flattering words collapsed at once. 'You are a tremendous woman,' he whispered, falling asleep consoled.

It was an impressive crossing of boundaries, which they would not forget among all the other events, that day he came downstairs, shuffling step by step into the living-room, dizzy from the effort, to drink a cup of coffee in an armchair that was hastily pushed by the fireplace. The bench in the garden was the next milestone. He won territory bit by bit in this way until, one day when he was alone at home, he grew too ambitious in his urge to conquer. Perhaps the absence of his wife made him anxious, perhaps he could no longer resist after months of suppressing the longing for an exchange of spiritual views. Giving in to a light-hearted impulse, he waddled over the plank across the ditch, into the wood, slowly and concentrating – his one leg limped a bit as a result of the thrombosis – his heart beating excitedly. When he reached the Koning family's house on the other side of the wood, in pure exhaustion he hugged one of the two dark green pillars supporting the porch over the door. He did not know how long he hung on there like that, fighting against breathlessness and palpitations, and the fear that the professor would find him in that state. He only pressed the bell when he had recovered a little. His friend opened the door himself, in a three-piece suit, a silver watch chain like a festoon on his breast. His beard bobbed up with fright. 'Heavens, what are you doing here? You're the last person I expected here. I regret...' he toned his voice down as though he were on the point of letting the other in on a secret, 'we're just expecting visitors, they'll be here at any moment. How could you have timed it so wretchedly? You had better come in, then you can leave via the kitchen door.' Lotte's father stumbled along the passage and sank into a kitchen chair. 'One moment,' he panted, 'I must just ... may I ... might I have a glass of water?' 'I'll have a look for you...' The professor threw open all the kitchen cupboards and slammed the doors closed with a bang. 'God, where does she keep the glasses? ... A cup will do.' The unwelcome visitor drank his water. The professor opened the kitchen door with a wave. 'Better luck next time, old fellow. Jesus you look lousy.'

Lotte's mother looked up when she heard crunching on the gravel. She saw her husband, whom she had thought to be in bed, stumbling along the garden path, seeking support from a pear tree half-way along and staring at the house with a dazed, hollow gaze as though he had sensed something dreadful there. When she looked more closely she saw he was crying. That same evening she told the professor by letter she was terminating the friendship. Her dip pen, scratching over the writing paper, called him an arch-egoist whose humanity disappeared on the threshold of sick-rooms and on the doorstep of his own house.

❦

'Yet it is striking,' said Anna, 'that you had a fantasy about travelling to Cologne at just that time.'

'Why?'

'Because at that time the urge in me to go to Cologne became stronger and stronger.'

❦

Anna had reached the age at which her own father had become oppressed in the symbiotic world between the church and the river: no more than a collection of farms and their inhabitants who watched each other being born and dying. Similarly in her case that mental tedium did not convert into fatalistic acceptance of destiny, but into rebelliousness. She tugged Jacobsmeyer by the sleeve of his soutane. 'How am I ever going to get out of this village?' Her voice disturbed the calm in the Landolinus church. 'Surely it isn't my vocation to lug pig muck for the rest of my life?' Jacobsmeyer nodded pensively. 'Perhaps I do know of something for you . . .' He stroked his chin contemplatively. 'The Archbishop of Paderborn is looking for a young woman to replace his elderly housekeeper in the long run. He wants to have her trained at an institute in Cologne where the daughters of well-to-do families learn about managing maids and servants. A school for ladies . . .' He laughed ironically.

Uncle Heinrich was not against it. Aunt Martha had more difficulty gracefully accepting the departure of an unpaid worker. 'You don't know what you're embarking on,' she said scornfully, recoiling at the thought of all that work she would now have to shoulder. 'It will come to nothing, I can tell you that.' Anna stirred the soup in silence; she had little inclination to get involved in another scene at this eleventh hour. 'Why don't you say anything? Do you feel you're already too good for us? I'll tell you something: it will work out badly for you there. I can already see the day that you . . .' her voice broke, 'come crawling back here on your knees, begging for a piece of bread. Don't think . . .' Anna sighed wearily. 'Why excite yourself?' she said coolly, without looking up from the pan, 'I'm going to die anyway; you've always said so. Surely I won't get to twenty-one?'

She was enrolled for the new semester. Uncle Heinrich contacted a cousin in Cologne for lodgings and ordered a tailor to make a coat of indestructible material to last a lifetime. In the same way that a bride in her wedding dress and veil is initiated into being a married woman, Anna predicted that this coat would usher in a totally new existence for her. Some days before the departure she was summoned to Jacobsmeyer. 'I have something awful to tell you, Anna: this job isn't going to happen.' 'You can't mean that...' She slumped down in one of the gleaming polished pews and looked at the statue of the Virgin Mary, which suddenly seemed self-satisfied to her. She couldn't go back any more – she had already stripped off her former existence – that was all she knew. Jacobsmeyer paced up and down in front of the altar, rubbing his jaw. 'You know what,' he turned round abruptly, 'we won't say anything to your uncle and aunt. I'll pay for the school. You say nothing, pack your suitcase, travel to Cologne and attend your lessons.'

On the first day of November Anna caught the train at Paderborn. She wore a trench coat made with room to grow, and to go with it a grey felt hat with a brown feather from the summer plumage of a pink-footed goose. Her possessions were in a cardboard margarine box. The train rode through pine forests and towards yellow deciduous forests, through meadows and ploughed fields. She closed her eyes and opened them again, hoping to see something she recognized. The landscape slid by neutrally. Yet she felt that she was coming steadily closer to her birthplace, that the thread which had held her tight for fourteen years had slackened, but it was being gathered in now – in the puff-puffing tempo of the train. But when the train roared into the station the feeling of being on the way home deserted her. The massive presence of the Cathedral right next to the station intimidated her, with its serrated silhouette of pointed spires protruding against the anthracite-coloured sky like a sombre warning. How futile your pleas would be in this outsized place of worship, given that it had already been hard enough to be heard up above from the Landolinus church. She clutched the cardboard box to her belly. And now for Uncle Franz, she said to herself, so as not to be sucked up into the innumerable parallel lines. She dug a carefully folded piece of paper out of her coat pocket. In Gothic letters of almost calligraphic beauty, Uncle Heinrich had written the name of a hospital where his cousin was chief maintenance technician. A passer-by told her in Cologne slang which tram she had to take. She suppressed the inclination to greet everyone when she got on, and passed down the gangway between all these fellow citizens – yes, fellow citizens. But no one noticed her. They were staring outside with a certain resignation, as though they had not personally chosen to ride in this tram through this city at this point in time. The tall façades, the bustle of people, the traffic; the density of life in the city of her youth overwhelmed her. In the village she had always been the daughter of old Bamberg's renegade son who died young; here, in the overcrowded anonymity, she was absolutely nobody.

As she pushed open the heavy door of the hospital, she had the distressing sense that she was stepping into a city within a city. There were births and deaths in both, in greater concentration here. She waited for her uncle in the foyer on the edge of a leather armchair. The glances of passers-by rested on her just a little too long. Suspiciously, she tried to see herself through others' eyes. She saw someone in a medieval coat, with a hunting hat and a droll feather and a shabby box on her lap – a rare example of a type that had become extinct in the city long ago. I look ridiculous, she judged. A man in a white coat came up to her. A look of horror slid fleetingly across his face, but he subdued it immediately and shook her jovially by the hand. She tried to remember him from the funeral, hoping to find something from the past in his face, now that she had not yet succeeded with Cologne in that respect. But she recognized nothing – he did not look like her father or Uncle Heinrich or her grandfather. His cheerfulness was definitely not a family trait either. 'Is this all your luggage?' he asked, taking the cardboard box from her. Anna nodded silently. She took off the ridiculous hat, so as to have something in her hand, and followed him, ashamedly stroking the feather with her finger.

His house was in the hospital grounds. He left her there in the care of his wife, who welcomed her with a baby in her arms. Aunt Vicki showed her round, chatting airily. She was plump, her reddish-blonde frizzy hair held in check by combs. There was a little dimple in the middle of her chin, which sometimes made her expression look bashful, as though someone were unexpectedly deceiving her, but then an unrestrained laugh brushed her face clean again. Anna walked through the citizen's house in a fuddle. A room with polished furniture – just for sitting in! The enormous horn of a gramophone gaped boldly at her. A real WC with wash-basin. Hot running water. A bedroom to herself: wallpaper with a medallion motif, a dressing-table with a marble top and washstand, a hanging cupboard – for the clothes she did not possess. The wooden privy at the back on the farm, the pump she washed under, the attic with the worm-eaten floor where she slept – these were abruptly banned to the hazy region of unwelcome memories.

Dizzily she slid between the stiff sheets that evening. Although she had tumbled into a different existence in a single day, she had the feeling of being further than ever from the city that had sur-vived inside her for all those years. The microcosm of a six-year-old, a covered-in city, where life was intact and round and where trusted voices sounded. Aunt Vicki put her head round the door: 'Schlaf wohl, Anna.' 'Gute Nacht . . .' she replied hesitantly. Her aunt and uncle's good nature confused her, accustomed as she was to surliness and suspicion.

At the school for ladies she was the only one who came from the country. No one noticed. She wore her aunt's dresses; she had always respected High German – her father's vehicle for distancing himself from his family. Yet she could only half follow the pupils' conversations; their language referred to an unknown world with its own jargon: an impending engagement, a *thé dansant* on Sunday afternoon. No *thés dansants* for Anna, but in the nearby bioscope the magical darkness recalled those vague memories of the theatre in the casino. Heinrich George and Zarah Leander with curls plastered on her temples and a rose behind her ear. *Die grosse*

Liebe, Heimat, La Habanera. The Ufa films were preceded by a
newsreel; images of reality acquired the allure of dream pictures.
Across the white screen marched lively soldiers. Germany had an
army again, it was busy at high speed pulling itself together out of
the malaise. Healthy, athletically built boys were sent out by the
Reichsarbeitsdienst to drain the marshes or to bring in the harvest.
Beaming girls, not wearing make-up, were helping on the farms;
they cleaned and polished and looked after the children; they were
working as health visitors. They smiled indefatigably, lived in
camps and began the day by hoisting flags and singing the Horst
Wessel song lustily: 'Die Strassen frei, die Reihen fest geschlossen'.
It was going well in Germany; everyone was helping enthusiastically with reconstruction; it was the end of chaos, poverty, unemployment. There was structure again, a structure which had the
colour of ripe corn and a summery sky, of blonde hair and blue
eyes. Despite her mistrust of flags and marching songs, her dislike
of the screaming Austrian and the warnings that came out of Uncle
Heinrich's Bückeberg adventure, she was at the same time swept
along by the optimism, together with the others sitting close
together there in the intimacy of the warm bioscope. The pictures
gave a comfortable feeling of confidence. Everything in the world
outside was under control, and on top of that they also got a film
into the bargain. The total improvement was no surprise to Anna –
it coincided naturally with the progressive line that her own life was
taking. Germany was climbing up out of the pit, so was she. This
was not a sober observation but an impression of the senses, a rising awareness of simultaneous ascent. The bar of chocolate Aunt
Vicki shared with her during the performance was the best proof of
it: who would have been eating chocolate previously?

Yet Cologne, with its history going back to Roman times, continued to intimidate and disillusion her. The sturdy round towers
with battlements that she often passed were subtly indicating to
her that fourteen years' exile on the edge of the Teutoburger Wald
amounted to nothing compared with being a Roman tower in

Teutonic Germany for nineteen centuries. And the Lippe was no more than a ditch compared with the Rhine. One Sunday afternoon she was walking in a park with her aunt and the pram; a wintry sun cast long white strips between the tree trunks. She still had difficulty about simply not having to do anything on one day of the week: walking about without a purpose, bending over the glittering surface of a pond, lifting the baby out of the pram and holding it up against the blue sky with outstretched arms so that it could waggle its limbs about. On impulse she said, 'Let's walk past the casino, where I ... where we used to live.' That 'we', said out loud, legitimized the idea: she ought to go to the casino on behalf of her father and Lotte too; they would accompany her and be looking over her shoulder. Aunt Vicki shrugged her shoulders: fine, it was all the same to her. In her innocence, chatting peacefully about trifles, she served as a lightning conductor for the sudden anxiety that clamped Anna's throat shut. As though she were an indifferent passer-by, she was strolling along the street from which, as a child, she had gone, carried off by hasty family members in the opposite direction. The street that was inextricably linked with the figure of her father walking over the cobbles in a black coat, leaning heavily on his stick and from time to time bringing out his spit bottle and quickly hiding it away again. By then the dark cloud on which he would float away – out of the city, the country, the world – was already hanging over the street, above the casino, the church and the school.

They passed the school; the windows began high up above the ground, it was impossible to see outside through them; passed the church in a merciless nineteenth-century style that inspired fear of the Supreme Being. She stopped a little further on. Her gaze ascended the façade up to the stained-glass windows, it slid sideways down towards the varnished double door with copper bell and small latticed windows. Wherever she directed her gaze it ricocheted back. The building shut her out, denied that she had breathed inside it, that her thoughts and feelings had filled its spaces, that her father and Lotte had been alive there. These walls had once enclosed family life; now they formed an immovable obstacle between her and the others. 'They have asphalted the street,' she said disdainfully. 'There used to be cobbles.' They walked on, as though it were any street. Everything was normal, the sun was shining, it was winter, 1936 was coming to an end, 1922 was unimaginably long ago. Her first six years, and those who had had a part in them, had left no trace: there was nothing to recall their existence.

The village on the Lippe did not exist any more either. Uncle Heinrich did not get in touch with her nor she with him. Only Jacobsmeyer had a letter from her now and then. When she was twenty-one years old the Court of Justice summoned her to sign the guardianship declaration so that her uncle could be released officially from his responsibilities. It was a long screed. She started reading it cursorily; she understood that her signature indicated her approval of the manner in which he had exercised his guardianship in the past. Did what it said in the declaration concur with reality? She felt hot, she felt cold. She simply could not read any further. This text referred to somebody else, from another life. She looked up from the document in confusion. Opposite her, in a sterile office behind a metal desk, the duty official nodded impatiently at her. She wrote her signature with an angry stroke. This Anna, smelling of soap, clothed in clean citizen's clothes, put the pen down, pushed the document brusquely towards the official, stood up and left the building. She went down the stone front steps and walked in the city, a city that would have to be reconstructed anew on the sunken foundations of her memory.

The ink on the certificate from the school for ladies was hardly dry before she had a job, as a live-in servant girl with one free Sunday every fortnight. She went into service with the Stolz family who lived in the east of the city in a neighbourhood of small villas, not far from the Bayer industrial complex where Stolz worked as a chemist. She had no notion at all about what it meant to be someone's servant girl, an organic component of your employer's household. Her expectation that she would be in charge of the Stolz family's housekeeping was already belied on the first day, when it became evident that legislative and executive powers were divided. The first, in the person of Frau Stolz, had devised a factory system to enable the household activities to proceed as quickly and efficiently as possible. Ever since her marriage, nine years ago, the skirting boards in her villa in the east were dusted at ten o'clock each morning, on Thursday afternoons the shirts were ironed at two-thirty, on Saturday mornings the windows were cleaned at nine o'clock. She had worked out to the decimal point how long each task required. The elements of the programme slotted so tightly into one another that the executive power hardly had time to breathe in between. As though in a silent film, Anna sped from one task to the next. With a hogshair brush she was dusting the skirting boards – half-way through this the doorbell rang, she put her brush in her overall pocket and answered the door. She resumed her work feverishly after the interruption, which had not been included in the programme. On her daily check Frau Stolz ran her index finger over the half-metre that Anna had overlooked because of the delay: 'You have not dusted here today.'

That her insistence on unquestioning obedience crushed all forms of personal initiative not only escaped her, she also blamed her subordinate for it. One afternoon she went out visiting. Anna had to iron all the shirts before she returned. It began to rain. Anna looked up, saw the drops on the window, was caught in a dilemma: if she went upstairs to close the bedroom windows she might not finish the ironing in time. She did not dare take the risk. A little later on Frau Stolz stormed in to the room, out of breath. 'I wouldn't have thought it,' she cried triumphantly, 'I say to my friend: I must go, the windows are open at home, it will rain in. She says: Isn't there anyone at home? Oh yes, I say, our servant-girl – but don't think that the idea will occur to her!'

Frau Stolz was convinced that, apart from laying down require-
ments, which she saw as a form upbringing, she also had a major
responsibility for Anna's welfare. She could not tolerate Anna
being alone in her attic room on free evenings, but invited her for a
cup of chocolate milk in the sitting-room. She taught her openwork and embroidery, in cross-stitch and *petit point*. Skills that a
young woman had to master, she explained, magnanimously providing Anna with the materials that were needed. They sat there as
a threesome like that, Herr Stolz with his newspaper, his wife and
the servant-girl united by a piece of needlework. Their daughter,
Gitte, a girl of eight with long plaits, was already in bed.

Whenever a speech was expected from the Führer, he switched
on the Volksempfänger – the standard issue utility radio set. Anna
listened and did not listen. It was the same as the embroidery that
she was working on: she did it but her head was not involved.
Goebbels spoke first, about issues that fell far outside her field of
vision. 'The plutocracy – the Wall Street Jews want to ruin us ...'
tatata, so it went on. This was only the prelude. Marching music,
military commands, Sieg Heil, Sieg Heil. Then he himself spoke,
directly to his people, too loud as usual, and kept that up throughout the broadcast. 'I must first of all reassure Mr Minister Eden
that we Germans do not in the least want to be isolated and also
that we do not feel isolated at all ...' Herr Stolz nodded in agreement. He folded his hands over the curve of his belly and listened
attentively. Anna impassively allowed the bragging to drift over
her, she waited until it was over, just as you wait for a rainbow to
end – meanwhile she continued to breathe quietly. The Führer had
become an institution. Everything was being decided and organized
at an abstract level, over her head; she had not the slightest influence in it. So she felt entirely indifferent about it. The silent struggle against Frau Stolz's authority was already exhausting enough.

Over the edge of her embroidery she had already peeked at the
walnut bookcase dozens of times, where the books were kept
behind glass as though they were jewels. She could not resist the

temptation any longer. 'Herr Stolz, excuse me, may I...?' She pointed towards the sanctuary with her embroidery needle, '...may I read a book one day?' 'Of course,' he nodded to her with surprise, 'choose one.' Avoiding Frau Stolz's staggered look, Anna stood up and went to the bookcase hesitantly. She pushed open the squeaking doors; a delightful smell arose from the bound volumes, many with gold blocking, a smell of thousands and yet more thousands of printed pages, of cardboard covers, of stories that begged to be woken out of their hibernation, of escaping from the foolish, unreal here and now – the promise of infinitely more fascinating worlds than that of cross-stitch and openwork. She read the titles giddily, Frau Stolz's eyes burned holes in her back. She dared not hesitate too long, took out *Die Leiden des jungen Werthers*. 'That is much too difficult,' sputtered Frau Stolz. 'Have you read it?' said her husband. 'No, but...' 'Well then, let her, culture is for everyone nowadays. It wouldn't do you any harm if you read a book sometimes too.' Frau Stolz fell silent, and laughed at Anna, to smooth things over. It was not clear whether the smoothing over referred to the humiliating remark from her husband or to the painful fact that she did not read. Anna opened the book and buried herself in it.

From this it seemed that the balding, wayward chemist was the weak spot in Frau Stolz's armour. Perhaps her domineering and perfectionism were purely means of preserving her self-respect. She recovered her strength whenever they were women together. The day after Anna had given evidence of her appetite for reading, she asked, holding the lid of the laundry basket in front of her like a shield, 'Don't you take any washing to your aunt on Sundays?' 'No,' Anna said, surprised. 'How is it that you hardly ever have any washing, a dress now and then...' 'I've only got two dresses.' '...And now and then some underclothes ... never a sanitary towel...' 'Sanitary towel? What's that?' Frau Stolz's eyes popped. She towered over Anna who grew smaller and smaller. She possessed nothing, two dresses, some underclothes, she was nobody.

'You're not really telling me that you don't know what sanitary towels are?' 'No,' said Anna, 'never heard of them.' 'But you menstruate?' 'Menstr . . .? No.' 'But every woman menstruates, each month.' Anna was silent for a moment, bewildered. 'I am not aware that I am lacking anything,' she said defiantly. 'Listen . . .' With maternal concern Frau Stolz laid her impeccably well cared-for hand on Anna's shoulder. In a lowered voice, creating an atmosphere of familiarity that aroused great distrust in Anna, she initiated her into the secrets of the female cycle. Frau Stolz's 'we', which referred to all women in the world, met with violent aversion in Anna. If it was womanly to lose blood every month, just as Frau Stolz lost blood every month, then she was proud that her body was having nothing to do with it.

But Frau Stolz made an appointment for her with her gynaecologist. During the examination he asked her how it could be that the hymen was broken. 'Have you ever been with a man?' It did not strike Anna that a reply was expected. She scanned the ceiling stubbornly – she had discovered cracks and colours, shapes and figures that were unintentionally expressing something, the significance of which she strenuously tried to comprehend, as diversionary tactics against the penetration by fingers, by metal, in an area that truly belonged to her but that she could in no way make her own. He posed the question more forcefully. She shook her head indignantly. 'Shhh,' he soothed, nodding calmingly at her, 'relax. Have you been examined before?' 'Yes,' she whispered, 'it was when . . . they tried to turn my womb.' The memory of the previous examination pressed itself forwards, the atmosphere of secrecy in which it had taken place, the presence of the phantom Aunt Martha who watched over her virginity from a corner of the consulting-room. 'You have indeed got a crooked womb,' said the doctor, 'something can only be done about it operatively . . . Moreover the ovaries are underdeveloped, but we've got a solution for that.' The animal word 'ovary' made her think of the births of piglets and calves in an odour of hay and muck, of sweat and effort.

While she was getting dressed behind a curtain, the doctor telephoned Frau Stolz to inform her of his findings. He employed lovely, poetic phraseology about her: the hymen, the uterus, ovaria, follicles. Anna had the uneasy feeling, just as she had done years before, that an entirely strange woman was involved in an obscure fight with her to appropriate her female organs. 'One every day,' said the doctor smiling. He handed her a prescription. 'Such a good-looking blonde girl ought to be able to have a whole lot of children!'

Every day Frau Stolz checked that Anna took her pill. She had assumed total responsibility for her fertility, as precisely as she had regarded it to be her duty to teach her embroidery. Anna's exterior and interior had to be orderly and flawless, like the skirting boards when they had just been dusted. Only Anna's thoughts escaped her all-seeing eye. She did not see that a rebel was biding her time beneath an increasingly thin veneer of servitude, provoked to the extreme. Months later, when the treatment first showed a dubious effect, she regarded this as a personal victory over chaos: something was being restored in the world order at the same time as in the order in Anna's abdomen.

There were further secret watchers over her fertility – equally concerned with order. That summer the Stolzs went travelling for a week, leaving Gitte behind in Anna's care. They went to the swimming baths together in the afternoon, beach bags dangling on their shoulders. Each day there was a clear blue sky above the roofs and the motionless tree tops. When they came home on one of their languid afternoons, a strange car was in front of the house. Two men were leaning on the doors, their hands in their pockets, their eyes screwed up against the sun. They hurried after Anna up the garden path as she put the key in the lock. 'Good afternoon, gnädige Frau, may we have a word with you?' Anna pushed the front door open; Gitte shot into the house under her arm, upstairs to her room. In the hall they remained standing, Anna with raised eyebrows, the two men – although somewhat embarrassed –

energetic. 'You see, we have come from the Erbgesundheitsamt, the genetic investigation branch of the health ministry: You have a servant, a certain...' Documents were consulted. 'Anna Bamberg? 'Yes indeed,' said Anna haughtily, 'what about her? 'Well, you see...' they both began together. They laughed apologetically to one another, after which one of the two did the talking and the other confined himself to nodding supportively. 'We don't know exactly, we're still investigating, but this Anna Bamberg is a bit feeble-minded.' 'Oh really?' said Anna icily. 'Is that what she is? She looks quite normal, this employee.' 'Yes, yes,' he breathed, 'that could well be so, gnädige Frau, but ... you must understand ... this woman has to be sterilized.' Once again she was hearing a word for the first time. Frau Stolz would certainly know what it meant. She kept her options open: 'Why?' 'Well, you see, we cannot ... feeble-mindedness is inherited; if she has children, they will be feeble-minded children too.' A ticklish laugh rose up from her chest. 'How do you make out that Anna...' 'Haven't you noticed anything about her then?' 'No.' 'Listen...' The one who had done the talking held up the documents like a trophy. 'It's all in the guardianship declaration.'

As she was listening to what he had to say, she was conscious that they represented a sort of bizarre unreality, standing together in the hall – as long as she was the lady of the house to them, regarding herself as feeling at her ease in her own hall, and at the same time referring to herself as though she were an absent third, an abstract person.

The men had been to the court and read the guardianship declaration that she herself had signed. The part she had left unread concerned the obligatory annual reports by Uncle Heinrich, in which he had to account for the fact that he was keeping Anna Bamberg, daughter of so and so, at the farm. He had filled it in conscientiously every year, saying that since the death of her grandfather he was exercising the guardianship, that she was feeble-minded and too delicate in health to be educated or look for a job. It was so matter-of-fact there, so unadorned, in the same phraseology every year, that no one from the guardianship board had ever contemplated going to look at the problem child with their own eyes for once.

There it stood in black and white, in the familiar calligraphy: Anna Bamberg is feeble-minded and in delicate health. A single sentence erased her, destroyed the only thing – except for two dresses and some underclothes – she possessed: that she, the daughter of Johann Bamberg, was equipped with a good brain and a parrot's memory. The hall was too small for the explosion in her head – of rage with retroactive strength, which could not be expressed anywhere in the absence of a target. The beach bag, still hanging from her shoulder, slid to the ground. She succeeded in channelling her rage and directing it at the functionaries in a super-cooled way. 'Gentlemen, she is standing here before you, Anna Bamberg. I am the delicate, feeble-minded girl you are looking for. What would you like to know? How much six times twelve is? From when to when the Thirty Years War lasted? Should I take a dictation for you? Just say!' They backed off in shock. One of the documents fell to the floor. They did not have the courage to bend down and pick it up. 'Just say! I've had enough of it now. More than enough. When my uncle wrote that in the guardianship declaration he did so because he had kept me at home to work for him for nothing all those years – in the sheds, on the land, day in day out, year in year out, without end. Because he beat me up, because he allowed me to be terrorized by his wife and because your dear Board of Supervision believed him all those years! That judge of yours, the one who's mentioned here at the top of the declaration – why did it never enter his head to find out if everything really tallied with the facts? And now on top of that you want to sterilize me. I have had enough, I really have had absolutely enough!'

One of the two glanced over his shoulder timidly to see the height of the door knob. The other snatched the document off the floor, laughing nervously. 'Entschuldigung, Entschuldigung...' they mumbled, going backwards out of the hall towards the door, 'wir haben es nicht gewusst das ... we did not realize that...' Suddenly they had disappeared. She stood there in the hall, left to the mercy of her bewilderment, which was much too great and violent for her alone. She heard the car start and drive away. She was nauseated, she was disgusted by the two gullible innocents who had come to convey the disastrous tidings to her. The whole story was so sickening that she felt the need to do something violent, to shatter something that was totally respected and valued, to destroy something. But it was too hot; now she just felt that it was altogether too hot for anything. Her dress was clinging to her body; it was too hot to think about anything. Yet they were within reach, the things it would be nice to destroy: all the objects around her, the interior with its compulsive Prussian order would be a lovely target. Dropping lengthways into a chair in the spotless room she looked round with weary eyes. She felt no urgency at all, the stolid neatness left her cold, everything left her cold, it did not matter to her. The rage imploded beneath her skull, the emotions ebbed away. She looked round the room that was utterly strange to her, even though she had dusted, polished and washed all the components a thousand times. She felt empty and exhausted.

Eventually the word 'sterilize' got her moving again. She stood up listlessly, went to the bookcase and took out the dictionary blindly. 'Make infertile.' Then her ovaries, which thanks to Frau Stolz's tenacity were developing very slightly, would be returned to their former condition by order of the county authorities, or even removed from her body, to be absolutely certain. So the court wanted to organize things in order that no feeble-minded children would ever be born again. But surely that was idiocy, she said to herself: it was just as feeble-minded as not tolerating for any reason any dust anywhere along half a metre of skirting board.

9

The day began with an absolutely clear sky and sharp sunlight – the snow hurt the eyes. Life was becoming extrovert. On the Place Royale it was busy opposite the Thermal Institute – an attempt to make up for lost sunshine? When they came across one another at the changing rooms Anna proposed going for a walk after lunch. To one of the springs perhaps, provided that was acceptable at their age, with their rickety joints, in the snow, in the hills, and so on. Lotte yielded to Anna's self-mockery.

Each equipped with a stick, they passed the Pouhon Pierre-le-Grand. Just for a second they looked right through the building. The view entered through high bow windows above the door and emerged via stained-glass windows in pastel colours illuminated by the low sun. They had decided to begin with the Sauvenière spring, the oldest spring in Spa, and not to go there through the wood – over difficult, impassable footpaths bearing such idyllic names as Promenade des Artistes and Promenade des Hêtres – but simply along the road to Francorchamps; then they couldn't get lost. In the discussion that preceded this decision, they secretly noticed the same fastidiousness in one another, the same profusion of fantasies when they considered what could go wrong on the way. Was that old age or a family trait?

There was no snow left on the branches of the trees. They were plodding up a constantly rising incline. Anna was panting prodigiously. Lotte was not troubled by breathlessness – she registered this small difference, not without satisfaction: she had often felt weak and weary in contrast to Anna's indefatigable vitality. She was instantly ashamed of her thoughts. Surely she wasn't engaged in a competition with this woman who was her sister? 'Let's catch our breath.' Anna laid a hand on her arm. They stopped on the verge, a car struggled past now and then in the melting snow. They stood there side-by-side and looked at the landscape of white hills stretching out in front of them, quiet and still, as though it had originated in their own fantasies.

'There is a legend connected with the Sauvenière spring,' said Anna. 'The patron saint of Spa, St Remaclus, fell asleep while praying by the spring. As a reprimand God saw to it that his foot sank into the ground and left an impression in the rock. Newly married men have taken their wives to the spring since the Middle Ages; it had a reputation for encouraging fertility. If the bride placed her foot in the impression of St Remaclus and drank water from the spring, they could be confident of being blessed with heirs. A lovely story, no?' She laughed. 'Perhaps there were hormones in the spring water!'

'It was medieval sales talk of course, to entice people to the spring,' said Lotte.

They continued their walk. The road ascended even further.

'We seem to be climbing Mount Golgotha,' Anna sighed.

The road now went through a beech wood; smooth dark trunks rose up on either side. A hollow opened on the left of the road, with a brook flowing in it, twisting blackly through the snow. After a single passing car they were entirely alone for the first time. Far more than the public places where they had already met, this desolation emphasized their being together. Only the two of them, in the Ardennes – somewhere in these woods, these hills, East and West had come to blows, twice.

'Ach, my poor feet,' said Anna.

A small hexagonal pitched roof appeared in their field of view, somewhat lower than the road. There was a small opening in the ground filled with brown water. A little house had been built around it to protect the sanctuary. The impression of the foot was there too, in the hard stone floor, close to a tap from which they did not dare drink. They had imagined something bubbling up out of the ground spontaneously, but here everything seemed to be concealed deep below the pathetic little construction, which would not have looked out of place at a Catholic cemetery.

'St Remaclus would be embarrassed,' said Anna with disappointment.

'The café is closed,' Lotte indicated with her head towards a tea garden, which looked dark and abandoned.

'There's no money to be made from two old women,' said Anna. 'Oh well, they have constructed a little brick wall for us, let's give our poor feet a bit of a rest.'

So this was the object of their pilgrimage, which had set their joints on fire: a spot by the roadside, lacking any romance, adapted to the demands of tourism.

'If there had been such a fertility spring in our neighbourhood,' Anna laughed to herself, 'I certainly would have drunk litres and litres at the time, for sure.'

'Those pills you took helped, didn't they?'

'Ach,' she waved the idea away as though chasing off a fly, 'that whole women's story never got sorted out in me, I must say. I've never had a normal cycle. Nor did my womb get back into position: years after the war X-rays showed that when I was growing, because of labouring on the farm, my spine had set too deeply into my pelvis. Otherwise I certainly might have been ten centimetres taller, like you.'

Lotte could see before her the group photo of her children and grandchildren taken on the occasion of her seventieth birthday, a photo brimming to the edges with offspring. She felt guilty, just for a while – it was an uneasy feeling when the roles were reversed. In a certain sense then, Anna had worked for two. If her own lungs had been healthy she too would have grown up in her grandfather's house and been put to work. A staggering thought. It was an incomprehensible arbitrariness; if Anna had been afflicted with TB instead of her, everything would have been the other way round. Would she have made the same choices then? She looked with confusion at the profile beside her. A dangerous vacuum resulted from all these reversible ideas. It would clearly be better to keep the relationships as they were. 'Never trust a Kraut – once a Kraut always a Kraut,' said her Dutch father, who could not be trusted an inch himself. In the war, those who could be trusted had been carefully distinguished from those who could not. It had to be so. Without that firm division they would not have managed. Either you were a collaborator with the Nazis or you weren't. This division did not suddenly cease to exist after the war, only a past participle was added.

'Let's go,' she shivered, 'I'm getting cold.'

They walked on through the pain in their joints, which were protesting at the resumption of the walk. The sun had disappeared behind the trees; the reflection on the clouds cast a pink glow over the snow-covered fields. As they were approaching the built-up centre of Spa, the silhouette of an old chalet towered above the trees on the right of the road. Lotte stopped.

'Look,' she exclaimed, 'what a lovely house.'

'A ruin,' Anna said coolly.

'That woodcarving...' Lotte walked to the edge of the bank. The house, dark and mysterious in the twilight, seemed to be built of dream fragments. It was lofty and square, with balconies of dark brown stained wood on each floor along the full extent of the façade, connected to each level by wooden stairs. Doors opened out onto the balconies with shutters of delicate lattice-work. The broad protruding eaves were decorated with lacy carving. It must once have been a pleasure to wake up in this house, she imagined, to throw open the shutters, walk out onto the balcony in bare feet and look down onto the garden in the early morning sun. The house seemed to have been victimized for that good life. Black holes gaped behind the broken windows, shutters hung crookedly off their hinges, parts of the sagging stairs seemed to have been hacked off for firewood.

'A house out of a Chekhov story,' Lotte sighed.

'A house of rich people, who never touched a duster themselves,'

Anna corrected. 'Pity the maid who had to keep such a barn clean.'

'They've simply let it collapse,' said Lotte indignantly.

'Who could afford such a house now? The heating bills, the maintenance, the staff...'

Anna's pragmatism annoyed Lotte. It sounded like: justice at last. 'Everything of beauty is disappearing,' she complained.

'Komm, meine Liebe.' Anna walked on decisively. This lament for an old house that was about to collapse. She, Anna, was also old; her shutters were also hanging crookedly off their hinges.

They walked on without saying any more. Anna, disapproving, was resolute in her silence; Lotte felt it with each step. The surroundings were becoming more densely built up, here and there the pavements had been cleared. Spa accepted them again – there was something reassuring about the lit-up shops, the bustle of people and traffic. They came to rest at a pâtisserie in Place Albert I, over a light tart of pears with whisked egg white. A pot-pourri of familiar melodies was playing in the background.

Lotte looked up with an expression of recognition. 'Isn't that ... "Lili Marlene"?'

'The number-one hit of the war,' said Anna scornfully.

'Yes ... I still remember what a stir she caused, Marlene Dietrich. She saw it all coming and left Germany in time.'

'So she could make her career in Hollywood, you mean.'

That scepticism again. Not anticipating which fire she would be stoking up she said with irritation, 'I still don't understand how all of you didn't see it coming. Hitler would not have got a foot-hold with us, despite the depression...'

'But you hadn't had your confidence taken away like we had. He, this buffoon, gave it back to us. With his marches, party rallies, his speeches. With the most impressive Olympic Games of all time. The foreigners stood cheering on the tribune and Herr Hitler was host to the world. No one was saying, You're no good. They all came. And then the newspapers, periodicals, the radio, the bioscope magazine, they all carried that one message – there wasn't anything else. You took it in, every day, there was only one version ... You swallowed it the way you swallow advertising. It ground its way into our heads, slowly but surely. Ach, you can't imagine it ...'

Anna sighed; she stuck her fork abruptly into the tart.

'Industry was flourishing. The young didn't hang around on the streets – they were in the Hitler Youth and came to school fresh and happy. They were training for military service so that they would make good soldiers later on. When the war broke out they were already used to camps and discipline ... it was all planned but no one realized it. The girls automatically became Blitzmädel, task force squads of young women in the Wehrmacht. And there was the Ideology and Aesthetics division for the educated youth – where they learned rhythmics, dancing, singing, making music: that's how they also won over the higher cadres. It was an orderly, beautiful, fantastic world.'

It was being said in an ironic voice, it is true, but so loud that Lotte made beseeching gestures and looked around nervously.

'You must understand once and for all,' Anna continued, just as loud, 'I can sense only opposition in you. The mothers were relieved of the care of their children, there was no boredom, there were no drug addicts, you didn't have the shambles we have now. Most people of my age who were involved in that still dream about it all the time. You should talk to a former BDM leader or an Arbeitsführerin, your hair would stand on end. It was their youth, the time of their lives, wunderschön!'

Lotte stared at her. It was as though Anna had become larger and larger during this hymn of praise, as though – with her cake fork in her hand – she had acquired pompous dimensions. This bumptiousness, this wunderschöne, fatal enthusiasm from before the war, filled the whole pâtisserie.

'Yet there were exceptions, people who didn't lose their reason!' Lotte was speaking into the wind, her words were blown back into her face, so weak did she feel in her defence. 'Even when a whole people loses its head like that, there are exceptions.'

'Of course. But the political opposition had been waved aside at once, you know that, they had neatly removed them. The rest of them, the intellectuals, the clever ones, like those who had contacts with foreigners so they could also get hold of other information, or people like Uncle Heinrich who understood it intuitively: all those people would have been in great danger if they had opened their mouths. That's why you didn't hear voices of dissent. All hands were raised in the same direction, the one direction . . .'

'But you, Anna . . . why did you do nothing?'

'I was a servant girl, someone's servant girl, a non-person. I had to be there all the time, for the gnädige Frau, I had to do what she wanted me to, like lightning. I didn't take kindly to Hitler, but beyond that I didn't care. It was all the same to me.'

The blood rose to Lotte's head. One way or another Anna was becoming increasingly elusive – she was putting up a smoke screen under the guise of candour. But Lotte would not permit herself to be misled.

'And the Jews?' she said fiercely. 'The disappearances, Kristallnacht . . . ?'

'The official answer to that was: we have taken them in for protection because otherwise the wrath of the people would kill them. Because the Jews had brought about all the miseries: the First World War, the scandalous Treaty of Versailles, the depression, degeneracy in art . . . that even persists now in some German heads, it had been so hammered in. Listen . . . Lotte . . .'

Anna leaned close to Lotte across the table. There was a fleck of egg white foam on her top lip. Lotte felt that the last opponents of the Nazi regime were represented by this trivial bit of foam – and at once a thick, shiny tongue came out to lick it away from its insecure position on her top lip.

'Listen, you can pose all these questions because you know about everything that happened. We didn't yet know where it was all leading so we didn't pose the questions. Why are you looking at me like that?'

'Wir haben es nicht gewusst . . . We did not know . . . we've all heard that one for so long.'

Anna started pricking the base of her tart with her fork, she really seemed angry. That pricking was getting on Lotte's nerves, she was very close to becoming angry herself.

'You all point with your accusing fingers,' Anna snapped. 'You've been doing that for forty-five years already, but that's the easy way. Why did the German people let it happen, you cry. But I turn that round and ask: why did you in the West let it happen? You allowed us to rearm quietly – when you could already have intervened under the Treaty of Versailles. You allowed us to march into the Rhineland without let or hindrance, and Austria. And then you bargained away Czechoslovakia to us. The German emigrants in France, in England, in America warned. No one listened. Why didn't they stop that idiot while it was still possible? Why did they leave us to our fate, turned over to a dictator?'

'So *we* did it, finally!'

'Why? That's what I ask.'

Lotte's eyes sparkled. 'You twist things beautifully, Anna,' she said with a hostile laugh, 'this really is the prettiest argument I've ever heard to exonerate the Germans.' She stood up angrily. 'Allow me to pay,' she said haughtily. She lifted her coat from the back of the chair and veered off towards the young woman at the cash till. Ow, the walk had severely affected her calves.

Anna stood up in a panic. Why was Lotte so piqued all of a sudden? She had set out her ideas in all sincerity. They had not been formed unthinkingly, just like that: you could not see past the piles of books she had read in order to fathom all those lurid patterns. It was doubtful whether Lotte had ever taken so much trouble to read up about it herself.

'Lotte,' she called, 'wait a moment . . .'

'I'm tired,' said her sister over her shoulder. Suddenly she looked very old and fragile. 'I think I really am very tired.'

As the door of the pâtisserie closed behind Lotte, Anna snatched her winter coat from the chair. She found it stuffy among all those women – it was smoky and her effortfully obtained insights had evoked nothing but the unwillingness and incomprehension of the only person in the world she wanted to convince. It was one big misunderstanding. She wormed between two chairs to the cash till. Lotte had paid for her too – was she wanting to justify her over-hasty departure in that way? Anna went out into the snow; she tried to breathe deeply but it seemed as though her lungs had shrunk. Her heart was beating fast and unevenly. Here, now, it could happen, just like that, suddenly, the discord with Lotte would never be set aside. Walking slowly, she tried to get her breathing under control; perhaps it was the sudden feeling of futility that was making her short of breath.

Lotte was relieved. The sabotage that she had committed just now uplifted her, she felt liberated – she had allowed herself to be taken in far too much by Anna, the limits of her empathy had been reached. It was as though they had been involved in a mock battle. They tossed worn-out arguments that had been heard a thousand times at each other's heads, ostensibly going right to the heart of their direct opposition to one another while, actually, something much larger was going on outside them. Something that withdrew as soon as you tried to bring it closer to you by observing it through a telescope.

They arrived at the Thermal Institute at the same time the next morning, except that Lotte was standing at the foot of the stairs while, for unknown reasons, Anna was on the opposite side of the road, waiting for a military procession to pass. Surely she hadn't been on the lookout? Lotte would not have noticed her if she hadn't been waving and calling out, between the vehicles driving past at a sedate pace towards the west. Lotte waited. She had slept wonderfully well that night after she had made up her mind not to allow herself to become so upset by Anna any more. And now there she was, waving; then she disappeared for a moment behind a jeep, a tank, a military ambulance. There was no end to the procession, creeping past her according to its own logic. Helmeted heads, looking ahead with martial bearing, as though they had just taken Spa by force, purely to enable them to drive through it. Lotte began to laugh. She saw that Anna was laughing too on the other side. Were they both discovering at the same moment that it was nothing more than a mock performance separating them? When the last camouflage-painted tank had passed, Anna crossed the street shaking her head.

As though nothing special had occurred the day before, they ascended the steps of the Thermal Institute, supporting each other. It seemed that the previous day had cleared out something thorny – you could not tell what sort of twists the human spirit followed. Later in the day they met up again in one of the corridors. On a long white bench they discussed the effects of the different baths on their muscles and joints like seasoned visitors at a health resort. Now the highest peak was over, the curative results would gradually have to reveal themselves. They decided to have dinner that evening in a restaurant opposite the Pouhon Pierre-le-Grand. According to Anna, whose scrutiny did not miss much, it looked convivial and affordable.

❦

Lotte's father did not emerge unscathed from his illness. The thrombosed leg limped a bit with every step. His heart sometimes began to beat faster for no reason. Then he would clutch his chest as though the moment he was going to die had actually arrived. The gesture immediately revived the old anxiety in everyone. Conversation stopped, music was turned off, a window was opened – although they knew that he exploited his heartbeats and feigned them at times when other methods for attracting attention failed. He had been the focal point at all times during his long period of illness; his wife had been completely devoted to him as she had in the springtime of their marriage before she became distracted by the children. After his recovery the youngest returned home and he fell into the old habit, worse than ever, of provoking the children (her children) with unreasonable demands and punishments. It was the simplest way of getting into a row with her; during the reconciliations he regained exclusive rights to her for a while. Instead of being grateful for the fact that he had survived three different causes of death, he was embittered, as though the regained life in no way fulfilled his expectations. He also developed the habit of sniffing repeatedly, first through one nostril, then the other – even the smell of his second life did not please him.

The sniffing got on Lotte's nerves; she could hear it everywhere. Behind closed doors, at the end of the passage, just round the corner, at night through the bedroom walls. She dreamed of escaping from this father and from the disharmony that he was constantly inducing in the family in different ways, on account of his inexhaustible inventiveness. She also wished to be released from his permanent grousing. About the impotence of Minister-President Colijn, who intended to combat the depression by cutting payments to the unemployed and loans to civil servants. Her father noticed it specially in the retarded growth of his record collection. Grumbling about the Communist Party, which had called on all political parties to sink their underlying differences in a collective fight against the National Socialist movement – now he could no longer draw his sword against the popes and Calvinists. Grousing about Hitler, who had merely been a half-wit at first, but had gradually come to enjoy the status of a dangerous lunatic. Grousing about the German people who marched behind the dangerous lunatic, whereby he conveniently overlooked that his own mother was German as well as his grandparents on her side – and also his musical niece. Sniffing violently, he took possession of the news-paper as soon as it dropped through the letter box and would not surrender it to anyone, as a dog grips a bone between its teeth. The more Lotte heard him carrying on against the German people, the more that people filled her with affection. Each negative remark on his part aroused her longing for a reunion with Anna. If her father thought that the Germans were good for nothing, she wanted to be one of them.

Nevertheless, Theo de Zwaan, Marie's fiancé, set out for Germany with two friends on the rumour that there was abundant work there. After two weeks he was back again. Instead of having earned something he had spent all his savings on a Leica that hung on his chest like a war trophy. 'How will you get it into your head!' said Lotte's mother. 'We don't buy German goods on principle and you come home flaunting a pricey Leica.' But he was not elated in the slightest about his purchase, rather it seemed like a sort of plas-ter over the wound. He was depressed and sparing with informa-tion. Yes there was work enough there, but he had no business being in that country. Half the people were in uniform, even child-ren; there was a revolting general enthusiasm about the *Anschluss* with Austria; there were posters, banners everywhere, placards with 'Ein Volk – Ein Reich – Ein Führer'. He had seen it with his own eyes and wanted nothing more to do with it. 'I could have told you that already,' said his future father-in-law, 'then you could have saved yourself that whole trip.' Lotte mistrusted the bearer of these bad tidings. Probably no one had wanted to take him on; you could see from afar that he was a drip. The way he had experienced Germany had been coloured by frustration of course; it spoke well for the country that it did not take anyone on just like that.

To compensate, Theo longed for the camera to provide him with glittering photographs. He asked Jet and Lotte to be guinea pigs. As neither of them could take him seriously, they put on men's trousers and jackets and Homburg hats, for a joke. With their lips made up to excess, they permitted themselves to be immortalized beside the water-tower in masculine poses, leaning on each other's shoulders, cigars in their mouths; staring into the camera with sphinx's eyes like Greta Garbo; in an imitation of Marlene Dietrich – 'I'm ready for love from head to toe'. Eventually they burst out in hilarious uncontrollable laughter. Theo took his photos, phlegmatic as always, setting the diaphragm and deciding the angle of view. When the minuscule pictures with zigzag edges had been developed, the worldly, sultry, negligent, independent women they perceived aroused their curiosity. Was this them? Their mother passed the photos round with a proud laugh among visitors: just see what good-looking daughters I have!

A Mahler symphony was on the turntable. Lotte attached herself to the group that sat in a circle listening as though at a religious confession – a waterfall was gushing down at the foot of a rock in a clearing in a wood, threatening rumblings sounded from behind the mountain tops, deer were on the run. Sammy Goldschmidt was listening with pursed lips; mentally he was performing along with it. For Ernst Goudriaan, who was gazing ahead darkly, the music seemed to arouse more sombre visions. 'Who was the conductor?' he asked when the last note had died away and they seemed rather dejected because the spell had broken. 'Wilhelm Furtwängler,' said Lotte's father, sniffing left and right. 'Furtwängler!' said Goudriaan. 'He plays for the Nazis now!' 'Furtwängler?' Lotte's mother repeated shocked. 'Oh well,' her husband muttered, 'that symphony was recorded years ago, we've already enjoyed it many times.'

Goudriaan looked round uneasily. He was just back from Germany, he explained. It sounded like an apology. He had been serving an apprenticeship with a famous violin-maker. During that time he had lodged with a Jewish family, and had more or less become a member of the household. A few days ago the violin-maker had come up to him. 'I have heard that you are staying with Jewish people. If you want to complete your training here you must leave there as quickly as possible.' 'But I have nothing to do with those regulations,' Goudriaan retorted, 'I am Dutch.' 'You are here in Germany, you have to go along with it. Either you leave that family or you do not remain here any longer.' 'Then I'll leave here,' said Goudriaan.

Disbelief and indignation filled the room. Goudriaan submitted to it with a dejected laugh. Hesitating between sympathy and suspicion, Lotte looked at the slender student. It was difficult for her to imagine him as a violin-maker – wood shavings on his impeccable suit, endlessly scraping with a plane – a craft that evoked associations with muscular arms and workmen's overalls. Her father put Beethoven's Ninth on, in a more kosher performance. Would they never again be able to listen to music open-mindedly from then on? The 'Alle Menschen werden Brüder' resounded magisterially; why wasn't it 'Alle Menschen werden Schwester'?

As the year progressed it became increasingly difficult to find excuses for her native country. Never before had the radio been listened to as much as it was in the September days, when Chamberlain flew to Germany three times to prevent war and, finally, with Daladier, sacrificed Czechoslovakia for peace. Everyone was relieved; only Lotte's father was agitated that France as well as England had reneged on their treaty with the Czechs in such a cowardly way. 'Out of pure fear of Bolshevism,' he sniffed contemptuously. 'In their hearts they admire the way Hitler has cleansed his country of Communists.' 'That fear isn't so crazy,' said his wife, with her predictable arguments again; 'when the workers seize power on a large scale, those people who come to the top also terrorize the people.' 'Do you know who you're talking about?' He was offended. 'You're talking about Stalin, he has to keep a whole continent in harness.' Then he became sentimental, everyone knew how the ancient discussion continued. Lotte ducked behind her music theory. The division of the roles had already been fixed in advance. Her mother appointed herself defender of democracy, made a plea for a natural equilibrium between the parties; her father jeered the democratic principle away: 'Do you by any chance want to claim that we have a democracy here? The poor are getting even poorer!' He allowed himself to be swept along by his feelings, took a sip of gin; the war that had been averted at the last minute was pushed into the background. Another much older war was being fought out here under the pretext of a difference in political opinions – a battle that always remained unresolved. 'Don't make me laugh,' her mother had the last word: 'you know best of all that you yourself would be a dictator here in the house if you had the chance.'

Lotte had had the funds saved up for a trip to Germany for a long time – the more the threat of war grew, the harder it was to speak about her plan out loud. They all listened masochistically to the radio together, to a summary of a belligerent speech by Reichsminister Hess. They reassured each other: the Netherlands would never get involved, we have always been neutral. Anyway, half of the Netherlands is related to the Germans: our prince, the former Queen Emma, grandmother in Amsterdam, you name them. Louis Davids' death was a greater tragedy than the annexation of Lithuania and the Italian invasion of Albania – Lotte's mother walked about the house wailing and slapping her forehead with the flat of her hands as though she blamed herself; she sang his songs melancholically on the bench under the pear tree.

'Now your Papa Stalin has made a poor showing,' she said when Hitler and Stalin signed a non-aggression pact. 'It's Stalin's trick,' her husband laughed at so much short-sightedness. 'There's something behind it. It suits him well to make a pact at this moment.' The Queen made a calm radio broadcast: there is no reason at all for concern. Mobilization was being proclaimed in order to preserve the country's neutrality. Theo de Zwaan left on one of the hundreds of extra trains: not discontent, at last he had something to do.

'Holland with its tin soldiers,' sniffed Lotte's mother, slipping a bag of apples and sandwiches into his hands. Two days later the Germans invaded Poland and another two days later England and

France declared themselves at war with Germany: there was nothing more to discuss with Hitler. Yet faith in the safety of the negligible little kingdom by the sea, which no party chose, was still intact.

❦❦

'So you see, you were just as naïve as we were,' said Anna.

Lotte nodded.

They continued eating, lost in thought. To Lotte's dismay, Anna mashed her potato croquettes; she cut hers into pieces of equal size, which Anna thought petty.

'Are they real?' Anna stroked her finger over a red flower that was blossoming with suspect luxuriance in a slender pot by their table.

'It's all plastic,' said Lotte, who had already seen this when she came in.

'You're right.' Anna withdrew her finger. 'It's much too dark for plants here. Ach . . . that makes me think of Frau Stolz's cactuses . . .' She grinned. 'They were fatal to me, you might say.'

❦❦

Thanks to the contents of the bookcase Anna's disguised serfdom did not become unbearable. The embroidery was hardly progressing; it was on her lap for the sake of form, getting creased by the book open on it. Herr Stolz divided his attention between the newspaper and the radio, which exclusively reported successes. 'Ten years ago we were the pariahs of Europe and now Chamberlain takes the trouble to visit us three times. Who would have thought it?' said Stolz with satisfaction. 'We have our Führer's genius to thank for that entirely.' On New Year's Day Hitler totted up the balance on the radio. 'The year 1938 was the richest in terms of events in the whole history of our people.' The Third Reich had grown to ten million souls by restoring the German minorities in the surrounding territories to the German community – Heim ins Reich. Frau Stolz said with satisfaction that at last she dared again to be proud that she was a German.

With a glass of Sekt they toasted the astonishing dynamism of the Führer and the big things he intended for them.

This euphoria left Anna unmoved. She had never been struck by the idea of being a German. When she heard Hitler and Beneš, the Czech president, blustering about each other on the radio she thought: give them each a club and they can fight it out between them. What is it to do with us? Tired of the villa district next to the enthusiastically smoking factory chimneys, broken in spirit by the suppression of her rebelliousness, she did her work in a deadly routine. But one weekday during the same winter, she suddenly reached her saturation point. From one small, innocent incident sprang that single inevitable spark.

She had to clean the dining-room on Thursday morning at half-past five. Everyone was still asleep; it was silent and cold in the house. Beneath a large window that overlooked the back garden was a large window-seat made of black marble, on which there were cactus plants. An exotic desert flower never appeared between the spines – it was unthinkable that anything could come into flower under Frau Stolz's regime. She had to take the cactuses off the window-seat one by one, then she polished it with wax until the gleaming black surface reflected her own face. Later that day Frau Stolz called Anna to her. 'Anna, you forgot the window-seat this morning.' Anna denied it. 'You are lying, look, here and here.' Copying her employer she sank to her knees. In two places the polish had not been totally wiped away. There were a few clouds left behind, which could not be seen against the background of the dark garden at half-past six in the morning. They stood up. Merciless winter light shone inside. Frau Stolz's face was flat and chilly, an icy shield against Anna's accumulated rage.

She started to take her overall off. 'Don't worry, Frau Stolz, about your window-seat, your cactuses, your skirting boards, I won't touch them with another finger, I promise you.' 'You need to be able to accept a bit of criticism,' said Frau Stolz. Anna looked at the cactuses, took stock of the whole room, all the objects that had been through her hands and, now that it came to it, sided with Frau Stolz. 'I can't work like this,' she said flatly, 'this small-minded order, the Prussian sense of duty, there is no place for me here. Put me in the middle of the desert and I'll lay out a lovely garden for you, but in my own way.' 'Ah . . .' it dawned on Frau Stolz, 'you want to sort out the linen here!' Anna looked at her, suddenly it was from a dizzying distance. She looked at her properly, for the first time and the last time, Frau Stolz, as she stood there, a sturdy, rectangular woman. There she stood, exactly as she was, with her shocking limitations. The woman was thinking feverishly; it was very difficult for her to consider an appropriate *coup de grâce* that would enable her to maintain her dignity. 'Do you know what it is with you? You have got too many big ideas . . .' She snatched the overall out of Anna's hands. 'You won't rest until you are in the banqueting hall at Bayer being waited on by two servants.'

Gitte would not let Anna go. On the day of her departure she had locked all the doors in the villa. She sat on the dark red velvet-covered sofa with her legs apart and arms folded, her bony knees sticking out apologetically: you can't leave me behind here alone. 'Where are the keys?' Her mother gave her a good shaking; Gitte did not move a muscle. Anna went rigid between her suitcases; she recognized, in painful comparison, the feelings of the girl. 'I threw them in the WC and pulled the chain,' said Gitte arrogantly. She was registering her absolute opposition to Anna's desertion. Formidably calm, Frau Stolz went to telephone a locksmith. Anna embraced Gitte in farewell but she turned away aggrieved. Finally Anna went to the kitchen with her suitcases, opened a high narrow window above the draining board, threw her baggage out and threw herself after it, off the sinking ship into the depths, which crunched pleasantly under her feet as she landed.

She returned to her uncle's house, to the bedroom with the medallion wallpaper, the living-room with the easy chairs and the gramophone and Uncle Franz's operetta music, but she was oblivious to it. Furniture and practical objects still came under the heading of compulsion – the compulsion of cleaning, every week, the eternally recurring tasks. Uninspired, she wrote off applications to advertisements. She had a bath, got out and stood politely before her dripping reflection in the mirror. 'How do you do, I am Anna Bamberg, my mother has been dead for years, my father too, then I also had a sister, Lotte, but to be honest she has not been around for a long time either. I, Anna, on the other hand, am alive and kicking, that is obvious . . .'

A reply came to one of the letters, an envelope of marbled paper with the sender's name in unadorned, businesslike handwriting. Charlotte von Garlitz Dublow, Countess von Falkenau. Instead of inviting Anna for an interview she announced her arrival, on the very same day. A countess! – Aunt Vicki excitedly ran to her clothes cupboard to find a dress for Anna. Anna stared at the upright, sober letters, overcome with misgivings – a countess, that recalled associations with serfdom; there went her tender, hard-won freedom. Through a chink in the net curtains she watched the Countess getting out of her Kaiser-Freser, beneath her open fur coat she was wearing a cream silk blouse. Aunt Vicki pinched Anna in the palm of her hand.

The sitting-room, which not long ago had struck Anna as the high point of luxury and comfort, became conventional and bourgeois with this lady in it. She kept hold of Anna's hand as she scrutinized her without embarrassment. 'I would like to ask you something,' she said. 'Are you related to Johannes Bamberg?' In a reflex Anna withdrew her hand, in no condition to reply to a direct question innocently posed. No one had ever spoken this name again: the family had buried his memory along with his material remains. She looked at the woman without seeing her. The tick of the pendulum in this room affected her for the first time – the tap of a stick on a cobbled street. Aunt Vicki looked from one to the other, wringing her hands, and when the silence had persisted too long said, 'Johannes Bamberg, yes, that was her father, a cousin of my husband . . . I never knew him because he died young . . .' 'Her father then,' the woman interrupted her, satisfied, turning her swan's neck towards Anna. 'Yes indeed, her father,' breathed Aunt Vicki obligingly. 'Then everything is in order.' A gloved hand descended on Anna's shoulder. 'Will you come with me? My car is outside.' 'But her things,' cried Aunt Vicki, breathless at the speed with which the transaction was being concluded. 'I'll send my chauffeur later on.' The Countess with the unpronounceable name guided Anna out in front of her, out of the citizen's living-room, along the passage; Aunt Vicki had no opportunity to open the front door for her, she did everything herself with great determination. As she gracefully swept one hand through her short brown hair, she held the car door open for Anna with her other. Anna stepped in blankly, as though hypnotized.

Cologne slipped past on either side, a mobile stage set. Time and place lost their normal proportions. Her father's name had set something going that still seemed mainly like a film rolling at accelerated speed. It was a blatant abduction; had he taken responsibility for her again after all that time, and was the woman behind the wheel an emissary fulfilling his commission in style? She steered the car with one hand, lit a cigarette with the other. An angel who smoked. They left the built-up area behind; did the inhabited world stop here? The car turned off the road, a manicured finger pressed the klaxon, wrought-iron gates opened. A broad drive, flanked by old trees whose crowns were enmeshed in each other. In the park landscape that flickered past between the trees, Anna recognized the Elysian Fields out of Herr Stolz's Greek mythology. Lawns sloping to the horizon, evergreen hedges, groups of trees and shrubs – all maintained with care and trimmed into shape like the driver's fingernails. They penetrated deeper into the tunnel beneath an arch of black branches, which ended in a circle of light. A motionless figure in a dark suit stood at the top of the steps of a majestic, blindingly white house; only his eyes followed the semi-circle the car described before it came to a halt at the foot of the steps. The woman got out. Anna, who was expected to do the same, remained seated, disorientated. 'Come, we're here.' The door opened, she squirmed out, blinking. Dizziness overcame her as she went up the wide stairs. She could see no more of the dark figure than a long arm with a hand on it that held the door open for them, thereafter he seemed to command two arms with which he helped them out of their coats, in the centre of an enormous hall with passageways, doors and stairs leading off it.

She was assigned a room on the first floor with a view onto a turquoise swimming pool – an unreal, poisonous element amid the natural green lawns. The governess, cook, servants, chauffeur, washerwoman, cleaning women, maids and gardeners seemed to live in contented symbiosis, each had their own territory. It was a centuries-old collaboration, a stylized form of servitude to the former Prussian nobility, which had proved its effectiveness in the centuries-long government of castles and country houses. Anna was entrusted with the care of Frau von Garlitz's wardrobe, replacing the previous chambermaid who had been dismissed. Whenever a seam was loose she had to repair it, she took the clothes to the washerwoman, picked up the evening dress that lay crumpled on the parquet floor and hung it in the cupboard. This luxurious life stood in such stark contrast to the daily battle of attrition in her previous job that she was ashamed of the size of the wages: double what she had earned with Frau Stolz, not counting the tips and gifts that Frau von Garlitz regularly slipped the staff with an intimate laugh.

In hours of idleness she floated through the house. *En passant* she learned how the table had to be laid when a general, a big industrialist, a baron came to dine; which dinner service was sufficiently respectful without overdoing it; she learned to arrange a seasonal bouquet on a half-moon table beneath an eighteenth-century still life with grapes and pheasants. Frau von Garlitz slept separately from her husband – their bedrooms, in a private wing of the house, were joined by a pink marble bathroom. A search for her night-dress, which had to be hung up in the morning, brought

Anna into Herr von Garlitz's bedroom, as a smirking maid had advised, where to her disillusionment the sought item lay carelessly on the floor by his bed – the Countess had gone to him!

Anna won the trust of the cook, who generously provided her with background information, legitimized by a devout attachment to her employer. The gnädige Frau was born a von Falkenau, related to the oldest Prussian nobility. Her husband, on the other hand, Wilhelm von Garlitz Dublow, merely came from the coal-scuttle. Anna raised her eyebrows. The Ruhr area, the cook explained. His father, captain of a ship that had brought the Kaiser to Norway, had fallen in love with one of the Kaiserin's ladies in waiting, Countess Dublow. He was ennobled in great haste in order to be able to marry her. Thus Garlitz came into his 'von' and Dublow was added on at the end. In recognition of Kaiser Wilhelm, the first-born was named after him.

The respect and affection with which the cook spoke about the gnädige Frau was at right angles to the disdain with which she disclosed Herr von Garlitz's curriculum vitae. 'He is a weakling, a Casanova,' she said, 'but she is crazy about him, the poor woman.' The management of the factory, Die Basilwerke, where vitamin preparations and herbal remedies were manufactured as restoratives for the Wehrmacht troops, he left to subordinates. 'Horses, he is always messing around with horses,' the woman sighed defeatedly, as though all the misery in the world resulted from it. Invisible behind a medieval rampart, the factory grounds bordered the park. Sometimes he spurred his horse and galloped around the nineteenth-century complex of buildings to remind the workers that the chimneys were smoking at his expense.

'Have you met my husband yet?' said Frau von Garlitz. 'Come, then I'll introduce you.' She rushed to meet him, down the entrance steps. Anna followed awkwardly. She was seeing a snippet from a Ufa film: the godchild of the Kaiser, in white uniform, bolt upright on his Lippizaner, trotting between the black shiny pillars of the drive. At the foot of the steps the Rider on the White Horse came to a halt; he dismounted and allowed himself to be embraced with self-indulgent absent-mindedness. 'Anna, my new chamber-maid.' Frau von Garlitz pushed her gently towards him. He gave her a hand fleetingly while his eyes looked for a baluster to tie the reins round. To him, Anna understood, I am less than a horse.

The discovery of the library put an end to the parasitic feeling. It was a spacious room, the walls clothed in books apart from three windows where bare vine tendrils tapped in the breeze – a treasury that was carefully maintained, supplied with fresh flowers and where even the fire was kept burning in the hearth. Everything for the satisfaction of an imaginary reader: she never found anyone there. *La Divina Commedia*, the *Petit Larousse*, *Der abenteuerliche Simplicissimus*, *Don Quixote*, the *Prophesies* of Nostradamus, Goethe's *Faust* and *Farbenlehre* were next to each other in no order. There were first editions: the books cracked peevishly when they were opened, the accusing smell of neglect rose up – a book that is unread does not exist, was being whispered. Anna saw that an immense task was awaiting her here.

One day she put the question that had been burning on her lips since the start. 'Ach ja...' Pensively Frau von Garlitz pursed her heart-shaped dark red painted mouth. 'My father was staying here when I was working through all those letters of application. Bamberg, I mumbled out loud, your letter in my hand, Anna Bamberg ... My father looked up from his newspaper. "Didn't I know a Bamberg ... wait a moment ... one Johannes Bamberg, a splendid chap, a first-rate employee, I have special memories of him, my God it must be thirty years ago..." I said to myself, if Anna Bamberg is related to him I'll accept her and regard it as a sign from above that my choice is correct.' Giggling, she continued: 'I don't believe in God or Jesus Christ but I do in signs from above, it's fun!' 'What sort of special memories were they?' Anna asked. 'You'll have to ask him that yourself, in due course. My father used to run the factory here. Your father must have worked for him – and made an impression!'

The house was an island in the effervescing twentieth century, and the library was another island within that house, where the seventeenth, eighteenth and nineteenth centuries were better represented than the twentieth. Anna rummaged round at her leisure, reassured about the legitimacy of her privileged position as chambermaid to Frau von Garlitz. She knew now that it was her rightful inheritance: her father's reputation was his legacy (how much more valuable than money and possessions). Long before her birth he had already bequeathed something with unconscious fore-sightedness. This same form of parental love, which extended from before birth to long after death, gave her the feeling that he was still concerned about her with retrospective strength.

Thus she came effortlessly through the winter, spring and sum-mer. Sometimes she walked about the house with an evening dress or a night-dress in her fingers, but mostly she read, with everyone's assent. She did not know that it was merely an interlude – a long held breath.

◆◆

The dripping candle that stood between the plates was reflected in Anna's eyes.

'The rigid discipline,' said Lotte, 'that the chemist's wife expected from you, that really was typically German.'

'Och, it was her view of household order,' Anna moderated her observation, 'simply: I could not function in such a system of total availability.' She began to laugh. 'Suddenly it reminds me of some-thing.' She pinched Lotte's hand from sheer pleasure. 'Somewhere in the fifties I met the Stolzs again. I was working in child welfare and was on a delegation visiting Bayer – I believe it was about an unemployment relief project for displaced children. We were grandly received in the banqueting hall, with two liveried atten-dants to each guest. Half-way through the meal I suddenly heard Frau Stolz's reproach again: You won't be satisfied until you . . . at Bayer . . . and so on. And now there I was! I choked, my neighbour anxiously clapped me on the back. After it was over I drove off, in my first Volkswagen – a thousand metres up to the house. They still lived there, only the bell was no longer polished spick and span with Sidol and the stairs at the front were no longer spotless. I rang the bell. An old woman stuck her head out of the window: Anna! Of course I must come inside. There were photographs of Gitte with husband and children on the sideboard – its doors had panes of glass that had to be cleaned one by one with a chamois-leather. Just then Herr Doktor came home from work. He was amazed: "Do tell us, what's brought you here by chance." I repeated his wife's prophetic remark. "And today I was sitting there, with two servants!" He burst out in uncontrollable laughter. His wife joined in in embarrassment, I felt sorry for her. "You see," he prodded his wife, "didn't I always say to you: you won't make a housemaid out of that girl in a hundred years!"'

Part 2

War

I

On Sunday morning there was a flea market in the nineteenth-century covered promenade that extended deep into the Parc de Sept Heures from the Place Royale. It was sunny, but there was a bleak wind from the east. The traders stamped to keep warm beneath elegant curly flying buttresses; others paced up and down between the wrought-iron pillars. Anna and Lotte strolled past the goods on display: vases, ornaments, old gramophone records, picture postcards. They stopped in front of an unpainted rocking horse that was staring inertly at the statue of a saint.

'You still remember, the rocking horse we always fought over!' cried Anna, so loud that the market-goers looked in their direction. Lotte thought she could see distaste in their expressions for having disturbed the Sunday quiet. In German, what's more! Firmly she said, 'No, I don't remember.'

'Yes ... yes ... it was painted blue and white with proper reins and a brown saddle; we pushed each other off until Papa intervened with a tactical proposition: today, Sunday, is Lotte's day for horse riding, Monday for Anna, Tuesday for Lotte again, and so on. What do you two say about that? I had completely forgotten,' she clapped her hands, 'how lovely that it's suddenly there again.'

The horse had no effect on Lotte, it just severed the gentle feeling of solidarity that there had been among all those objects from the past. How was it that her memory only functioned properly from after the sick-bed in the garden, in the care of her Dutch mother? It was handicapping her for the first time; it made her incomplete.

'The war is in fashion,' Anna observed, 'there's still money to be made.' Military helmets and belts were laid out on a piece of velvet cloth. Yes, the war was peacefully present everywhere: a soldier's water flask lay next to an ancient coffee grinder; beneath crumpled romantic novels and detective stories there was a richly illustrated treatise on military insignias and uniforms in the Third Reich; on a stall with old portraits of married couples, baptisms and confirmations there was a framed photograph of a young soldier who looked defiantly into the lens.

'He did not yet know that a monument would be erected for him here,' said Lotte.

'Look how he puffs out his chest, the poor boy; he solemnly believed in his mission.'

'Not really ... He wasn't fighting for an ideal, he had to defend his country.'

Her sister took her arm and pulled her away. I won't be provoked, thought Anna. Behind in the park, the Chalet du Parc had stood for at least a century by a steep rock wall; here they came to a halt, the sun shone inside horizontally, the vapour from the coffee curled upwards, blue in a beam of light.

We always get together in public places, thought Lotte, as though there was still something improper about our meeting.

❈❈

The sky did not take on the colour of fate, the cook did not break off kneading the dough for a second, the chauffeur did not let his newspaper drop, the servant walked through with a fully laden tray as usual, Anna's darning needle did not stray off course for a moment, no one anticipated that in the margin of innocent, everyday activity a fracture had occurred that morning, when a familiar voice which they had already heard so often that for a long time they had no longer been listening to it, resounded into the kitchen on the Volksempfänger: 'At dawn on the firrrst of Septemberrr Gerrrman trrroops crrrossed the Polish borrrderrr ... Frrrom today bomb will be rrrepaid with bomb...'

A few hours later too, when Anna was just standing in the middle of the lawn to enjoy the unreal beauty of the house and grounds, she did not realize that there, beneath the same sky, in the same daylight, something had been set in motion that was far more unreal – a process of total alienation that they would all be dragged into together. Something indefinable glistened high up in the air. She narrowed her eyes into slits. Simultaneously with an exploding sound in the far distance, white clouds appeared from nowhere and removed the thing from view. At that same moment the house began to speak; it shouted at her from all its openings: 'Are you mad? Get away from there, come inside, it's war!' 'What?' called Anna, walking towards the house, cupping her ears in her hands. 'It's war!' Frau von Garlitz hung out of one of the windows gesticulating wildly; she sent her husband outside to prevent Anna's kamikaze. They bumped into each other at the doorway. 'It's a British reconnaissance aircraft,' he said curtly. 'Our anti-aircraft guns are bringing it down. You had better stay inside.' His Clark Gable moustache moved up and down emotionally, despite his masculine composure. Ridiculous, Anna thought, all that fuss. War – it was no more than a word, she almost wished that something really would happen, something that was more than a dot in the air, so that the word would acquire meaning.

Three days later, after England and France had declared war on Germany, Frau von Garlitz gathered her children, her staff and the most essential possessions and breathlessly handed the premises over to Anna. 'Put the upper floor in order for the Saarland refugees,' she laid her hands on Anna's shoulders, a gesture symbolizing the transfer of goods and chattels, 'we are going to the east.' On her head an asymmetrical cloche hat like a crooked helmet, on either side a child, and in her wake the obedient, giant household, she departed for the family estate in East Brandenburg.

Anna, in her new function as the housekeeper, opened her book and continued where she was, in calm expectation of the Saarlanders. No fear was aroused in her of being alone on the ship after the rats had deserted it – her nervous system was not sensitized to vague threats. During the eighteen days that the Polish campaign lasted, her body benefited, uninhibitedly, from the enormous provisions in the cellar, her mind from those in the library. One day, instead of a group of dispossessed refugees, the whole troop was there at the main door again and daily activities were resumed as though they had not been away – except for Herr von Garlitz, who had marched off to Poland as an officer, and at the Tucheler Heide had had the good fortune to dislocate his kneecap, thereafter the expensive godchild was immediately removed from the front line.

The war became a farce. The troops at the Westwall and Maginot Line lay in wait like boy scouts. Opposite each other in their ambushes, they grew cabbages and potatoes between the fortifications and toasted each other's health with beer mugs raised high. After his recovery, Herr von Garlitz, who was stationed somewhere in the district with his regiment, came home every Sunday with a company of officers who fell upon the supplies of drink in their reckless boredom. Despite rationing, all through the week his wife was busy obtaining the ingredients for a celebration meal. But Anna was only half aware of it. Shortly after the Polish campaign she had received a letter from Holland.

❦

Disturbed by the political developments, Grandmother travelled from Amsterdam to Cologne to find an old bosom friend, in case the borders were about to be closed. She came back mortified to the depths of her soul and swore that she would never set foot over the border again. One rainy day in October she came to give an account of her stay. The whole afternoon she kept on her black hat with purple velvet violets, which undoubtedly came from the Albert Cuyp market stall with the frilly bits and pieces. She had caught a streaming cold in Germany, she said, from the emotions. Lotte did not move from her side. Grandmother sighed, in the shade of the hat brim, 'It was a very unpleasant situation...' Her German accent had deteriorated. Continually interrupting herself to wipe her nose with a lace handkerchief, she related that whenever they spoke about the war her Cologne friend put a tea cosy on the tele-phone, fearful of being overheard. When a daughter-in-law came to visit with a child in Hitler Youth uniform, the friend nervously changed the subject to an insignificant topic. 'German women adore the Führer,' she explained afterwards. 'I am ashamed,' Grandmother coughed, 'I am ashamed for all those crazy German women.'

Grandmother had also been to her second cousin Franz, 'a sym-pathetic chap...' She had heard a few things about Anna from him. She looked fleetingly at Lotte's mother as though seeking support. She nodded indulgently. The blood rose in Lotte's head, she did not know where to look. 'And...?' she said with a pinched voice. Grandmother applied her handkerchief again, it seemed interminable... Anna had ended up well, according to Franz, with an aristocratic family on the outskirts of Cologne.

Lotte stared at the network of broken veins on the ruddy cheeks and tried to locate the eyes above them, which hid behind slits through the heavily drooping eyelids. Grandmother was somewhat impenetrable, despite her readiness to communicate; one day she would suddenly not be there any more and would take away with her for ever a wealth of images, sounds, secrets, pieces of informa-tion, smells from another period, irretrievably. A sudden anxiety came over Lotte: the old woman was the only umbilical cord that joined her to the formative past. 'Do you have her address?' she asked agitatedly. 'Why?' said her mother. 'Then I can write to her.' The two women exchanged a knowing glance across her, the rain came over the field in waves, lashing against the windows. 'Yes, I have her address,' Grandmother said softly. 'I want to go and find her,' Lotte explained. 'Now...?' her mother cried shrilly, 'in this situation?' 'It will have to happen sooner or later, of course' said Grandmother pensively, 'we can't prevent her.' 'It's war there!' Lotte's mother argued. With both hands Grandmother lifted the hat from her head – to supply herself with air or to acknowledge her powerlessness against the force of attraction between two halves of twins? She placed the hat in her lap and stared wearily and dejectedly at the violets as her fingers mechanically fingered the brim. 'If an old person like me can come back unscathed from this dreadful story,' she said, shrugging her shoulders, 'then a healthy young woman will certainly manage it too.'

Lotte wrote a letter in which courtesy and romantic yearning created a peculiar friction against one another, and ended with the statement of her readiness to come to Germany. In reply she received a formal letter, elegantly signed by Anna Bamberg, with the invitation to spend New Year's Eve at the estate of the von Garlitz family. Up to the last minute Lotte was worried about whether she would get a travel permit. Eventually she was able to travel on 30 December. In her coat pocket was the embroidered handkerchief that she had kept in her suitcase all those years, being returned to its original owner with her.

When they crossed the border and the customs officials asked for her papers in German, she said to herself: my country. She tried to see the image of her father before her, but that other father kept pushing himself into the foreground. It suited her better to think of 'the country of my birth' or: the country of composers and conductors, of symphonies and songs – how much easier it would be to sing a song such as 'The shepherd on the rocks' in a country with mountains instead of meadows. That each second was bringing her closer to Anna was almost incomprehensible. She had depicted the reunion in numerous versions in her fantasies, and still it remained a blind spot. The nearer it came the more her longing was further thwarted by anxiety – an irrational anxiety without any logic. To distract herself she looked outside with exaggerated attention. She bit into one of the apples that her mother had put in the bag. Just for a moment a slight feeling of guilt flared up, or treason, but it changed into pity immediately: from Germany she looked insignificant, puny.

At last the train slowed down and came into the station. Anxiety won. She wanted to stay inside the intimacy of the compartment for ever, but the train stopped and began to unload its passengers who thronged outside, mesmerized by the journey. The cold hit her in the face, she swayed back, put her suitcase down on the platform and loathed the pressing throng around her, the winter, the strange station, herself in her sudden cowardice. Shivering, she fished the handkerchief out of her winter coat. Instead of waving it, as had been arranged, she held it up awkwardly between thumb and forefinger. The reunion was suddenly so unavoidable that she observed the passing faces without attempting to look for anything familiar in them. A conductor blew his whistle somewhere. The sound skimmed over the travellers' heads like a bird's shriek. Then behind her she heard her name being spoken softly, hesitantly. It sounded like a quiet sigh from the mouth of the crowd. She turned round slowly, a pale face lit up between the winter coats ... a round and yet pointed face where the contrasts seemed to balance each other. Lotte thrust the handkerchief forwards in a reflex, the other accepted it cautiously. 'Anna?' The woman opposite her closed her eyes in acknowledgement. In the poetic picture in Lotte's head the two sisters fell into each other's arms, on the platform in Cologne they shook hands formally and their smiles made little clouds in the frozen air. Then the woman picked up Lotte's suitcase and began to walk towards the exit, exhorting Lotte to follow her with a nod.

Everything was enormous and overwhelming: the lofty, sooty roof of the station, the immense hall dominated by an advertisement for 4711 in coloured glass, the monumental presence of the Cathedral, the towers like two guards watching over Cologne – a double warning to the above, twins, in fact. Everything was enormous and overwhelming except the reunion, which was proceeding with such aloofness and efficiency, as though they were both operating on behalf of someone else and it was not about each of them. At a dry fountain at the foot of the Cathedral Anna shifted the suitcase to her other hand to get money out of her pocket for tram tickets. It occurred to Lotte that there was a greater degree of intimacy between the numerals of Route 11, which was taking them through the narrow streets of the inner city, than between Anna and herself. In vain she looked for family features in the pale face. 'So this is Cologne,' she remarked with a stiff laugh, to break the silence. 'Yes, one can indeed say so,' said Anna ironically. She leaned towards Lotte: 'And ... do you still remember this song ...?

With a teasing expression on her face she sang softly:

> 'Ding ding ding
> comes the tram
> with the conductor
> and if you don't have fifteen pence
> you have to run behind it ...'

Nothing in the children's song, which could have been the key to their mutual recognition, the renewal of the old bond, had aroused anything in Lotte – perhaps too many arias and cantatas had slipped in between. Anna looked at her expectantly. Lotte replied to the test of authenticity with an embarrassed shrug of the shoulders. Silently Anna turned away from her and transferred her attention to the dark grey surface of the Rhine. The tram rumbled over the bridge. It seems as though she rather reproaches me, thought Lotte, perhaps she has seen me as a deserter for eighteen years.

'Eighteen years ...' she now said aloud, 'it's eighteen years ago ...' Suddenly the spell seemed to be broken. The tram reached the other side. 'Why did you never write to me ... at the time?' Lotte asked, like a tentative defence and attack combined. 'Because I heard nothing from you,' Anna snapped. 'That can't be so,' Lotte lashed out, 'I wrote dozens of letters to you and each letter ended with: Anna, why don't you write back?' Anna seemed disturbed from her composure just for a moment. But it was no more than a ripple – she shrugged her shoulders and said flatly: 'Then they intercepted those letters. I never received them.' Lotte looked at her with bewilderment. 'Why would they do a thing like that?'

Anna stared outside ostentatiously, as though it did not concern her. 'You don't know them,' she said disinterestedly. Disconcerted by excitement and indignation at Anna's detachment – this was a crucial point – Lotte cried: 'They couldn't do that, just like that?' Impassive, Anna turned her face to her: 'That's how they are.' Irritably she added, 'It's best to get the bad things said straight away ... You have come here full of expectations but I ... I'm telling you honestly ... I really do not know what that is ... family ... or a special family feeling. I'm sorry, but now that you've suddenly returned like a female Lazarus I don't know what to do with you ... Long ago I had already reconciled myself to my fate of being alone on this earth ... I belong to no one, no one belongs to me, those are the facts ... I have nothing to offer you ...'

'But yet we're ... we have the same parents ...' Lotte repudiated weakly, 'that must count for something surely? In order to know who we are we must surely know ... how it all began ...?' 'I know precisely who I am: nobody. That suits me very well!' Bitterness shimmered through her provocative position, making her voice loud and rough. Some passengers looked round. Lotte remained silent, intimidated, she was in a cold sweat. Again she had the feeling that Anna was blaming her. But for what? For still being alive? For wanting to give the term 'sister' meaning? Was this her punishment for the long-cherished illusion of two orphans who would finally plunge into each other's arms, pure and unsullied by time, distance and family matters? Grandmother's description of the small-minded Catholic milieu of primitive farmers was now really taking shape.

Later she would reproach herself that she had not decided at that moment to come straight back on the same tram. There was no more doubt that the reunion was a disillusion and that the stay could only make everything worse. It would still be possible to spend New Year's Eve at home, with mulled wine, lardy cake and music. But a misplaced sort of stubbornness compelled her not to be daunted. In the German fairy-tales that she had been over-fed on as a child, many-headed monsters and dragons had to be slain to free the magic princess. Perhaps she was refusing to admit the failure already at this stage, perhaps she wanted to put off the moment when she would return home without illusions, perhaps she hoped to break through the armour and learn about what was still hiding beneath it.

The tram stopped. Anna indicated that they had to get off. This was her last chance: I'm sorry, Anna, I believe it would be better if I went back – but she stood up and snatched her suitcase; all of a sudden she could not bear the thought of Anna appropriating it again. They got off, it had become dark, and icy cold, the suitcase knocked against her leg with every step. 'All cars have been requisitioned,' Anna explained coolly. 'Now we do everything on foot.' Iron gates opened, a drive lined with dark tree trunks stretched out before them, the moon performed a sinister shadow play with the branches above her head. We are going the same way for the first time, she and I, thought Lotte, and a misplaced sentimental feeling flowed through her. She still had the inclination to embrace her sister, who walked next to her in fierce silence ... let's give up this charade for God's sake. But they walked along the endless drive a metre apart from one another, together and yet separate. A white house fluoresced in the dark, with blind, black windows. Wide stairs describing an elegant arc, first curving away from each other and then coming together, led to a baroque entrance.

Preparations for New Year's Eve were under way within the darkened house. Herr von Garlitz was expected home; his wife was trying to estimate how much food and drink his companions would get through. Helped by her status, money and charm, she knew how to get hold of a variety of products that had been unobtainable for ordinary people for a long time. Anna displayed feverish industry from Lotte's arrival to her departure. In between the activities she introduced her sister to the Countess, the cook, the butler, the governess and the other members of the staff, all exactly as was

proper but without any kind of enthusiasm. The two sisters were
compared. You could see it in the eyes, pronounced the cook, the
same blue, but beyond that the differences were greater than the
similarities. Frau von Garlitz complimented Lotte on her German.
Eighteen years and still quite without accent! The work was hectic.
You could already smell New Year's Eve in the kitchen, its arrival
was tangible in the staff's tense activity. Lotte stood at the window
of her guest room in pyjamas and looked out through a chink in
the black-out at the reflection of the moon in the swimming pool.
Anna had said a curt 'gute Nacht' and not exchanged another word
with her. The day ended in greater mystery than it had begun.
Instead of 'How will Anna be?' it was 'Who is Anna?'

The following day was also about staff busily walking back and
forth, involved in dim preparations, until an invasion of officers
forced them back to the wings. Lotte fled into the grounds. If at
first she had only felt unwelcome, the uniforms and caps, loud
voices – some with drawling eastern sounds or an ugly rolled 'r' –
made her into a confirmed outsider. Shivering, she walked in the
park. German ground. German grass. German trees . . . Country of
her birth? The kitchen garden at home and the neglected fruit-
trees struck her as a paradise compared with this emphatic wealth
per linear metre of lawn, per square metre of swimming pool, per
cubic metre of German air. The rest of the day she wasted in the
staff sitting-room, leafing through the *Illustrierte Beobachter*,
already contemplating the return journey and the way she would
disguise the disillusion at home. The evening meal in the kitchen
was bolted hurriedly; Anna appeared at table in a black dress with
a white, starched collar and a cap on her head. 'Here you see what
a chambermaid's life is like,' she said, again managing to make it
sound like an accusation. 'Can I help anywhere?' Lotte stammered.
'Why not?' said Anna sarcastically. 'I have another uniform like
this, that will be a splendid metamorphosis.'

Lotte let the waitress's dress slide over her shoulders – a desperate attempt to creep into Anna's skin, or at any rate to be twins on

the outside for once. She entered the dining-room with a soup tureen in her hands, her gaze straight ahead on the bow of Anna's apron ribbons, which had been tied with mathematical precision. The officers, who had exchanged their uniforms for dinner-jackets, were seated on either side of a long table decorated with evergreen sprigs. Candles in branching candelabras glittered in the table silver and in the dark red sequins on the Countess's low-cut dress. She sat at the head of the table, twinkling; her husband sat opposite her in his dual role as host and officer. Anna and Lotte were unnoticed as they put the dishes down – as though they were transparent. Anna's phrase 'I am nobody' acquired an additional dimension. They went back noiselessly; serving was the waiters' job.

That is how the festive evening slipped through their fingers in dull servility. Dirty plates, glasses, spoons, empty dishes. The guests became increasingly boisterous, it was hard to keep up with the pace at which wine and Sekt had to be fetched. One of them, a well-fed officer with a shining red face, performed an improvised sword dance with one of the weapons taken off the wall, around his half-empty glass which had been uprooted and placed on the parquet floor. Anna's arrival with a strawberry bavarois disturbed the acrobat's concentration – losing his unsteady equilibrium he thudded backwards onto the solitary piece of family crystal. With bloodshot eyes he crawled back onto his feet, the fragments sticking out of his backside like crows' feet. Enthusiastic applause rang out. One guest roared, 'The first victim has fallen at the Westwall!'

At that moment Lotte, also carrying a dish of bavarois in her hands, became convinced of her sister's fearlessness. Anna set the dish of gently wobbling pudding on the table, bent over the affected area and picked among the pieces there with a neutral expression, as though she were gleaning corn. Then she supported the wounded one towards the bandage cupboard. Just before leaving the room, he laid his hand on her bottom, to indicate that his spirit was unbroken – Anna coolly pushed the hand away.

Around midnight the staff crowded together in the communal sitting-room and at twelve they hugged each other with foaming glasses in hand. The sisters kissed each other like ice queens. Something external immediately provided them with a magnificent excuse to distance themselves again: a rifle shot, and then another, made everyone rush over to the windows. Lights out, someone roared. They rolled up the black-out curtains and pressed their noses to the glass. 'Dear heaven,' groaned the cook, 'they've gone mad!' Some officers, laughing and hawking, were aiming at a white bath towel hanging over a low branch. They shot again, the material moved a little and fell back slack. The cook went to the door. 'It's a scandal,' she cried angrily, 'I'm going to do something about it!' The governess stopped her: 'Calm down, Frau Lenzmeyer, it's not up to you to call senior officers to order.' The cook knocked back a few glasses of Sekt in frustration. The shooting continued. Lotte slipped out to her room unseen, where she let herself drop onto the guest bed.

The shots in the night and the image of the riddled towel brought to mind the disquieting stories of Theo de Zwaan and Ernst Goudriaan on their return from Germany – stories that had only increased her longing. It was only now that they took on meaning: she felt the threat that emanated from each shot, fired out of boredom and the lack of a more suitable target. Up to now 'enemy' had been an empty word – here it was acquiring significance. A significance that replenished itself with Anna's cold New Year's kiss, with a gloomy walk in the grounds, with the failure to retrieve anything as vague as country of birth. The shooting stopped, a song started up instead. In utter loathing she screwed her eyes shut. She took the cap off her head, untied the apron and looked at herself in the mirror. The black dress exactly suited the funeral of her illusions.

She had already put her suitcase in the hall when she went into the kitchen for breakfast. It looked as though they had worked the whole night through – not a dirty glass or scrap of pudding recalled the previous evening. Everything was focused on a hearty break-fast; on no account could the guests return to the Westwall on half-empty stomachs. Anna hurried to and fro, composed, without a trace of weariness, her blonde hair correctly waved around her cap. Lotte approached her about the tram departure times. She would enquire, she called over her shoulder, disappearing down the pas-sage with a silver dish full of rolls. Ignoring Lotte's objections, Frau von Garlitz decided that one of the officers would take her to the station.

The guests automatically allowed Anna to help them into their heavy coats, embroiled in their conversations right up to leaving. Lotte stood by stiffly, holding her suitcase. The acrobat grumbled noisily to his neighbour about the tenants on his property in Brandenburg. 'They are so stupid, so dirty, indolent – actually they're not people, but somewhere between person and animal...' Anna froze, his coat in her hands. 'It is easy for you to talk,' she said sullenly, 'I'd like to see you if you had to drudge like a farmer.' All heads turned towards her; the Countess looked on open-mouthed. In pure astonishment at such impudence, the officer per-mitted her to help him into his coat as willingly as a baby. His face went the same colour as the previous evening after his fall; it was probably the recollection of her efficient management of him that restrained him from demanding her immediate dismissal. At that moment the signal for departure sounded on the other side of the vestibule. Lotte grasped her suitcase. Anna came up to her to shake hands. She smiled again for the first time since Lotte's arrival – perhaps less from friendliness than out of satisfaction at the way she had cut an arrogant landowner down to size. 'We'll write some-time...' she said looking over her shoulder – Frau von Garlitz was calling her. The last thing Lotte heard was her cultured, enraged voice: 'Who do you think you are, offending our guests! If I ever see anything like that again...' A short, stocky officer seized Lotte's suitcase and hurriedly pushed her outside. She climbed into a military car. She let herself be driven away without turning round, down the drive, into a suburb swathed in profound quiet. Anna kept reappearing with raised chin, a coat in her hands, and each time she heard her angry retort, which had to be a justification for her own past. The designation 'barbarians' resonated in a remote corner of Lotte's mind. Curiosity overcame her: Anna's unflinching honesty had admirable aspects. But it was too late, they were crossing the Rhine – inaccessibility through distance would be less chafing than inaccessibility in proximity. She stared at the Cathedral. The two towers propelled upwards – already centuries ago they must have found a method for remaining joyful beside each other at their point of origin.

Throughout the journey the officers were silent to the parcel from Holland that had to be delivered to the station.

2

In a gust of cold air a boy came in, followed by his father who had bought one of the helmets at the market. He put it on his son's head, grinning, after he had ordered two Cokes. Even from the table where Lotte and Anna were sitting it was evident that the father–son romance was revived by the purchase of the helmet. As long as the glow lasted they were participants in the same adventure, a war in which neither of them had been involved. If there had been a feather headdress in the market, then the battle of Winnetou against the whites would have easily had the same effect.

'American Coke and a German helmet...' Anna shook her head, 'I'm getting old.'

Lotte's thoughts had not disengaged from that unfortunate New Year's Eve. 'I'll never forget it,' she murmured, 'all those drunken, shooting officers ... I had the feeling I was among fanatic Hitler-supporters.'

'Are you mad?' Anna sat up straight; something needed putting right. 'The von Garlitz family, they were old nobility, they were industrialists! Of course they had helped that buffoon into the saddle; in return he polished off the communists and got them their Greater German Reich. But you don't really think they thought much of the son of a customs official? They were able to use him well, for a while; only when it was their turn to die on the battlefield did they realize that that parvenu had used them too.'

She burst out laughing.

'What is there to laugh about?' said Lotte tetchily.

'I can still see myself running through that house in cap and apron. What a misery. All the time I was trying frenetically to forget that the visit was for me – think about it, for the first time in my life I was being visited. You have no idea what difficulty it caused me. Those officers were a lovely alibi. How I worked!'

Lotte was silently building a pyramid of sugar lumps. 'It has stayed with me like a decadent image,' she murmured, 'those officers in the night ... an enemy you can expect anything from if he is capable of shooting at towels...'

'They were dancing on top of a volcano,' Anna interrupted her. 'Why do you think they drank so much?'

✦

Anna paced about in her bedroom. Her body hurt with every step, as though someone had given her a beating. She struck her fist into her palm. The recurring silence was unbearable. It was a silence with a double foundation, left behind by someone who had now gone away for good. Not because others had arranged it so, but through her own guilt. She was besieged by images she had seen fleetingly in between work duties: her sister's figure – in the grounds with coat flapping about, alone at the long kitchen table by an empty plate after the meal, seen from behind as she went upstairs despondently. Piece by piece, silent indictments. Rewinding and playing the film again – differently. Too late, too late, too late. Why, that was what she wanted to know. The answer would not be found in the best-equipped library but was hidden in herself. The only thing she knew was that, from the moment Lotte had turned to her on the platform, she had come face to face with her father. His long curved nose, his narrow face and dark wavy hair, his melancholy, stubborn gaze. There was something improper – as though Lotte had robbed him or caused unfair competition. In Lotte she did not encounter the thickly swathed six-year-old sister who had been abducted by a woman in a veil. Now there was someone else who could exert rights over her father, someone who was perhaps more entitled than herself because she looked so staggeringly like him. So this was Lotte. Why now?

Restless and self-reproaching, she wrestled on that double trail all through the winter, that pushed drifts of snow against the house and deposited a crow at the top of the steps, frozen to death, so that Hannelore, one of the maids, saw it as a bad omen, on finding it in the morning, after which the washerwoman warned her that superstition brought bad luck, and Anna, forgetting everything for a while, had to laugh at this rare form of recursive superstition. The past revisited Anna for the second time without her having intended it to. Hannelore, eighteen years old, recently extracted from Lower Saxony by the Countess, had been placed under Anna's care since her arrival. The girl boldly announced that she was going dancing at the casino on Sunday afternoon. 'You can't permit her to go,' said Frau von Garlitz, 'unless you go too.'

The casino seemed to be flirting with the new socialism. The walls no longer shut her out; the doors with the copper handles stood wide open. She wore a Marian blue dress; red silk shimmered though the skirt; her employer's perfume still wafted out from the material. Anna handed the tickets in with a chaperon's characteristic lack of enthusiasm. Thus she gained entrance to her own hall. The field of marble, the leapfrog square, the hide-and-seek pillars, the high dome where the songs collected ... the marble staircase where she had fallen over ... everything was still there ... Somewhere she must, they must still be there ... behind the pillars, in the passages ... clouds of condensed breath rose up into the dome. Hannelore disappeared in the foyer. There were the sofas – Anna's trampolines. She heard a deep rushing silence through the hum of voices, through the dance music, through the clapping and tapping of heels on the dance floor inside. Hannelore had saved places, wine was ordered and gone was Hannelore. Anna caught a glimpse of her now and then, waltzing round in the arms of a soldier whose shaved, thick-set neck kept coming back into view. The Westwall seemed to have been emptied; the cat-and-mouse war had transferred to the casino foyer on this Sunday afternoon in April.

She drank her wine without tasting it and looked ahead of her fixedly – all of a sudden somebody placed himself between her and her memories. 'May I have the pleasure . . . ?' She stood up dejectedly and allowed herself to be led to the dance floor. 'Was machst du mit dem Knie, lieber Hans' seemed like something from a former life. The soldier carried himself impeccably. She stared at the silver V on his sleeve with a vacant gaze. After the dance ended he returned her to her seat. Just as she was going to sit down a new number started up; he nodded briefly and invited her again. The images slowly ebbed away during the second dance, which was more compelling than the previous one; she now perceived this soldier clearly. His face seemed remarkably trustworthy to her – it was more the face of a person than a soldier, she reasoned, without interest.

She moved her gaze away and discovered a large framed photograph of the Norwegian fjords on the wall. Were conquests already being flaunted? 'They are suitably topical with their wall decorations here,' she said gruffly. 'It might also have been the bridges over the Moldau,' he added. His accent surprised her. 'You are an Ostmarker . . .' 'Austrian,' he corrected her with a courteous nod. 'But they are all soldiers out of operettas with red roses in their rifles instead of bullets.' His face set. 'Not much to laugh or sing about in Czechoslovakia.' 'Being a soldier is not your vocation, so it sounds.' 'I was called up,' he smiled, 'I'd a thousand times rather be at home in Vienna . . . with roses in my rifle.' He spoke so melodiously that it seemed as though everything he said was in jest. Holding her more tightly, he began to describe passionate circles over the dance floor. When the number was over he brought her back ceremoniously – a pattern that kept repeating itself, as soon as the orchestra started on a new number he raced across the parquet floor again and stood before her. At about half-past eleven he excused himself. He had to be back in the barracks by twelve. 'May I see you again?' he asked. 'Excuse me, I haven't introduced myself: Martin Grosalie.' 'You can telephone me,' she said flatly, 'number fifty-two thousand.' 'Are you serious?' He looked uncertainly at her. 'Why?' 'It is such an improbable number.' 'You don't really think I'm imagining it,' she said annoyed. Blushing, he leant forward to kiss her hand. 'Ich küsse Ihre Hand madame,' said Anna ironically, pulling her hand away from beneath his lips.

The soldier was not deterred. He telephoned two days later. No argument instantly occurred to her to refute the request for a meeting. They met in a café on the Alter Markt; it was raining incessantly. A feeling of alienation, shame, overcame her as they sat opposite one another without the dance's option of escaping. But with the bravura of a schoolboy he took upon himself full responsibility for the meeting. He described Vienna to her, Schönbrunn, the Nashmarkt, the Prater, the house where Schubert was born, the house where Mozart lived, the house where Haydn died. The survey reviewed all the sights; he recreated his city and strolled through it with her, pointing everything out on the way, lively, enthusiastic – not in order to win her over but to put something else at a distance, something that was increasingly present in the background and was biding its time. Anna too, who thought she had nothing to do with it, felt it was there. Yet it still broke through unexpectedly. 'And now we're here,' he sighed, 'opposite the French, with all that equipment, and they are opposite us. Why? I hope that joke is over soon, then we can all go home again.'

Other meetings followed. He collected her from the house; everyone called him a nice, polite boy, which needled her. She harassed the nice polite boy with teasing, which he openly enjoyed – she poked fun at his accent, his courtesy, at Austria. One evening there was a dancing party at the Stadthalle. When it was drawing to a close Anna dragged him towards the exit. 'Come, it's over.' 'No, no, they're playing a couple more numbers,' he implored her. 'Shall we have a bet? If I win I can say *du* instead of *Sie*.' He won. They sauntered silently through the deserted avenues in the suburb, the moon curved behind the clouds, there was a sweet smell of young foliage. I can't start saying *du* just like that yet, thought Anna. At the bottom step in front of the house he kissed her, abruptly, as though he were settling a score with a voice that had forbidden him to do so all the way there. 'You're crying...' Anna was shocked. 'Not *Sie*, *du*,' he corrected her hoarsely. Under these circumstances she did not dare to take her leave: she could not abandon a weeping soldier at the foot of the steps. Although she would have preferred to run inside to think about it behind a locked door, she pulled him into the grounds towards a stone bench that seemed to be pointed out in the moonlight, surrounded on three sides by a shining, clipped yew hedge. They sat down. Fragments of films and books shot though her head, in which the characters turned out all right in the next phase; embraces, official declarations ... but a weeping admirer was not included among those. Although she regarded crying as a sign of weakness in herself, it occurred to her that on the contrary, for a man it demanded courage. The last time she had cried – an eternity ago – it was in rage, humiliation and pain. In the soldier's case it had to be something else; she did not dare to embark upon it. He pressed her hand and looked serenely ahead towards the sleeping house. Something in her that had been waiting all that time fluttered away. An agreeable languor overcame her. 'I'm so sleepy all of a sudden,' she yawned. 'Lie down,' he whispered, 'put your head in my lap.' Without hesitating she stretched out, dozed off, stupefied by soldier smell.

During her sleep the sickle of the moon moved to another place in the sky. She woke relaxed, in a condition of complete submission such as she had not known since her childhood. She observed him unnoticed. Sitting there, motionless, he reminded her of her grandfather's dying soldier who lifted his face to a descending angel. It looked as though he were communicating wordlessly in an intimate way with something that was invisible to her. He swallowed. His Adam's apple rose and fell, which gave him back his earthliness. Ashamed of her clandestine observation she said his name. He bent over her. 'I had never thought ...' he laid a finger on her lips, 'that anything so beautiful could exist as when a girl falls asleep on your lap.' 'Didn't I say so?' She remained sober: 'You are a Rosenkavalier.'

In the following days her thoughts went on circling round the soldier like a cloud of summer flies. How could he be simultaneously trustworthy and mysterious? – this paradox held her in pleasant confusion. There did not seem to be a way back. They arranged to go to the Drachenfels at Whitsun. A picnic basket was packed. But that eponymous dragon did not wait for their arrival. It had been woken from a sleep that had lasted about two decades, it stretched, yawned, looked in the mirror to see if its eyes were in place and its scales were shining, sharpened its claws on the rock face, opened its mouth wide to check the fire and sulphurous fumes mechanism and descended from the mountain, thrashing about with puffed-out chest and sweeping tail, in a westerly direction.

The telephone rang on 9 May. 'For you,' said Hannelore. Anna picked it up. The soldier was out of breath on the other end of the line: 'All leave has been cancelled.' Alarm, quick march. He had climbed over the barracks wall to telephone her. He had to go back immediately. If they found him he would be shot dead, without mercy. She was still standing there with the receiver in her hand long after he had put the phone down. There it was again, no longer in the background. It cast its entire shadow over her, settling itself in her diaphragm. Tears slid down her cheeks entirely of their own accord. 'Jaja,' said Frau von Garlitz, 'that's war, eh?' The laconic observation made Anna furious. Tears that had been conserved for years now flowed out. She had read enough to know that crying for a soldier who was departing for the front joined her to the company of millions of women throughout the ages. It had been written and sung about over and over again, but even so her grief was the only one, the worst one of all. Again she was powerless against the things that were happening; this time it was a powerlessness for two.

His first Feldpost letter came from Bad Godesberg. 'I am here in a gymnasium, I have a candle, pencil and paper, and I am writing to you because I care about you. Please let me hear something.' So began a correspondence that would last for years. It would survive the campaigns in Belgium, France, Russia, up to the last letter, which was not written by him. The love really developed on paper, with all the self-denial that was associated with it: ... all's well with me ...

'The French are coming!' Frau von Garlitz fled to the east with her retinue again. Anna and Hannelore were left behind to take care of the house. The door of the air raid shelter, which had already foresightedly been built in 1934, would not close any more. The swimming pool had been plentifully filled with fire extinguishing water as required by ordinance. Everything was well organized.

⟡

They were drifting like the sole survivors of a shipwreck in an ocean of coffee, tea, wine, Ratafia de Pommes – bad for the arthritis, good for the soul. A warm gulf stream repeatedly brought them in sight of new, unfamiliar coasts without them going ashore anywhere. It was still Sunday. They ordered lunch. Instead of exploring the environs of Spa on painful feet they preferred to go down the paths and avenues of the past, even though the risk of land mines was gradually increasing.

⟡

Years later Lotte's children were taught that the war began on 10 May 1940. But for the Germans it had already begun earlier, in September, or before that – a matter of perspective – in 1933, when the frustrated Sunday painter came to power. On that tenth of May the family did not leave the radio for a moment. Lotte looked outside through the tall windows. The unreal events that the broadcaster reported in a neutral voice were counteracted by the cloudless sky. Parachutists? Bombing raids on airfields? German troops crossing the border, like German housemaids had done all those years ago?

But the German army made swift progress. Rumours and facts jostled each other: the German parachutists were disguised as postmen and country policemen, it was teeming with spies, the royal family had fled, Rotterdam was in flames. The Germans were threatening to bomb other towns as well. Dutch soldiers defended themselves with the courage of despair. The Netherlands was small, but not small enough to be able to hide itself – from a bomber you could see it in its entirety.

The capitulation was frustrating but it also removed the anxiety. Threatened towns were spared, the occupier knew how to behave: no plundering, rape or slaughter as had been described in the books. Nevertheless, from then on marching columns constituted part of the street scene and the echoes of stamping boots and battle songs could be heard there. On the way to her singing teacher, Lotte chanced upon a group of Germans walking abreast, blocking the cycle path. Ringing her bell emphatically but in vain, she turned on to the road in order to pass. One of the soldiers ran after her, insulted that she had dared to ring a warning, and tried to grab her luggage rack. She stood up on the pedals to go faster; the blood whooshed in her ears. His swearing pursued her. She could hear the roaring and shooting in the night again. The soldier expanded, he swelled up behind her into something of monstrous dimensions that wanted to overtake her, pull her back, punish her. But she gradually gained ground. She did not dare look round until she was three roads further on and it had become quite quiet behind her.

Music was a good chaser-out of devils. For some time the choir's accompanist in radio broadcasts had been a well-reputed student from the conservatoire, David de Vries. Lotte asked him to accompany her studying Mahler's *Kindertotenlieder* at home, so she could concentrate fully on the singing part, which was already hard enough. Thus together twice a week they submitted to the magic spell of pain transformed into beauty:

I often think they have only gone out
and will soon be coming home again.
It is a beautiful day – do not worry,
they have gone for a long walk.
Yes, they have only gone out
and will presently be home again.

The songs suffused her with an indefinable homesickness – her voice, unhampered by false breath, no longer came from her chest but from her whole body. She became a single accumulation of music, of diffuse longing; in between she saw the profile of her accompanist, in heart-rending abandonment as though he were effortlessly identifying with the grieving father. When they stopped, the feeling continued to float, it was difficult to part, they turned around one another with the music still in their ears, full of disinclination to break the spell and dissolve into ordinary life separate from one another. He lingered increasingly before putting the music in his case – at such reluctant moments he was an easy prey for Lotte's father, who permitted him to hear his newest acquisitions.

He was also a diligent sailor, so as not to become an anaemic and languid musician like Chopin. On a fine day in summer he hired a boat and invited her out for a trip on the Loosdrecht Lakes. He praised her father as he initiated her into sailing: so sympathetic, and what impressive apparatus he had built! It would be blasphemy to say anything against him. Blasphemous of the fine day, of the water lapping syncopatedly against the boat, of the wind that gave her goose pimples that were smoothed out again by the sun; blasphemous of the sight of his sun-tanned body and long fingers, which were not now dancing over the keys but were involved in an active game with ropes, boom and rudder.

The compliment seemed to be a way in for him to complain about his own father. Originally a cantor in a synagogue, he had been unable to resist the attractions of popular song. He enjoyed a reputation among a large public, in the Netherlands as well as Germany: gramophone records of him were in circulation. The fame brought him pleasures and sorrows. Young women crowded outside his hotel room; he waited in a shiny dressing-gown, champagne in an ice bucket, until the very loveliest of them forced their way in to him. He bought his way out of his guilt about his sick wife with gaudy jewellery, but his sentimental songs remained innocent and cheerful in tone: after his performances the audiences went home emboldened – they were prepared for life again. David, who accompanied his father on tour, sat in an adjoining compartment in the train the next morning: he could not bear his father's presence. He closed his eyes in disgust and mentally escaped to Palestine, musing about studying medicine there after the conservatoire – you would get more out of being a pioneer there. The trip always ended with his father's remorse. Moved to tears by his only son's rejection, he begged him for understanding and affection, in exchange for laying the whole world at his feet. 'You'll get a sailing boat from me, boy,' he implored him, 'but let's wait until the war is over.'

Lotte, who was letting the water flow over her feet, did not yet know that the imaginary sailing boat mentioned here for the first time would become the symbol for something that would cast a shadow over the rest of her life. Something too that would not be compatible with a cloudless sky, billowing white sails, and a joint dive into the lake – where they stealthily touched each other for the first time; the water was a good alibi.

The early days of the war shambled along at a level of groceries. More and more necessities were rationed; Lotte's mother encountered few problems with it at first – because they lived out of the way, she always kept large supplies in the house. She got chests of tea from China from a former colonial who lived in one of the country estates, milk was fetched warm and foaming from the farmer, she baked bread herself. She did not go along with hoarding, but only stocked up on green soap. No extra measures had to be taken to comply with the black-out: drawing the horsehair curtains completely closed was sufficient. Theo de Zwaan was released from captivity in June. He had noticed no warlike activities, he had been stationed in Limburg at a place where nothing happened. 'He had hidden himself in a haystack of course,' said his mother-in-law, 'and waited quietly until the smoke of battle had lifted.'

3

The heavy lunch had driven them, even so, into the fresh air. Shivering, Lotte sheltered behind her collar: it seemed that the east wind had become even more vicious. Anna, who commanded a robust layer of natural protection and was anyway less inclined to allow herself to be influenced by weather conditions, walked cheerfully into the Parc de Sept Heures. It was deserted now that the flea market had packed up. A clump of man-sized yellowed bamboos was rustling in the wind. Anna wondered whether the bamboo would recover in the spring; Lotte thought it certainly would and added the intelligence that once in a hundred years bamboo bushes all over the world flowered at the same time. This struck Anna as a myth, although she granted that there were plants that bloomed for just one night, though no one had witnessed it.

Suddenly they were standing in front of a small natural stone monument that leaned against a steep rock, which seemed to close Spa off on the north side like a wall against the rest of the world. The monument had been erected to the designers of the footpaths around Spa. They were listed: from the Comte de Lynden-Aspremont in 1718 up to Joseph Servais in 1846. At the bottom there was a basin filled with frozen water; two copper frogs crouched on the edge with their heads thrown back; in summer, water probably spewed out of their open mouths. Anna had the bizarre sensation that they themselves were the two frogs, shut out by the ice and holding themselves in equilibrium on the edge, in expectation of the thaw.

They turned right in unison, walked along Avenue Reine Astrid and a little later found themselves in front of an iron gate that was the entrance to a building housing the Musée de la Ville d'Eau. They nodded to each other and went inside. An old woman sold entrance tickets, huddled behind a table with picture postcards. Her face, round and red like a shrivelled star fruit, was ruled by an intricate network of wrinkles that got in each others' way. But somewhere between the creases her eyes shone as she handed them their tickets with a gnarled hand. Anna asked for a guidebook – something faltered in the mechanism, then the head began to nod fiercely and a pale mimeograph appeared.

'Scandalous,' Anna whispered, 'a woman of a hundred still put to work.'

Suddenly they felt very young. With a certain bravura they went into the first room. The illuminated glass cases contained a large collection of 'Jolitées', objects that had been used by the visitors over the centuries: snuff and tobacco pouches, water bottles, walking sticks with the head of Napoleon or a wild animal, watch cases, quadrille boxes, delicate pieces of furniture – all painted and carved out of the celebrated wood proudly called 'Bois de Spa' – as though it were a kind of marble. The Arcadian images of elegant strollers with or without wig and crinoline on the routes laid out by Lynden-Aspremont and Servais elicited cries of wonder from Lotte. Anna felt annoyed at the frivolous baubles and saw the exploitation of underpaid craftspeople in the painted miniatures. She held the mimeograph up a long way from her eyes and began to read out loud in her wobbly accent.

Long before Spa became Spa, Pliny the Roman had already praised the curative actions of the water that bubbled up in that area. Ever since Henry VIII's physician had ordered his patient to drink the water from these springs, Spa became known in all Europe and the water, in flat bottles packed in plaited willow, found its way along all points of the compass. In 1717 Tsar Peter the Great honoured the town with a visit. The European aristocracy followed his example, surrounded by adventurers and parasites – statesmen, famous scientists, artists and ladies of royal blood strolled from fountain to fountain, a stick in one hand and a bottle in the other, and drank eagerly of the miraculous water that even enjoyed a reputation for curing the pangs of love. They were called 'Bobelins' by the inhabitants of the town. There was one firm rule of behaviour that the Bobelins had to stick to: all serious matters were absolutely prohibited. Quiet, harmony and loose reins were the ingredients of the cure. Famous names followed: Descartes, Christina of Sweden, Bollandius, the Margrave of Brandenburg, the Count of Orléans, Pauline Bonaparte ... Anna fanned herself with a hand. Pfff – yes of course, only the rich people could afford such a cure, they had all the time in the world while the staff worked themselves into the ground. It was a miracle that they managed to become ill on top of that: from their earliest youth they had eaten well, played sports, had not had to lug muck carts ...

Deaf to Anna's philippic, Lotte leaned over a trinket case on which two ladies with corseted waists and wide hats full of waving feathers were drinking glasses of water. 'Look at this,' she pulled on Anna's sleeve, 'what an elegant fashion that was: a really feminine silhouette. They were women with style ...'

'Of course they had style,' Anna retorted, 'they were brought up like that. I worked for them for years, I know exactly what they're like. It is all a façade – they were not a whisker better than us, these people who were nobility on the outside. I feel I am on a decidedly higher level than that so-called élite.'

Lotte pulled her along from one display case to the next. She refused to allow her pleasure to be spoilt by carping at the aristocracy. She simply wanted to enjoy the curious paraphernalia with which that class had surrounded itself – life in that period seemed so much more intense and richly coloured than life now. All at once they were in the hall again. The old woman had fallen asleep or, perhaps, even died. They left the museum – the wind pursued them two blocks further into the, by now, trustworthy pâtisserie, where they once again took seats beneath the hideous wrought-iron lamp fitting and ordered merveilleux, this time with coconut.

After the French campaign the family returned from the east. The Führer had done it again! The Sekt flowed in torrents, the flush of victory lasted until the first English bombing raids over Cologne. Anna made attempts to learn to swim – she floated on her back in the fire-extinguishing water and looked at the blue sky through her eyelashes. Weightlessness ... to be there and not there ... to forget for a while that Martin was in Poland with his division. After their first meetings, which subsequently seemed to have taken place in a dream rather than in reality, he began to be an ordinary person in the Feldpost letters in his choice of words, his observations: a tree in Odrzywót that was a thousand years old, a richly gilded baroque church in a village where there were more pigs than people, a weathered old man who lisped three words of German in which he bragged because his forefathers had been with Garibaldi on the barricades, a locality with hundreds of lakes that reflected the sky so that you ended up not knowing what was above and what was below. Warlike matters were not mentioned at all, though marriage was – a proposal full of Viennese flourish and elegance. From the moment he had seen her on the other side of the dance floor, in her blue dress, lacking any form of coquetry, even sending out a mildly aggressive 'don't come too near me', he had known it. On his next leave he wanted to ask her father for her hand. But he is dead, she retorted. Her guardian then? She had declared him dead. He had to ask someone for her hand surely? She found his obstinacy on this point old-fashioned but endearing and suggested that Uncle Franz should take that role upon himself. The idea of a marriage was so extravagant that she burst out laughing from time to time. I'm going to get married, she said to herself. It sounded as though it concerned somebody else – something like marriage could not possibly have anything to do with her. But at the same time the seriousness of it did permeate her, as expressed in the stereotypes: one body, one soul – till death us do part ... Never to be alone again – her fate would be coupled to his for ever in the practical and metaphysical sense. She would no longer be 'someone's chambermaid' but 'someone's wife' ... Yet stronger than all these considerations was a feeling of tranquillity – events overtook her in any case.

One afternoon in the autumn Martin got off the train safe and sound. The smoke from the locomotive hung under the roof. Coughing, she allowed herself to be embraced. Then he held her away with outstretched arms to look at her. She was shocked. During his absence he had become transparent in the physical sense. On paper he was as familiar to her as someone whom she had known since her youth, someone to whom no detail was too irrelevant. Now everything switched round at high speed. The old friend from the letters evaporated; in his stead was a soldier with a tanned face and shining eyes. To conceal her shyness she forced a way to the exit for him through the thronging masses.

The cook, housemaids, governess, washerwoman, he won them all over again with his courtesy, the flawlessness of his appearance and a rare combination of natural authority and boyishness. After the news of the imminent engagement they treated Anna with a new respect. Frau von Garlitz arranged two rooms for them in a small hotel in the Eifel; they deserved some undisturbed time together after all those months of separation and uncertainty, she thought.

Through a landscape that the autumn had set on fire the train puffed southwards with interruptions. A cousin of the hotel owner, who was himself at the front, fetched them from the station in a rickety jalopy that, preserved as a museum piece for years, was standing in for the requisitioned car. Wheels rattling on the road, forest air and an unfamiliar destination. At any moment Anna expected to see a convent appearing on the crest of a hill next to the von Zitsewitz castle at a bend in the road. One glance at Martin's profile brought her back to 1940 – times had moved on, don't look back. Under his care they would be able to bring her everywhere. Although up to now in spirit she had withdrawn as much as possible from reality as it presented itself to her, and in compensation had been in league with the world of literary imagination, now, as each bump in the unmade road threw her against Martin, she felt reconciled with everyday reality – she even loved the bumps in the road that were throwing her against him.

The hotel had an atmosphere of charming, dilapidated chic. The only guests, they dined in the faded dining-room in the company of an invisible élite who ate in a whisper at the scattered tables between dusty palms. Via the radio the owner's wife was in permanent contact with the nocturnal threat that was flying over the sea towards Germany. Instead of calm music from a string band, during the evening the meal was repeatedly graced by the familiar tick-tock, followed by a report of approaching danger. Determined not to let this one evening that was meant for them to be disturbed by any calamities, they let the woman show them to their rooms, which were pointedly at the opposite ends of a long passage, as though an extremely sensitive pair of scales had to be kept in balance.

But a little later on there was a knock at her door and he surprised her with a bottle of Sekt. They drank it all at a frivolous pace on the edge of the bed. The war disappeared from their consciousness – they were seized by a sense of freedom, separated from the external world, separated from time, in a room that belonged to someone else, among objects that had been seen by thousands of others. They touched each other, raised up from themselves by the tingling Sekt and a dizzying lightness. He began to undress her with trembling fingers, draping her clothes carefully over a chair. They crept into the bed shivering and pulled the sheets over them. 'I have not been with a woman before,' he confided in her ear. His erect member seemed to want to bring something to her memory, a warning, a reflex that had nothing to do with the here and now. Veiled by the vague recollection of a recollection, she lay still while he explored her body with his lips. He could do what he wanted with it, it was worth little – there had always been others to decide about its amenities.

'The sky, Martin, look, the sky!' Anna raised her head from his chest. They got out of bed and went to the window. In the north behind the hills a red glow fanned out in all directions. Dull roars sounded, like an approaching thunderstorm or drumroll. Anna felt a great disgust at the disturber of the peace on the horizon and at the unrelenting employer who could claim Martin back again at any moment. 'It's on fire in any case,' she said. 'Come.' She closed the curtains with a brusque gesture and pulled him back towards the bed with her. Above it hung a Lorelei swathed in clouds, brushing her blonde hair on the fateful rock.

A mountain of debris a metre high blocked the tram rails; the passengers got out and continued on their way, clambering over twisting paths that had come into being in a few days. The route passed between burnt-out blocks whose scorched façades were still standing half upright. Anna thought of a line of verse by Schiller: 'Horror dwells in the bleak window caverns...' In an intact window frame curtains flapped; further on, like a doll's house, the blasted-away front façade gave full view of completely furnished floors; the residents had not returned to hang the chandelier that had taken wing back in its place. They got lost in the disrupted lay-out of streets; a man with a sweating face clearing rubble told them the way. Peculiarity was the norm. Life had resumed its course – the ordinary noises of the city prevailed instead of the reverbera-tions of explosions and collapsing buildings, of crackling sheets of fire, of frightened screams and wailing. People clambered with their shopping bags over the rubble beneath which perhaps fellow citizens still lay.

Aunt Vicki seemed to have lost some of her talkativeness because of the terror. Uncle Franz was quiet and controlled as always – if the hospital caught fire he would also have to remain quiet and controlled. During the evening meal he tossed Anna an approving look: bravo Mädchen, you've brought an excellent chap with you. Aunt Vicki was beaming too: Martin was so polite and attentive – a man who knew instinctively what a woman was due. Uncle Franz played operetta songs in honour of the Austrian, until the siren sounded right through 'Mein Liebeslied soll ein Walzer sein'. Pre-programmed, Aunt Vicki went to the child's room, lifted her asleep out of bed and hurried with her to the shelter. They followed her mechanically. The tumult of hasty footsteps and voices was every-where. They settled on an empty spot in a corner. Anna looked up anxiously at the gas pipes and sewers and imagined how they would all go under in a porridge of sewage if the pipes burst. The prospect was so disgusting that she prayed silently that if the pipes did have to burst it should be the gas. This alternative calmed her. Every time the thought of the sewer threatened to gain the upper hand she performed the praying ritual with the help of the gas. But for the time being nothing happened. Aunt Vicki's child slept on – it was unthinkable that anyone would want to kill an angel with blonde hair and gently fluttering eyelids. Perhaps she was a talis-man that made everyone in the immediate vicinity unassailable. Anna herself felt sleepy at the sight. She leaned against Martin and slowly dozed off. She continued to sleep peacefully when the ground began to tremble. 'Wake her!' cried Aunt Vicki, upset at the idea of an adult woman meeting death sleeping. From her slumber Anna heard Martin's calming voice: 'Let her sleep, what difference does it make?' The ground shook again. His arm was round her. Nothing could happen to her.

In the face of this permanent menace from the English squad-rons, Frau von Garlitz finally fled for good to her parents' estate in Brandenburg. Although the house was far from the city centre, on the other side of the Rhine, the chemical factory immediately bor-dering the grounds seemed an attractive target. Martin returned to Poland; once again, Anna stayed behind alone as housekeeper – a strange, vacant position, a lengthy, inert waiting – for what? An old feeling – to be deserted by everyone, remaining behind in hos-tile surroundings – drove her restlessly through the rooms of the house. Even the library offered no solace; her attention evaporated over the pages. Her powers of imagination failed, except on the point about the different deaths a soldier could die. She exercised virtuosic indefatigability in creating threatening scenarios that took place in unfamiliar locations in Poland. A primitive country, they said. To pull herself together she cleaned the antique cupboards and polished them fanatically. After the cupboards she started on the beams – everything had to shine. When it got dark she descended to the luxuriously appointed air raid shelter where her bed was, resisting the feeling that she was entering a tomb, to stretch herself out in her quilted coffin, hands crossed, eyes closed, so.

At the end of the winter she was instructed to close the house and come to the east. In order not to leave it to the wolves just like that, she packed everything of value – table silver, crystal, dinner services – put it in the polished cupboards, locked them and stuck the large iron keys to the floor with plaster. She took the curtains down from the rods, folded them up and stored them away together with the expensive linen. Then she went into the garden to look at the house from a distance once more. It looked vulnerable and transparent without curtains in the pale March sun. She left it behind in no man's land, hollow, lifeless, chilly in all rooms. To the extent that the house was riveted to this spot, so she herself was being uprooted again: she was going away – the series of departures and arrivals, of attaching and detaching, was growing ever longer. With a suitcase in each hand she walked down the drive to the tram stop. In Cologne she boarded a train that would in any case take her in an easterly direction to one end point.

On first acquaintance with Berlin she was shocked by the inhabitants' blunt common sense. Dazed from the journey, encumbered by her suitcases, she accosted two passers-by on the platform. 'Excuse me please, could you tell me where the Schlesische Bahnhof is?' After a disapproving look, as though she had begged for alms, they hastily walked away to the stairs. She stopped another traveller, leaving aside the 'Excuse me please' this time, but she had not finished speaking before he too walked away shaking his head. Now she dropped all politeness. 'Schlesische

Bahnhof!' Her voice resounded beneath the roof. A man with a Homburg hat like a gangster stopped sarcastically: 'It's staring you in the face, can't you see?' He pointed upwards with his head to a sign on which it was shown in thick letters.

The ancestral castle was situated on the Oder in extensive estates with twisting paths, ponds, a family chapel and mossy gravestones in the shadow of conifers and yews. A central section topped with a tympanum, hiding the porch behind two tall white pillars, divided the façade in two symmetrical halves. The neo-classical severity was compensated for by southern yellow plasterwork and by geese scratching about freely on the terraces. Her arrival had been badly needed. Rudolf, Frau von Garlitz's son, had contracted tuberculosis of the spleen. A guardian angel was needed day and night, who would watch over his strict diet and his rest periods and relieve the seven-year-old's boredom by reading aloud. Separated from his contemporaries, he was confined by his illness, which was threatening not only his own survival but also the future expectations of his grandfather, whose only male descendant he was. The old man came every day, twirling the tips of his white moustache, enquiring about his grandson's health. Every day Anna had to forbid him to bring sweets. Thus her status as guardian angel inclined more and more to that of gaoler. Uncles, aunts and cousins who brought delicacies surreptitiously, as with a saw blade inside a cake, to release the poor patient from his rigid diet, were unwittingly smuggling his death inside. She read to him from his favourite books to make him forget about the sweets that had been thrown away, and to forget that the only thing she was waiting for was a letter from Poland. Waiting, you could calmly say, was something which she had been adequately steeped in.

Meanwhile, however, she obtained an answer to the question of why her father's name had had such a magic effect on Frau von Garlitz. She had asked von Falkenau point-blank. 'Johann Bamberg ... yes ... wait a minute ... I'll never forget him ... an exceptional young person, very dedicated and ingenious, he thought up various

improvements within the business to make things work more efficiently...' He looked at Anna thoughtfully. 'Outwardly you don't
look like him but in you I detect the same effort and incorruptibil-
ity. Alas we were not able to profit long from your father. I remember that he was offered another job ... he was a socialist, well yes,
that was his affair ... an extraordinary person, that Bamberg...'

'You yourselves had begun to bomb towns,' said Lotte, who was
annoyed at the way Anna depicted the inhabitants of Cologne as
victims. When she thought of the bombing of Rotterdam and
London her sympathy froze.

'Yes of course we had started it,' said Anna.

'Then you shouldn't have been surprised that there was
retaliation.'

'We weren't surprised, we were afraid – just like the Londoners
when they were packed on top of each other in air raid shelters.
That fear is actually universal!'

'With the difference that you had yourselves to thank for it.
You had chosen the regime that would shrink from nothing to
bomb towns.'

Anna sighed. She rested her plump arms on the table, leaned
forwards and looked wearily at Lotte. 'I have just explained to you
how the poor stupid people let themselves be blinded. Why won't
you accept that? We still aren't getting anywhere this way.'

Lotte sipped from her empty cup. She felt the rage rising to
her head – she was being lectured here, would you believe! What
arrogance!

'I'll tell you now in exact detail why I can't accept it,' she said
angrily. 'Perhaps then, in your turn, you'll also understand something for once.'

The water that had lapped against the keel of the boat was scraping
beneath their Friesian skates six months later. They were gliding
over the ice in a cadenza, hands criss-crossed in each other's. It

186

looked as though together they made one skater. Frosted reed borders and willows shot past; above them the sun hung low and was slowly turning red. Lotte stumbled over a scar in the ice. David caught her. Twisting on the narrow blades they stopped, facing each other; he kissed her frozen lips. 'Ice queen...' he said in her ear, 'what would you say if we were to get engaged...' 'But...' Lotte began. She looked at him in amazement. He laughed and kissed her on the end of her nose, which was numb from cold. 'Think about it...' he said. He grasped her hands and they zig-zagged onwards. Mist formed; minuscule particles of water took on the colour of the setting sun. The cold penetrated through her clothes. A line of verse from the song cycle went round in her head: 'In such a stormy weather, I never would have sent the children out...'

In the dark they cycled back. Outside her home he said goodbye. 'I wouldn't want to give you a fright,' he said, 'but I'm simply mad about you.' She blew on her hands, he took them in his and rubbed them warm. 'I'll come on Saturday,' he promised, and then we'll talk it over.' 'No, no...' she said in confusion, 'I mean ... I can't on Saturday ... let's wait a little...' He kissed her cheerfully. 'Fine ... fine ... we're not in a rush...' He rode off humming, turning round to wave once more.

For days, absent-mindedly, she did the things that had to be done. The as yet unnamed love should last for ever for her; she loved the secrecy, the unspoken and the painful. A concept like 'getting engaged' made her nervous. Yet she knew that ultimately she would not say no. Before their relationship accelerated and everyone interfered with it she wanted to harbour ambivalent feelings and the reliable solitude. Perhaps he felt it – she heard nothing from him.

The illusion that the war was turning out well came to an end. In Amsterdam's Jewish quarter there were clashes between WA men, stirring up trouble, and Jewish gangs; a WA man was killed. As a reprisal, on 22 February, hundreds of young Jewish men were picked up arbitrarily. In the official report there was mention of 'a murder so horrible and bestial, as only Jews were capable of committing', but the illegal newspaper *Het Parool* demythologized the affair: it was a question of manslaughter in an ordinary fight – the dead body had been found with a cosh round the wrist! Lotte's father brought home a manifesto from the underground Communist Party, exhorting resistance to the Jewish pogroms: 'STRIKE!!! STRIKE!!! STRIKE!!!' the working people were urged. The strikes that broke out in various parts of the country thereafter were stopped by the Germans with executions. Calm apparently returned again.

Just as Lotte was beginning to grow restless – it had been ages – she was telephoned by David's father. In a dull tone he asked if it would be convenient if he and his wife could come round the same evening: they had something to discuss with her. Blood rushed to her head. Why was David sending his parents instead of coming himself? After everything he had said about them? They were received solemnly (the famous singer!). Lotte's father shook hands in silence. The singer smiled sadly, turning his seducer's moustache into a stripe. His glance slid over the four sisters. 'And who is Lotte?' Lotte nodded cautiously. David's mother hurried to seize both her hands and squeeze them delicately. Overcome with emotion she clicked open her crocodile skin bag and took out a handkerchief. 'We did not know that he had a girlfriend . . .' she said, moved.

Her husband did the talking after they had sat down. The reason for their visit was a postcard from David from Buchenwald, in which he asked his parents to convey his greetings to Lotte because he had not been able to say goodbye to her. 'Buchen . . . wald . . . ?' Lotte stammered. De Vries swallowed and stroked his forehead in a gesture of despairing resignation. Staring at the floor he explained that David was arrested on Saturday 22 February in Amsterdam's Jewish quarter while he was making music with a group of friends. The Grüne Polizei had burst in suddenly; they had to stand with their backs to the wall. 'Which of you is Jewish?' was screamed at them. Without thinking for a second, his head was probably still in the music, David had taken a step forward. Two other Jews in the group wisely kept their mouths shut. He was taken to the Jonas Daniël Meierplein, where rows of companions in misfortune were already waiting. Without a charge, without any form of trial they had been transported to a camp in Germany.

David's mother sobbed into her handkerchief. Desperately looking round him, the father took heart: 'You'll see that after a few months of labour camp the boys will be sent home. The Germans wanted to make an example: think about it, no more disturbances. David is well, he's done a lot of sport ... He isn't having a bad time there ... here, read it...' Lotte bent over a few miserable lines on the card buried beneath rubber stamps: '...I am fine, we are working heartily...' He had had this card in his hands. It was rather alarming, a card that could leave the camp freely and find the way home while the sender was held in captivity. Yet the full extent of the seriousness did not immediately get through to her. It was so bizarre, so absurd, so senseless, that it could not be comprehended. Automatically she looked at the piano – the sheet music still lay open at the page they had been on. Everything in her resisted the thought that he had disappeared just like that – just like that. Immediately she also clung on to the idea of a labour camp, a sort of scout camp – chopping wood in the open air, planting trees.

'We are sending him back a card,' said his father, 'would you like to write a line?' 'Dear David...' she squeezed into the little space under the fully written card. Her pen stopped, floating above the paper. She felt his father's eyes on her, driving her pen. She wanted to write in code, something personal, something essential. A line from the song cycle came to her – without thinking it over she wrote a variant of it: '...I hope you have only gone out and will presently be home again...' As she reread the line it suddenly evoked a strong fear in her. What in God's name had she written down? A quotation from a poem of mourning, an elegy. Too late, too late to change anything. She gave the card back with a trembling hand. She could not bear to be in the room any longer. The sight of his parents upset her, but nor could she bear the sympathy of her parents . . . a world that could let someone disappear just like that took her breath away. She stood up abruptly and went out of the room without polite phrases, out of the house, outside. She sat down on a step at the garden house with a throbbing heart. It penetrated through to her like a slow-acting poison, something that was almost as intolerable as David's disappearance: on 22 February he would have come to her . . . if she had wanted that.

For weeks she subjected herself to strenuous self-analysis, put herself on the rack: why had she not gone along with his spontaneous suggestion . . . why did she have such a need to keep her options open, for the sake of form . . . if she had wanted to put him to the test a bit, provoke . . . why all that reservation . . . ? She lashed herself with questions that she could not answer, questions that bit by bit gave her an increasingly monstrous picture of herself, which invariably brought her to the same merciless conclusion.

His father telephoned again. They had received a second card, this time from Mauthausen, with the cryptic text: 'If I do not catch my sailing ship quickly, then it will be too late . . .' He cried desperately, 'He is imploring us to help, my boy, but what can I do? I wish I could take his place – I am an old man, he has his whole life in front of him.' Lotte sought for words in vain – when she really needed to find them they seemed not to exist. If David did not survive then the whole idea of justice was an illusion – only arbitrariness ruled, chaos, in the midst of which one person, with all his plans, expectations, hopes, fantasies, signified nothing – nothing. At night the ship with the billowing sails drifted through her dreams. The Loosdrecht Lakes swelled into an ocean – now he sat beaming and tanned at the rudder, then he was in the water again and trying frenetically to haul himself into the boat, holding on to the edge with petrified fingers while she looked on.

She received a recent photograph from his father. Painfully innocent, David was laughing at the photographer. That naïvety had cost him his freedom, perhaps his life. He had been in the wrong place at the wrong time – she could not look at the photograph without that thought. Reverence prevented her from tearing it up, again and again she forced herself to look at it. David had cycled out of her life waving cheerfully; that movement of his arm, back and forth, stayed longest with her as though something more was being conveyed, which was of great significance. And what had he been humming as he disappeared in the darkness?

Music irritated her. All those melodies, measures, subtleties, struck her as ridiculous – useless frills, false sentiments. Her voice refused to work in the upper registers, in the lower it vibrated uncertainly. Catharina Metz sent her home: 'Pull yourself together a bit first.'

4

Where did all the water come from and where did it go to? Anna lay in a shining copper bath-tub. Bubbles of air took off from her skin, a network of scales. Her body lay pale and fish-like in the water. There must be an ingenious system of pipes through which the water flowed from the springs to the Thermal Institute and, via the bath-tubs, was conveyed away again – the body it lapped around for half an hour was merely a way-station. All that water, invisible, flowing inaudibly, like blood in the arteries, the bath-tubs a pumping heart. In how many bottles of mineral water am I lying? she thought.

Long ago this same body sat in a bath-tub on the kitchen floor. Uncle Heinrich drummed mockingly at the closed kitchen door: you must be really filthy if you have a bath every week. It seemed a loaded silence reigned in this bathroom, as though the guests of the past were invisibly present and anxiously ensuring that they did not reveal themselves. How many, which famous dead had been in this bathroom, in this bath-tub? Were their thoughts left behind here, could the silence be top heavy from it? What they had thought wouldn't have been up to much, she chuckled.

From those unknown dead it was but a small step to Lotte's death. Shame, rage, sorrow had prevented Anna sleeping the whole night. Yet we are sisters, she remonstrated stubbornly with herself. But didn't age go together with leniency, with wisdom? If the two of us can't surmount all those barriers, how do others manage? Then the world will stay in the grip of irreconcilability for centuries, then you can multiply the duration of each war by at least four generations. Of course – Germany had been able to extort the reconciliation with all its money, but one football competition was enough to reveal that the old enmity was still alive and kicking.

Something in the angle of the light, in the green reflection off the tiles, in the peaceful privacy, brought her back to the casino. Lotte was sitting opposite her in a bath on lion's feet, a dark woman (Aunt Käthe?) leaned over them and poured a thin trickle of cold water down their backs from a blue enamel jug. They took it in turns to shiver, trembling with pleasure. She could see Lotte very sharply before her, with her damp dark hair, her eyes screwed tightly closed – the picture was clear, more lifelike than that of Lotte as she had sat opposite her the previous day. It is still all there, she said full of surprise. Although the bombing had left no tile, no stone of the casino intact, it is still all there in my head; those years in between signify nothing.

What history has subjected us to we cannot weigh on the scales, she thought. Suffering does not separate us, but connects us – as pleasure connected us then. This insight, however absurd it seemed, relieved her. At the same moment the woman in an overall came in to help her out of the bath. She offered Anna an inviting hand. Without strange antics, upright and dignified, she stepped over the edge of the bath and descended below. Like Pauline Bonaparte, assisted by her chambermaid, she grinned inwardly.

They found each other in the coffee-room at the end of the morning. Although the door was always invitingly open, they had never come across anyone in there. Now and then a guest shuffled through the labyrinth of passages but mostly it was quiet and empty – January was the slack season.

'I slept so badly,' Anna confided, 'the whole night I saw the image of that one young man who stepped forward unsuspectingly.'

Lotte nodded absent-mindedly, sipping her coffee and a glass of mineral water alternately. Anna had the feeling that she did not want to go on with it.

'I don't want to give the impression that I am bidding against you in terms of the distress that befell me,' she said carefully, 'but my husband was killed in the war too, in the same bloody war, after I had gone through years of worry...'

◆◆

The first notes of Beethoven's Fifth Symphony sounded in the dining-room. 'Ta ta ta ta ... The Wehrmacht High Command announces: The twenty-eighth infantry division on the advance to Russia...' Anna was preparing a piece of bread for Rudolf. Slowly she spread some butter on it mixed with tears. Old von Falkenau, sitting opposite eating breakfast, watched her pityingly. 'You mustn't cry, Fräulein,' he shook his head, 'after all, your fiancé isn't in the infantry! He isn't in any danger with the signals troops. Anyway, you'll see, the whole operation will be over in six weeks. Did you think that that nation was going to defend itself? They are glad to be being released from Communism.' Anna laughed deject-edly. Although von Falkenau, a war-horse with connections in the highest military circles, got his information first hand, no reassur-ance from outside was adequate to soothe her anxiety. What was one soldier among a million soldiers? – a bit of fluff in the wind over the tundra, in the wastes of a country where the sun rose on one side as it set on the other. It was a nonsensical war, chiefly expressed in huge numbers that far exceeded the powers of imagination: 'Ta ta ta ta ... The Wehrmacht High Command announces...': thirty thousand Russian prisoners of war, forty thousand, fifty thousand. What happened to them, where did they manage to live? Questions that the practical spirit, at home, posed itself quite inno-cently while the victory chatter zigzagged outside from the radio through the open garden doors and whipped the roses up into more profuse flower. When a letter eventually arrived it was already fourteen days old. Meanwhile perhaps Martin had already been killed in action. She went to see the newsreel in the nearby town, she read the paper, but the more efforts she made to assess his chances of survival in relation to the advancing armies, the more she felt a powerless outsider. Sitting at home and unable to do anything – a front that nobody spoke about.

A telegram arrived at the end of October. 'Please come to Vienna. Immediately. We will get married.' Her suitcase, containing a home-made wedding dress and an officially authenticated family tree, had been ready for months. She travelled to Vienna in great haste. As she got off she hesitated. For one moment it was as though a strong gust of air was pushing her back inside the train. There he stood in actuality, after having died a hundred deaths in her imagination. He was there, returned from an immensity in which an ordinary person would be lost. Time and space had brought him back here as though it were the most ordinary thing in the world. He was flanked by his parents. She envied him slightly for having two parents with whom he could wait for her: look, that's her now. Father and son both wore suits and hats, Martin's was crooked, the other's was straight. The father was slim and youthful, but there was a troubled expression on his face in the shade of his hat brim, as though he were constantly looking into a strong sun. The mother also gave the impression that existence demanded a superhuman effort from her. She pursed her lips together stiffly as though she were blowing up a balloon; she wore her heavily permed black hair like a cap on her head. Between these two people, who seemed to be ignoring one another, Martin stood and beamed.

The father said goodbye in a wide, treeless shopping street where trams rumbled past, at the entrance to a massive six-storey building. The moment had now come for him to go back to his wife again, he explained courteously – but by the way, she warmly invited them round. Anna looked from one to the other in amazement. Why hadn't Martin told her that his parents were separated? The father raised his hat and walked to the tram stop. The three of them climbed the steps of the building where Martin had grown up, on the first floor, above a chemist's. Anna, having become used to large rooms with carpets, antique furniture, paintings and family portraits, recoiled when she entered the small rooms crammed with knick-knacks.

After his mother had sent Martin out on an errand she led Anna to her guest room with exaggerated hospitality. 'So,' she said, glad to be closing the door behind them, 'now we can talk to each other as woman to woman. Listen. I want to warn you, for your own good. Don't get married. Abandon the wedding while you still can. Marriage is men's invention, they are the only ones to benefit from it. Through that one transaction they acquire a mother, a whore, a cook, a worker, entirely for themselves. Everything in one go, gratis. You never hear anything about the wife. She sits nicely locked up, in those few square metres, with her scanty house-keeping money. She has walked into a nasty trap, but by the time that dawns on her it is too late. Don't do it, dear, be wise. I am saying this to you in friendship.' Anna tried to release herself from the black hypnotic eyes. 'I can assure you that I love Martin very much ...' she declared to her. 'Ach, love ...!' said the woman condescendingly, 'all lies and deceit to drive the woman mad.' Anna began to open her suitcase with trembling hands, she took out a blouse at random. 'Would you excuse me,' she said weakly, 'I would like to change.' 'Think it over!' The woman left the room triumphantly. Anna sagged onto the edge of the bed. She finds me unsuitable, was her first thought. What kind of mother is this who tries to upset her son's plans behind his back? The plans of a soldier who has to return quickly, to the war! Staring at her wedding dress in a state of shock, she subsided into a tangle of thoughts and reflections until Martin knocked on her door, full of impatient happiness. 'May I come in ...?' Courageously she decided to hold her tongue.

After the evening meal the mother placed a porcelain plate with a flower pattern in front of her son. 'I have another surprise for you my boy, something you're absolutely crazy about.' With a mysterious laugh she conjured up a jar of apricot compote and began to fill the plate with it. 'Doesn't Anna get any?' said Martin. 'But I kept it specially for you ...' a mischievous, warmongering glitter in her eye. Martin sighed. 'I would like you to lay another plate.' The mother stood there without moving. In the cluttered rooms she was queen, whoever ventured into her territory was exposed to strange specimens of deranged maternal love. Warmongering made way for being the injured party. 'Ach so ... therefore I have to do it for her ...' 'Yes, otherwise I won't eat a mouthful of it.'

Outside the four rooms she had no hold over them. Breathing more freely, they went into the city that showed itself off stylishly with its churches, palaces, symmetrical parks and ponds, botanical gardens and orangeries, cake shops. This was his city, the preview of her future. Here she would live as soon as the war was over. In a museum they admired the Habsburg art treasures, they looked down over the roofs from the Leopoldsberg. Tickets for the opera and theatre were scarce, except for a soldier with a leave-permit. To every performance they went to he also invited his mother. She insisted each time that her close friend should accompany them, an ample Viennese, quickly moved to emotion, with many frills and lace – during the performances she felt impelled to inform them of every whim that fluttered through her head. 'Mother,' Martin said eventually, 'I am happy to take you with us, but please ... that friend doesn't always have to be there?' 'So ...' she raised her chin, offended, 'isn't my friend to your liking? Though you didn't ask for my approval in the choice of your friend.' Martin apologized for her in the bedroom, watching Anna wearily. 'I am sorry, don't blame her ... she has been like that since the day my father left her. I was only small then. She has never been a normal mother, as a mother ought to be. She has always wanted to possess me, in a tyrannical way. To provoke him. Nothing can be done about it, that is simply how it is now.'

The sense of expectancy that the city had aroused in Anna slowly ebbed away. It seemed to her that her mother-in-law was floating over it with outspread wings – no district, no building escaped her shadow, wherever they went. One day when they came home, the house had an atmosphere of a morgue. The curtains were closed, a sharp smell of vinegar struck their throats. Cautiously they opened the bedroom door. The mother lay in bed with eyes shut; her close friend sat next to her and reverently applied a heart compress soaked in vinegar. 'Shhh...' she whispered with a finger to her lips, 'your mother has had an attack of nerves.' Martin clenched his jaw muscles. After a cool look at the scene he turned round and left the room. Anna lingered at the foot of the bed, looking down uneasily at the ashen mother. My God, she thought, if he deals with his mother like this, how will he deal with me later if there's anything the matter with me? She found it stuffy. She tiptoed out of the room with her hand on her throat. Martin was sitting at the kitchen table, depressed. 'I know what you're thinking,' he said, 'but I tell you: it's all play-acting. There's nothing wrong with her.' 'How can you be sure of that now?' said Anna indignantly. 'Fine,' he sighed, 'you're being sympathetic in spite of everything. Go back there and feel her pulse, then you'll see how serious she is about it.' Anna returned to the bedroom timidly. She put a finger on the substantial pulse. The friend nodded blandly to her. The heartbeat was calm and regular, just as it should be. The eyes did not open a chink; she was lying on the pillows like an enormous black dahlia.

'I have something to confess to you,' said Martin, 'I have already been walking round all day with it and didn't dare say it to you ... We cannot get married now...' Anna went rigid. 'Why not?' He put an arm round her. His leave was actually illegal, he explained, he had a forged leave-permit. After his company had been in action for weeks they could have three weeks to recuperate. In Russia, mind you. The company commander, a pleasant chap, had suggested: 'Before you all have to be in that hell again I advise you ... go home for two weeks. On my authority.' Martin would have betrayed them all by getting married: it was an official event that had to be notified to his superiors. Anna nodded without saying anything. Suddenly the war was hugely present again. He laid his head on her shoulder contritely. Everything paled into insignificance beside the fact that he would soon be returning to the east again. And she to the north. That they were no more than pawns on a world-sized chessboard. 'That hell...' Anna repeated thoughtfully. 'Just tell me honestly, Martin, what is it like there? – don't protect me...' He put a finger on her lips. 'Shhh ... don't talk about it,' he whispered, 'I'm here precisely to forget it.'

As the attack of hypochondria began to leave her, the mother rose again from her apparent death. Pottering about the apartment, she took up her positions. Martin and Anna made plans for their last week. 'I think I'll go to the savings bank,' he mused, 'I don't want us to have to penny-pinch.' On the way to the hat stand they heard the front door slam shut. They left the house; the sky, which promised rain, was the colour of the façades in the tenth district. Martin gripped her arm. 'Well, just look...' A block ahead of them on the opposite side of the street his mother was dashing in the same direction as they were, head forwards, a large leather bag in her hand like a weapon. 'What a hurry she's in,' he said astonished. They passed a shop window with dirndls. 'Can you see me in a thing like that?' Anna said jokingly. Martin turned up his nose. 'That's for gushing types who like an Alpine glow and forest horns.'

'That's odd,' said the bank official, smiling slightly, 'two minutes ago your mother withdrew the last of the money in the account.' 'But there was a hefty sum in there,' Martin cried, 'years of savings.' He had to sit down. Dazed, staring ahead, he shook his head. 'Before I left I gave her a letter of authority,' he said flatly, 'for emergencies.' Anna pushed him gently outside. He threw his hat in the air. 'I'm broke,' he cried with a shrill laugh that echoed round the walls, 'O mein lieber Augustin, alles ist hin...'

He went inside the apartment gruesomely cheerful. His mother was already in the kitchen as though she had never been away. Martin picked up a kitchen chair and stood on it. 'And what was left in my bank account...?' he cried rhetorically, 'nothing...!' He picked up one of the carefully labelled jars of apricot compote from the shelf, let it slither out of his hands onto the floor and reached out to take a new jar. 'I've been taking care of him all those years,' his mother began to lament to herself, '. . . gone without food myself . . . not a shred of gratitude . . .' Martin looked down on his whining mother with a jar in his hands. Suddenly he put it back quietly on the shelf, turned it decoratively so the label faced outwards and got down from the chair. 'Come,' he said calmly, gripping Anna by one arm, 'we're going to pack.' In a cloud of self-pity, the mother traversed her paltry empire; she threw herself pathetically on her son's half-packed suitcase on the bed. Anna pushed her wedding dress, which she had hung up, into her suitcase and closed it. A dull throbbing headache located itself between her and the outside world; she followed Martin mechanically out of the house, into the street, onto the tram.

They were received by the father and his second wife with calm, silent understanding. Anna, who had thought her initiation as a member of the family was now behind her, was brought into the know about the latest mysteries. The father had recently renewed his paternal role after an involuntary interruption of twenty years. All that time Martin's mother denied him access to his son, and depicted him to his son as a frivolous womanizer and profiteer. When Martin was in the fourth class at the grammar school she refused, for reasons perhaps only she knew the logic of, to accept the father's monthly study allowance any longer. To the son she said the father no longer wanted to pay, to the father that the son had had enough of studying. She had found a place for him as a pupil in a first-class hairdressing salon just by the Opera in Kärntnerstrasse. Since then, instead of Homer's hexameters it was the heads of moody divas that he bent over. Her manoeuvres had only come to light when Martin had sought to contact his father on the occasion of his imminent marriage.

With retrospective force Anna now understood the strange, three-headed reception at the station. The one did not want to yield to the other; the father would not allow himself to be bypassed any more. All that involvement in family entanglement befuddled her. She was inclined to count herself lucky to be someone without parents – although in a certain sense Martin too had become an orphan years ago, with the absence of the father, under the domination of a hysterical mother.

They resumed their trips with desperate energy. They climbed from the Untere Belvedere, the seventeenth-century summer palace of Prince Eugen of Savoy who liberated Vienna from the Turks, to the even larger Obere Belvedere, the symbol of his power. They visited the Karlskirche, where Martin wanted to be married. They got drunk at the Heuriger tavern. During the days that remained it was as though a reservoir had to be filled with joint pleasures and enjoyments that they would be able to draw from for the rest of their lives.

She took him to the train with his father. 'I'll manage fine…' he cried from the window of the departing train, 'Russia is large and the Tsar far away!'

❧

'I still well remember how afraid we were,' said Lotte, 'that autumn, that the Russians would lose.'

'I only thought about the life of that one…' Anna stared at her nails, 'that was the only thing that interested me. Beyond that I didn't see, didn't hear. I hoped and prayed that he would come back. People totally forget that now, the continuous anxiety within which every one of us, at home, had to live – there were millions of boys like Martin there.'

Lotte felt compelled to help her recall that millions of Russians had been slaughtered by those same boys.

Anna sprang up. 'We simply didn't think about that. With us all you heard was: Advance, advance, Bialystok, Leningrad, Ukraine. Hermann Goering delivered a major speech: "We have conquered the most fertile country in the world…." He promised: "We will do some fine things there. From now on we will have enough butter, enough flour." Germany was getting thinner: anyone who had skills to contribute was sent there to give advice about farming, health services. Even the greatest fool was somebody there and could do something. The prisoners of war were brought back here to work in the factories. It became a crazy organizational machine, a huge achievement in a certain sense. People at home became ingenious too – you made a jacket out of an old table-cloth, you made your own shoes . . .'

'The Dutch did that too,' Lotte snapped.

'Naturally . . . an emergency mobilizes all the forces that normally lie fallow. That's why people are so bored now. They have to go on creativity courses. That is the malaise of this age.'

Lotte cut Anna off vindictively, sensing that her defence was increasingly acquiring the character of a hymn of praise: '. . . And then the winter set in.'

'Yes, General Mud. Then the swift advance was over.'

'Napoleon had already got stuck in the mud and cold – we fervently hoped history would repeat itself and it did. Now Hitler has lost the war, we said straight away.'

'We thought: we must help the boys get through the winter. They wrote home that they were cold and everyone got going – even the children and the patients in hospital. Everyone got on with knitting. Sheets and table-cloths were sewn together, fur coats sent, all via the Red Cross, behind the party leaders' backs. Everyone took care that their husband, their son, their father wouldn't be cold. Ach ja . . .' She stared outside; the air was the colour of the slate roofs. 'I still have his Gefrierfleisch-Abzeichen at home – the decoration for that dreadful winter in Russia when there were so many frozen toes, fingers, noses. The order of the deep freeze, the people dubbed it cynically.'

◆◆

Herr von Garlitz's mother, at one time a courtier of the empress, decided to spend her last days in the inhabited world and moved to Potsdam. The forty-five-room castle she left behind was on the other side of the Oder in a Frederickian ribbon-built village, of which there were many in Brandenburg. At one time Frederick the Great had reclaimed and populated this border province – he put a prince there; in the middle of the fields a castle was built for him, a road was paved, to the right and left of it houses for the farm workers were built, there was a church, a small school. In exchange for their total availability, the workers were given grain and a piece of land large enough to keep a pig and a cow.

Because it was far away from where the bombs were falling, Herr von Garlitz decided they should all move to the estate where he had grown up. He travelled ahead with his wife in order to make the arrangements, leaving the children behind in Anna's care in his parents-in-law's house. Six weeks later she received a summons from Frau von Garlitz: 'Come over here. I need you. We have tracked down Adelheid, Rudolf's former nanny, she will assume care of the children.' And once again Anna set off with her two suitcases, one with the wedding dress and Martin's Feldpost letters, and one with her other possessions. She was fetched from the station in a horse cart; her employer sitting on the box, less *soignée* than before, appeared slightly dishevelled. She had acquired a charming indifference, a *laissez-faire* that surprised Anna, accustomed to her good manners and self-control in all circumstances. 'You'll laugh to death,' said the Countess at the top of her voice, trundling over the unmade country road, with the same abandon as when she had carried Anna off in her Kaiser-Freser a century ago. 'All you can do is laugh, the castle is so dreadfully run-down, you can't imagine it, you'll have to see it with your own eyes.'

After a half-hour journey through an uninhabited world where even the succession of forests and fields conveyed a certain monotony, they drove into a village. All the ingredients were there: church, school, workers' houses on either side of the road. Only the castle was hidden from view on account of a wall, draped wearily with the branches of old chestnut trees and maples. The gate was opened by a man who had such a squint that it looked as though he was welcoming other people alongside Anna and the Countess. The cart bumped inside. The gate was closed behind them. And there was the castle, massive, robust, light grey walls covered with creepers, white window frames and a forest of chimneys on the red roofs. It was turned in on itself, shy, as though it were an individual who would not readily divulge its secrets. Out of a Frederickian need for symmetry, a porch had been introduced in the middle of the front façade with a staircase that began broadly and invitingly but narrowed as it approached the double front door. Square pillars either side of it supported a tympanum above which the family coat of arms had been sculpted in relief. They drove round the side to the service entrance. Various outbuildings and sheds enclosed a cobbled inner courtyard.

Frau von Garlitz led her into the house. Scarcely had Anna set foot on the landing when various craftsmen who were busy with restoration work on the second floor shook the dust and grit from their clothes – it fell down the staircase onto Anna's Viennese hat. Hilarious laughter filled the space. 'Now you know what it's like here,' said Frau von Garlitz.

A thorough inventory that same day proved that she had not been exaggerating. As well as the structural problems resulting from years of maintenance backlog, the interior was filthy and threadbare. The smell of an old lady who for fifty years had obstinately demanded that everything should stay as it had been in her youth hung in every room. Rickety suits of armour flapped in the draughty hall and passages – there were whimsical tree trunks with phosphorescent lights that with spooky kitsch woke the unsuspecting passer-by who, half-asleep, had to go to the WC at night. Frau von Garlitz's bedroom was an urgent case. Since her arrival six weeks ago she had been sleeping in the same night-dress, the same sheets, in a bed whose satin canopy sagged low beneath the dust. Everything was so filthy that you were already infected just by looking at it. 'My heavens,' Anna whispered, 'what a pigsty.' Frau von Garlitz raised her hands helplessly. 'I don't know where anything is, by God nothing, I mean sheets and so on.' 'But they must be somewhere,' said Anna huskily, throwing open the windows. It began to dawn on her that with that one candid, timid gesture the Countess was transferring full responsibility for the decayed estate on to her. 'How glad I am that you are here,' she sighed girlishly.

Thus the renovations began. For a year Anna went from room to room with a succession of Polish labourers and cleaning women from the village until all forty-five had undergone a transformation. The German tenants – sent off to war – had been replaced by Polish forced labourers and Russian prisoners of war, housed in the stables, permanently guarded by four armed soldiers. There were no tractors or petrol. At six o'clock in the morning eighty oxen teams manned by Russians, supervised by an agricultural inspector exempted from military service, went into the surrounding fields with rattling carts, where they worked the whole day at an un-Russian pace to fetch in the quota of grain decreed by the Reich. Potatoes, grain, milk, butter, everything had to be handed over, apart from a small ration for individual use. For the castle inhabitants a wall cupboard had been constructed with compartments in which each kept their own store of butter – one hundred and twenty-five grams per week. They had to hand over half to the kitchen for cooking, the other half was for bread. Humanity seemed to be divided into two camps: the one spread everything on one piece and had dry bread for the rest of the week, the other carefully spread each piece with a puritanically wafer-thin layer.

Before the great refit could go like clockwork, Anna had to do battle with traditional ways. Unsure, because she had to direct a complicated, unfathomed household on the basis of the pathetic certificate from the School of Housekeeping for Young Ladies of the Better Circles, she roamed through the rooms in the hope of discovering a domestic structure. She ended up in the wash kitchen where four jovial fat women from the village scrubbed sheets in oval wash-tubs, singing, laughing and chatting. The little procession traipsed from there to the cellar where the sheets were put through the mangle and smoothed with irons that contained a piece of glowing metal. They did not rush themselves, the wash was done in fourteen days, then a new lot arrived and they began all over again. Each day was punctuated by an ample lunchtime break. Mamselle made coffee and baked biscuits. It was really pleasant – it was beyond their range of interests that this sociability could be taking place against a backdrop of forty-five rooms in a state of disintegration. 'Good Lord,' thought Anna, 'that surely can't go on like this.'

At the back of the wash kitchen she discovered, under a thick layer of dust, an enormous washing machine with a centrifuge. 'Broken,' the women waved aside fatalistically. Long elevated transmission belts crossed the courtyard and ended up at a generator in a distillery, where gin was made from potatoes. 'What's wrong with this,' she asked the mechanic, 'is it broken?' 'I don't know,' he rumbled, shrugging his shoulders. Anna had the feeling that she was swimming in treacle, in a river of listlessness and indifference. 'What sort of an answer is that: I don't know,' said Anna sharply. 'Perhaps you could just have a look at it.' Sighing, with a vacant gaze, the man bent over the machine. A few hours later he had repaired it in spite of himself. The next morning at six o'clock Anna put the washing in the machine; the enormous thing, about a metre across, started to move; a lively wood fire was burning beneath it. On their arrival the washerwomen were greeted with joyful sounds: boom, boom, boom, tch, tch, tch, klop, klop, klop. They blinked nonplussed, and then they were furious. What did this Rhinelander imagine, did she think she could interfere in their lives just like that? They had washed by hand as long as they could remember, it suited very well, there was no need for change at all now. 'Why should you wash and iron for fourteen days?' cried Anna above the din. One load was already spun. The sun was shining outside; she hung the washing on the line and hurried back to the wash kitchen. She taught the women how the machines had to be used, ignoring their disapproving looks. 'You can go and sit next to it quietly.' Anna trudged back and forth to the line. At the end of the day the washing smelled delightful and had been folded neatly. Everything was ready – thirteen days remained to clean the house. A little revolution. When the women realized that, their rage turned to hate – which gradually melted in the winter when they and their children were ill and Anna brewed camomile tea for them and wrapped them up warmly and drove to town at night with them when they were about to have a child. In this way she compensated silently for Frau von Garlitz's negligence – it was the nobility's traditional duty to care for the welfare of the tenants.

Room after room was mucked out. Anna's amazement at the cobwebs, the dust, the mould and dead insects, which the old countess had collected over the years, soon turned into robust perseverance. There was one room that outdid all the rest: the Emperor's Room. It had remained a locked sanctuary since Kaiser Wilhelm had spent one night there as the guest of his wife's former courtier. As soon as they opened the door a musty sour air came at them. They took down the curtains and drapes, they pulled the sheets and pillows from the canopied bed in a cloud of dust and mites, but even when the whole room had been stripped, that penetrating imperial smell still hung there. Finally they unstitched the mattress: maggots teemed where his excellency's body had rested, gladly jumping out of the horsehair – into sudden freedom. Anna was horrified. It is wartime, she thought feverishly, we can't throw expensive horsehair away just like that. Suddenly she remembered the still she had seen in the distillery. They crossed over the courtyard with the mattress and toppled the contents into the boiler, beneath which a gentle fire burned. The maggots exploded like popcorn. When no further form of activity could be detected between the hairs the horsehair was washed and dried in the sun. Finally she took the expensive load to a mattressmaker, armed with two litres of gin.

The attic was full of objects that the age had already vomited up years ago. The only valuables Anna discovered were a series of English engravings, old hunting scenes in mahogany frames, which were found a place in the corridors and the hall. A staggering amount of kitsch was found there under the filth, from a period that seemed to have a preference for curls and gilding. They brought everything up into the courtyard for a public sale. The announcement went from mouth to mouth: 'Everything going for fifty pfennigs'. Polish women from the nearby dwellings crowded forwards in threadbare, shapeless clothes with scarves tied tightly round their pale round faces. They brightened up at the sight of the luxury articles: they fingered the symbols of a rich and carefree existence with shining eyes. After they had hesitated endlessly over their purchases, eventually they rushed off as though someone could take them away from them – a silk-covered tabouret or a tea cosy in the form of a rococo lady.

After the sugar beets had been harvested they were washed, sliced and pressed in a nauseatingly sweet smoke by the Polish women. Then they were made into a syrup; everything was sticky and clinging. Each one got a sack of beets for themselves as payment. 'May we use the press ... ?' they gestured, shyly demonstrating how hard pressing by hand in a cloth was. 'Of course,' said Anna, 'we've finished, we don't need it any more.' Some hours later Herr von Garlitz came up to her in riding attire. 'Listen here,' he called her to order, 'now what have you done? You have given the Poles the press.' 'Yes, why not?' said Anna defiantly. She was irritated by the fashionable, indolent element in the middle of the hum of activity. 'Do you think,' he raised his chin, 'the Poles would give us a press if we were in Poland?' He looked challengingly at her and answered for her: 'They certainly would not do so, precisely because they hate us.' 'But after all, we don't hate them,' Anna retorted, 'anyway, if the Poles are so much worse than us, as you say, and I am meant to follow their example and be like them, then that makes us not a whisker better and we have no right to behave as though they ought to obey us.' He shook his head at the paradoxical reasoning. 'They are Untermenschen,' he said with dignity. 'If they are Untermenschen and we are the Herrenmenschen, as you say,' she tried to put it diplomatically, 'then actually I can't be like the Poles, so shouldn't I be like us, namely a Herrenmensch?' The whole idea of Untermensch, Herrenmensch, Übermensch struck her as ridiculous, but she had just enough political awareness to understand intuitively that she could not say that out loud to a lackey of the Führer. Von Garlitz frowned; this dialectic was going over his head. Somewhere he sensed he had been put in his place by a self-opinionated, unfortunately indispensable, member of the staff who impudently deployed her power against his, as employer, over his household. It was all too much for him; shaking the confusion off him he walked away with short, measured steps, his head bent, thwacking a tree here and there with his riding whip.

The excessive work shortened the time between two Feldpost letters. Martin wrote about the beauty of fields full of sunflowers; he had found a case of books at a weekly market; a recipe for borscht followed. There was a strange contradiction between the tumultuous triumphal processions of the Wehrmacht on the radio and the peaceful calm in Martin's letters in which a rifle shot never sounded, a house never burned. In the autumn he was stationed near Tula. When it began to freeze and knitting needles were clicking everywhere to drive out the tundra cold, Anna sent him a parcel in the blind hope that it would find its way into infinity. Rumours of people who had died in action came ever closer, an anonymous threat that was denied in the newsreels, where the soldiers smoked cigarettes cheerfully in their snow caves. At first it was second cousins, student friends, friends of friends, then it was brothers, fiancés, fathers. But winter had a Chekhovian beauty in Martin's letters. With his comrades he had come across a farm where there was a grand piano. One grand piano amid endless fields of snow, but badly out of tune from the cold. The family slept on a platform built over the stove. The soldiers hauled the mattress off and combined their strength to lift the piano up. It thawed quickly; there was music night after night. Martin's courteous apologies were passed over by the farmer: he thought it was more important to hear Mozart and Bach than that they should be warm at night. The more colourful the events being described the more suspicious Anna became.

One of the Russian prisoners carried unusual responsibilities: he had to light the stoves in the castle and keep them going. Day in, day out, he went from room to room with a basket of wood. No one said anything to him – it was punishable to regard Russians as human beings. One day Anna found herself in a room with him. Shy, almost invisible, he did his work as though he had realized that he had no right to exist except as the bringer of fire. She spoke to him, without preliminaries, simply because they were two individuals in one space. To her surprise, he replied in broken German – moreover he appeared to be called Wilhelm: after the German Kaiser had visited the Tsar, all new-born babies had been called Wilhelm. Another godchild of the emperor, Anna grinned to herself. His explanation was full of softly vibrating Russian consonants. After the first introduction, she could regularly be found in rooms where the stove was being lit. They were suffering from hunger in the stables, he whispered, there were shortages of everything. She stole food for him from the kitchen. In the evenings she cut discarded blue checked quilt covers into pieces and made them into handkerchiefs for the prisoners. She collected discarded toothbrushes, remains of toothpaste, pocket combs with a few broken teeth and soap. Wilhelm smuggled the spoils to the stables where they were eagerly put to use. She did not ask herself why she did it; subversive intentions were strange to her – she simply could not tolerate the disharmony between the relative comfort in the castle and the hardship in the stables.

Between stoves Wilhelm brought her up to date with the rumours doing the rounds among the Russians and the Poles, rumours that revealed a world in the shadow of the jubilant newsreels: the German offensive was stuck; precisely when they thought the Russian army had been exhausted by the millions of losses, one hundred living Soviet soldiers came forward for every dead one. And Tula? Anna asked with a shrinking heart. He apologized: the rumours were not that detailed. How did they reach them in fact? Well ... he spread his hands with an eastern smile. Where the information came from remained a mystery to her. Had the news been brought by the last flock of birds who pierced the grey sky, or had they had the benefit of a well-trained marathon runner who covered the distance to the Polish border in Olympic time and on the way called in at all the estates where Poles were working?

❦

'You really are a proper German,' said Lotte shaking her head.

'How so?' Anna was on her guard.

'A proper, efficient German ... as when you solved that washing machine problem ... all thoroughly in the spirit of the economic miracle. But what I ask myself...'

'Yes...' Anna was nothing if not obliging, so as to explain everything, but also to dispel every misunderstanding.

'Were the washerwomen ultimately better off in that organized housekeeping of yours? Could they still laugh, sing, gossip?'

'Pfff...' Anna shrugged her shoulders wearily. 'They still got their coffee and biscuits, you know. But you can't halt progress. In the days of the landlords the workers learned to read and write; more was not thought necessary. Then came the time when the workers refused to allow themselves to be kept in ignorance any longer – I was such a person – they got trained, television arrived, the computer ... If you want to go back to laughing, singing and gossiping you'll have to eliminate technology and the benefits we get from it.'

'But a lot has been lost.'

'You mustn't romanticize it.'

And so they were back again at their old point of difference.

They stared outside past the woman with the swan, attempting to organize their thoughts, which were fluttering in the wind in all directions, like scraps of paper, as they retrieved memories.

'I can well understand that you did something for the Russian prisoners,' mused Lotte, 'somewhere you were hoping that the Russians themselves would do the same for Martin if he were taken prisoner...'

'No...' Anna pursed her lips, 'I did it to be helpful, without thinking further about it.'

'Other motives could nevertheless be hidden beneath it. From the moment the first people in hiding came knocking at our door, at last I had the feeling of being able to do something – as though we were still doing something for David ... in the abstract, with each person in hiding we could keep out of the occupier's hands.'

'So you had people hiding in the house...'

Lotte nodded.

'Jewish?'

'Mostly.'

Anna sighed, and all her curves sighed too.

5

They lunched in a restaurant on Place Albert, with a view onto a colossal angel that had alighted on a tall plinth and was observing humanity from there with perplexity. Afterwards they made a small excursion round the town, their daily dose of therapeutic activity. They wandered into a grey granite church with three towers, whose steeples pointed firmly to the sky like schoolmasters' pencils. For once they were in agreement that it was an exceptionally ugly church. Uninspired, they strolled through the dim space, a leaflet about its history in hand. 'Built in 1885 in Romanic-Rhine style following the Cologne school,' Anna read. 'I didn't know we exported such hideous architecture then.' They dawdled by a sculpture that had come from a much older church on the same spot: a group of angels with swords and bishops' staves. Bored, they walked out of the church into a café directly opposite – a consolation for the disillusioned church-goer. They were both in urgent need of coffee. A fighter jet crossed the sky diagonally, behind the misanthropic steeples, as though it wanted to erase them.

❧

When the Frinkel family, an elegantly dressed trio, came to the door one day in the summer, nobody realized that with this apparently innocent visit, a period in the lives of Lotte's mother and her family was coming to an end that would never again return. Bram Frinkel, eighteen years old by then, had arranged the meeting; he had remained friends with Koen all those years. They drank something that had to pass for coffee. Lotte's father put on Bach's Double Concerto in honour of Max Frinkel, who had acquired a certain fame as first violin in a radio orchestra since his emigration from Germany. The gathering listened attentively; it was as though the guests had come specially to hear the concert. But when the last sounds died the war immediately took its place – in the sudden silence, in the surrogate coffee, in the presence of the Frinkels. 'You luff muziek...' began Frinkel, stroking his chin uneasily. These circumstances emboldened him to ask Lotte's parents for hospitality, in return for payment of the costs, of course, and only for a short time, until a definite solution had been found. 'All ze Jews from Hilversum haff to assemble in Amsterdam,' he said meaningfully. 'You live so splendidly out of the way here,' continued his wife Sara in faultless Dutch, 'Max could do his daily violin practice without anyone hearing.' She was small and vivacious, her lips and nails the same colour as her dress.

Bram's bed was put in Koen's room, the Frinkels took up residence in the nursery, from where dizzy runs and flageolet harmonics made the walls tremble. When the father stopped, the son took over with gypsy music and Slav dances. They were looked up by a friend from Germany whom they had taken into their confidence, Leon Stein. He had left his country at that time to fight Fascism in the Spanish Civil War. After that he worked in Harlem for many years for his uncle, a manufacturer of barrels and crates, who was allowed by the Germans, for a lot of money, to get away to America. He had been able to take his horses but not his nephew, who had become stateless since his Spanish adventure. The New World, on the other side of the ocean, which was open to all nationalities, closed its borders hermetically to anyone who had no nationality. Stein needed to go into hiding urgently. But it was only from time to time, he said. The old flair of the Spanish anti-Fascists had not been extinguished in him and had driven him to the Dutch resistance – in his case it was a strong instance of contempt for death because he looked thoroughly Jewish, even when he wore a German uniform during a surprise attack on a distribution office and gave orders in his mother tongue.

A bed was put up for him in Lotte's father's office; he slept there like a soldier on a narrow wooden plank, feverishly devising plans, always nervous – only when he was in the greatest danger would a mild calm come over him, he confessed. He was elusive, his life hung together on secrets – at one point he would shelter with them for three weeks, then he disappeared for a month without warning.

One morning at dawn they were woken by rifle shots. People ran about the house in pyjamas, the Frinkel family desperately looking for a way to make themselves invisible. Koen went to see how the land lay – the allure of danger shone in his eyes. He wandered into the wood quasi-casually. There he came upon three Austrian soldiers, hardly older than himself, who were out hunting, to break the monotony of their daily rations. He was given a cigarette, they chatted about hares and rabbits. Later that day they would be starting a raid in the neighbourhood, they said carelessly, sometimes it was easier to catch a Jew than a rabbit. Koen led them to a hill on the other side of the wood which was riddled with tunnels and holes. They departed with fraternal shoulder-slapping.

Breathlessly he reported back. 'They are only hunting hares and rabbits now but in a couple of hours they will be hunting for ... for...' He could not get the word past his lips; ashamed, he looked at his friend standing barefoot on the tiled floor, numb with cold. Shots sounded again in the distance. Max Frinkel massaged his fingers nervously. 'The Noteboom ladies...!' he cried. His wife nodded emphatically. 'Two admirers,' she explained, 'they sat in the front row at each concert. If you get into difficulties, come to us, they had once offered. However, they are a bit eccentric...' They were taken there at top speed. The ladies lived with forty-eight cats in a large ramshackle villa held upright by creepers and ivy. Although one was the mother of the other, there was great difficulty telling which of the captivating ladies was the elder, with their grey buns and Karl Marx glasses. They could take a hint. Of course the famous violinist was welcome – they took in all strays, whether they walked on two feet or four.

After the Frinkels had gone, the raid was awaited calmly.

Lotte's mother enjoyed the sudden peace of mind. Only now did she realize how much strain the Frinkels' presence had caused. The continual fear of an unexpected visit, that the youngest children would let their tongues run away with themselves, the anxiety of a small, fatal slip, so insignificant that you overlooked it – the fear of reprisals that no one dared to imagine ... a fear that went along with a sense of guilt: all that time she had been putting her children at risk. We won't start that again, she decided. They are fine there, with the Noteboom ladies.

There was more than enough to be anxious about. If the Russians did not lose, for example, because then everything would be lost. During the Stalingrad period Jet sleepwalked through the house at night. Lotte woke up, discovered the bed next to her empty and found her sister bolt upright and pale as a statue in the living-room, where she slowly and dreamily negotiated the tables and chairs without colliding with anything. To prevent her falling down the stairs Lotte locked the bedroom door from then on, but the urge to walk had to find an outlet: one night Jet opened the balcony door and walked out into the rain in her night-dress. Lotte was woken by the wind blowing across her forehead. Not just the bed, the balcony appeared to be empty. Disconcerted, she peered into the night: had Jet got wings? Only when she looked out over the balustrade, into the depths, she saw her lying – soaking wet, in a bed of overblown asters that had been spoilt by the rain. For many weeks Jet lay in a darkened room with severe concussion. A persistent headache had taken the place of her somnambulism. Even so, she demanded to be kept up to date with the latest developments in the east – without sparing her.

Rain in the Netherlands was snow in Russia. It seemed as if an unusually large amount of rain fell that autumn. One evening even Lotte's mother's good intentions were rained off. The bell rang; two men had braved the rotten weather. The face of one of them was hidden behind heavily framed glasses misted over from the rain. The other seemed to be Lotte's father's barber; he did not immediately recognize him as he was – what was left of a barber without his customary entourage of knives, razors and mirrors? Authenticating themselves by dropping Leon Stein's name, the barber asked for temporary hiding for his companion who was in great need. It would only be for a couple of days. No one said anything. Lotte held her breath. The silence was heavy with tension that was not so much the result of doubt as of inevitability. The possibility of a free choice was only apparent – in actuality it had already been decided, at a suprahuman or even primarily human level. It was impossible to say no, go back outside into the storm, the rain, make sure you find a roof over your head. 'We aren't taking people any more,' she heard her father saying, 'it's too risky.' 'The Frinkels' bed is still there,' her mother proposed. Her hands began to fiddle with the unwelcome guest's coat; she took the wet thing from him and hung it on a clothes hanger next to the stove. She offered him a chair, took his glasses, dried them with a piece of her skirt and put them back on his nose. 'So, at least now you can see where you have ended up.'

Ruben Meyer discovered that there was a sleepwalker bored stiff in one of the rooms upstairs. He sat on her bed and began to read aloud to her; he brought her tea and improved on the news from the front for her. After six weeks, when still no other address had been found for him, he admitted that he was suffering from sleeplessness because of anxiety about his family. The baker in an Utrecht village with whom they had been hiding had been blackmailed by his sister-in-law, who had noticed that in the store behind the oven it smelled not only of bread and currant buns but also of cold sweat. Ruben had been smuggled to the Gooi region by a laundry in a basket of dirty washing, to search for a safe place they could go. 'The barber was going to organize it . . .' his eyes darted back and forth behind the thick lenses, 'I don't understand . . .' 'We can't wait for that,' said Lotte's mother.

She sent Lotte out on the job. The train rode through a barren landscape beneath a drab, joyless sky. The woods, the hay were not themselves any more, they had lost their innocence under the marching of strange boots, they had become hiding place and tragic scene simultaneously. That she could calmly ride through there, while Ruben could not, distorted the landscape into something that never again, just like that, could be called beautiful. Absurd, senseless movements were being made in it, she was on the way to his family, he had settled with her family – everything was an expenditure of energy, a fundamental disorder. No one could follow the rhythm of their own lives.

In the bakery, squeezed together in a small oppressive room, she discovered his mother, brother of ten, sister and brother-in-law, emaciated and beside themselves with fear. The mother clung to her: 'Please take my boy with you, take him out of here!' 'We'll come and fetch you as soon as possible,' Lotte tried to calm her, 'but it has got to be properly organized.' 'My little boy, my bubele' the mother pleaded, 'take him along with you...' A boy was standing somewhat to the side with an exercise book in his hand. It seemed as though he was consciously distancing himself from her, in masculine shame at his mother's pleas. He looked much too Jewish to be able to travel in the train. 'Sums?' she asked, buying time. 'I am writing a story,' he said with dignity, 'about ship-wrecked people washed ashore on an island in the Pacific Ocean.' 'And what else?' she encouraged him, feverishly asking herself what she ought to do. She was not equipped for such a dilemma; she was no more than a pawn who had been pushed out to start exploring the situation. This was not a decision that she could just take on her own initiative ... 'They think it is uninhabited and they will be able to live there safely, but there are cannibals who hunt them with spears and...' 'Here,' the mother ripped a dia-mond ring from her finger. Lotte shook her head, an unbearable heaviness pressed on her temples. 'It is not a question of money ... The Germans will just pick him off the train, it would be irrespon-sible, but we'll come and fetch you ... we'll come and fetch all of you as soon as possible...'

That same evening contact was made again with the laundry boss via the barber. He could take no more than three people, at the end of the week. Because Mrs Meyer looked the least Jewish of the four of them, Lotte's mother decided to fetch her straight away by train the following day. She took a broad-brimmed hat with her. They travelled back together like chatting women friends. The nervous tics on the face of the one, because she had to leave her children behind for a few days, were camouflaged in the shadow cast by the hat. The laundry boss came punctually as arranged; so did foresight: the Germans had been there just before him – all three were picked up the night before.

'My little boy, my bubele, take him along with you...' Lotte had to hide her desperation; she felt she was being judged by an invisible tribunal. If she had known that the child would be carried off she would certainly have taken the risk of the train journey. If he had been picked up on that occasion she would definitely have been guilty, but less so than now: now she hadn't even tried. This was a lacerating, dead-end thought that went back and forth like a diabolo between guilt and guilt. She was being confronted with an intrinsic, subtle cruelty of existence that offered her no possibility of a choice. She had not been prepared for life to become so serious. What made it even worse was that no one thought of blaming her at all and she was seemingly struggling with a luxuriously self-indulgent problem in comparison with Ruben Meyer's legitimate sorrow and loneliness. It was decided to be silent about it in front of his mother: what could they come up with for a Jewish mother who was beside herself? They led her to believe that her children had been taken to another address that evening. Every day she complained: 'But couldn't they write a letter all the same?' 'That's still much too dangerous,' her son mollified her with a breaking heart, 'the post is also being intercepted. No one must know where they are.' He walked about the house with drooping shoulders; it exhausted him to lie to his mother every day.

David's father came over carrying a box. Although he had not received any more news from his son he had regained something of the old indestructibility that had characterized the mood of his songs. 'We are also going into hiding,' he said, 'I've got some knick-knacks here ... some bits and pieces...' He tapped the box. 'We would be very sorry if they were lost. Would it be all right with you if we buried it here in your garden or in the wood?' 'It's fine with me,' said Lotte's father casually, 'but not in the garden because every inch of it is in use now.' He was alluding to the tobacco plants that he had sown and for which he would also have sacrificed a large part of the kitchen garden if his wife had not set limits. Lotte leaned on the balcony and watched the two men walking into the wood with a shovel – it made her feel uneasy, although she did not know why.

❦

'You are still as angry as ever,' Anna remarked, assessing Lotte accurately, 'you have been hoarding your rage for almost fifty years. Get it out! I am the obvious person, I offer myself, I've certainly stood in hotter fires before in my life. You have every reason to be angry!'

'I'm not angry at all,' Lotte's hands were clenched into fists on the table. She spread her fingers out hastily. 'I am merely telling you what happened.'

'Why deny you are angry? You have been projecting all that rage onto me for days now, selbstverständlich.' Anna leaned back contentedly. 'I am offering myself. Go on, blame me!'

'But I have been doing that continuously,' Lotte sighed, 'and you keep shooting back in defence.'

'I won't any more, come on. You must first blow off steam ...'

Lotte looked at her sceptically now that they were onto the therapeutic tack, in this coffee house with big-city allure, among business people and housewives who were calmly sipping their coffee.

'I'll help you a little bit. We'll order another cup of coffee and then I'll tell you something I'm still as deeply ashamed of as ever.'

-❧-

Martin's letters were coming from deeper and deeper south. That mobility stopped just before the Caucasus – he had caught a dangerous intestinal infection; Anna received letters written by his comrades. She did not allow herself to be misled by their blatant attempts to disguise the seriousness with anecdotes and pleasantries; the anxiety made her throw herself into her work with monomaniac industry. Then one day his writing was on the envelope again. The crisis had been averted with a diet of milk and tomatoes; they were crossing the Ponto-Caspian plain towards Taganrog. Anna received several letters in close succession: defects in the lorry were dictating the pace, the vehicle was weary of travelling, Russia was too large. Eight days too late they reached the town on the Black Sea from where they would have to fly to Stalingrad for the grand finale. They had not been expected, had been given up for lost, so the lorry's crew stood outside the Grand Plan – they were officially sent on leave. One year after the dress rehearsal Martin obtained permission to get married.

'Anna, Anna, come here, there's a telegram for you.' Frau von Garlitz's voice resounded through the passages. One of the cleaning women from the village, who had been keeping a fattened goose at the ready for the postponed marriage, hastily slaughtered the main course of the wedding feast. A pigskin suitcase was packed full of provisions, another with the wedding dress, necessary papers and other bits of the trousseau. 'You don't really think it'll really happen now?' Herr von Garlitz smirked. Ottchen, the old butler, took her to the station with the last remaining horse.

The crowded train was about to depart. Ottchen grabbed the cases from the cart and shoved them inside over the bellies of the soldiers who lay asleep on the platform. 'Go to the devil with a capital D!' they protested. Anna exhausted herself apologizing, stepping carefully between them. After a trek along crowded corridors she found a space in a first-class compartment. The train roared through the night like a maniac; they halted in the protectorate of

Bohemia-Moravia, orders were yelled, and then they continued as far as just before Vienna, where the train had to wait four hours for an air raid alarm to end.

On arrival the pigskin suitcase seemed to have disappeared. A soldier remembered that someone with a suitcase had got off in Bohemia, perhaps he had scented the goose. In the commotion about the lost item Anna did not realize that it was Martin touching her discreetly, accompanied by his father. She shrank back. Thousands of kilometres lay between them; for weeks he had only existed in his comrades' handwriting; he had been a concentric point drawing all her feelings to it, a magnet for anxiety and longing ... now he was standing there, it was somewhat banal. They greeted each other formally – not here, in front of everyone. In the tram on the way to his father's house, his clean-shaven neck fascinated her, a vulnerable, timid neck, so complete despite snow, illness, inhospitability – despite the war.

They were married in the Karlskirche. The bridegroom had made a final attempt to get his mother's approval and to persuade her to be present. 'The day of my life!' he cried, giving her a good shaking. 'It is the day of my life!' She pressed the tips of her fingers to her temples and screwed her eyes shut tight. So he left her behind for ever in her domain, where now she only had herself as victim of her domination. Overwhelmed by the scale and excess of the interior of the domed church, Anna let herself be led to the altar. Pillars, wall panels and galleries of pink, brown, sandy and black marble. Behind one of the pillars, she assumed, her future mother-in-law had positioned herself under cover, with a great sense of timing waiting for the critical moment to spring out and perform a tragic drama that would make the bedroom scene of a year ago pale in comparison. But the paintings on the ceiling in the dome distracted her, as did the golden rays that came out of a triangle with a Hebrew inscription and angels floating between them, above the altar, a window with golden glass through which a bronze glow shone and enveloped the small bridal procession –

somewhere in the heavenly spheres there had to be a higher organization, a secret plan laid out in detail, delineating their lives from moment to moment, with a deeper, unfathomable purpose. She looked sideways at the bridegroom's profile – his Adam's apple went up and down as the organ, much ornamented with gold, began a hymn.

After the ceremony was over they floated down the steps between Greek columns, obelisks and two white marble angels holding crosses up to the sky. Anna looked round mechanically. The right one was staring at the horizon full of inner calm, the left one looked more stern – and a snake was entwined around her cross. A feeling she had presumed dead, but that was suddenly brought to life by the ceremony, went right through her. Lotte. Not the stranger who had visited her in Cologne, but Lotte as she was then ... there she was ... if anyone must not be absent from the wedding it was she ... and why shouldn't she be there in the form of an angel? In which case she herself was the other one, with the snake ... They were looking at the world with marble eyes as though they understood something of it ... The bridal gathering had crossed to the other side opposite the Karlskirche, the wind caught hold of her veil – for a moment tangible reality was something hazy and vague to her, through the fine mesh of tulle.

They moved into the apartment of Martin's dead grandmother; the woman's hairs were still in a comb left behind on the chest of drawers. A house of one's own ... they turned to each other with an insatiable hunger as though the thousands of lost hours had to be caught up. The city and surroundings were a fitting backdrop for their honeymoon, except for one small flaw, when they came across a small group of people with yellow stars on their coats strolling slowly down the worn steps in the Mölker Bastei in the old city. Martin went rigid. With a strange sort of piety he took his arm out of Anna's and stared at them, affected by it, as they passed in silence. She shrunk more from Martin's involvement than the procession, which was silently manifesting something that was new and yet immediately obvious to her. 'Come,' she pleaded, pulling at his sleeve, 'don't look, please, come on.' He allowed himself to be led away with difficulty. The whole day she reproached the procession for having appeared in their way, like a sombre admonition.

She wanted to live, to live intensively, in the three weeks that they were allowed – enough for a whole life.

When she was packing her suitcase listlessly the evening before the departure, the voices of Martin and his father could be heard faintly from the next-door room. 'Here, my son, I've bought long under-trousers for you because it is so cold there, take them.' 'No,' Martin protested, 'that's not necessary.' 'Why not? Anna won't be around there.' A short wry laugh. 'It's not that . . .' 'What then?' 'Ach, father, that cold doesn't mean anything compared to the other dangers we are exposed to.' 'But surely signals troops run less of a risk, you don't fight at the front?' Incomprehensible mumbling, Anna brought her head close to the door-frame. There were partisans everywhere, she heard Martin saying, especially where you least expected them. The signals troops were also vulnerable when they were working in a small group behind the advancing front, placing masts, laying cables, hauling wires. One day a technician high up on a mast couldn't find his pliers. 'Hang on,' cried Martin, who was supervising the work, 'I'll just go and get them.' He walked to the lorry, which was hidden behind pine trees. As he was looking for them he heard short staccato screaming in the distance, followed by an abrupt silence. He sneaked back cautiously, seeking cover behind the trees. Where just a moment before his comrades had been busy with hammers and pliers twelve bodies lay with their throats cut, between motionless stems of tall grass. The perpetrators had dissolved into nowhere, a hasty, soundless hit-and-run operation beneath a cloudless sky.

Her father-in-law's comment escaped her. Anna sank down on the edge of the bed next to the half-full suitcase. This then was the other side of the blossoming fields of sunflowers, of an untuned grand piano in a farmhouse, of a case of books in a flea market. It happened like that, from one second to the next, at the edge of a soft green pine wood amid blossoming grass. It did not matter whether the landscape was idyllic.

There was no convention for saying goodbye. They stood awkwardly on the platform. Whenever their eyes met they smiled encouragingly. 'We'll see each other soon,' he said with forced lightness, 'my guardian angel never leaves my side, even at forty degrees below zero.' I must imprint his face on my memory, she thought, his face as it is now. I'll take it home with me and make it appear whenever I want, whatever happens. It was painful, all the more so as they lacked the art of separating; no tears, no suitable words, at the most a certain impatience, on both sides, to be released from something that was too large for ordinary mortals. The delayed sorrow only burst out in the train going north. 'My husband . . .' she apologized to a surprised fellow passenger, 'my husband has gone back to Russia.' It was the first time she had designated him with that term. It filled her with a melancholy pride, which was immediately shouted down by the association 'widow, war widow'.

When she got back the park around the castle was strewn with chestnut leaves. There was a frost at night. Thousands of stars glittered in the blackness; they were keeping out of the war, whether you saw them from Brandenburg or from the tundra. Martin was there, a hundred Russians were here and sleeping like pigs propped up against each other in the stables. On one particular day two of them managed to escape the permanent guard. At an observation post in the forest, a simple wooden construction with steps and a plank to sit on, they discovered an aged forester intending to shoot a hare for Christmas. He had been shot dead before he could defend himself with his hunting rifle. The escapees took the rifle and ammunition. The body was found the same day and the starvation rations of ninety-eight Russians were halved. Two thousand troops from a nearby airfield combed the cordoned-off wood. The two Russians had buried themselves beneath a covering of leaves;

the closing circle passed them without seeing them. They had almost done it when one of the soldiers, who kept his pores wide open as well as his eyes, sensed that two eyes were piercing his back and he turned round.

By this time, the news had also reached Herr von Garlitz. He hurried to the hunting room, took down a horsewhip and raced through the corridors, hitting out wildly about him with the leather straps, cursing all Slav people. 'Murdering an old man, that scum, I'll beat them to pulp, they are going to suffer!' Anna went into the courtyard, nauseated by the sham masculine courage. The procession arrived there, the two prisoners stumbling at the front. Von Garlitz flew at them with his whip, roaring; two officers held him in check and urged him to calm down. Primitive revenge was not acceptable; officially they had to stick to the rules that applied to prisoners of war. One of them gave the order for the escapees to be freed – hesitantly, in disbelief, they began to walk towards the stables. At that moment he shot them in the back. They fell down silently onto the stones. He turned to von Garlitz: 'Shot dead while escaping.'

The incident caused resentment among the Russian prisoners. From then on Frau von Garlitz had personal escorts for Anna and the other members of staff whenever they went for walks in the woods. Anna brushed aside the surveillance, she was not afraid. In her view there was merely a dreadful misunderstanding; through an absurd, senseless exchange, Russian men had ended up in Germany and Germans in Russia. While Russian prisoners waited in frustration and resignation, somewhere in the heart of their native country their fellow countrymen were engaged in a bitter struggle against a backdrop of snow-covered ruins with icicles in the burnt-out windows – there were deaths on a huge scale in order to take one house, one barn, one wall. The fate of the whole world seemed to hang on the outcome of this icy battle in a slowly capsizing town.

The news that Stalingrad had held firm got through to the stables faster than the castle, where the raw facts were camouflaged in euphemism: we are returning home. The big turning point had arrived. The castle, restored from the rafters to the cellars, prepared itself to receive guests on its shining polished parquet floors, between its white painted walls in the comfortable warmth of the ever-burning stoves: old Prussian nobility who were also going to make a contribution to history. Anna, averse to interest in strategic developments, averse to political opinions, had but one burning desire: that he would emerge unscathed from the gunsmoke.

Lotte stared outside, her gaze glanced off one of the granite church walls. 'We were putting our lives at risk for those whom you yourself did not wish to look at...' she said incredulously.

'Now you see it,' Anna nodded, 'that's how it was. I am not a bit better or worse than most people. For a whole year I had anxiously expected news of his death, now he was there in a living body for three whole weeks. Then it was back to the beginning again. All I had for it was that little bit of life we had been allowed. But if I had gone to the Mölker Bastei alone I certainly would have seen them, believe me. I had probably asked myself painful questions, but that bit of luck, you understand, dominated everything at that moment.'

'That's the way you always have an excuse for yourself,' said Lotte bitterly, 'but all of you were without pity for the Jews.'

'Hold on with that "all of you" ... that little bit of luck was all I had, I had the right to it, I think, I had to make do with it for the rest of my life.'

The sun broke through, a wintry white ray shone on their hands – on a spreading network of blue veins. Skin, blood vessels, muscles – fragile and mortal.

'Here I believe we have the kernel of our disunity...' said Anna pensively, 'and we have arrived at the cause of your rage...'

'Will you leave off my rage as something to be regarded as constructive, which will transform itself into forgiveness if I air it sufficiently.'

'Forgiveness doesn't concern me,' Anna said sharply, 'I haven't done anything wrong.'

'Let's drop it shall we,' Lotte sighed, overwhelmed by a feeling of predictability, 'things are simply as they are now. You mentioned Stalingrad ... I still well remember how relieved we were ... our euphoria ... and yet afterwards it became really difficult...'

❦

Papa Stalin was not going to let himself be pushed aside just like that. The Allies had swept North Africa clean and marched off to Italy. For a short time they lived under the illusion that it was merely a question of waiting and persevering. The Frinkel family had returned in a overwrought state, having narrowly escaped two raids and forty-eight cats. At each meal the animals ate with them as full companions at table; the Noteboom ladies placed pieces of raw heart between their teeth so that the cats, decoratively standing on their hind legs, could tug them away. Excessive maternal love and spoiling had turned them into selfish nest soilers who began to miaow *en masse* when Max and his son did their daily finger exercises.

Since Lotte, as a member of the radio choir, had refused to register with the Nazi Department of Culture, singing had officially ended too, and she became an essential cog in the fourteen-person giant household. Life became increasingly complicated not only in a practical sense but also in the abstract. From then on anxiety was permanently present, slumbering, subcutaneous. A sudden silence, a strange noise, hugely swaying tree tops, rumbling in the distance, a vague rumour – a trifle was sufficient to inflame it. It could happen at any minute, no particular moment was in principle unsuitable. No one could imagine it yet they imagined it, their powers of imagination forcing the unthinkable, unbearable. The anxiety drove the Meyers and the Frinkels into the wood on a false alarm, winter coats hastily thrown over their pyjamas. They lay for hours in a wet ditch beneath layers of overhanging spruce branches; in the distance there were voices and dogs barking. Mrs Meyer chewed the soggy tails of her fox stole, Max Frinkel massaged his finger joints to prevent the moisture affecting them. Eventually the master of the house constructed a more refined hiding place in a deep built-in cupboard in his bedroom. He reduced the cupboard door to a hole in the wall and hung a full-length mirror in front of it, which clicked open on a cable and was closed again from the inside after the hatch was shut. Everyone could fit in. They dived through their own mirror image into the hole – an ambiguous form of existence and non-existence. After that Lotte's mother shoved her dressing-table in front, with purple and dark red perfume bottles sparkling attractively on it. From then on Mrs Meyer would only sleep in the cupboard; from their bed they could hear her crying and praying in a strange key.

It was not easy to call a halt to the constant expansion of the household. For example, the doorbell rang. Lotte was alone at home – except for five invisible, inaudible personages who were playing whist upstairs. A young man with short red hair was at the door, his right hand on the shoulder of a small, very old man wearing a black hat, who raised his wrinkled face expectantly to Lotte. 'I've come to bring the father-in-law of Mr Bohjul of the gramophone record shop,' the young man declared. Mr Bohjul had been arrested, he explained, while his wife and daughter were in Amsterdam. Someone had caught up with them at the station and warned them not to go home. Bohjul had managed to smuggle the message out from the police station that his father-in-law was still in the attic and undiscovered. He advised the old man to go to a good client of his, more a friend actually, who would certainly be able to find accommodation: Lotte's father.

'He's not in,' she said, 'I can't decide here on my own initiative.' She stood holding the door. No one said more, they looked at each other shyly. It seemed as though the old man, in his total dependency, was the only survivor of a catastrophe, as though he had been deemed too small and too light to go under with the others. Suddenly she was ashamed of her reticence. 'You can wait for him inside,' she said, opening the door wider. She led them to the din-ing-room. The old man waited meekly, his hat on his knees, his white eyebrows curling downwards over his deep-set eyes. His companion took in the surroundings as though he were sitting in a waiting-room. When her father got home he scowled at them with a frown until the name Bohjul was mentioned – ah, the owner of the record business where he was one of the family, how many heated discussions they had had about specific recordings. Indeed he had certainly once seen his father-in-law – Grandfather Tak – shuffling through the shop. Of course he would do his best to find him a good address. 'Apropos...' he said, turning to the old man in surprise, 'I don't understand, your son-in-law is a Persian Jew isn't he? I have nothing to fear, he said to me last time; because Germany is not at war with Persia, we can go about freely.' 'Don't ask me,' sighed the other, 'until 1914 the world could still be understood by an ordinary person ... since then it has gone over my head...' 'Hat,' his guide teased him, pointing wrily to the black hat that lay in his lap, now suddenly like a *corpus delicti* that had brought about the loss of the former world.

The TB-house was patched up provisionally. Because his stay was temporary he was not to know that he was not the only one in hiding. When the sun shone he sat dreaming on a rickety folding chair, an amber pipe in the corner of his mouth. Lotte brought him his meals. He told her about the diamond-cutting business, long ago, when the world was still worth living in. His white hair, in which the sun spun an aura of better times, his defeatism, his transparent skin – she felt despondently as if he had just popped over from death to cast a surprised glance at chaos, in the safe knowledge that he could go back whenever he wished to. There was no success at finding him another address; new categories were going into hiding: students, soldiers at risk of becoming prisoners of war, men who wanted to avoid forced labour in German indus-try. Theo de Zwaan joined the people in hiding – as did Ernst Goudriaan soon afterwards, who was so endearing in his heroic efforts to hide his anxiety that Lotte's mother empathized with him. He was put up with Grandfather Tak; he enlarged with a stylish extension the more frivolous than solid TB-house that squeaked in the wind, and there he got on with his violin-making, with a view onto a field of blooming tobacco plants. Koen had to hide too because he had reached the age for military service. His temperament did not suit him to waiting quietly at home until the war ended. He slipped out of the house onto the road, got picked up and taken to Amersfoort. At the end of a column of randomly captured fellow victims who had been picked up off the street, he was walking in the twilight through the old town centre towards an unknown destiny. The road was narrow; unseen he slid sideways into a porch and pushed backwards against the door, knocking on the wood with his knuckles. 'Open up, open up,' he pleaded. 'Are you a Catholic?' 'No,' he moaned. 'Pass on then,' said the voice.

They were taken to a barracks near Assen, where a plague of lice was in charge. Disgusted by the millions of crawling insects, he could not get any sleep. He slipped outside and gently dozed off, sitting against a wall. At the crack of dawn he was woken by a wood-fuelled post van driving in through the barrack gates. The postman climbed out and slowly emptied the letter box, then reversed and turned, the chimney smoking. The following day, the instant the man climbed back behind the wheel, Koen opened the back doors and hoisted himself in among the mailbags. He emerged at the ferry over the IJssel. The postman blanched. Although he was impressed with Koen's ability to improvise, he was not inclined to take this unorthodox postal parcel further with him across the IJssel. 'Boy, I absolutely cannot do that,' he complained, 'it is much too dangerous.' 'Hide me under the pile of wood,' Koen suggested. The official had to give in in the face of so much ingenuity. 'I must be absolutely mad,' he growled, carefully covering the stowaway with sawn fruit-tree logs. Koen returned home with undiminished self-confidence. His mother took him in her arms after two sleepless nights, trembling with fatigue and relief. He freed himself from her embrace to make a sudden clothes inspection, for fear that he in turn had brought a stowaway with him from the barracks.

While Grandfather Tak took root between the apple trees and the tobacco plants and dreamed of his dead wife, beneath her photograph pinned up on the wall with a rusty drawing-pin, his daughter and granddaughter were adrift. After rambling from address to address the latter had joined her fiancé, who was in hiding somewhere in the Beemster, and the former arrived in a provocative tailor-made suit one summer evening – from no one knew where – looking for her father. Lotte's mother smelled trouble instantly. Her husband was defenceless from the first glance. He yielded to Mrs Bohjul's request to be allowed to stay, no match for the transparent tempting manoeuvres, of which a pouting mouth painted red was the strongest card. She was given a bed in Jet and Lotte's room. From then on they slept in an atmosphere saturated with cigarette smoke and exotic perfumes. More and different dresses with low-cut *décolletés* kept being draped around on the beds and chairs, more and different necklaces were conjured out of a jewel case inlaid with mother-of-pearl. If she was deprived of attention she collapsed; she flourished on admiration – everyone was exhausted from having to provide her with more of what she needed for peace and quiet. No one type of pastime could occupy her for longer than five minutes. She walked back and forth like a caged panther; the click of her nail scissors disturbed the others reading, playing cards, doing crossword puzzles. It was unbelievable that she was the daughter of the man in the orchard, who smoked his pipe in meditative tranquillity and grew cress in a narrow strip along the sagging terrace.

In the evenings when the horsehair curtains had been closed they all came downstairs to eat at two long tables. Lotte's mother did her best within the restrictions to put kosher meals on the table. Afterwards Max Frinkel sometimes played a virtuosic piece by Paganini; his son took revenge with a melting gypsy song. Flora

Bohjul sang a popular American song, exaggeratedly jazzy. Finally all eyes turned to Lotte, as usual, who bit her lip and shook her head. To compensate, Mrs Meyer recited a poem. The favourite was an iambic elegy about a mother who had to sell everything she possessed in order to fill stomachs. The only thing left to pawn was the youngest daughter's doll, which she had with her day and night. The children were crazy about this drama, the adults hoped it would not prove prophetic.

They listened to Radio Orange and the BBC. Since May, when all radio sets had had to be handed in, they managed with a receiver improvised by Lotte's father without external casing but with very sharp reception. They could hear the Queen breathing during her broadcasts in London. There was a constant hunger for reliable information. Illegal newspapers and pamphlets went from hand to hand, someone read a bit out of an article now and then. 'What's this...' said Koen in amazement, 'listen...' Without thinking he read out a piece from *Het Parool* that mentioned the existence of gas chambers where 'captive opponents' were driven inside naked and gassed under the impression that they were entering a bathroom. The capacity of those gas chambers would soon be increased from two hundred to a thousand persons. Mrs Meyer burst out in desperate sobbing; Ruben leaned over her and squeezed her hands fiercely in a clumsy attempt to comfort her. Lotte's mother cast a devastating look at Koen, who slowly realized what he had done. The news was immediately made light of. Of course it was no more than a sensational story from the overactive journalists' distorted fantasies. Bram Frinkel threw his napkin on the table and went to the door, his head lowered between his shoulders. With the handle in his hand he turned round and said to Koen with a grin, 'Perhaps you'll want to be the chosen people for the next two thousand years.'

6

The beneficial effects of the peat treatments, carbonated baths and underwater massages were gradually becoming apparent. During the first week of the cure guests usually had to struggle with an unfathomable weariness bordering on depression, caused by the release of obstructions in the joints and poisonous materials stored up in the adipose tissues. For the two sisters there were, in addition, the toxins released during their talks, alongside the obstructions in their relationship and their memories, which were being put to severe test. But usually a turning point was reached half-way through the treatment. As each movement was no longer plagued by pain, patients moved more easily, the blood flowed more freely, breathing became deeper. Anna and Lotte experienced some of this effect too. They were both reviving physically; only their spirits were lagging behind, but then they were undergoing a quite different cure, the therapeutic effect of which was much less certain. They went out of the Thermal Institute after a morning of intensive bathing; before commencing the risky descent of the steps, they looked at the sky, which was sheer blue over the green dome of the Heures Claires hotel. The snow had melted to a grey slush. The two stone female figures that had been guarding the entrance to the Institute since its construction in 1864 – one with a staff in her hand and a fish at her feet, the other with a small harp and a fallen pitcher at her feet, with water flowing out of it – jumped off their plinths, dawdled nimbly down the steps and crossed the road to the Place Royale. They stood with amusement next to a *fin-de-siècle*-style square kiosk. One raised her staff and pointed it at one of the four sides, on which was written:

Quand il est midi à Spa il est:
13 heures à Berlin, Rome, Kinshasa
14 heures à Moscou, Ankara, Lumumbashi
15 heures à Bagdad
19 heures à Singapore
 7 heures à New York

The other played a few chords on her harp and sang in a hoarse voice, '... the mystery of simultaneity, when one lunches in Rome, one dines in Singapore ... while bombs rain on Berlin, breakfast is being prepared in New York...' The words became soap bubbles that drifted over the Place Royale. Spring water flowed out of the pitcher, or was it melted water? – it flowed away over the Rue Royale and Avenue Reine Astrid. Lotte and Anna took each other's arm as they crossed the wet road, the water lapping inside their shoes. They passed a simple restaurant and decided to go in – when one breakfasted in New York one lunched in Spa.

❦

Martin's company had been recalled from Russia to construct the air defences round Berlin. From then on he spent the weekends with Anna – something like married life was under way at last. She watched out longingly for the first signs of pregnancy. In early autumn she had had an operation; it now remained to be seen whether they had succeeded in correcting the damage done at an earlier stage by hauling muck carts and pig feed. A child seemed the only thing, the most important thing she had been missing up to now. She herself would be born again with the birth of a child; the youth of her child would cleanse away her own youth. Her child would lack nothing. A child would also replace her lost sister. A child would reconcile her with everything that had gone wrong.

There was an extensive lake in the wood. On the banks were rowing boats in bright Viking colours, with which to go over to an oval island. Hidden there, behind the willows and grey birches, was a wooden house with a pitched roof that had belonged to the castle for centuries, just like the lake and wood. Frau von Garlitz gave Anna the key. In sunny weather she strolled to the lake with Martin. They tied the boats together and rowed to the island towing the whole fleet so that they would not be disturbed by unexpected visits. They swam, lay in the sun in the tall grass, slept in the house that smelled of sun-baked wood and marsh spirits who, when the wind rose at night, moaned and creaked between the planks. The war was far away and unreal. Wind, the gabbling of geese, croaking frogs, instead of air raid sirens and the Volksempfänger blaring. At night as she listened to his breathing, it seemed miraculous that he was lying beside her. An invisible hand had led him through Russia to safety three times and had guarded him from stealthy murderers, freezing, fatal illness, because he had to be preserved for her. Their being together on this island in space and time seemed something sacrosanct to her, a form of being chosen. Through the window she saw the moon reflected in the water behind swaying willow branches – the island was drifting in the lake and time stood still. On Sunday afternoons the fleet returned in the opposite direction again. The walk back through the wood was the last thing they shared; Martin went to the barracks, Anna stepped through the gate into her old life.

At the castle they took in five housekeeping students, on behalf of the state, who had to be trained. They were placed in Anna's charge. Frau von Garlitz had had limitless faith in her since the castle and housekeeping had undergone a metamorphosis under her direction. And again Martin was to everyone's taste – when he stayed at the castle the trainees put on their best aprons. Anna was beside herself when she realized that their preening coincided with his visits. 'Those aprons,' she cried, 'are only for serving in. We haven't got enough soap powder to wash them if you wear them meanwhile.' Sniggering – with their female instinct they had correctly seen through her motive – they changed out of the aprons. From the kitchen window one Sunday Anna saw Martin give one of the girls a present in the garden before he left. 'What was it?' she asked, after she had waved him goodbye, 'that you received from my husband?' The girl gave her a brief guilty look. 'Well?' Anna insisted, grabbing her by the shoulder. 'I can't let on.' 'Tell me . . .' 'It is a present for you for Christmas.' 'Now? In August?' She nodded. 'In case your husband is stationed somewhere else at Christmas and can't come over for you . . .' Anna looked at her in disbelief. In the girl's eyes she saw indignation and contempt because she had forced her to divulge the secret and because of the insinuation that lay behind it. She walked away piqued, leaving Anna alone with her authority – dispensed in shame and emotion, which the shame magnified: that Martin, now, in the middle of summer, was already attending to how he could comfort her in six months, at Christmas.

Activity picked up at the castle. The refurbished rooms were continuously filled with guests – highly placed officers came there to have a breathing space between missions. After dinner they retired to the library, leaving the ladies behind in the salon in the care of Frau von Garlitz, who was friendly, as always, elegant and entertaining, as though the war and her husband's promiscuity had no claim on her. In the corridors it was whispered that he had had an affair with Petra von Willersleben, the daughter of an industrialist who had had a meteoric career in the army. Since he had dislocated his knee in the Polish campaign, von Garlitz occupied a vague staff function, for which he regularly had to go to Brussels. Anna could not imagine that this society figure could be trusted in the army with an important function, since he ran his factory in Cologne by galloping round it like a hussar – this smart alec who could not actually do anything and was no good for anything but constantly gave the impression that he was terrific. Mysteriously, he seemed to succeed in maintaining high-level contacts. Lineage and money, she muttered to herself, that's how you get on in the world instead of working hard.

Recklessly, von Garlitz officially invited his lover to a dinner. She infiltrated herself into his house under the camouflage of her weighty father. She wore a provocative dress to intimidate his wife. Anna served at table with her trainees. Among the guests she only knew Frau Ketteler, an aunt of Herr von Garlitz, who lived in the district and visited regularly. A woman of indefinite age, never married, she lived with a handful of staff in a villa that was hidden from view by tall spruces. Before the war she had had a stable full of sleek thoroughbreds, the cleaning women related; she loved to make the woods unsafe by riding a black stallion through there at a gallop, a hunting rifle on a leather strap on her back. Since the horses had been requisitioned, she indulged in long walks with her dog, a sturdy sheepdog who obeyed only her. It seemed that she had given her fallow maternal instinct full vent on her nephew since his birth – she adored him, blind to his shortcomings, and still tried to mother him from the sidelines.

Anna followed the developments at table in snatches as she went to and fro with crockery and glasses. Herr von Garlitz, as Fräulein von Willersleben's host, concerned himself courteously with her. The conversation dealt with painting: the nudes by Adolph Ziegler and Ivo Saliger. She seemed to have studied art history in Berlin; he feigned surprise and amazement, asking her innumerable questions, to give his wife on the other side of the table the impression that his table companion was a perfect stranger to him. The latter nimbly played along with the game – she got them both excited, it was almost as though they were making love, via painting, in front of Frau von Garlitz's eyes. She observed the performance coolly for a while, having been in the picture about the affair for a long time, as everyone was, until she had had enough of the role of naïve, deceived wife and spectator that had been imposed on her in the presence of a table full of guests. With control she stood up, raised the glass of red wine that Anna had just refilled, as though she were going to make a speech, and flung the contents in her husband's face. Fräulein von Willersleben jumped up with shocked cries, worried that something had got onto her own dress. At the same time Frau Ketteler rushed round from the other side of the table to dab her nephew's face with her napkin in order to wipe out the scandal as quickly as possible. Anna breathed again. The exasperated tension she had felt, because von Garlitz apparently did not find it sufficient to cheat on his wife, but also created further perverse pleasure in belittling and provoking her, flowed away. She slipped out of the dining-room with an empty dish, laughing at the grotesque helpfulness of his aunt.

The same evening Frau von Garlitz had herself taken to the station by horse and carriage. She disappeared without ceremony, leaving the company behind in bewilderment. Von Garlitz was beset with unspoken reproaches. He had to call his spouse, their hostess, the mother of his children, to order – a man at his level, with his background, function – he had to bring his wife to heel. After all, they weren't gypsies, or Slavs, who dissolutely let themselves be carried away by their emotions. A few days later he fell ill. Hurt pride, remorse, shame? At night the fever crept up high; he lay between the soaking sheets, sweating and delirious. Anna sat by his bed, eagerly adopting the function of avenging goddess over him. She moistened his forehead and temples with wet facecloths; she gave him drinks and whispered him to sleep with soothing words. But when the fever began to subside she told him what a Schwein he was. 'You can count yourself lucky to have a wife like that,' she said contemptuously. He had no strength to retort. Like a dying front-line soldier he lay on the pillows, with swollen eyelids and a stubble beard. Mercilessly she continued. 'A woman with so much style, charm, character! Get it into your head once and for all. You've got all the time to do so now.' He stared at her with the feverish eyes of a sick child being told a cruel fairy-tale, with the difference that he was being accused of identifying with the monster, the dragon, instead of the hero.

After two weeks Frau von Garlitz returned home, a model of aristocratic self-control through which a touch of cynicism shimmered. A sigh of relief was breathed; this was no time for marital conflicts that, however passionate, paled next to that single gigantic conflict in which the whole population was involved. Martin tried all month long to get long leave to take Anna to Vienna, even if it was only for two weeks, to be able to live as husband and wife in their own home, which they only knew from the honeymoon. But his ardent attempts came to nothing. There seemed to be only one possibility for getting long leave: to declare himself prepared to go on a short course of officers' training. Although the thought of getting promotion in the army disgusted him, he finally succumbed out of longing for Vienna and for a little shred of freedom, just to be able to escape from the military treadmill of total availability and self-denial that had already been going on relentlessly for four years, in the interests of a war that he could do without. He was stationed at a junior officers' school in Berlin-Spandau. During the course he lived shut off from the outside world. On the day he was discharged, Anna waited for him at the gate, suitcase in hand. 'Who are you?' The sentry stepped forward quickly, 'May I see your papers?' 'I've come to fetch my husband, Martin Grosalie,' said Anna, offended at so much suspicion. 'He goes on leave today.' The sentry blanched. 'Oh, God, please don't go in.' She put her suitcase down and looked at him affably. 'They are being punished,' the soldier whispered, shyly scratching behind his ear. After some hesitation he explained what had happened. The group was already standing in the courtyard, ready to depart, with one foot already outside the gate, as it were. They had to take their leave with an enthusiastic 'Heil Hitler!' in unison. In the commandant's opinion it sounded too weak. 'Louder!' he cried. The company repeated the obligatory salute once more without conviction but with more volume. 'Louder!' roared the commandant as though his honour was at stake, next to that of his Führer. 'Heil Hitler' . . . it was still too dim, they were exactly like a gramophone record that will not spin at full speed. 'We'll just see once more whether you are going to go home today . . . !' They had to change, pack the clothes in their lockers, turn the key. Then they were chased outside, left, right, knees bend, crawl on the ground in the mud. One lesson in humiliation and humility that they would remember as long as the war lasted. 'Please,' whispered the sentry, 'come back in an hour and make out as though you don't know anything about it. They are ashamed, all of them.' Anna glanced at the emphatically closed gate behind which Martin was crawling in the Berlin mud, mud of the Thousand-Year Reich, for which he had to be prepared to sacrifice his life, which was also her life. She picked up the suitcase and went into a street at random and other random streets, which were neither friendly nor hostile but indifferent. When she got back to the barracks he was already waiting for her, immaculate, glistening, alert – a wonderful *tabula rasa*. 'You're late,' he said, surprised. He made no mention of the punishment session. They had become well-versed in denying the war in each other's presence, like superior outsiders, deaf to the drumroll, blind to the lightning.

After their stay in Vienna he was posted to Dresden. It was autumn. Anna, who had already sewn and knitted a suitcase full of baby clothes, was still not pregnant – Hannelore was. She had got married in the spring and since then had been living in Ludwigslust in Mecklenburg, from where she kept up a nostalgic correspondence with Anna. Frau von Garlitz, who sympathized with the ups and downs of her staff, prepared a parcel of fortifying foods for the welfare of the mother-to-be, and sent Anna with it to Ludwigslust. Once again she was sitting in a train to Berlin with a suitcase. Involuntarily she thought back to the day she had travelled to Cologne in a trench coat with a hunting hat on, her possessions in a cardboard box. She felt slightly ashamed as she thought back to her provincial naïvety, the long way she still had to go then, from pig muck to table silver on damask. She jerked out of her reverie as the train slowed down abruptly and stopped; then it continued wearily on until they were riding into Berlin with jolts and blasts. A grey steel wall rose up outside the window of the compartments, without beginning or end, like the precursor of a tunnel. But the wall was moving ... it seemed to be made of smoke, grit, thick smoke. The train rolled backwards, then it drove hesitatingly into the station. Anna got out, still used to the unblemished neutral atmosphere inside the compartment.

It happened to her at that moment, just as it did to hundreds of fellow passengers: as soon as they set foot on the platform their reflexes took control of their sense of direction, they scattered, everything around them was on fire, the roof was cracking as though it would give way at any moment. Someone pulled her away from collapsing wood or steel, the smoke stung her eyes, her throat, she walked blindfold away from the fire . . . air raid warning, someone pushed her into a shelter. There she became part of a trembling, sweating tangle that was listening, huddled together, to the screaming and rumbling; the ground shook, the tangle shuddered with it, buildings, trains, people, everything would perish into dust, a ridiculous, communal downfall without meaning. For a suitcase of sausage and salt pork.

It took three days and nights to reach Spandau in the west, from the eastern part of the city where she had arrived. Three days and nights in an inferno, sometimes dragged into a shelter at the very last moment by someone whose face she never got to see. Someone gave her something to drink; she stumbled onwards, tripped over an electricity cable; a wall collapsed somewhere; she cowered, too tired to be afraid. Then it was night again, wailing sirens, a shelter, dozing off with exhaustion, going on further through the stage set of a horror opera; somebody gave her something to eat. Berlin-Spandau? Always the same question in the chaos – she was standing on a disintegrating map whose edges were being incinerated. Did Spandau still exist or was she on the way to a smoking heap of rubble? Why did the bombing go on day and night – did Berlin, did Germany have to be removed from the face of the earth?

Suddenly she seemed to find herself at Spandau station with her scorched suitcase. It was still there: a bulging train was on the point of departing for Mecklenburg. Someone lifted her up and shoved her inside through the window, followed by the suitcase.

The train started off immediately. Dazed, she sat down on her suitcase; she seemed to have survived: it left her feeling indifferent.
She made the journey in a state of semi-consciousness – she could
not fall over, propped up as she was between other overtired
bodies. They reached Ludwigslust in the middle of the night. She
was the only one who got off. She wobbled towards the vague silhouette of a house in the pitch dark. Her trembling hand found the
bell with difficulty. A light went on in the passage, the door was
opened, someone appeared on the threshold, saw what was standing on the step and closed the door in shock. And she was in the
dark again, collapsing from exhaustion. It was cold. A primitive
fear crept over her, stronger than during the bombing, direct and
ensnaring – the anxiety of being refused, shut out for ever like a
piece of dirt, like a creature that (an orphan who...) did not
deserve to live. She began to beat on the door in agitation. 'I come
from Berlin, please...' she moaned, 'open the door. I only want to
sleep, please...' But nothing happened, the house shunned her.
'This is a person, a decent person, who only wants to sleep...!'
Beneath her hammering fist the door moved open. A blanket lay
on the tiled floor in the passage. She stumbled in, fell down on to it
and slept without a glance at her slow-witted benefactor. The following day she had just enough strength to complete her mission.
Unrecognizable in a disguise of soot, scratches and tears, she
handed over the suitcase to Hannelore who was oblivious to bombing raids, floating on her pink cloud of blissful waiting. In her spotless home, organized for the coming event, the sausages, pork and
hams were a perverse, animal element, emerging unviolated from
the suitcase – in honour of the new life, stained by death. Anna
looked at it and burst out in a joyless, overwrought laugh.

◆◆

'Ach, Berlin...' Anna sighed. 'I happened to be there a couple of
years ago with a friend. We rode through the city on a bus. She
suddenly cried: "Look, the Anhalter Station!" I saw a splendidly
restored station but a second later it was on fire. It was burning

before my eyes ... just like then ... and everything caved in ... "Is anything the matter?" my friend asked. I had a light-headed feeling, hissing in my ears. "It's on fire...!" I cried in a panic. It was the first time that I'd remembered it – I'd not thought about it any more, it was so awful. I had suppressed it for forty-five years.'

'How is it possible,' said Lotte pointing at Anna with a piece of Ardennes ham on the end of her fork, 'that they could send you into a burning city with a suitcase of meat?'

'Frau von Garlitz didn't know, none of us knew. It was the first big bombing raid on Berlin, at the end of November. Your liberators lit up their Christmas trees above the city and threw their carpet bombs down below. Systematically, no square metre was to be spared. But something always remains standing ... Me, for example.'

Lotte stopped chewing at the cynical 'your liberators'. However hard she tried to imagine a burning Berlin, Rotterdam always appeared, or London. Berlin remained abstract, a point on a map.

'Martin wrote a letter to Frau von Garlitz: "I forbid you to send my wife out in such circumstances."' Anna laughed. 'But those were different times. The longer the war lasted the more important food became.'

Lotte endorsed this with a full mouth, in front of a salad so richly garnished that someone could have lived off it for a whole week in the hunger winter.

⋙⋘

Lotte had not yet got down to guilty feelings, swallowed up by the Moloch of housekeeping. Endless stirring of buttermilk porridge in gargantuan pans; next to them stood buckets steaming with washing; two meters further on the iron was glowing ready. Her mother, the linchpin of the constantly expanding family, was ill; a tumour had been discovered in her uterus, which had to be removed immediately. Before the operation she took three of her daughters – Marie, Jet, Lotte – to one side: 'You must promise me something – if anything goes wrong with the operation ... and I should suddenly not be there any more ... then you will take over the care of the people in hiding. I'm worried that Pa is in a state where in a bad mood he could put them all out on the street. He threatened it again last time ... it's getting too much for him...' She looked pointedly at them one by one, almost solemnly. 'I have calmed him down again ... managed to conceal his attacks from everyone ... They shouldn't have to put up with that extra strain...'

They stared at her in shock. The thought alone took their breath away. All three immediately understood that their mother's anxiety was far from unwarranted. They had known him a long time. At certain times he needed rows, preferably at the children's expense, his greatest competitors. Why not one day at the expense of the people in hiding? Of course they were his too, but his position was ambivalent in relation to them. When an appeal had been made to him on their arrival, he could not permit himself to refuse. Didn't he have a name to keep up? As a music lover – the Frinkels, Grandfather Tak, Ernst Goudriaan? As a Communist – Leon Stein? A pure impulse from the heart, which couldn't be helped – as with their mother – was out of the question for him, although he had his sentimental moods, of course, provided he had the exact background music to help him.

When the patient came round from the anaesthesia, Jet, Lotte and their father were standing either side of the bed. She lay between the sheets, pale and worryingly delicate, the chestnut brown hair with grey streaks in it dull on the pillow. Her gaze was muzzy, as though she still dwelt in hazy spheres of non-existence. She grasped her husband's hand with unexpected strength. 'Take good care of ... of everyone,' she whispered. It was something between a plea and a command. Lotte walked round the bed and stood next to her father and nodded on his behalf, her eyes shut tightly, as though presenting a guarantee of everyone's safety from the notorious mood swings of the master of the house. He stood in anguish beside the bed, waiting until he could honourably escape from the hospital, the death palace stinking of ether, where he had only turned up in the interest of exceptional self-sacrifice.

When she came home she was a shadow of her former self. She had seriously lost weight. Nothing seemed to remain of her original vitality, that mysterious primeval strength. With a forced laugh she made her way through the room, seeking support from the edges of the table and the arms of the chairs. Thrilled that his Eurydice had indeed returned from the underworld, her husband put on Gluck's *Orfeo* for her, but that was his only contribution to her recovery.

Eefje had received a piece of blue velvet on her birthday, to make dolls' clothes. She had hidden the valuable gift deep in a secret drawer in her bedroom. One day she opened the drawer and grasped thin air. She looked in the other drawers with a thudding heart, the whole bedroom, the house. She did the rounds of all the residents, crying in disbelief and disappointment. 'Have you seen my material?' became a rhetorical question that seemed to symbolize for them everything about what was lacking because of the shortages. Eventually she tossed back her plaits and pushed down on the door handle of a room she had not so far included in her search, because the prohibition on entering had been strictly maintained for years, even in the war: her father's electro-technical sanctuary. From the threshold she looked with bewilderment at the still life on the workbench. Between fittings, screws, lamps, flex and fuses, lay a packet of butter amid fresh bread, cheese and liver, like a pheasant by a seventeenth-century master. He looked up, wiping the crumbs from his mouth, trapped. With his mouth full he shouted: 'How did you get it into your head to come in here just like that?' Hastily he began to pack the bread and cheese away. 'But I am looking for my velvet material,' she whimpered. Right opposite her on the wall hung a map of the world with little flags indicating the Allies' progress. The map was mounted on blue velvet fixed to the wall with tacks. 'My material, my material . . .' she pointed in astonishment. Her father followed her trembling finger with raised eyebrows. Was a more glorious purpose conceivable for a piece of material than to serve as the background for the Allied victories? She turned her back on him and ran down stairs sniffing. She told Jet and Lotte, busy in the kitchen, what she had seen, tripping over her words, not realizing that the greater crime was not pinching her material but the secret enjoyment of bread and butter and cheese while everyone else went hungry.

The origin of these delicatessen was cleared up at the next hospital checkup when Lotte accompanied her mother, and the doctor took her aside to express his surprise and concern about the patient's extreme underweight – after all, her husband had taken away a stamped card authorizing extra food rations on the day he had fetched her. It was almost unbearable to know this; she confided to Jet but kept it a careful secret from everyone else. It had a paralysing effect on them both. It is true they had known that the boundaries of his egoism were flexible and reacted seismographically to his tempers and needs, but that there seemed to be no boundaries at all was so shocking that it went beyond their comprehension.

'I'll go and get the rest of the coupons,' said Lotte, 'at least if there are any left.' For the first time she felt a crack in her self-control. Calm thoughts, tactical strategies became impossible. She was not herself any more, in a manner of speaking, or perhaps at last she was now herself. Grimly, she set off upstairs, invaded his sanctuary without knocking. There he sat ... he was smoking a home-grown cigarette and looked up interrupted from reading an underground newspaper spread open on the workbench. It seemed as though two broken wires at the top of her skull made contact ... as though twenty-one years had evaporated ... She saw a dark figure standing in the doorway of a classroom, his black wings tightly folded ... 'How dare you...' his voice intoned in the distance, '...to two children who are weaker than you...' It was merely a glimpse, an echo that came and disappeared, but left a strong emotion behind it. 'How dare you...' she said with a trembling voice, 'to mother, who is so weak...'

'Just come in once again,' he said, 'and knock first.' There was a short circuit between the two wires ... she took a step forward and held out her hand ostentatiously. 'Give me the rest of the coupons that were meant for mother...' Raising her voice she added: 'Immediately!' He began to laugh in disbelief. 'Where in God's name did you...' he said stupidly. 'You know very well what I am talking about.' She wanted to injure him as he sat there and played the innocent – too cowardly to come out with it. But her contempt was even greater than her hate. This had to be settled quickly and efficiently, then she would have nothing more to do with it. The map hung behind him framed in blue velvet. Little flags everywhere, stubbornly stuck into it as though they concerned personal victories. Germany, flag free, apparently had nothing to do with the war. Germany was a vacuum, an absorbent hole into which her gaze disappeared. How many ways were there for you to hate yourself?

He laughed in her face. 'Give those coupons back,' she said icily, 'otherwise I'll tell everyone what a scoundrel you are.' The grin disappeared from his face. He stared at her as though he was seeing her for the first time, overwhelmed, still not ready to believe it. Then the realization began to move up his neck in a red flush; angrily he pulled open a drawer beneath the workbench, rummaged about randomly in it and pulled out a mostly used sheet of coupons. He came at her with it threateningly. Lotte did not move a muscle and stood where she was – she felt no trace of fear. If he asked for it she would squash him like a flea. He pushed the sheet of paper into her hand angrily. 'A proper Kraut...' he hissed, 'as you see, after all those years ... still a proper Kraut.' She had just enough strength to get to her bedroom, apparently composed. In a false scent of perfume and expensive soap she fell down onto her bed. Her heart was throbbing in her head. How did he know how to find her weakest spot so mercilessly ... perhaps because he himself in effect was half ... She was nauseated. With closed eyes she lay there until the knocking in her temples was less and the drone of English bombers got through to her, flying to the east. How many ways were there for you to hate yourself?

When no one was expecting him any longer the barber turned up with the news that an address had been found for Grandfather Tak and his daughter: a miller who lived in a remote spot on the polder. If it had been for the old man alone they would not have accepted the offer, but everyone breathed a sigh of relief at the thought of being free of the daughter, who believed herself to be too beautiful for this planet and all imaginable worlds. Marie took her away late in the evening by bicycle. Lotte followed the next evening – the old man who weighed nothing sat behind and anxiously held onto her hips. It was freezing, the frosty meadows reflected the light of the moon. Bent, pollarded willows formed a guard of honour either side of the narrow path, of long-dead grey-beards who were welcoming Grandfather Tak into their ranks. But he was still alive and sighed nostalgically. 'Ach Lotte, would you believe it ... if I were young I would kiss you here in the moon-light ...' Lotte turned round laughing, the bicycle swerved danger-ously. 'If you say any more naughty things,' she threatened cheerfully, 'we'll end up in the ditch.'

With regret she handed him over to the miller, who stood in the doorway like an apparition in his long white underwear. It was an unreal, disturbing transaction. Grandfather Tak leaned over and kissed the back of her chilled hand. The last she saw of him was his little bald pate shining in the moonlight, because he thought a keppel, such as his Persian son-in-law wore, humbug.

The news of what happened to him subsequently reached them indirectly and in crumbs. There was one constant: the rapid decline of the thread of the old man's life. His daughter suffered from claustrophobia in the flat, frozen no man's land where her charms were wasted; she had bitten her manicured nails until they bled. When the miller was visited by his family she beseeched them to rescue her from dying of boredom and to take her with them to the inhabited world. They yielded to her despair. That was how she landed up in a village street. She took up a provocative pose by the window. At least ten times a day they asked her to move away from there because she brought not only herself into danger but also them and the chain of people who had taken care of her in the past. But for Flora Bohjul to be seen was an essential of life; she would rather give herself up and be interrogated in a risqué striped prisoner's uniform by a charming commandant than let her days slip through her fingers between pillar and post in a horrible anonymity smelling of cabbage. She slid out of the house and reported to the Ortskommandantur, confident that she was inviolable through her marriage to a Persian Jew. When this news reached the miller he threw the old man out of the house in the dead of night, fearing that she would squeal. Torn out of his deepest sleep he wandered displaced through the meadows. The guard of honour of pollarded willows offered him hospitality again, but he could neither see nor hear anything – the only thing his organism probably desired was a warm bed. No one knew how long his freedom lasted that night. In the dawn light he seemed to have walked into the hands of the Germans, exhausted and numb with cold. To save themselves the formalities and the problems of transport, they put a permanent end to his weariness with a few bullets, in the back garden of the villa where they were billeted.

Dismay was everywhere at Lotte's home. A very old person who scarcely took up space on this planet. Why? And if an old man's life was dealt with this carelessly so near home, what was the fate of those who were put on transports? The dismay had double foundations for Lotte – who had neatly delivered him to the one who would send him on to his murderers? Who, in her so-called innocence, had once again become a willing tool in the hands of the occupier? Watch out for me! I am even worse than those who openly make war. I am friend and foe in one. I? There is no I, only an ambivalent treacherous we, who deceives itself in itself ... She immersed herself in housekeeping with an almost sardonic devotion, simply eliminating herself – her despicable self.

As though crocuses and budding branches were out of tune with the phenomenon of war, spring got off to a hesitant start. Ed de Vries deserted his shelter address to fetch the box; he needed a couple of things that were in it, he said vaguely. Lotte's father picked up a shovel and dug an immense hole, allowing for shifts in the earth and growth of tree roots, but the box did not surface. Perhaps they had made a mistake about the tree. Another spot was tried. The deeper the holes became the greater the suspicion he was loading onto himself. He took it very seriously. His image to the outside world was at stake. He set the children to work on it. All day long they poked the ground in vain with long iron poles. Max Frinkel advised engaging a renowned clairvoyant; before the war there had been one in Curaçao Street in Amsterdam. Lotte's father dismissed the suggestion cynically, allergic to anything to do with religion or the supernatural. It was his wife, sufficiently recovered to contradict his prejudices, who sent Lotte forth – you never knew.

No glass globes, playing cards, eastern trinkets. The psychic looked like a bookkeeper in a grey suit; his office was bare and businesslike. Sobered, Lotte took her seat by his desk. She looked at him expectantly, not knowing how to begin. 'You have come because something has been lost,' he said calmly, 'I will tell you: it is still there. There is a path with trees. Parallel to it is another row of trees...' She nodded in bewilderment. '...It is there ... in the vicinity of the fifth tree ... I would say.' It was as though he were walking around in the wood with her and *en passant* pointed out the spot to her with his walking stick. And that without evident display, without magic tricks or rituals. He spoke in a tone in which one discusses business matters. She did not know what she ought to think about it; a bit of hocus-pocus might perhaps have made him more credible.

'Then I'd like to ask you something else...' she said shyly, fishing a photo out of her bag, 'can you say anything about ... him?' He took it. She watched with a calm that surprised her – she could always disregard his findings. He took the photo in, glanced at her, at the photo, at her – without seeing her. The photo began to tremble; it seemed as though the person who was depicted in it was coming to life of his own accord. But it was the hand holding it that was trembling. The whole man began to shudder. With eyes that were bulging from fear he looked at the photo spellbound. He loosened his tie, wiped randomly over his forehead. 'I ... I ... can't tell you anything...' he uttered breathing heavily, turning the photo over tormentedly as though he could no longer bear the image. Under his hand he shoved it towards her. '... But can't you say ... anything ... at all?' Lotte attempted. He shook his head, with tightly closed lips. She put the photo back in her bag and stammered a polite phrase. As she went down the stairs she felt slightly ashamed for leaving him in that condition.

7

It had become a familiar pattern by now: tired of eating, talking, raking up the past, tired from listening, softened up from the conflicting sensations, they were leaving a restaurant. Anna put her arm through Lotte's, who accepted it with a certain resignation.

They found themselves in the Place du Monument. Anna stopped at the foot of the monument, bending forward to read the text on the plinth.

'Cette urne renferme des Cendres provenant de Crématoire du Camp de Concentrations de Flossenburg et de ses commandos, 1940–1945.' She exaggerated the pronunciation like all foreigners.

Lotte pulled her away, annoyed by so much perverse German curiosity.

'Mensch, Mensch, are you still troubled by a guilty conscience?' Anna exclaimed.

Now that was going too far. 'You twist things so beautifully,' she said irritably. 'I have absolutely no guilty conscience, why should I? That at the time I did take all the guilt onto myself . . . I was young and egocentric, thought I was the linchpin the world turned on, that I had influence over the fate of another. The arrogance of youth . . .'

'You're saying something there . . .' Anna looked at her, touched. 'It was like that with me too, young and egocentric. You hit the nail on the head . . . With heart and soul I only cared about that one person . . .'

Lotte shook her head with annoyance. The egocentricity of her youth could not be put on a par with Anna's just like that in one line – there was a chasm of difference between the two. Anna had a crafty habit of turning everything round. She sighed. She could not find the arguments fast enough to enfeeble this presumptuous equal treatment. She walked off, offended.

'Wait ... wait ... Lottchen ...' Anna pleaded after her.

That sounded like a very long time ago. As a child she had already been much faster than her plump sister. A whiff of nostalgia for her youth threatened to surface.

'Listen here, do wait a minute ... I want to tell you something, something you'll be flabbergasted at ... wait ...' Anna was panting. 'Did you know that I could have changed the course of history? There was a moment when I ...'

Wearily Lotte turned. That tactic she recognized too from long, long ago. Anna would try to tempt her by making her curious: 'I have discovered a jar of sweets somewhere, a jar of marbles ...'

Anna caught up with her. 'There was a moment,' she grinned, 'when the war turned on a stupid housekeeper in West Prussia, a certain ...'

'Anna Bamberg,' said Lotte laconically.

'You don't believe me.'

⊰⊱

With the flow of a caravan of refugees from Berlin, which probably no longer existed, Anna returned to the estate. Frau von Garlitz had received a billeting order. The castle swarmed with homeless townspeople who had to be provided with everything in the way of food and clean clothes, and, on Anna's shining parquet floors, were trying to come to terms with the trauma of their burning, collapsing city.

When the castle was already thoroughly saturated, the wife of a senior officer arrived, with a baby and a whining toddler.

'My husband holds the Knight's Cross,' thus Frau von So-and-So introduced herself, reckoning that all doors would now be opened for her. Those who were awarded that cross had killed a lot of people, Anna knew. Whenever it was mentioned on the radio that someone had received this medal, Martin always said, 'Somebody will have a sore throat again,' because the order was worn hung tight around the neck. Anna had no idea where to accommodate the hero's wife. She crossed the courtyard brooding until her eye fell on the coachman's house above the stables. The coachman had disappeared at the same time as the horses. He had left an adequate dwelling behind, a large living-room, two bed-rooms, a bathroom and a kitchen. We could let the high-up lady live here without us needing to feel embarrassed, Anna decided. But three days later another young mother arrived with baby and toddler – the wife of a factory worker without a 'von'. Anna rea-soned: if the noble lady gave up one room, and they shared the bathroom and kitchen in a friendly manner, they could live together in the coachman's house. *En passant* she buttonholed Frau von Garlitz half-way up the stairs for her approval. 'What?' she cried scandalized. 'You can't saddle a lady of status with a woman from who knows where.' 'She's just a mother,' said Anna calmly, 'with two children, nothing else, and that other one is also a mother with two children. She will still have two rooms to herself all the time.' Frau von Garlitz looked at her as though she had a dangerously mentally ill person opposite her. She shook her head. 'It is not on.' War or no war, she was not allowing a headstrong housekeeper to remove with one stroke her conviction that different sorts of people existed who, from their birth – each at their own level – had a dif-ferent destiny and therefore lived in different worlds. 'Then I'll give her my own rooms,' cried Anna. 'Out of the question.' Their argument blared down the staircase; everyone could enjoy it. 'You are a Bolshevik!' the Countess accused her. 'Fine, then I'm a Bolshevik.' Anna turned her back on her and left her standing there. At the foot of the stairs Ottchen was waiting with a stern expression, he who had licked his superiors' boots since childhood. 'How dare you take such a tone with the gnädige Frau,' he hissed. Anna positioned herself right in front of him. 'Otto, I'll tell you something. What I have to say to her I say to her face. I'd give my life for her if needs be. You bow low but with a knife in your boots. You say "Jawohl, gnädige Frau" slavishly but at the same time your eyes sparkle with hate. I've seen it, you don't fool me.'

For the mother, who was unaware of the storms raging over her head, Anna eventually found a draughty attic room without stove, without water, without window. The unsuitability of it deprived her of all the pleasure of continuing to have civilized contact with her employer. She had been accustomed to waking her in the mornings, drawing open the curtains and having a gentle morning conversation with her from the end of the bed. For Frau von Garlitz this was a precious ritual that reconciled her with the umpteenth day of war in the scarcely manageable chaos that had the estate in its grasp. Now Anna snapped her a contemptuous morning greeting, tore the curtains open and disappeared fast. After five days the Countess could endure it no longer. 'Damned mule,' she cried unladylike from her four-poster bed, 'can't you say good morning at least?' 'I said good morning.' 'Yes, yes,' she sat up against the embroidered pillows, 'but how! Come...' she tapped her fingers on the edge of the bed, 'don't be cross any more ... sit down. Go and fetch that woman and take her to the coach-man's house ... do what you wish ... you understand so much more about that sort of thing than I do...'

One Sunday in March a younger sister of the Countess was getting married. Frau von Garlitz set off with her children before the crack of dawn to her parents' castle, where the wedding was to be celebrated: her husband would come by aeroplane from Brussels to Germany. *Deo gratias*, thought Anna, the empire alone at last. As she was turning over in bed once more, a popular song went through her head: 'This is my Sunday delight, in bed till ten o'clock, then nobody can get me out of it...' But at nine o'clock there was a merciless knocking at her bedroom door. It was Ottchen, so agitated he could scarcely get his words out. The military aircraft that was to bring Herr von Garlitz to Berlin had crashed over Bohemia: none of the occupants had survived. Anna was quick to get over the shock. She did not delude herself into believing that she was sad. The only one she was anxious about was Frau von Garlitz, who reappeared at the gate half-way through the afternoon. The wedding had been postponed. She gave orders with the remarkable self-control required of her position – only her nostrils were trembling slightly. She kept a cool head about everything: a state funeral had to be prepared.

Anna was sent to Frau Ketteler at great speed to tell her in person of the tragic death of the apple of her eye. With a horse and carriage she rushed to the remote villa. Through a dark tunnel of spruces that exuded a damp spicy smell she walked to the staff entrance. She pushed the door open. No one was there. The only thing that was sounding, with regular interruptions, was the electric bell with which the lady of the house summoned the maid to her room via a pedal next to her armchair. Surprised, Anna walked along the corridor. Where was the staff? Did they all have Sunday off? What was the point of calling them then? Although Anna did not know Frau Ketteler's villa, it was not difficult to find her room – she only needed to look for the source of the staccato sound. The door stood open a crack. She looked in on a dim room, spruce branches pushing up against the windows. On a Persian carpet in front of the hearth, where a professional fire was blazing, lay Herr von Garlitz's aunt – on her back. She was being mounted by her favourite sheepdog: both were at full gallop, which explained the continual on and off of the bell as she was lying on top of the pedal. Apparently she had not allowed herself enough time before the ride to pull this out from under her back. Anna held her breath. She had never suspected that what she saw here, illuminated from the side by the flames, could exist at all and even now, as she looked at it, she did not believe it. With fascinated horror she stared at the animal lover's flushed face – this was an unsuitable moment to trouble her. The sheepdog looked into the distance with glazed eyes. Suddenly Anna was afraid that he would get a scent of her presence. She fled down the passage, out of the house, between the antiseptic spruces to the ordinary world where the spectacle easily seemed like a bizarre dream.

Back at the castle she said she had not found Frau Ketteler at home. The truth could not cross her lips – it would be thought that she was imagining perverse fantasies. Moreover, everyone was preoccupied with the mystery of how the military aircraft had crashed over Bohemia. That was surely far off the route from Brussels to Berlin? There had been no bombing raids that day that one would have had to avoid. Secretly it was suggested that a political reason existed for taking Herr von Garlitz out of the way; discredited individuals were increasingly having accidents. Anna remained level-headed. She could think of no single reason why the life of this clever dick would be worth the sacrifice of a military aircraft. Yet she also slowly realized that another truth might exist behind the generally accepted one. Just as beneath the exterior of Frau Ketteler something lurked that was completely, inconceivably different.

The coffin with the material remains was delivered after a few days. It was entrusted to the gardener. He grabbed her behind the hedge and said, looking round with panic: 'Did you know there's absolutely . . . nothing in the coffin . . .' 'Oh no,' Anna swayed back. With a weathered hand, which had toiled in the earth for half a century, he led her by the elbow to an outbuilding where the coffin stood on trestles in the semi-darkness. It was too small to contain an adult man. When they lifted it up it seemed remarkably light, something rattled back and forth inside. 'I don't know what it is,' the gardener whispered, 'not a whole person in any case.' 'Frau von Garlitz mustn't notice,' Anna said hurriedly. 'Put stones into it before the funeral so that the coffin weighs as much as a person. That thing will have to be carried. Cover it with flags, decorate it with flowers and greenery . . .'

Until late into the night she sat at the sewing machine in her room making a mourning dress out of a black evening dress of Frau von Garlitz's for her daughter, fourteen-year-old Christa. 'What are you doing Anna?' the Countess's voice suddenly sounded through the noise of the machine, flat and robbed of any inflection. 'Christa doesn't have a dress for the funeral,' Anna mumbled with three pins between her lips. Frau von Garlitz dropped down into a chair in her night-dress. She followed Anna's actions with an empty gaze. 'What would I do without you,' she whispered, 'no one has done so much for me as you.' Anna, who had little experience of receiving compliments, blushed up to the hairline and cranked the sewing machine with double force. Her employer was seated on the upright chair, nodding off, as though Anna were her last remaining refuge. Her head sagged onto her chest – now and then she lifted it with a jerk as though the inner realization of early widowhood kept occurring to her. Anna's head was reverberating with worries about the funeral the following day: the state guests had to be offered a welcome fitting to their status and function; no element must be missing from the military cere-monial ... the whole farce in memory of a nonentity had to go off faultlessly.

When the sun rose the dress was ready. There was no point in going to bed. She felt a strange lucidity that overcame her tiredness and would have prevented her sleeping. She took Frau von Garlitz, leaning heavily on her, to bed, and hurried downstairs. It was a chilly, lustreless day. Everyone conformed to the scenario: the official guests played their parts with a practised, abstract dig-nity that led to the suspicion that funerals were just as much a commonly occurring and obvious aspect of their careers as thinking up strategies or inspecting troops. In the front rank, behind the coffin professionally draped with Nazi flags and flora, walked Goering's representative with clenched jaws, broad and massive as a tank. Frau von Garlitz, flanked by her children, floated behind like a black angel, pale and serene and not of this world. To the accompaniment of speeches, in which his services for the father-land were made much of and rhetorically vanished between the chestnut trees, the deceased was placed in the family grave on the estate where he had been born – not for long, as history would relate.

The undermining thing about the war, thought Anna, was that it continued as a matter of course and that you could not dwell on any single disaster or tragedy. Fresh problems immediately presented themselves anew which demanded an immediate solution. Onwards, onwards, onwards, one cog slotted into the next. Work went on, plodding on, purely in order to keep everything turning in expectation of . . . of what?

There were also those who opposed the apparent inevitability. One evening, a month after her husband's death, Frau von Garlitz received a notable visit. From her window on the first floor Anna saw a group of gentlemen arriving – they walked towards the front door discretely but purposefully, briefcases under their arms. She recognized some of them, officers in civilian dress, who had also been at the funeral. They were received in the great hall, immediately below her room. Murmuring voices ascended through the hot air duct that began in the fireplace and had an outlet in her room.

Anna put the inkwell on the table, dipped the nib of her pen, bent over a sheet of pale blue notepaper. But the words had difficulty forming themselves into sentences in her head, drowned as they were by the fragments of conversation that entered her room from downstairs – apparently they were sitting in a circle around the fireplace. There was repeated mention of the Wolf's Nest and the Bendler barracks. It sounded as though one of those present had to fulfil a mission at both locations, the details of which were being comprehensively discussed, and the timing arranged to the second. Beneath the controlled, rational tone in which they spoke she could hear a subdued tension that sharpened her attentiveness. Frau von Garlitz's voice did not join in. Her only typically female contribution apparently was to offer the place for this rendezvous. Although Anna tried to regard what was coming to her ears as not intended for her ears, the more the evening went on, the more her dry pen floated inactively over the paper; the importance of all those words pressed upon her as though they were specially meant for her. She felt cold. It started with her feet and crept slowly up her legs to her middle. But in her head she was dominated by the feverish awareness that she was the only one in the world who knew about a breathtakingly bold plan. A plan that would interfere profoundly in the order of things and bring about changes too dizzying for her alone to grasp. Her head felt top-heavy, the responsibility was too great. In sudden desolation she considered entrusting everything she had heard to the blue paper, but her pen hesitated at the thought that it could be fatally danger-ous to entrust a letter with such contents to the post. So she sat motionless until the visit had broken up and left an ominous quiet behind in the castle where, within its walls, beside the unfortunate emperor's bed, it was now also keeping a secret whose timing mechanism had been set.

❦

As though guided by an invisible hand, they ended up in the pâtisserie with the unrivalled merveilleux. At the other tables well-groomed contemporaries spooned in their cakes with ladylike mouthfuls, chatting pleasantly about everyday things. Why were Anna and Lotte doomed to dig endlessly over that war, at this age, in a history that really would not change for the better?

They looked at each other expectantly over their empty plates. 'What I heard through the chimney then was precisely what was executed' – Anna interrupted the silence as was only to be expected. 'I read about it years later – about that one unforeseen chance, of course. They had had enough of the Sunday painter. It began with the Stalingrad catastrophe. Then there was a turnaround in the disposition of the nationalistic nobility because their sons too were perishing there. It was the end of the great dream. The military experts among them realized that the war could not be won, their estates were in danger as the Russians approached, their whole status was in danger. Thus was the conspiracy created. Frau von Garlitz had offered her services, probably under her father's influ-ence – that fierce Prussian of the old guard with his connections. And I in my maid's room heard them talking as though I were

261

sitting there! All the conspirators were there and devised the plot to the minutest detail. It would have worked if they hadn't had such dreadful bad luck. It was all fixed up in the Bendler barracks in Berlin – at a password the officers would revolt, take the government prisoner, form a coalition and offer peace immediately. The war over! If it had succeeded Martin would still have been alive, and millions of others, many towns would had survived intact. I would have had a totally different life. Whether it would have been a better life I don't know, more interesting, certainly not – my God, as a housewife in Vienna! But I did not see that at all then. I was very badly shocked, did not know what I ought to do. I was law-abiding although I had not much faith in the Führer. I believed in the necessity of authority, still do for that matter, I was in charge myself . . . in that I am very German, I admit it. Martin came the following Sunday. I told him what I had heard. He went white round the gills. 'Keep quiet about it,' he said, 'you've heard nothing. Absolutely nothing. God grant that it succeeds!'

Lotte ordered another pot of tea. 'Yet, it would, with hindsight, not have mattered much if you had disclosed the plan or not,' she made light of Anna's secrecy. 'The plot would have failed anyway.'

Anna did not go along with her. 'If I had betrayed it at that stage, perhaps an alternative plan would have been devised that really would have succeeded. In that case it would have been better not to have kept quiet.'

On this speculation a senseless discussion followed, in which the word 'when' often appeared with the meaning of 'what if'. With their invented variations they still steered the course of history by their hands, in an argumentative tone because it mainly fell to Lotte to contradict Anna. Eventually they left the establishment squabbling wearily: Anna provoked and exhausted – it seemed impossible ever to convince her sister (with what artillery ought she to approach?) – Lotte angered on account of the fact that Anna imputed a central role for herself in an event which had proceeded completely beyond her.

8

'If you had a revolver in your hand at this moment and Hitler came walking round the corner would you shoot him?'

Leon Stein looked at her with an anguished laugh. They were walking in the wood; he was a head shorter than Lotte. In broad daylight he was strolling cold-bloodedly along the beech path and took her arm as though they were engaged. That cold-bloodedness was part of his survival strategy – up to now he had survived all daring exploits. He did not worry about his own death; he dealt with that of another more carefully. 'I think I would,' she said hesitantly, 'but I don't know if I could really do it.' They passed the row of trees that was still keeping the secret of the box despite the clairvoyant's prophesy. They had searched exhaustively following his advice but had found nothing: the earth there was loose and uneven as though colonies of moles had contested the territory with each other. Moreover, 'In the vicinity of the fifth tree' really was very vague.

'I have a problem . . .' said Leon. 'A month ago we took a Jewish family – husband, wife, children – to three separate addresses. Meanwhile the wife was betrayed and picked up but set free a short time later. Since then she has been walking about unhindered and a number of us have been arrested, those who gave her coupons, identity card, a hiding address. We have followed her, we can work it out. You understand that we are not going to wait quietly to see who the next victim is going to be.' He looked at her with partly closed eyes, as though speaking while half-asleep. 'We have taken a decision: she is going to be liquidated.' His arm held hers more tightly. 'Sometimes it is necessary to sacrifice one life to save other lives.' Lotte looked at him, shocked. 'To save my family I would also be capable of a lot, I think...' 'Exactly so,' he nodded. 'Who's got to do it?' she asked after a long silence. The little man, who could not permit himself to shirk the answer to the big questions, poked at a tree root that crossed the path with the point of his shoe. 'That's exactly the problem.'

After a few days' absence he returned hurriedly; agitated dots of light shone in his glasses. There was no time to ask him anything. 'A raid's coming,' he waved his hands in a vague direction, 'they could be here at any moment.' In the house there was the usual chaos. Those who did not exist officially, who were not allowed to occupy a square centimetre of the surface of the earth, dissolved into nothing. The game of cards, still warm from their hands, the forbidden books that they read, their unmade beds – they had an astonishing routine for wiping out life that should not exist. The ordinary Dutch family who lived there applied themselves to their daily activities with ostentatious industry, hoping that the deafening beating of their hearts would continue unnoticed.

They were mistaken in imagining that Ernst Goudriaan was, as usual, in the hiding place behind the mirror, until he appeared in the kitchen in a long leather coat with a kit bag on his back and misted-up glasses, where Lotte was doing the washing for the sake of form. 'I have come to say goodbye.' He held out a trembling hand. Lotte wiped her hands on her apron. 'Goodbye? Why?' 'I ... I ... can't take it any more ...' he stammered, taking his glasses off and putting them back on. 'I ... that tension ... increasing again ... I ... I am going away...' 'Away?' Lotte repeated, positioning herself in front of him. 'You'll walk straight into their arms! How do you get it into your head – you'll betray us all!' He shook his head nervously. 'I've got some arsenic...' he reassured her. Her mouth fell open. 'Arsenic...' she emphasized each syllable, '...you're crazy ... give that coat and bag here...' She put her hand out authoritatively. He stood motionless opposite her. Was that the sound of voices in the distance? Barking dogs? Drone of an engine? Instead of his eyes all she saw was his stupid steamed-up glasses, his narrow face behind them, white and fixed in tension – perhaps this time he had to be thoroughly rattled. They hypnotized each other, a silent test of strength with the background sounds coming ever closer. 'Come...' ordered Lotte. She began to tug at his bag, helped him out of his coat – suddenly he let her do as she pleased, like a dog who submits to its master in blind obedience, against its instincts. 'But I'm not going in the cupboard any more,' he cried rebelliously. Without allowing himself to be prevented he turned and rashly walked out of the kitchen into the garden, straight to his studio, leaving Lotte behind with his coat and bag.

A police van drew up in front of the house. A dozen soldiers began to spread out according to ludicrously strict stage directions. Some positioned themselves like macabre guards at strategic points in order to close off possible escape routes, others searched through the house and showed themselves at the windows to check whether there were any camouflaged rooms. An officer strode through the apple trees to the TB-house. In the parental bedroom they allowed themselves to be enticed to the three-bay window by the lady of the house to admire the view on to the meadows and edge of the wood. The cloudless sky and sun shining through the branches seemed to be ignoring the danger. Lotte, mesmerized by the quiet and stillness around the studio, kept going to the window expecting to see Ernst Goudriaan coming out with a rifle in his back and his hands raised. Eventually she could not bear it any longer and went the same way she had seen the officer go. She looked mock-casually inside through the window at the back. Ernst, his glasses half-way down his nose, was holding up a half-complete violin and pointing at something, giving enthusiastic explanation. The officer had put his cap on the workbench and was listening in fascination, nodding now and then and stroking his chin. Lotte opened the door. Distracted, they both looked over their shoulders. The German was stroking his middle finger caressingly over the back

plate of a violin hanging on the wall. 'Ein sehr schöne lacquer...'
'I make it myself without pigments,' said Ernst proudly.
'Wunderbar, wunderbar...' the other cried euphorically. He stood
up and inhaled deeply with closed eyes. 'It smells good in here
too,' he discovered, 'marvellous...!'

Disconcerted, Lotte took large strides back to the kitchen, putting her feet down without thinking. But even before she reached
the door she was overwhelmed by a feeling of triumph: at one
moment he was prepared to take poison from fear of the occupier,
the next moment he welcomed him in – enthusiastically – to the
secrets of violin-making. A wonderful alchemical transformation
that enabled her to forget all danger. She was just going inside the
house when violin music sounded behind her. An ardent, heartfelt
passage from the Beethoven concerto arose from the studio and
penetrated through the pale blue planks. The soldiers, losing their
interest in the insides of the house, assembled in the garden to listen
to the officer's musical intermission. They listened in a controlled
way, as though it were part of military discipline. The sun glittered
on the buttons of their uniforms. Now that the raid was being
graced with a famous concerto, Lotte's father also came outside to
listen with his hands in his pockets. After the last notes had died
away, it was more quiet than ever before, until a magpie flew off
noisily from a branch and the officer dreamily left the studio. He
swayed through the fruit trees, drunk from the music. Suddenly he
saw his subordinates in view; he ran a hand through his dishevelled
hair, put his cap on and adopted an expression suited to the war.
'Well then...' he said gruffly, 'what are you waiting for...'

The engine drone died away. Those who did not exist emerged
sweating and smelly and gave vent to their surprise at Beethoven's
wonderful intervention, which had even been heard behind the
mirror. Max Frinkel had plenty to say about the power of music.
Only Ernst Goudriaan stayed behind in his studio and went on
planing the back plate of a violin. 'You seduced the commandant...' said Lotte delightedly; she sat down among the wood

shavings. 'Thanks to you...' he grinned. '...She is doing the washing as usual, I said to myself as I walked to the studio. If the people in hiding are discovered, there's a huge chance that the whole family will be put against the wall and yet she is doing the washing as usual. Why, I thought, don't I get on with the plane then? Someone who is at work has something inviolable, something invulnerable ... as though he is placing himself outside the war with it...' She was shyly silent. She did not feel indifferent to his singing her praises. It brought her into an enjoyable confusion that now for a change she had had a positive influence on the fate of another. 'And he even played a solo for you...' she sighed, as a diversionary tactic. Ernst nodded. 'An enthusiastic amateur. He said: if we weren't in the middle of a war I would buy this violin from you.' With a craftsman's pride he repeated, 'He wanted to buy a violin from me!'

The incident pepped her up and brought the credit–debit balance more or less into equilibrium. Chastened by the thought that this person in hiding actually belonged to her, since she had held him back from his ridiculous kamikaze action, she offered no opposition to the feeling of being in love that flooded over her as an apparently natural result: with him and with all the activities that are necessary to making a violin: sawing, planing, polishing, lacquering. That the front and back plates were of fine-grained Yugoslavian maple wood, the fingerboards of ebony on the other hand, that a bad lacquer affected the tone, that the sides were bent with steam, all of it moved her, as when she also caught the stink of the bone glue that was used for sticking various components together. But the loveliest thing of all about him was that he seemed unlike her father in every respect.

❧

In a guidebook promoting Spa's fame as a health resort it says: 'The resort guests at Spa should forget about everyday life. They are urged to live according to a slower, a more regular rhythm. They are gathered up into a caring and protective milieu, which is closely connected to the medical world, which is in itself a symbol of reliability and certainty.'

A fat lot the two sisters cared about these good intentions. None of the 'slow and regular rhythm' showed up. The more they confided further to each other about their incompatible lives, the more the tension and the awareness of the irrevocability of the past grew. It was the last chance they were being offered for *rapprochement* and reconciliation. The one wanted to, out of profound need, but was already too willing; the other was still bracing herself, because of a mistrust at least as deep. The war was overrunning their health cure. They summoned up ghosts and the ghosts came ... with their frayed souls, in a deserted landscape, under leaden skies in a smell of gunpowder and phosphorous ... one great lament against remaindering the right to life, freedom, humanity, Christian charity ... values that had once had significance, words from an archaic language, an Esperanto of naïvety. The ghosts came past in columns and left deeply ingrained traces behind them.

It is true that Anna and Lotte were lying full-length on their couches in the Salle de Repos, but they did not keep their eyes closed and they were not listening to the cooing of the doves. As there were no other patients in there that morning, they continued as usual with the war, horizontally.

'The twentieth of July, the day Hitler was not killed,' said Anna, 'I remember it as though it were the day before yesterday. Frau von Garlitz had the radio on. She knew precisely when it would happen of course. There was a brief mention of the attempt, nothing more, she had been expecting it. "Thank God!" she cried, delirious with joy, "The Schwein is dead!" It echoed through the corridors and staircases. I went rigid. Then Ottchen suddenly appeared and said: "The Führer is alive, he is talking on the radio now." Oh my God, I thought, let no one have heard Frau von Garlitz. The house was full of strangers! We only found out later what had gone wrong. The Führer, who never left his seat at meetings, had walked round the table to the other side – just before the bomb went off. The conspirators were arrested immediately, von Stauffenberg was shot that same day. The gentlemen I had seen on the front steps with their briefcases, including a nephew of Frau von Garlitz, not one of them survived. All those senior officers from good families whom the Schweinerei did not want any more ... most of them were hung at Plötzensee, on meat hooks.'

'An exhibition ...'

Anna nodded. 'As a terrifying example. Their wives and children were taken off to camps. They had a great purge right away and absolutely everything with a bad smell was picked up and sent off.'

'And Frau von Garlitz?'

'No one knew that she had been involved in it.'

❦❦

'I am lying on my back and watching the aircraft fly over,' Martin wrote from Normandy. He had enclosed two photographs. In one he was sitting in a military coat on the rocks of Mont-Saint-Michel, looking out over the sea to England – the other showed him sitting on the wing of a shot down English aircraft with a star on its side. One week later he telephoned unexpectedly. 'I'm nearby, I'm here, in Stettin.' His signals unit had been disbanded. They had to go for brief infantry training at a Wehrmacht barracks on the Baltic Sea. The inventive company commander, who had once rustled up the illegal leave from the Ukraine, had thought up a new trick. All spouses received a telegram with the news that their husbands were seriously ill. With this official document in her pocket, which authorized a journey north, Anna got on the train. And again at the end of this journey, a steep grey wall rose up as the train tipped over sharply to one side. What would they be hiding behind that one? Anna thought. The miracle weapon that had been highly praised on the radio occurred to her, the weapon with which Germany was going to win the war. Perhaps V2s were indeed being deployed behind that wall! But wrinkles appeared in the enormous wall, it was moving – the train swayed simultaneously, it toppled back, and for the first time in her life she suddenly saw an unending grey water surface with a boat drifting on it.

The train stopped at a seaside resort. A conspicuously large number of young women with two suitcases got off. You could be forgiven for assuming that one suitcase contained clothes and the other was stuffed full of comestibles. Hesitantly they trudged to the square in front of the station, to and fro, until they discovered that they had a common problem: how could they get to the hotel with their heavy suitcases? Two tanned women with a handcart smelling of fish approached Anna, after having searched round to look, holding up one of her wedding photographs. 'Are you Frau Grosalie?' 'Yes,' said Anna in astonishment. 'Your husband has sent us. We have to fetch you and bring the suitcases.' Without waiting for her reaction they took her suitcases and put them in the cart. The other women burst out in a torrent of abuse. Why had their husbands not made arrangements for them? 'Dear heaven,' cried Anna, 'what's the matter? We'll load the cart full and all push it together.' A bunch of women in summer dresses of wartime floral prints pushed the top heavy cart over the bumpy cobbles to the beach hotel. Martin had apparently explained the problem to a fisherman the previous evening and had arranged with him that Anna would be fetched in exchange for cigarettes.

The hotel stood resolutely on top of a dune and seemed to challenge the sea: rise up, then. The barracks were three kilometres further on. Every evening the company went swimming with the commandant's permission. They left their uniforms behind on the beach, walked three kilometres in their wet bathing trunks, and spent the night with their wives in their hotel rooms. One warm evening Martin and Anna went swimming as they had done in the lake. The smooth water reflected the light of the moon. They swam out next to each other at a calm, even pace. The element of water gave a sense of freedom, as though the war's rules only counted on land. 'I've just heard on the radio,' said Martin with unrestrained joy in his voice, 'that the Russians are in East

Prussia.' 'Then it can't go on for much longer...' Anna spat out a mouthful of sea water. He dived under and came up a bit further on. 'When that stupid war is over,' he cried, sneezing, 'we can go to Vienna for good at last.' They swam on in an excited fuddle until Martin turned and said with surprise: 'We really are rather far from the coast.' Anna looked round mechanically. An unreal white strip on the horizon was all that was left of the coast. They turned round and began to swim back in equanimity. But when the strip did not seem to come a millimetre closer, their strokes took on a grimmer character. The moon accompanied them impassively, Martin looked round frequently, encouraging her to keep going. The sea water was heavy, it seemed as though litres had to be displaced with each stroke. She became breathless. The more fiercely she tried to keep calm, the more forcefully the panic struck. The strip of land continued to distinguish itself by keeping its distance. 'Martin...' she cried weakly – she disappeared beneath the water, came up again, 'let me...' 'I'll help you...' Although his voice was coming from far away she felt his arm around her shoulders, '...right at the end of the war we surely can't dr...' suddenly sounded much nearer. She surrendered to him. Her sense of time was distorted. She did not know if hours or minutes stretched out before he no longer had enough strength to keep them both above the water. His cry for help, which skimmed over the surface of the water, vaguely got through to her. She was resigned to disappearing with him, to being sucked into the mother sea and never more needing anything. Unnoticed, without resistance, she allowed herself to float into a silent no man's land.

An eternity later she was lying on her back on the still warm sand, and someone was blowing his breath into her. A nauseated disgust flowed though her arteries along with her returning life. She was being rubbed dry and warm with a rough towel. Why hadn't they left her where she was? It suited her there absolutely. But Martin was sitting next to her, blue-white in the moonlight, and watching out anxiously for the return of signs of life at the hands of their skilful rescuer, a sergeant from his company who had the shoulders and biceps of a gladiator – Martin even permitting him to give her the kiss of life. She could not yet know that a few months later, looking back on this evening, she would once again become consumed with regret that the arrival of the industrious sergeant had prevented her from dissolving into nothingness with Martin.

The following day the illegal holiday came to an abrupt end: the Waffen SS had permitted its eye to fall upon the group doing infantry training. Upset, they ran to the hotel that evening. They had had more than enough of the war; the approaching peace was already singing in their heads; they refused to join the corps of fanatics. Martin drummed his fists into the pillow. What could these orthodox officers, these war-horses in whose vocabulary the word surrender did not exist, be planning, other than to prepare themselves for collective suicide? Closed in by the English and Americans on the one side and the Russians on the other, would they stop at nothing to bring about the sacrifice of young warriors to old Germanic custom in order to placate the gods once more? It was the first and last time he rebelled. Anna rocked him to and fro, without conviction trying to calm him. 'We have nothing to say . . .' he capitulated finally, whispering, 'nothing.'

The company was moving to Nuremberg. From up on the Baltic Sea all the way down the Third Reich, in wagons for transporting goods or cattle. The wives travelled with them to Berlin – except Anna, Martin would not permit his wife to have to travel without any form of accommodation. 'No question of it,' he said proudly, 'there is no toilet, no sink. My wife is not travelling in a cattle truck like an animal.' He climbed in irritably. She would wait for the next passenger train. Anna shoved the suitcase with provisions in after him. 'What's that for . . . ?' His glance grazed the suitcase. 'Provisions,' Anna said. He put it back on the platform. Anna lifted it up and put it in the train again. 'Take it with you, I get enough to eat.' He heaved the thing out again with pursed lips.

Does this have to be our parting? Anna thought. The departure signal sounded. Martin held her face in his hands and kissed her grievously. Wringing her hands she was left on the platform, hemmed in by two suitcases.

The news that the Russians were in East Prussia blistered into the summer heat, causing anxiety on the one hand and secret joy on the other. In and around the castle everything was as before, farming and housekeeping were turning at full speed – a *perpetuum mobile* cranked up by the war. But the Russian prisoners of war and Polish forced labourers, Wilhelm whispered, found themselves in a state of permanent excitement that they only managed to hide from their guards with extreme collective self-control. Anna nodded; it could not go on for much longer now. They were in the kitchen garden, behind a tall rhubarb plant. He took her hands and brought his furrowed face close to her ear; she thought he was going to kiss her. 'Warn the gnädige Frau ... the day the Russians come to liberate us the Poles will kill everything German here. They are patriots, they will take revenge for what has been done to their country. Everyone will be murdered, except you. A finger won't be lifted against you, they have promised us that. The Russians are protecting you.' 'But Wilhelm ...' Anna stammered, 'you can't mean that ... Frau von Garlitz ... and the children ... surely they haven't done anything ...' He lowered his eyes, let go of her hands and walked away with drooping shoulders as though a lead ball hung from each arm. Anna stared at the powerful stems of the rhubarb; the association with barbarians occurred to her. The well-tended kitchen garden, the smoothly cut lawns, the glistening castle, the washing as white as snow hanging out motionless on the line ... she could not imagine the possibility of this self-evident order being disturbed. The human linchpin of this order, the inhabitants of the castle, the family whose name had been associated with this spot since the seventeenth century, Ottchen, Mamselle, the cleaning women and chambermaids, even the refugees – all these people with whom she had been involved day in, day out, had to pay the penalty? What had they done? For the first time she began to sense that the liberation they had yearningly looked forward to would perhaps be no liberation at all, that the war would continue as usual – wearing a different mask. She began to move, walked straight in to Frau von Garlitz, who reacted with neither surprise nor shock. She had long understood that the hordes from the east would not bring liberation; her evacuation plan was ready.

A letter came from Martin, an SS letter from an SS barracks. The Russians were approaching West Prussia, he wrote; resign and go to Vienna – that will be safer, you will be at home there. A sensible, understandable message. Martin, who had already travelled though Europe for six years like a gypsy, spoke about her departure from the estate as though it concerned a random change of posting. As though she did not have ties to cut, for the first time in her life. The tie with her employer, the two children, the staff – her surrogate family, that unwieldy, tried and tested, capricious rag-bag that she had been involved with so profoundly over the years. The renovated castle, her own creation, how could it function for a day without her? Did she have to leave all that behind, prey to . . . ?

She left it all behind; goodbyes were said with tears and promises. Frau von Garlitz was touched and hurt as though her own mother were abandoning her. The children clung on to her like monkeys, the cleaning women blew their noses, Ottchen sniffed loudly to proclaim his contempt for members of staff who did not regard their function as a lifelong calling – he climbed up onto the box sullenly. A period was coming to an end with her departure, everyone felt that and no one knew what would take its place.

Anna heaved herself up with her eternal suitcases and rode down the castle drive with red eyes, out of the gate, waving one more time. They drove along the Frederickian village road, the emaciated Russian prisoners of war formed a row on either side, in their worn-out clothes, waving their blue checked handkerchiefs. Their guards looked on from the sidelines. Wilhelm was standing at the front, with a tortured grin from ear to ear. They stood there like the last faithful followers of a queen who was being taken to the scaffold. The queen of the handkerchiefs, the toothpaste, the combs with a few teeth missing, burst into tears. Wilhelm stepped forward to give her his handkerchief. It was her last sight of the village, through a veil, the sentries on either side with their sadly waving rags, their drawn faces – who was disappearing out of whose life? The village ended and the fields began and there was only desolation – apart from Ottchen who stared unfathomably at the horse's hindquarters swinging to and fro.

❦

'Yes, they loved me,' Anna concluded.

Lotte did not react, she could not reconcile all that adulation with her own, less flattering picture of Anna. Anna was romanticizing the past. 'And . . .' she said rancorously, 'was Wilhelm right?'

'It happened just as he had predicted. The castle was ransacked, many did not survive it. Frau von Garlitz fled at night to the west with the children and a few trusted ones across the frozen Oder. I heard it years later from Mamselle, whose tracks I came across by chance.'

'And the castle, have you ever been back to see it again?' Lotte, with her weakness for old houses, was curious despite herself.

'Don't talk to me about it!' Anna sat up in pure indignation. 'The Poles have the same mentality as those fat washerwomen when I came to the estate. They don't know what work is. They never will, I'm telling you.'

The bed, not intended for guests who sit up and talk emphatically, protested with strenuous creaking.

'I have been to Poland by car with a friend last autumn. Warsaw, Kraków, Auschwitz, Zakopane, Poznań. I had an inspiration. "Let's go to the village where I worked during the war." "But surely that doesn't exist any more," my friend spluttered. "Of course it's still there," I said, "only it's called something different." We went in search, without a map, in an area with Polish place names that gave you nothing to hold on to. I drove purely from memory: a gnarled tree, an old barn, a three-forked road that struck me as familiar, were my only points of orientation in this empty country. All of a sudden we were driving along a straight road with chestnut trees – ramshackle farms, chickens in the road, tipsy chaps round the door of the post office that was also the village café. I got out and asked about the village, calling it by its old name. They looked at me indifferently without answering. A drizzly rain was falling, which made everything even more impoverished. I walked along the village street a bit, stopped in front of a colossal neglected house of . . . a landowner, I thought. Grass was growing in the gutters, which were hanging loose, the unpainted shutters were coming off their hinges, some windows were boarded up, the porch over the front door was shored-up crookedly, cracked plaster everywhere – geese were scratching about on a stubbly patch of grass, further on a pig was rootling in the mud, a mangy guard dog bared his teeth. I thought of our immaculate farms in Germany. See, I said to myself, this is how the Polish farmers go about their business. They simply haven't a clue. An old man walked past. I buttonholed him, I used the old name of the village again. He stared at me through thick pebble lenses as though I were an apparition, then he began to nod slowly. "Stockow now . . ." he said in broken German. I nodded with him, suddenly excited. "Familie von Garlitz?" He said nothing. "The castle, where is the castle?" He smiled; he had a broken denture, the poor man. "Das Schloss . . . ?" he repeated in surprise, "but it's here . . . right in front of you . . ." I was standing in front of it and looking at it and did not recognize it. Can you imagine!'

Anna's face had become flushed. The walls of the Salle de Repos looked as though they were bulging out from the indignation that she exuded. She opened her plump arms. 'There used to be a wall round it, and the grounds with old trees. All gone. There was the castle, threadbare, pitiful, between the mud and the exhausted grass. I can't tell you what was going on inside me there. It was as though my last remaining trust in humanity – and there is not much left of it now – was being disposed of. As though every-thing, everything had been for nothing. "Can I see the house from the inside?" I asked, "I used to work there during the war." He nodded but I don't know if he understood. Twelve Polish families had been living there since the end of the war, he explained, the farm had become a co-operative.'

She turned up her nose. 'One of those kolkhozes. We got per-mission to see a part of the castle from inside. My God, what an ordeal. We started in the hall, that same hall of the conspiracy. Washing lines were strung across it, with some yellowed sheets and shirts hanging up. The walls were grey, the tiles cracked. We opened the door to the dining-room. I put a hand over my mouth. "Look at that, my parquet floor!" I cried. There was my pride and joy, my best floor that had endlessly been rubbed with wax – dried out and cracked, whole pieces were missing. A couple of rusty bicycles leaned against the wall, a thin pale ginger cat slunk off with its tail between its paws. I was staggered, as you can imagine. "Let's go outside, please," I pleaded. We walked to the back door along an empty, ominous passage – without runner, unpainted walls without hunting scenes – I almost stumbled over a bucket of dirty suds. Outside I took a deep breath. "The cemetery," I sug-gested, "there must be something there from earlier times." The old man shook his head. "Alles kaputt," he mumbled. I walked to the place where we had buried Herr von Garlitz in the earth, or what had had to pass for him. The old paths were still intact but dark holes gaped instead of the graves, overgrown with creepers and ground ivy. Here and there a fragment of marble. The branches of mature shrubs bent overhead as though they wanted to cover up the shame. "They have not even left the dead in peace," I cried. "Everything ruined," said my guide resignedly. So it was. They had been so vengeful they could not even leave undisturbed the graves that went back to the seventeenth century.'

'But that's easy to understand really,' said Lotte over the edge of her sheets. 'They certainly had enough reason to.'

'Yes, yes,' said Anna impatiently, 'but as I stood there looking into those gaping holes I didn't understand any of it.'

It was quiet for a moment. Then she said, in a voice suggesting she was entrusting Lotte with an intimate secret: 'I picked up a conker. A large shiny conker. I always have it with me, as a memory of those days . . . when I was very happy, without realizing it.'

◆◆

Vienna. You will be safe in Vienna, Martin wrote. When Anna arrived her father-in-law was just packing his suitcases. 'I am going to Nuremberg,' he declared, 'the SS is inviting the parents to come and have a look.' He came back content after a few days: 'You need have no worries about Martin, he is having an excellent time. Order prevails, comradeship prevails, they've got brand-new kit. Everyone is friendly and polite.' 'You're telling me stories,' said Anna suspiciously. 'I swear to you, he is like a fish in water.' 'But he hates them, those Nazis.' 'You'll see for yourself, the wives will be invited soon.'

She received a travel permit; she set off in the last week of August for a fortnight. Bombing had not left much of Nuremberg, but the press hotel taken over by the SS was still standing and undamaged. Luxury suites had been reserved for the married couples – in the mornings the officers had gentle training, the rest of the day they could do what they wanted. The barracks too were an island of peace amid the chaos. Everything shone and glittered – respect prevailed, for people as well as things. Her father-in-law had not exaggerated: Martin, who put so much store by good manners, neatness and courtesy, had thoroughly come into his own there. They took advantage of the unexpected reunion, it was just like a honeymoon – the army leadership pampered its youngest scions. A bomb fell now and then, a small aberration that had long since ceased to surprise them. There was a mania for photographing each other: Martin, good-humoured, in his uniform – Anna in a cream suit constructed out of what had been a tennis outfit belonging to Frau von Garlitz.

The wives of the Baltic Sea adventure were all there. They enjoyed each day, each night that had been given to them, with fatalistic eagerness – except for one of them who confided to Anna in a desperate fit of crying that her parents had forbidden her to become pregnant by someone who might soon be dead. 'Every night I have to turn my back on him,' she sniffed. Anna, still fervently on the lookout for signs of pregnancy, gave her heart: 'If he were to die, it would still be a tremendous comfort if you had a child of his at least . . . but what are we talking about, the war really is almost over! Then they'll come home and we'll live together under one roof and . . .' she raised a finger laughingly, 'then it really will be war, Liebchen.'

Martin's concern for her welfare sometimes took grotesque forms. One morning the women met in the swimming pool. One of them came rushing over while Anna was floating on her back. 'Get out, get out, a column of officers is coming.' They heaved their wet bodies hastily into the dry and fled to the lockers. Anna looked round with astonishment and drifted on, relaxed, without paying attention to the distant singing that was fast getting louder. Only when the officers were on the point of diving in did she sense that perhaps her presence in the water might be unwelcome. She swam to the side with languid strokes. In a decent black swimsuit that definitely covered her ample figure but did not conceal it, she walked between the officers to the lockers. As she passed she saw the pursed lips and furious expression on Martin's face. That afternoon he erupted. How did she happen to be the only woman in a swimsuit on show to all those men. She shrugged her shoulders. 'Simple. I was swimming.' He shook his head, deeply offended. 'My wife . . . among all those chaps.' 'But the swimming pool is for everyone,' she laughed innocently. 'My wife doesn't do such a thing.' 'Seemingly she does.' Their ideas about decency were irreconcilable. 'I won't have them making jokes about you, I know them.' She was oppressed by it. 'If you go on like that I'll leave you,' she blurted out to shut him up. He was so badly shocked and in such an endearing way that she flew to his neck, from regret and empathy. It was stupid to squabble about inanities. Time was pressing.

She awoke shaky and teeth chattering on the last night. Martin, who responded to her utterances in his sleep too, opened his eyes and held her. 'You're frightened...' His voice was dark from sleep. She laid her head on his chest. 'I don't know what's the matter.' He pulled her tightly to him. 'We must talk about it,' he said calmly, 'I think this is the moment. Listen. Millions are dying in this rotten war, up to now I have had a lucky escape. Who can guarantee that will work until the end? Why, so many have died, why not me? For me it will not be bad to die, it happens very quickly, don't you worry. The only thing that will be bad for me is that then I won't be able to help you any more. I know what will happen to you, I know exactly. You are as delicate as porcelain, but no one knows it. You always play the strong one and the sturdy one, but in reality you are emotional and vulnerable and you need me. But you must live even if I am not there. Promise me one thing: don't put an end to it. I won't look at you any more if you commit suicide! I won't salute you any more!'

There was silence in the room apart from the beating of his heart in her ear. It was out of the question that the beating could stop from one moment to the next – that a connection could exist between the things he alluded to and the precious beating of this heart and this warm breathing body which belonged not only to the army but to her and him too. The well-being of that body was so closely tied to that of her own that she did not want to hear what he was saying and yet it was engraved on her memory, word by word.

'Nor do I want you to stay in sackcloth and ashes for the rest of your life. Even if I am dead I want to have a beautiful wife. Will you promise me that? I'll tell you what you should do. You will only bear it by helping others who are worse off than yourself. Go and work in a military hospital or something like that, only then will you survive, I know you...' Instead of seeking comfort and courage from her for the possibility that he would die just before the peace, he was giving her a manual for the rest of her life, with serenity. Defence replaced her anxiety and eventually an immense calm – he had spun a cocoon of safety and invulnerability around her where there was a peaceful, reliable tranquillity – where life and death flowed naturally into each other. They fell asleep entwined; entwined they woke in the morning.

It was brilliant weather. Martin had never looked so well. Tanned, alert, full of good spirits. Anna leaned out of the window of the train that was about to move. He ran alongside the train and waved. 'Auf Wiedersehen until Vienna, this bloody hell will soon end anyway!' he cried cheerfully. She stiffened – such a tone of optimism was unforgivable from the mouth of an SS officer. And it resonated along the platform too! Anna narrowed her eyes, anxiously expecting that they would pick him up. But he was still standing there and waving and no one bothered him.

Vienna was not that safe. In order to cut off the German troops' retreat from the Balkans the Americans were dropping a wide swathe of bombs that ran right through Vienna. Because they did not dare fly over the Alps at night, they only flew during the day. The windows of the new apartment were shattered. Anna fixed them with cardboard. The alarm sounded. She ran to the nearest shelter. On the way she saw an old woman hiding in a porch. 'What are you doing here?' Anna yelled, dragging her along with one arm. 'Come, hurry into the shelter.' It was a crush inside. 'Get up,' she said to a boy, 'I've got an old lady here.' The warden of the block, responsible for citizen's safety during attacks, rushed over to her, 'What possessed you?' 'How do you mean?' asked Anna, 'what have I done?' 'Do you know who you've got with you?' She looked at the woman who was sitting huddled up, like a bird in winter. 'It makes no difference to me, obviously, an old woman.' 'A half-Jew!' he barked. 'Well and...' she shrugged her shoulders, 'there's a dog over there, can't a poor old woman be allowed in?' She was stared at with anxious eyes from all around; what recklessness to challenge the warden of the block. He tensed his jaw muscles. She looked at him defiantly. He lowered his eyes and slunk off to another corner of the shelter, as though his presence were urgently required there.

The whole month she waited in vain for a letter from Martin. She wrote to him at the beginning of October. 'I am sitting here with a pen in my hand but I have the feeling I am talking into the void.' She bought a bunch of asters to comfort herself. She was climbing the stairs to her apartment with the flowers in hand when she met the neighbour half-way who usually greeted her noisily with a rolling Viennese 'r', but now he shyly quickened his pace. She opened the door. To her surprise her father-in-law was waiting for her in the living-room. 'No post again,' she sighed with a glance at the empty table. 'Yes,' he said, pointing to the sideboard with his head, ' there is post.'

A parcel. She leaned over it and read: Nachlass-sache – estate matters. Wildly she tore it open. On top there was an envelope, she ripped the letter out. 'Dear Frau Grosalie ... As Company Commander it is my duty to inform you of the heroic death of your husband...' Feverishly she read on. '... In the Eifel ... grenade explosion...' The letter ended with, 'In the belief that there will be ultimate victory and that this war is justified, I remain ... Heil Hitler! SS-Hauptsturmführer, Company Commander...' The asters fell to the ground. 'It's not true,' she contradicted the contents of the letter in a quiet voice. She began to walk about, round the table, around her father-in-law, faster and more rebelliously, calling out 'not true, not true...' as though a ritualistic denial of reality could undo the facts. Catatonically she kept repeating the same words until her father-in-law managed to force her onto the sofa. Above hung a framed portrait of Martin; she lifted it off the wall. With the photograph in her lap she rocked back and forth. What a tasteless paradox – the unbearable would have to be borne in some way or other. She glided about the apartment, wanted to put on something dark, saw a repellent stranger in the mirror – the curls of her perm had disappeared instantly. Look at that, her hair was already dying, the rest would from now on.

She hadn't promised him that she would eat! For days she did not eat, drink, sleep or cry. At night she wandered about among the shattered apartment blocks as though she were looking for something among them. All she wanted was to be there where he was, nothing else. Her restrained father-in-law, who was staying at the apartment with her on his wife's instructions, tried to see her behaviour as a normal phase in the mourning process. He brought her a long widow's veil for the requiem mass at the Karlskirche. Where she had advanced down the aisle in a long white veil two years before she now walked vacantly in a black one. 'The German woman doesn't shed a tear...' she heard being whispered in the pews. She allowed the sounds of the requiem to come over her like a deaf mute.

After a week her father-in-law gave up his chaperoning. Because he alone had not been able to end the hunger strike he made her promise to come over to his home that Sunday, in the hope that his wife could persuade her to eat something. Hesitantly she went outside. The world was unmoved by his death; there was no shadow of him even in his own city. She was alone, in a strange city, it was war – those were the facts. In that constellation there was no place for her, just as there was no place for the facts in her life. She sleepwalked into the centre, along the Ring, the glittering Ring, past the theatre, the Hofburg, the opera. She followed her own footsteps towards the Karlskirche in a vague need for religious support, but mainly in the desperate hope that He would give her a sign, an affirmation of His ubiquity – a proof of His existence. She could barely push the heavy door open. The Sunday mass had just started. The voice of the pastor reverberated in the dome. The baroque gold trembled with it. At first she was in no state to let the content mean anything to her. Weakened by the fast, she slid down somewhere in a pew. Eventually, within the walls of the mother church, trusted since her youth, she was threatening to doze off, a result of the persistent lack of sleep. But suddenly she jerked out of her slumber. 'Every death at the front...' warned the voice, 'and every devastated home here is a punishment for our sins...' A punishment? How did he get that into his head, the idiot! This was the most insincere, the cruellest message she had ever received from the church. In protest she stood up. She managed to walk past the rows to the back. Despite her weakness she had just enough strength to close the heavy door with an ostentatious bang. Still shaking with rage she descended the steps. In a reflex she looked round: on either side there was still an angel, each carrying its own cross and staring ignorantly ahead over the world.

And further she went. The Hitler Youth was marching enthusiastically across the Ring with brand-new flags. Anna was shuffling past in her black veil. One of the boys barred her way. 'Heil Hitler!' She stared ahead silently. 'Can't you salute the flag?' he snarled. He was at least a head taller than her, she tapped him on his chest. 'I'll say one thing to you. My husband has just died for that very same flag.' She brushed him aside and continued on her way. Exhausting himself with apologies he came after her. Anna did not look up or round; she had reached a state of collapse that made her immune to someone else's shame.

She did not know how she got to her parents-in-law's house. As the door opened she slumped onto the threshold. All that time she had been on the point of fainting but her organism had waited decently for a suitable moment. They laid her on the divan. In her muzzy twilight state she could hear arguing in the room next door. 'You haven't taken enough care of her...' sounded her mother-in-law's voice. 'You promised Martin you would take care of her and now she collapses in our hands.' Anna threatened to faint again. A pot of strong coffee was made. A cup with real coffee made from coffee beans was moved back and forth under her nose. Anna herself did not react. It was primitive life spirits that forced her to open her mouth and take a swallow, provoked by the irresistible stimulus. Similarly she ate a piece of cake mechanically. In this way the suicidal idea was driven away very prosaically with coffee and cake, in order to make room for being merely unhappy. That she still knew; she had been familiar with it for years.

Then the second part of the promise had to be kept. A black Mercedes with the SS emblem on it drew up in front of the cardboard-patched apartment where she continued her marriage on her own. The SS took good care of its people. The Head of the SS and Chief of Police in the Danube region welfare board came to give the widow his condolences. He was friendly, knew faultlessly how to find the right words of comfort for which she had gone to the Karlskirche in vain, asked if there was anything he could do. 'I would very much like to work in a military hospital,' said Anna in a flat tone of voice, 'I promised him. But in my employment papers it says "Housekeeper" so I'll never be able to get a nursing position.' 'Come to the office and we'll give you an official testimonial,' he promised, shaking her hand sympathetically.

After the visit by the high-up, which had been observed by all those living around Anna, she was no longer 'that German' but 'the SS aunt'. The more the bombing increased in severity and Hitler lost further ground, the more openly she was stigmatized. That's how it is, she consoled herself, as long as it's going well they cry Hosanna, when it goes the other way: crucify him. She reported to the employment office. The necessary document was already waiting for her. 'Frau Grosalie is an orphan and childless and now that her husband has been killed she would like to be taken on as a sister in the Red Cross. I request you to issue a dispensation and to put nothing in the way of her commencing work with the German Red Cross. Oberscharführer Fleitmann.'

❦

At the Chalet du Parc, where they had walked from the Thermal Institute, a woman made of stone stood ringed by soldiers, trying to fend off a bayonet. There was no inscription, not even a list of names. Anna and Lotte stopped, each sheltering inside their upturned collars.

'Where was ... Martin buried in fact?'

'In Gerolstein in a military cemetery. But first in ...'

'But didn't they bring him home?'

'Are you crazy? He was ripped to pieces by an artillery grenade in the Eifel. They gathered him up and put him in the ground. Did you think they brought the dead home in 1944? There were far too many of them! In Russia, France, the Ardennes, they lay all over the place, the torsos here, the legs there. Come off it, it's a wonder they even mentioned where he was.'

Lotte was hurt and silent. Anna adopted a tone towards her as though she were stupid, as though she, Anna, had exclusive rights over the war because her husband had been killed.

'He had seen it all coming,' said Anna thoughtfully, 'that night in Nuremberg. Instead of being frightened of death, because he was the one that was going to die – he was concerned about me. A boy of twenty-six, so mature and well balanced, as though he had achieved the inner development of a whole life at an accelerated pace. He knew it all, that night.'

9

The younger children, a risk factor, had been well tutored; as well
as the four times table they had learned never to speak about it
under any circumstances whatsoever. If they brought a school
friend home unexpectedly then they called out from the wood:
'Mum, isn't it nice, Pete is with me!' In other words: get them all
upstairs. The war had made them suspicious and inventive. Bart
had been accosted in the wood by the gardener's wife from the
next-door property. 'Tell me, who is that woman at your place
who sits at the sewing machine?' He understood immediately that
she must have seen Mrs Meyer who did sewing and mending from
time to time. 'I went to borrow sugar from your mother but there
was no one there, only that woman in the dining-room.' 'Oh,' he
improvised casually, 'that is one of my aunts, a sister of my mother,
who sometimes does some sewing for us.'

Lotte's mother was back in charge. She baked potato cakes and
enormous loaves. The people in hiding took it in turns to grind
grain in the coffee mill. Meanwhile she rushed upstairs to settle a
dispute that had arisen about whist. Her husband, who played it
fanatically, was not a good loser. Mrs Meyer cheated if she was
driven to it. The Frinkels were immersed in an English correspondence course in preparation for their emigration to America as
soon as the war was over. As soon as the war was over! A lofty
phrase, a toast, a hopeful expectation, now that the Allies were in
France and no one any longer looked up at the English bombers
daily flying east in formation – everyone was agreed that the peace,
alas, could only be achieved by means of destruction. Meanwhile
two more people arrived to come into hiding. A saboteur who
worked at the post office and read all the letters for the Security

Service had discovered that Sammy Goldschmidt and his wife's address in hiding had been betrayed. They had to be taken somewhere else at once. Without wasting words, two beds were added and everyone shoved up a bit.

Two large brooms were slowly coming closer, one from the east, one from the south. Brooms with long bristles that were sweeping the Germans up into a heap, like dust. It was awaited impatiently all round. On Monday evening, 4 September, Radio Orange reported: 'According to Dutch government sources the Allied armies have reached Breda.' The people in hiding hugged each other, laughing and crying; the master of the house fetched a bottle of gin out of his war supplies. But some days later the report was already being weakened. The Allies had only liberated a vulnerable corridor crossing through Brabant. They were marching north through this groove. A number of bridges over the rivers had been taken in a lightning raid, but at the bridge over the Rhine outside Arnhem it had failed. The onward march had been brought to a standstill. Lotte's father had to withdraw a couple of premature flags.

In the pale blue studio Lotte allowed herself to interpret everything in terms of millimetres of thickness; Ernst Goudriaan took off his glasses and brought his face close to the wood – he seemed to be involved in a secret conspiracy with the emerging violin. He forgot to put his glasses back on as he embraced her clumsily amid the shavings and a pot of bone glue, which fell on the floor and immediately began to spread a sickly rotting smell. Perhaps it was love, perhaps they used each other as an antidote to the war that put his nervous system and her conscience too much to the test. Unconsciously he was banishing her tarnished origins from her, releasing her from her earliest memories that had to do with a previous life. *Tabula rasa* – with him, through him, she was becoming undilutedly Dutch.

In broad daylight they were walking in the wood; he was coolly tempting fate with her at his side. They rested on a fallen oak.

Over his shoulder he discovered a beefsteak fungus on one of the heavy branches, a tongue-shaped red-brown piece attached to the bark – he loosened it carefully. That evening Lotte fried it quickly on both sides watching that the blood did not run out. The fungus appeared at table like a *pièce de résistance*; everyone was served a portion of this gift from the gods, because everyone was always hungry.

The food shortages were becoming dire. They took it in turns to walk to the soup kitchen in the village, lugging back a churn of watery cabbage and potato stew. In response to the rumour that geese could be bought in Barneveld, Lotte and Koen, who still couldn't stay at home, went over on their bicycles. Just before Amersfoort they came across a caravan of evacuees from Arnhem including two little girls who were stumbling along with a cat on a rope. Further on they swerved into the verge, ahead of a bus full of Blitzmädel dashing past at full speed. 'Bats,' said Koen scornfully, 'to hell with those bitches.' They cycled on in the stink left behind by the bus. It began to rain. An aeroplane skimmed so low over the road that the birds flew out of the trees in terror. A second later they were startled by an enormous bang – right in front of their eyes, in the distance, the bus exploded. A column of fire shot up, the smoke evaporated into the rain clouds. Koen, astonished that his wish had been fulfilled so rapidly, stared at the scene open-mouthed, hesitating whether to think it was great or terrifying. Lotte, on impulse, in a dumb reflex that she was not responsible for, thought of Anna. They had still been there a minute ago, they had whizzed past in bird flight in their spotless grey uniforms – the war was visible in a bizarre manner here, between the meadows in the drizzle. Imagine that Anna had been in that bus, then she would have just lost a sister. Then she was actually, definitely free now. The thought did not arouse a single feeling in her. Anna had already become so blurred into a shadow figure that it was all the same to her whether she went up in smoke right in front of her nose or not. Yet she cycled on with a slight reluctance, until an evacuee stopped them and told them breathlessly that the station at Amersfoort had been bombed and all the transport trains were ablaze. It was no place to cycle through, for a goose. They heaved their bicycles over the ditch into the meadow and went round the town in a semi-circle, from where the wind carried apocalyptic sounds. They found their goose. With the goose and a bag of wood shavings, in which fresh eggs were packed a safe distance from each other, they returned home via a short cut.

There was a shortage of flour. Sara Frinkel remembered a gentleman farmer in the vicinity of Deventer, before the war a vigorous admirer of Max's antics on the violin. She volunteered to make the journey herself: nothing could happen to her, she had an impeccable identity card in the name of an Aryan seamstress from Arnhem. She dismissed Lotte's mother's objections: 'He won't give you anything without me.' On a wet autumn day Sara and Jet set off for Deventer by train armed with two empty sacks and Bart's old pram. Max Frinkel's fame had not yet faded: they left the farm with full stomachs and an overflowing pram. On the way back they found shelter for the night in a stately manor house on the IJsselkade in Deventer. The next day another address flashed into Sara's mind. She was becoming ambitious: the one time she had left her hiding place she wanted to come back laden with provisions – there was still room in the bags. They left the pram behind under supervision and walked out of the town. There had been a storm in the night; the road was strewn with broken branches. Autumn rain assaulted their faces. A German police van stopped half-way – the window was wound down. 'Where are you going?' Daringly Sara named the village. 'Get in,' invited the driver jovially. 'Two lovely women in this beastly weather, that's not on.' They got in the front between the driver and an officer with a tight, tense face. They drove on in silence. Although the driver needed all his attention to keep the van on the road as it was being buffeted by the wind, he smiled roguishly at them in between. The other cast furtive looks to the side and discovered one of the famous noses of the Rockanje family, the hallmark of authenticity. 'You are a Jewess,' he cried, shocked. 'Stop ... stop ...!' The driver braked. Trembling, Jet took her identity card out of an inner pocket to show it. He was not at all satisfied with its innocent contents. 'Nevertheless you are a Jewess,' he said stubbornly. 'Come now,' said Sara in High German, 'if she is a Jewess then I certainly must be one.' 'Let them be,' said the driver. The rain beating on the roof created an intimate, oppressive atmosphere in the cab. 'But she is a Jew...' droned the other, 'a child can see that.' He threw the door open in anger because he could not prove anything: 'Get out, both.' 'You'd better get off,' said the driver, giving them a defeated look. They did not know how to get out of the van fast enough. When it had disappeared behind a mist of raindrops they fell into each other's arms. The rain streamed down, but they did not feel it, wet as they were with anxious sweat. The *élan* for filling the bags had passed. They now had to conserve their strength for the journey home the next day with a laden pram.

But it did not turn out like that. That night the town was bombed. They fell into a shelter and waited, crammed together in the semi-humid darkness. At the moment when the attack seemed to become more intense and the floor and walls were shuddering so violently that they no longer knew what was up or down, left or right, Jet began to scream incredulously, indignantly. 'The whole shambles is coming down like this all at once...' She went on ranting and raving, slumped, her hands over her ears. The fear gave her voice a volume that exceeded the din of the air raid. Sara tried to calm her in vain. Hours later she was still on the verge of a breakdown – rigid and unapproachable, she crouched on the floor, only prepared to leave the shelter if she could go home on the first train. 'And what about the pram then...?' said Sara. Jet looked at her witheringly.

They could only think in terms of food. A pram full of flour, that was so many loaves, which so many people could eat for so many days. This simple logic drove Lotte to Deventer, where Sara had left the pram behind with a bleeding heart. She went on a man's bicycle without tyres but with panniers, oversized lace-up shoes from Ernst Goudriaan on her feet over a pair of worn-out socks held together by Mrs Meyer's home efforts. In Deventer she loaded the contents of the pram into the panniers. The big barrier was the bridge over the IJssel. First she went without the bicycle to take the pulse. There was a wooden building at the entrance where WA men were inspecting the traffic; half-way along was a shelter where a German sentry went through things once more. He noticed her and winked. 'You want to bring food across the bridge?' he said softly. 'If possible,' she whispered. She would not be the first he had helped, he told her. He had thought up a system to lead people unseen past the Hollanders who stole everything edible. The bridge consisted of two parts, one for motorized vehicles and one for pedestrians. Between the two was a high wall, interrupted half-way along by his sentry box. If she navigated through the ruins of the Sperr district with the laden bicycle and, as she walked via the pedestrian part, ducked towards the back of his sentry box, he would take the sacks of flour from her. Then she would have to walk back with the empty panniers and go past the Hollanders on the official road. Finally he would load the bags up again. She took his advice. They ordered her to go inside the Dutch post with the bicycle and all – a promised land of confiscated potatoes, bread, butter, cheese, bacon. The sentry peeked into her empty panniers, saw from her passport that she was far from home and said cheerfully: 'We'll give you some bread to take with you.' He took a loaf from an enormous pile and shoved it in her pannier. She could continue. Wheeling the bicycle she approached the German sentry. A squadron of Spitfires swerved over the bridge like a storm out of nowhere. 'To the wall, quick...!' she heard shouted in German. She threw down her bicycle and pressed herself against the dividing wall. The bridge came under heavy fire, it groaned right through the infernal racket. From the corner of her eye she saw that one of her sacks had been hit; the grain was beginning to flow out like a column of ants. Her breath caught: as the shells flew all about the German crawled towards it to stop up the hole with a rag, as carefully as though he were dressing a wounded soldier. The Spitfires circled over the bridge once more then disappeared leaving a gloomy silence behind. Beneath the bridge the IJssel flowed on impassively. Crumpled, Lotte struggled to her feet. She was still alive and everything was going on as usual. The German heaved the grain over into the panniers. His generosity so confused her that she thanked him in his own language. 'You remind me of my wife,' he said, melancholy. 'We have two little children. I am looking forward to the end of the war with longing and fear. Hamburg has been bombed heavily. I don't know if they are still alive...'

The grain, the grain ... only the grain mattered. She set off on her journey. On the road from Apeldoorn to Amersfoort the broad-leafed trees flamed orange and yellow between the permanent green of the pines. The sun was low and cast a sharp, uncompromising light on the colourless pedestrians wrapped up in old coats who were trudging along the road with anything that could be ridden, exhausted, hungry and continuously on their guard, fearing that at the very last moment they could still be deprived of the meagre supplies they had obtained in exchange for a ring or a brooch that had been their great grandmother's. Lotte walked among them and lugged her spoils of war with her. Two men were stumbling just in front of her; the contrast between them and the autumn colours on either side of the road was striking – they looked as though they had come out of damp dungeons and had not seen daylight in years. Their coats seemed mouldy, their hands and feet were wrapped in filthy bandages. The moment she caught up with them a deafening tumult broke out. The shadows of bombers slid over them, explosions sounded behind the copse. German soldiers appeared out of the crêpe-paper shrubs. The two men looked around bewildered. 'Come, help me push,' yelled Lotte to give them an alibi in case there was a sudden checkpoint. 'Push!' They seized the handlebars, the luggage rack. Something exploded nearby; the three of them fled into the ditch, dived into a manhole. Gradually they realized that the railway line, parallel to the road, and soldiers' transports were the target. Hidden in the earth, a grey film over their thin faces, in the pandemonium around them, in fits and starts the men told the story of their flight from Germany. As prisoners of war sent to work in a steel factory, at morning roll-call they had to jump up high like circus artistes because the guards, for amusement, whipped them under their feet. Feet that were hurt became ulcerated; the ulcers did not heal because of the chronic malnutrition. When the factory was bombed they fled in the chaos through the woods at night to the west – sleeping during the day. Their families lived in The Hague; they doubted whether they would get to them, the soles of their feet were festering away, their strength was exhausted by persistent delirium from hunger.

It grew quieter around them, except for the soft crackling and hissing of burning trains. The rumble of bombers died away; they disappeared over the horizon like angry insects and left an empty road behind, which soon became populated again with those who had to continue. In a village Lotte exchanged some grain for rye bread in the hope of bolstering the escapees' fortitude a little. Although they were slowing her down, she did not dare leave them to their fate. 'Let's sit down...' wailed one of them. Lotte was unrelenting, anxious that he would never get up again. 'Keep going ... keep going.' 'It's finished,' he said, three kilometres further on, 'I can't any more...' 'Just a bit ... just a bit ... you're almost there.' It was already dark; they were approaching Amersfoort. Lotte showed them the way to the hospital – it was known that the gates were always open for everyone. 'They will certainly take you in there.' But they held on tight to their talisman. 'Don't leave us alone,' they pleaded, 'we will be picked up without you.' She shook her head. 'I can't go with you, with all that grain.' The grain, the grain ... she had lost so much time already, she had to get out of the town with the grain before the curfew.

Hastily she disappeared out of their sight with her top-heavy bicycle. She quickened her pace. It was one of those same evenings, without moon, without clouds, ruled by an absolute blackness made even stronger by the window black-outs. The suspicion that she was in the process of getting lost crept up on her. A man passed her with a cart behind his bicycle. She spoke to him. Yes, she was on the right road, but why didn't she put her things in his cart? Then she wouldn't have to push so hard. He had a lamp. He could accompany her for a bit. She went along with his offer gratefully. He cycled at walking pace with her; nothing was said. What was there to talk about after curfew to an invisible stranger? All of a sudden, next to him, she became aware of an acceleration in his movements – her guide gained speed; cold-bloodedly he cycled away from the silent get-together. He disappeared into the darkness, swerving like a will-o'-the-wisp in a marsh. All she heard was the dumb mechanism of her heart pumping. An emphatic absence of sound prevailed outside. Now the anxiety got to her. On the bridge over the IJssel it had not succeeded, nor in the bombing of the railway – it had bided its time quietly. She began to scream. In the pitch blackness intended for no one she screamed straight through the curfew. The volume, with which she had once rocked the water-tower to its foundations, gave her voice an exceptional carrying power. A police surveillance car arrived; a policeman gripped her by the upper arms to calm her. She gave her account in fragments. He pushed her into the car and began the pursuit; the headlights bored a tunnel into the darkness. Beyond emotion, a strange apathy came over her; she did not care whether they caught him; the once clearly delineated concept of friend or foe had become blurred, the undertaking had got out of hand, it was no longer her affair, others seemed to have taken it over. He was caught, forced to stop, scolded. Perhaps he had twelve starving children waiting for him at home for the proceeds of the nocturnal raid. She looked uninterestedly at the figures in the light of the headlamps. The grain was handed over for the umpteenth time – it would get worn away.

They had settled in the Chalet du Parc. Once again they ducked behind a menu card; they did themselves proud. Their arthritis cure was mainly happening within the privacy of the bath house, the restaurants, pâtisseries and cafés because it was January and they wanted the heat of the peat baths to last the whole day – but chiefly because it was easier to talk over a meal, a pastry, a cup of coffee as lightning conductor.

'Well...' Lotte contemplated, 'if you hadn't ransacked our country such scenes would not have happened.'

'We had our rationing too...'said Anna weakly.

Lotte raised her eyebrows. 'You were the storehouse of Europe.'

Affronted, Anna let the menu drop. 'The French took revenge after the war. They starved us in the French zone.'

'Ach...' Lotte sighed. Always that explaining away. Always that: but we didn't have it easy either.

'What are you having?' said Anna. She had got an appetite from all those stories about shortages.

'I think...' Lotte hesitated, 'an Entrecôte Marchand de Vin ... or shall I have a Truite à la Meunière...?'

❦

Anna got her military hospital. It was run by nuns; she learned fast, in her eagerness not to disappoint Martin ... She was given responsibility for two wards, one for soldiers and one for officers – all had lost limbs at the ever-shrinking front. The alarm went at ten o'clock every morning: enemy aircraft on the way! The wounded had to be rushed to the shelters on special stretchers with wheels on one side and two handles on the other. Wooden rails had been fixed to the stairs. 'Sister Anna, hurry up!' cried one of the nuns. Needless to say, Anna was already running half-way down the stairs to the hairpin bend, a precarious moment for the amputees. Whipped on by the sirens, she hurried back and forth until the last patient had been taken to safety; as the first bombs fell she rushed back up to fetch their prostheses. No assistance could be expected from the nuns, they were completely preoccupied with getting the monstrance to safety. They prayed and sang and carried the Blessed Lord to a small improvised chapel so that he would not be hit by the bombs. Anna had no time to take a breather. The daily programme continued with energetic relentlessness despite the bombing: washing, distributing medicines, cleaning bandages. High and dry in the sky her beloved puppet-master could see his suspicions confirmed. The wounded were concerned – clearly seeing that Anna, driven by a motivation that was not of this earth, scarcely managed to eat or sleep. One day those who could move a little with the aid of their prostheses knocked together a regal couch for her made of coats, jumpers and pillows in a corner of the shelter. She allowed herself to be driven there under protest, thermometer still in hand – to fall instantly into a bottomless sleep, after they had put a blanket over her with brotherly tenderness.

In another ward there was a patient with an inoperable splinter close to his heart. He could not move or be moved. He simply had to wait for the bombing raids in his hospital bed, in complete tranquillity – excitement was a greater threat to his life than a bomb. The sisters took it in turns to watch over him together with his doctor. So Anna regularly sat there by his bed next to the window like a living target and chatted gently about innocent subjects. Opposite her on the other side of the bed the overworked doctor sat wearing an anti-aircraft helmet. Her idle chatter did not often misfire on him either. She saw his eyelids, his head, slowly droop. Before he dozed off he was still sufficiently conscious to remove the helmet from his head and put it in his lap. If a bomb fell close by them he sat up and put the helmet on in a reflex, and then it began all over again. Not unaware of this slapstick effect, Anna suppressed her laughter with difficulty, in the interests of the splinter.

While looking for one of the nuns, she lost her way in the hospital's building complex. She opened a random door that seemed to be the way in to a large room, and froze on the threshold. She could barely control the impulse to run away again immediately, through the labyrinth of corridors outside. It was a ward without beds – soldiers missing all their limbs were lying on the floor. The wounds had healed. Their bodies had been wrapped in leather so that they could roll over the floor like babies. The skimming autumn sunlight slid over what was left of them. All they could do was talk and roll. Anna shut the door abruptly. This was forbidden territory. She had seen something that did not exist – the other side of military grandeur, of sabre rattling and insignias, of heroic words. Which soldier going off to war was warned that this too, as well as the hero's death, could be his hinterland?

In the evenings she walked home through darkened streets, a journey full of surprises. The damage done during the day was continually altering the familiar look of the city. With difficulty she pushed her front door open – two window panes had come out again, an icy autumnal wind had blown the Feldpost letters she had been rereading the previous evening around the apartment. She felt her way to the chest of drawers to light a candle, she reached into a hole and almost lost her balance. The chest of drawers was lying down below on the street. A day later a woman collapsed before her eyes at the entrance to the staircase. Anna recognized the pale face. After Martin's death the woman had given her condolences on the staircase. 'I think it is so hard for you,' she had whispered with a bowed head, 'you probably think that the worst thing of all has happened to you, but there is something worse.' She had run up to the top apartment in tears, leaving Anna behind with her cryptic prediction in riddles. Anna brought her round with a wet cloth. 'I'll murder them!' cried the woman, getting up. 'Gently, gently . . .' soothed Anna. 'I'll know how to find them when the war is over, I shall drink their blood, I swear it,' the woman raved. The outburst brought some colour to her cheeks. Anna held her by the shoulders: 'What's the matter then . . . ?' Immediately slumping into a position of resignation, the woman confided to Anna in a dull voice her husband's unexpected arrest some months ago. He had been picked up while leaving his daughter's watch for repair with an old acquaintance who had a watch shop. The daughter was a nurse and what is more she wore the brown uniform with sincere conviction. Unaware that the watchmaker was suspected of communist activities, her husband had been wrongly taken to be one of them. Since then he had been in prison under sentence of death, chained up, unable to move. Water was dripped on to his head every minute, day and night. The thought of it was driving her mad. 'But they have really made a terrible mistake!' Anna cried indignantly. That an innocent had been convicted, that they had acted so unfairly, she could not understand, with her sense of justice and her orderly efficient approach, but on top of it all she immediately felt the urge to take action because it was so unacceptable that they could let the poor devil die an endlessly slow martyr's death in a cunning way that could only have been conceived by a madman. She put an arm round the woman. 'Leave it to me . . .' she said grimly.

In the old parliament building of the former Habsburg monarchy, which had become the administrative headquarters of the Ostmark under the Third Reich, the Gauleiter resided. Anna was in one of her tempers. She marched there, up the stairs, into the historic buildings that were evidence of superabundant riches, through a long columned corridor with every ten metres motionless SS soldiers like stuffed corpses with rifles. Although no one ever came into this sanctuary uninvited they were too dumbfounded by the appearance of a hurtling Red Cross sister to intervene. Anna was not troubled by anxiety or modesty. The ring of her footsteps on the marble floor sounded like a confirmation of her righteousness. At a crossing in the corridors she became confused for a moment. Eventually a sentry barred her way. 'Where do you wish to go?' 'To the Gauleiter.' 'Why?' 'I want to see the Gauleiter!' Two others came over; they looked at each other quizzically. What was a hysterical hospital sister doing here? 'My husband has just been killed serving with the Waffen-SS,' haughtily she held the letter of condolence from the Obersturmführer under their noses. They had no reply to that. They escorted her to the required place as though she were a diplomat.

In her fantasy the Gauleiter had acquired monstrous proportions. In reality he sat in a gaudy room that must once have been the emperor's study, behind an immense desk: a kind-hearted old man with a long beard – a sort of Santa Claus. Surprised, he gave her an encouraging nod. After taking a deep breath she cast the scandalous error at his feet. 'I know those people, they are Nazis, their daughter is a brown sister! The Führer would not stand for such a thing! He does not know that an error has been made here, someone must inform him!' The Gauleiter nodded like a weary grandfather who can refuse his granddaughter nothing. 'Do me a favour,' he said slowly. 'Go home and see that the wife writes a letter requesting mercy. And bring the letter to me personally.'

The fruit of Anna's efforts was the return home, fourteen days later, of a man who could only whisper about the forms of entertainment they had thought up for him in advance of his execution. He had lost the knack of eating, each movement was painful and exhausting. He slid into his bed with the last of his strength and stayed there, too weak to live or die. His wife had to go to work during the day. That was why she was not there at the end of March when a bomb fell on the block and blasted a hole ten metres wide. When Anna came home all she could see instead of her flat was the flats behind it. There was a heap of rubble up to the supposed first floor – beneath it they had found the one sentenced to death, a neighbour explained. 'God, you are a sadist...' cried Anna. The wind whispered in her ear: Do you still believe in justice, idiot? She clenched her teeth. She could not complain to the Gauleiter about this ... she had to look for a higher authority ... in more rarefied Gauen ...

That same wind also carried the smell of dried mud – the Russians were advancing. During a staff meeting the sisters heard that the hospital would have to be evacuated in two hours. A hospital ship was ready on the Danube; all the wounded had to be transported there. Anna crept out unseen to say goodbye to her father-in-law. She pressed the packet of Feldpost letters into his hand hastily; since the apartment had been bombed she had kept them in the air raid shelter in the military hospital, stuffed into two suitcases with her other paraphernalia. 'Please burn these,' she said hurriedly, 'otherwise they might yet be published in *Izvestia*.'

When she got back there was a line of buses at the entrance to the hospital. She had just finished helping the patients from her wards in and was going to sit at the front, flanked by her suitcases, when she was pulled out again by her apron. 'Wait a moment, sister, you can't do that!' Before she knew what was happening, the medicaments and medical history notes of all the wounded, numbering one hundred and sixty, were handed over to her, Anna, Red Cross sister *à l'improviste*, by the nuns who were staying behind. She was pushed with these into a bus containing seriously wounded men she did not know; it set off immediately. Hopefully her suitcases were travelling behind her in the other bus. The bus moved off at a cracking pace as though it wanted to shed the imminent deaths of its passengers – unfortunately it was forced to stop half-way there at a tunnel that was too low. Another bus was ordered. Meanwhile Anna unloaded the wounded with the driver and laid them on stretchers on the verge. It was getting dark – the Russians were coming – they stood there and waited and looked at the tunnel as though that was their last connection with the world of the living. Another bus, of more suitable dimensions, appeared in the darkness. The patients, chilled to the bone, were shoved inside it and it proceeded to the banks of the Danube.

One hundred and sixty wounded were laid in the damp grass. Hastily rustled-up orderlies carried them into the ship one by one over a narrow gangplank. Anna was buttonholed by a husband and wife couple drenched in the rain. 'The boy being carried in now is our son. He has a pistol on him. We are frightened he is going to do something to himself. He can't bear it that we are losing the war.' She promised them she would keep an eye on him and went to look for her suitcases. In the distance she heard her name being called in unison: 'Sister Anna from 3C, here we are!' In her ears it sounded like a *missa solemnis* whose passages were being carried in the wind in fragments – she ran towards the sound, criss-cross between the wounded, and found her own wounded, who had refused to go into the ship without her. They were sitting in a large circle with their prostheses on the grass and guarding her suitcases. Their sister, her patients – during the previous months a mutual craving for possessiveness had come into existence; they were a big family who would only board the ship together.

After doing their task the orderlies vanished, leaving Anna behind in an overloaded ship. To assist her in the care of the wounded, who lay round about in no particular system, she had five hastily recruited middle-class women, without training or nursing experience. They wore aprons and caps and were regarded as being endowed with a natural talent for the business of caring purely on account of being female. It became clear all too soon that their talents resided at another level, and that they had a completely different idea of their duties. Whenever she needed them to hand out the urine bottles, medicines, meals, Anna found them after a long search back in the arms of soldiers. They had been grass widows throughout the whole war; now they were making up for their loss under the charitable pretext that they were providing a divine medicine for the poor devils who had been wounded in the battle for the fatherland – perhaps even fatally: an extra *frisson*.

From sheer necessity Anna split herself into one hundred and sixty parts; the one changed bandages, the next assisted the emptying of the bowels, a third mopped the fever – all at the accelerated pace of a silent film. At night those fragments could not all get back together again, they continued as usual with their own activities. After two days she was stumbling about with eyes red from tiredness. No one noticed it except Herr Töpfer, a high-ranking SS officer from her own ward who had lost a leg on the Hungarian front. 'You will fall over,' he observed, pushing her into a chair, 'sit down.' Leaning on his crutch he looked around like a general; he raised his voice to address his officers: 'I say the following to you. Sister Anna cannot cope any more. She must have sleep. We need a couple of walking volunteers who can take over the duties from her. She has a list and she can tell you where the people are – it's a question of organization.' His audience nodded in agreement. 'Secondly,' continued Töpfer, 'there is a spare bed in my cabin. I am offering it to Sister Anna. If any one of you has any reservations I will gladly hear them now. Woe betide anyone who I only get to hear from tomorrow morning. I'll shoot him dead. Do you understand?'

He took her to the cabin and tucked her in tenderly. Anna slept instantly. When she woke the caring Töpfer was lying next to her; he had retreated to a corner and held on to the edge of the bed even as he slept, so that he would not roll onto her. He had given his own bed to a dying man who was hawking incomprehensible swear words.

The following evening they moored at Linz. The seminary stood like an impenetrable fortress in the rain, a colossal dark building, which was to be set up as an emergency hospital. When Herr Töpfer, who had limped up to it, supported by Anna, used the weapon of his voice, the door opened a crack. A fat sleepy man appeared in the doorway in silk pyjamas over which he had slipped a uniform tunic and looked at them with bad grace. Oh yes, the ship with the wounded ... he scratched his head ... but they would have to be deloused first, of course. 'Verdammtes Schwein!' cried Töpfer, beside himself at such ignorance and incompetence, 'Watch out that you don't have lice, we don't have them, we come from a tidy hospital. If you don't find us beds immediately...!' The man opened the double doors trembling.

Everything had been prepared inside: there were wooden platforms with sacks of straw in the former classrooms, large cavernous rooms. At least the wounded would be getting beds again. The ship departed immediately after unloading; the surrogate sisters went back with it, satisfied from overwork, leaving Anna alone as mother superior of the wounded. Everyone tried to sleep, including her, seated at a large table in the centre of the room with her head on her folded arms. Töpfer woke in the middle of the night. 'What are you doing here? You can leave us alone peacefully, everyone is sleeping! Go to bed!' 'But where is that bed . . . ?' Anna yawned. What? His blankets moved, he grasped his crutches and limped out of the room indignantly. Silk pyjamas was bawled out of bed: 'If you don't immediately . . .' 'Yes, yes, yes . . .' he cried nervously. He found a bed for her somewhere; it was still warm from whoever had to make room for her, but Anna did not ask herself any more questions of conscience.

They had both chosen trout – easily digested – with boiled potatoes. Lotte thought of Schubert's song 'Die Forelle' that she had once studied, and of the tragic ending: '. . . The little fish wriggled on it . . .' She associated the image of a powerless fish that only had a body and a head, floundering on the line, with the fourfold amputees in the Viennese hospital. 'It had never occurred to me,' she said, 'that anyone could lose all his limbs . . . Gruesome . . .'

Anna put her fork down. 'They were young men. I certainly asked myself what became of them. I've never read a word about them in a paper, a periodical, a book. Yet they were still alive! Where have they gone?'

They ate on in silence, each at the mercy of her own speculations.

'Your husband's letters from Poland, Russia, Normandy . . .' Lotte remarked, 'were they actually burnt?'

Anna sprang up. 'I could still kick myself . . . they would have been a lovely memento now, a document. Unfortunately my father-in-law bravely did what I asked him. Burned everything. It was the effect of the propaganda: when the Russians come they will take everything they fancy. Then if they find my letters, largely written in Russia, I reasoned, they would find them very interesting and print them in their communist newspaper. That's how we thought then.'

Lotte laughed ironically. 'As if they would have been interested in them! One soldier's life meant nothing to the Russians ... At any rate, a human life represented nothing under Stalin ...'

'Nevertheless we were still being brainwashed! Up to the end of the war. "The Führer would not stand for such a thing..." I said to the Gauleiter. Imagine it! In all sincerity. Although I had never marched behind him and just like everyone else I knew that he could not win the war, I was still so naïve I could not imagine that the innocent were being sentenced to death and martyred under his authority. End of 1944! God how naïve I was ...'

From pure anger she forgot to eat any more; her trout was threatening to get cold.

⬦⬦

This was the second atheist-Jewish Christmas they celebrated together. Everyone had lost weight; the stew from the soup kitchen had become so thin you could drink it. Lotte's father, who secretly supplied electricity to the doctor, the liquor merchant and befriended farmers, had come home with a perversely large piece of pork and a bottle of gin. His wife disappeared to the cooker with it and basted the meat simmering gently in the casserole. Lotte fetched the dinner service from the cupboard. Mrs Meyer came downstairs, alarmed by the distinctive smell of fricandeau with ground cloves. 'Er ... we're not allowed to eat that,' she said, looking peevishly into the pot. 'What would you rather be,' enquired the cook sensibly, 'a dead orthodox Jewess or a sinner alive and kicking?' Mrs Meyer capitulated, no match for such healthy opportunism.

The table was laid, the candles were lit, everyone drew up a chair. Lotte and Ernst were still in the kitchen peeling a second batch of potatoes boiled in their skins, when they heard the distant rumble of an aircraft that was approaching fast. They stiffened with the potato knives in their hands. A bang, as strong as a lightning strike, took the ground from under their feet and made the windows rattle in their frames. A bizarre change of air pressure beat them to the ground amid the scattering potatoes. 'We're going to die,' squealed Mrs Meyer's voice. The whole gathering fled from the dining-room with the fragile bay window into the walled-in kitchen. They crouched there – Mrs Meyer, in the idle hope that youth was immortal, hung round Eefje's neck, who bravely remained upright. Then it became absurdly quiet and they straightened up suspiciously one by one. In the dining-room they found Sara Frinkel who had meanwhile gone on with the dislo-cated Christmas meal on her own. She was eating with gusto. 'I didn't want my potatoes to get cold,' she uttered with her mouth full. All the windows had cracked; the glass hung like fine lace cur-tains. Sara pointed to the meadows with a piece of meat on her fork: 'I saw an enormous flash.' 'It sounded like a crashing air-craft...' said Bram. 'If the pilot has ejected ... we can expect a large-scale operation here...' suggested Ernst Goudriaan, with increasing panic in his eyes. He was still holding the potato knife in his hand as though he thought he could defend himself with it. He looked round in terror. 'The Jews ... the Jews ... must go upstairs...!' 'What "Jews",' cried Sammy Goldschmidt, offended, 'that's how it all started, they swept us all into one heap.' 'You're right, you're right...' Ernst raised his hands guiltily, 'but what ought I to say...?' '"Person in hiding",' said Sara carefully. 'After all, you yourself are person in hiding too.'

While they were disappearing behind the mirror upstairs – those who coincided with their mirror image neutralized them-selves and ceased to exist – Lotte's father went to take the pulse, as his job permitted him to leave the house after curfew. On going out he discovered the front door had vanished; he retrieved it undamaged in the meadow. The other members of the family had to create the illusion of an ordinary Christmas celebration in case there was going to be a house search. The plates of the people in hiding were taken away – they were sitting crestfallen behind the cold turnips; the candles flickered and dripped in the draught. A chilly wind blew through the curtains; now and then a piece of glass fell to the floor. They sat round the table like actors waiting for the curtain to rise. Lotte was aware that it was a long time since they had been by themselves – it seemed that they had forgotten how to be like that. Covertly she looked at her mother, who was still the linchpin. She was sitting bolt upright ... she still puffed her chest out against the wolf and kept her cubs from his jaws ... But the chestnut glow had disappeared from her pinned-up hair, even the tortoiseshell comb had dulled. Somewhere during the war she had begun to go grey and to abandon some of her invincibility. A strong gust of wind blew all the candles out. The door was thrown open, her father came in. 'They can all come down,' he said, 'it was a bomb. Where's the gin?' After he had knocked back the contents of his glass in one gulp he told them that a stray bomb had blown a deep crater in the lawn of a nearby eighteenth-century manor house. The neoclassical entrance porch had been rammed into the salon, pillars and all; the lady of the house, who had gone to stand by the window to see where the row was coming from, had been taken away screaming with her eyes full of glass.

Life narrowed down to survival – the increasingly frequent poaching expeditions inclined more and more to the demonic. Lotte and Jet, Marie and Lotte foraged about the tip of the province of North Holland from farm to farm like peddlers with linen, rings, strings of pearls, watches, brooches, light-headed with hunger. On the gate a placard said 'We don't give out water'. The dog was set on them. Somewhere people were threshing – uninvited onlookers waited patiently until a few grains fell by the wayside. A nasty polar wind raced across the frozen fields, the ice groaned in the ditches and canals. Near the Afsluitsdijk the road passed a German outpost. To comfort the hungry hordes who were stumbling by with the promise of a better world, a world of plenty, the officers had put the dining-table outside – ostentatiously they sat at their steaming plates piled high with vegetables and sausage, the buttons burst off their uniforms from the guzzling. Lotte looked at it with a dry mouth. By means of an intricate psychological manoeuvre she forged the inflamed feelings of hate into contempt, which was more bearable on an empty stomach.

There were generous farmers too, who gave food and drink to passers-by and laid out straw sacks in the stables. The most cynical stayed awake at night to rob their dozing companions; as a matter of course Lotte slept with her head on the jumper in which the jewels were wrapped. When they had already given up all hope on the way back, in the Beemster, their sacks were filled with potatoes by a farmer's wife who refused to accept an item in exchange. To return home with full bags was the only triumph on earth still worth achieving. In Amsterdam they crossed the IJ by the ferry – a thick chilly mist was hanging over the water. WA men turned up to search through the passengers' bags. Jet and Lotte made themselves small – depriving them of the potatoes would rob them of their souls as well. A boy of about eight was standing by the handrail; his worn-out trousers flapped round his legs. There was a resigned expression on the sharp old man's face beneath his cap. He had a cart, its load covered by a piece of sailcloth, yet the approaching inspection seemed to leave him cold. He was staring out over the IJ into the mist; screeching seagulls were emerging out of it. He saw no reason to turn as the two uniforms came up to him decisively. 'Young man,' said one of them ironically, 'would you be so kind as to lift up that sail so that we can look at the cargo?' The boy looked ahead impassively, motionless. 'Looks like he's a bit deaf.' They became impatient. 'Lift that sail up!' Lotte's throat went thick with rage. He is a child, leave him in peace, she wanted to shout, but the potatoes disabled her tongue. 'Get a move on, lout, do what I say!' The boy leaned over stiffly, a thin wrist came out of the frayed sleeve as he gripped a corner of the sail and dutifully pulled it back. Beneath it lay a dead man, with bent legs – emaciated, with hollow eye sockets and ears sticking out from his bony skull. His body was strangely twisted midway, as though it had snapped. 'Who is that...?' said the guard, vainly trying to make his question sound like an order. 'My father,' said the boy flatly. He drew the sail back and stared across the water again. Fragments from 'Der Erlkönig' came back to Lotte. The boy was

the representation of the opposite: '... it is the child with his father
... in his arms the father was dead ...'

It started snowing a week later. Misery hid beneath unspoilt
whiteness; from the air the occupied north seemed to be united
with the liberated south, thanks to the snow. The iron stove in the
studio fed with damp kindling gave out more black smoke than
heat. Ernst tried to keep the plane under control in his numbed fingers, forced to squint through his sooted-up glasses. 'And meanwhile at home in Utrecht I still have sacks of coal,' he grumbled.
Lotte volunteered to fetch them; he did not refuse her offer, convinced as he was of her indestructibility. She set off – she made her
way through the snow with the bicycle, pausing now and then to
take a sip from the beetroot stew her mother had given her to take
in a small pan. It snowed again from time to time, she made slow
progress, the little flakes stung her face. Bent forwards she pushed
the heavy bicycle onwards, her consciousness solely on that one
radiant point of coal glowing on the horizon, which was already
spreading heat into her spirit. Outside of that there was only the
white void, absolute desolation. Her hands and feet froze away; the
cold penetrated in from those extremities and settled itself within
in a not unpleasant heaviness. She had no idea how long she had
already been on the road, how far she still had to go. Every notion
of time dissolved in the abstraction of all-encompassing whiteness
– a benevolent peace descended upon her. Clods of snow stuck to
her lace-up shoes; the contours of a lumpy fort were vaguely
revealed in a snowy expanse of white through a fine network of
crystals that had settled on her eyelashes. An irresistible temptation
emanated from a tree with white branches like a photographic
negative: a brief repose. She leaned the bicycle against the trunk
and let herself sink into the snow, a soft blanket beneath her and
soon covering her. She could not finish a single thought any more
– like white butterflies they fluttered through her heaviness. All
contradictions and paradoxes dissolved in a woolly nothing; she
vaguely remembered a corresponding perception from long ago,

when she sank through the ice and a few seconds stretched into an eternity. She forgot that she had a body. The sound of falling snow ... was the last thought before she sank away into a ruthless, delightful oblivion.

'Come ... if you lie there you'll die...' Someone was pulling her roughly by the arm back to reality. The snow slid off her. She was too far gone to resist. The bicycle was pushed into her hands. 'I'll walk with you...' She walked like a wound-up mechanical doll, accompanied by a man in a long black coat with a snowy hat. He was breathing heavily – the only sound to be heard as they trudged onwards. He asked nothing, said nothing, but confined himself to brief exhortations when the pace slackened. 'Keep walking...' She had the sense of being on the threshold of an important memory, but one which could not break through the screen of her dullness. It was already dark when the town loomed up and they trudged along empty streets to the centre. At the Fish Market he suddenly took his leave of her by removing his hat, piles of snow falling from it ... it seemed again as though the shadow of a memory was catching her unawares as a dark street swallowed him up.

Only then did she realize that the one she was staring at had saved her life. He had turned up out of nowhere like a *deus ex machina* – he had disappeared again into it as though he were no more than a hallucination. It had stopped snowing. The town was deserted, the snow lay on a few corpses in the shelter of a wall, hunger had left clear traces behind on their upturned faces. An astonished landlady let her in. His rooms were still intact; his possessions, mainly books about violin-making and family portraits, were waiting stoically for his return – she looked at them as she slowly came to the right temperature. The only thing missing from the interior was the coal. The landlady, who cleaned the rooms, gave herself away in the exaggeration of her denial. Coal? No, if there had been any coal she would have known about it. Lotte could not prove anything. She spooned the last remains of beetroot stew out of the pan and crept into his narrow, chilly bed.

10

'Œufs à la neige' is the poetic name of a dessert that was a means of conquering hunger with air during the war. At that time Lotte got cramp in her wrists by whisking up the miracle of the age from the whites of two eggs into an ever-expanding foam.

'I made that for the children in the hunger winter,' said Lotte, spooning one of the islands out of the vanilla sauce, 'to chase away the empty feeling in their stomachs.'

Anna sighed. 'I did not know that you had endured so much hunger.'

'It was a better weapon than the V1,' said Lotte curtly.

Anna switched tactically to another subject. 'And you were almost snowed up ... I recognize the feeling of absolute desolation in the midst of nature, which is essentially indifferent ... and the longing for death that can assail you against the background of the war ...'

❦

The doctors and nurses turned up the day after they had arrived at the seminary and it was business as usual with normal equipment. Herr Töpfer, who was already in the convalescent phase, asked official permission for Sister Anna to accompany him on his practice walks in the garden. They walked very slowly between the snowdrops and budding hazels. There was a watery sun. They rested on a mossy bench. 'Sister, it's over with us,' Töpfer stated mercilessly. 'Up to now the pendulum still swung back and forth to the east, to the west, but now it has come to a halt in the middle – they are advancing from all sides and will crush us.' 'We still have the V2 ...' Anna interposed. 'You don't really believe that, Sister. It simply is finished. My parents, my wife, my children –

311

they are all hoping for my return, but when the Russians come they will shoot all the SS here.' Anna nodded mechanically – the Russians' revenge was proverbial. The SS were even recognizable naked by their tattooed blood group on their arms. She looked around. Soon the snowdrops would be trampled under Russian boots. A sense of fear came over her for the first time, not for herself but for the wounded whom she was trying to patch up, and for whom she sacrificed her night's sleep. 'Ach Sister...' the sombre Töpfer held her by the chin and looked at her dolefully, 'we had such beautiful dreams.'

The feeling of approaching calamity no longer left her alone, it was difficult to wait calmly and yet not to wait. At any rate, waiting calmly for the collapse of the Third Reich was not on for the boy with the pistol. Anna kept her eye on him, waiting for the opportunity to filch it off him. She went to sit on the edge of his bed in between her duties and listened to his feverish plans that concealed his inability to face up to the fiasco of his ideals. He had been active in the Hitler Youth even when it was illegal; he had lost an eye in a street fight with communist youths. With his flair he had reached officer rank in the Wehrmacht – even though he was in the military hospital with a shattered knee he was not contemplating capitulation! One night as he slept, Anna carefully removed the pistol from beneath his pillow. She threw it into the Danube with relief. The next day she went to sit with him with an innocent expression. He grasped her hand, his eye shone. 'Sister,' he said conspiratorially, 'come with me to the Werewolf!' She shook her head. He aroused her pity with his naïve fantasies about the Werewolf movement, a group of desperadoes who were withdrawing to the Alps to continue the fight to the death. 'You're crazy, Junge, it's over,' she said softly. 'If you are right I will shoot myself in the head,' he cried vigorously. 'They won't get their hands on me alive.' To demonstrate that he meant it he rummaged under his pillow. The emptiness he found there enraged him – where was the thief who had stolen from him the right to decide on his own life? He twisted himself out of his bed and limped through the ward with a flushed face and clenched jaw, dragging the leg with the shattered knee behind him. Anna barred his way. 'Stop screaming! The pistol is in the Danube. I took it, no one else did. Your father and mother asked me to, I promised them I would.' The one eye stared at her in bewilderment. He stiffened and clenched his fists: she must not see the shuddering tension suppressed in his body – then he burst into tears. His lust for battle collapsed; he crumpled up as though she had given him a beating – leaning heavily on her he allowed himself to be led willingly back to his bed.

The war quickened. The front was just twenty-five kilometres away from Linz. A night-time transport to Germany was impro-vised for all the patients who could move at all or who could some-how be carried. All reported except twelve patients with serious back injuries – they could only lie on their fronts. Anna was given the task of watching over them that night. Moved, she went to say goodbye to her old patients from Vienna. 'Open that box a moment...' ordered Herr Töpfer, pointing with his crutch. Anna fiddled with the lock; inside there was a packet on top. 'Take it out and lock the box again please.' She obeyed his instructions care-fully. Her heart was thudding: it was as though he had been watch-ing over her all that time – now he was going away. 'Come...' he beckoned, 'come with me.' In a recess in the long cold corridor he opened the packet. His hands were trembling. 'Listen carefully. I am giving this to you, it is chocolate. I had been keeping it for my wife but I think you can make better use of it now. We are all leav-ing, tonight you will be all alone: eat the chocolate then, you will need it.'

He had prescience. That night as the seminary emptied silently, Anna sat by the light of a candle near the twelve wounded whom she recognized by the nature of their injuries, not by their faces. She sat there and obeyed Töpfer's last order: she ate herself into a delirium with his chocolate so that it would not strike her that they had all absconded. By morning she emerged from her stupor.

Wobbling from tiredness and nausea she stumbled out of the ward. The seminary seemed just as deserted as on the night they had arrived: the doctors had disappeared, the nurses with their bandages and the medicines, even the caretaker in his silk pyjamas had fled the sinking ship. A solemn, almost pious, silence prevailed – was this the silence that preceded the ultimate slaughter, like the squalls that presaged thunderstorms, an oppressive, charged silence? What was she doing in this godforsaken spot, far from home? Far from home? She had no home, there was nothing to long for, no fireside, no apple orchard ... no one waiting for her with yearning. She heard the echo of her footsteps on the tiles as though she were chasing herself. Each cavernous room that she went in to emphasized her solitude ... a house with empty rooms from a dream, every room led on to yet another empty room ... 'Sister...' the wail of the patients who had been entrusted to her like terminally ill babies drove her back to the ward. But she could neither relieve their pain nor cleanse their wounds – she had nothing but some pieces of paper at her disposal to wipe away the pus, as she calmed them with hollow words. Thoughts, ideas, perceptions went through her without touching any other emotional thread but morose long-suffering. The day slipped through her, gradually changing into evening, and still no one came to take her place. Had they been forgotten by everyone? Did they not appear in any plan, no single scheme? Had they already been crossed out? The electricity had stopped a week earlier, they had managed with candles – these too had been taken away. She sat at her post in the dark. You might have thought they were already dead. Although there were thirteen of them, each one of them was alone and fighting against despair in his own way. It was clear that she had come to the end of her peregrinations; this was the point all lines had been leading to. Her soap bubble burst and left an emptiness behind where only the smell of dying soldiers hung.

But she was not alone. A familiar companion of old emerged: he was trustworthy, a precise allure emanated from him that suited the circumstances. He did not burden you with an unreliable strategy for living, he laughed at all the senseless striving, he asked nothing, demanded nothing ... the only thing he desired from her was that she did not resist him. She left the ward without looking round; she picked up one of the suitcases, which contained baby clothes. Hypnotized, she walked outside, went down to the river. The Danube was black. She hesitated: if she went in from the bank she would not be able to prevent herself swimming. She walked up onto the middle of the Baroque bridge. I promised you that I would not do it, she murmured, forgive me. The words dissolved into the sound of the rain. The bridge was there, and the water beneath it, and the promise of peace that lay enclosed there. She lifted the suitcase up onto the balustrade, which came up to her shoulders, and tried to pull herself up. But the mossy stone edge was wet and slippery; she could not get a grip and suddenly lacked the strength in her arms, which used to be so tough in the old days. Once again she tried, and again ... she scrabbled up and slid back again ... She refused to resign to failure ... how could something as banal as the balustrade of a bridge stand in the way of a matter of life and death? In frustration she seized the suitcase and flung it over into the depths below. What worked for the suitcase would work for her too. But the balustrade was just a bit high and slippery everywhere. Up there, there was laughter at her ludicrous efforts: Anna, always so resolute and efficient, went about her suicide so pitifully and clumsily!

She gave up and trudged off the bridge up the slope back to the seminary. It was all over: she had left her life behind, tossed it into the Danube, it was floating away in the suitcase – only her body was still there; there was nothing else to do but let it move the way it usually did. She went back into the room and waited with resignation until the waiting could come to an end. But only the rain ceased: she stared outside indifferently and saw, without actually taking it in, that the sky was slowly clearing. She had no sense of time – somewhere in that endless night there was a knocking on the door. Half-asleep she shuffled down the corridor. They seemed to be in a hurry, the doors were flung open. 'Where is the military hospital?' cried impatient SS orderlies. 'What hospital?' said Anna. 'Surely this is a military hospital!' 'I don't know if this is still a hospital . . .' she hesitated. 'I should have been relieved but no one . . .' They had no time to listen to her, the front was very close, they had to unload and get back. The wounded were laid each side of the corridor in a great hurry; the stretchers were taken away for the subsequent victims, the blankets too. Before she had realized it they had gone away, and she paced to and fro between rows of badly wounded – at least a hundred. Boys who had been taking part energetically in the battle a couple of hours before lay naked on the chessboard motif of the stone floor, reduced to a memo that stated where they had been operated on. Moonlight came through the high, gothic windows onto their unconscious, pathetically young bodies. The romantic moon, patron saint of lovers, shone without compassion upon their nakedness, in a perverse aesthetic. Anna walked up and down, taunted; she could do nothing except witness their deaths. Her disgust at the phenomenon of war became greater with every soldier who died. This was how it was, everything that she had gone along with up to now had been merely a prelude. This was it – all care, fostering, sacrifices of anonymous mothers, all dreams and expectations, everything was felled by an obtuse, premature death . . . The son, fiancé, father, no more than a naked, numb, redundant thing, a name on a card.

A soldier came to. 'Schwester . . .' he rattled. Anna bent down over him. He seized her arm, his eyes glittered. 'Schwester, we're still holding out!' 'Yes, my boy,' Anna nodded. He wanted to add something else, opened his mouth with elation, but at the same moment something invisible happened in his body. The unspoken died on his lips, his body went rigid – the frozen expression of stubborn passion was so unbearable that she quickly closed his eyes.

Somehow or other the dawn broke. The dead were grey in the dull morning light. Once again the doors were flung open, doctors and orderlies swarmed inside the building. They looked around fleetingly. What they saw seemed not to surprise them, except for Anna's presence: she was stared at as though she were a ghostly apparition. 'What are you doing here . . . ?' cried one of the doctors in astonishment, stroking his ginger moustache. 'Have you gone mad? The Russians are coming!' 'So . . . ?' she said indifferently.

A day later it was teeming with industrious Red Cross sisters. Anna did not know where they had come from. She had long ago given up wanting to understand anything about it: suddenly there was talk of organization again, everyone got on with their own duties – but she was not taken in by it, it was no more than a cover for the chaos that could gain the upper hand at any moment. A meeting was called too. The adjutant summoned all the doctors, orderlies and sisters together to receive the Gauleiter's instructions. 'The Upper Danube region is holding fast,' he announced. 'We will remain here at our posts under all circumstances. The sisters too. They have no reason whatever to be anxious about the Russians. Their safety in this hospital is assured.' Anna, sceptically letting his soothing words fall off her, stepped forward from the middle of a group of nurses and shouted, 'But you have already sent your own wives and daughters away, eh?' The sisters pulled her back into the group in a reflex so that she became a uniform among uniforms again. 'Who was that?' said the Gauleiter sharply. He sent his adjutant over; the sisters were asked in turn who had called out but no one answered – they closed ranks.

After the meeting the doctor with the moustache took Anna aside. 'Listen, Sister,' he said confidentially, 'I have four wounded patients here and only their arms are bandaged – they can walk. Now I am going to give you and two other sisters a marching order to accompany them to Munich.' Anna nodded mechanically. Naturally, she still did what she was told, even if it was something rather pleasant like leaving the seminary. 'Incidentally,' he scratched behind his ear with his pen, 'did you hear that yesterday, that woman who called, "But have you already sent your wives and daughters away"?' He looked at her with such a shrewd but at the same time faithful dog's expression that Anna replied in a tone that implied a confession, 'Yes, I heard it.' At once she realized why he had thought of the marching order to Munich. Because she could not thank him openly she let him know with her eyes that she knew that he knew that she knew.

❦

'It seems like something from a former life...' Anna murmured.

Lotte was staring at her. Behind the face opposite her for the first time she could see the young woman Anna must have been – on a stone bridge in the rain, in a corridor with dying soldiers. It touched her more than she could concede to herself. Making an effort to get her voice to sound matter-of-fact she said, 'How could all those badly wounded soldiers possibly be left behind?'

'You have to imagine it: the front is close by...' Anna gesticulated, 'orderlies carry the wounded out of the battle and take them to the field hospital. The most severe cases are dressed there, something is scribbled on paper – such and such was done – then they are chucked into a vehicle and ordered to a military hospital behind the lines. Then they dump them and have to go back straight away. They were SS, the Waffen-SS were the ones fighting to the last, the youngest, healthiest boys. One after the other died before my eyes that night. There was no one to nurse them. That long, dreadful corridor. I was alone and I could do nothing. I have repressed that night for years, I could not talk about it. There's a song, "A moonlit night in April", that always makes me think of it.'

❦

Seven insignificant little figures progressed with difficulty beneath a heavy sky. Anna was lugging her possessions in a fat leather suitcase. They slept in schools or churches on the way – villages were obliged to provide shelter for them on presentation of the collective marching order. One of the soldiers discovered a cart somewhere into which they could put all their baggage and they trudged on, day and night, ever further, until they came to a railway junction that professional bombing had turned into a moribund moon land-scape with craters where shining pieces of twisted rails protruded. They manoeuvred through with their cart; the wheels were creak-ing dreadfully. Suddenly Anna saw that her suitcase was no longer on it. She ran back, stumbling, tripped in a hole with one foot. Was that her case, that shiny black thing floating in a crater's inland lake? She fished it out. Now it really was heavy. When they put it back on the cart a wheel broke – they left the cart behind in the company of capsized railway carriages.

Anna stopped to empty her shoe. Her soles were full of holes – her feet were sliding about in the worn-out leather. One of the sol-diers gave her the extra pair of boots he had with him, and his hel-met as protection from the rain. Still not satisfied, he took her suitcase from her with his one arm and she carried his rifle instead. During the evening it cleared up. The moon peeped out onto the plodding travellers between scurrying clouds. Two guards sprung up from nowhere and barred their way. 'Mensch, Meyer, look...' one of them called in amazement, 'That soldier here is a female!'

From now on reality consisted wholly of having to put one foot in front of the other. Every metre was a metre closer to Munich, a metre further from the Russians. One evening, when every metre had become a metre too much, someone took them to an old school. There were wooden bunk-beds. Anna was shown to a bed, apathetic from tiredness. She lifted herself up with a last effort – still wearing her helmet she collapsed onto the bed there and then. But the bed could not bear so much tiredness, she fell though the middle and onto the one sleeping below, straw sack and all. He rolled the weight off him without waking up, she landed on the floor with a bump and went to sleep immediately. Early in the morning she opened one eye – a dwarf-like old man with a knobbly face above a narrow, sunken chest was looking at her from the bed with shock. 'Jesus Maria Joseph, what a dragoon fell on me during the night. I thank God I am still alive!'

Every kilometre on the other side of the border had to be

conquered on foot too. Stabbing pains in her knee warned her that it could not go on much longer, the joint was swollen out to the top of the boot. Defeated army units were hurrying to the middle of Germany: cars and freight lorries whizzed by, loaded with women, soldiers, officers. They tried to get a lift but nobody stopped – the ghost of the defeated was breathing down the military neck. The pain became intolerable – her body now refused for the first time too. Anna dragged her suitcase into the middle of the road; she took off her helmet with a bow, as though greeting the traffic, and sat astride it. 'Have you gone mad?' cried her companions indignantly, 'you'll be killed.' Anna laughed disparagingly. 'I couldn't care less whether they take me with them or run me over!'

A freight lorry approached. There was something comforting about the dumb mechanical strength that took no notice of living creatures – she waited for it with an inviting smile: do it quickly. The screams of panic from the others sounded like a choir singing in the distance. The justice of a primitive fairy-tale was being invoked in the middle of a main road: if the maiden completely surrendered to the monster it would turn into a prince. The lorry came to a stop at a polite distance. A young officer got out; he invited her to get in with military respect for her cold-bloodedness. Stoically she stood up. She beckoned to the others over her shoulder and got in.

The reception at the hospital was not what they had expected after their brutal journey. 'What do you want here?' the sisters were snarled at, 'we don't need you here at all!' Only the wounded soldiers were allowed to stay. The three Red Cross sisters got a new marching order: back to the Bavarian Alps, to a military hospital on the Chiemsee. They were back on the road again and everything began anew. They took it in turns to hold their hand out, listlessly, at the kerb. 'We don't need you...' echoed in Anna's head. Now I understand, she thought bitterly, how it is possible that a hundred soldiers could die in a cold corridor while there were no sisters to care for them: there are too many here.

A military lorry stopped. The driver stuck his head out. 'Who knows the way to Traunstein?' 'I do,' cried Anna. They had been past it on the way there, it was not far from the Chiemsee. Anna had to go and sit at the front. The driver drove on slowly and watchfully. A soldier on the bonnet was scanning the sky with a telescope. 'What is he looking for?' Anna asked. 'Fighter bombers,' her neighbour grimaced. The corners of his mouth were still twisted when the cry came from outside, 'Get out! Bombers!' They jumped out blindly, threatening circles were being described above their heads. They dived into a deep trench. Anna was buried under her own suitcase. At that same moment the lorry bringing them nearer to the Chiemsee exploded. It was as though it was being hit repeatedly – one explosion set off the next in a chain reaction, debris rained on her suitcase. Only when nothing more could be heard did they creep out from their hiding place. They stepped timidly into the silence that followed the bomb – everyone was still intact. There was a smell of ammunition in the air. 'It is . . .' the driver began, 'it was a munitions lorry.' The scorched remains were smouldering. Looking at it was not helping to get them further so on they all went, silently ruminating on the thought of a narrowly escaped death. A freight lorry from Hitler's construction organization, TODT, stopped. They signalled. 'Only the sisters,' cried the driver sternly. As though he thought he would be tempting the irate gods above if he spoke, he took them without saying a word straight to the military hospital by the Chiemsee, which had been set up in a former hotel. It proclaimed itself from afar because – with an eye on the same gods – on the road big white circles with red crosses had been painted.

At the side of the road two men without lower limbs were sitting in wheelchairs. They watched as the TODT lorry unloaded sisters instead of building materials; they saw Anna with her impossible suitcase twist her knee and land on the asphalt. They were not unmoved. One of them wheeled over smartly, gathered her up and put her on his lap, the other took her suitcase. At a brisk pace they traversed the two hundred metres to the chief doctor's office, where they left her on a bench in the passage, proud of the compensatory strength in their arms. A passing soldier reported their arrival. 'Don't drop them in here just like that...' they heard the doctor storming on the other side of the door, 'we don't need anyone! The war will be over the day after tomorrow; we have nothing to eat, they'll have to manage for themselves.' Anna let her head sink onto her chest. She looked at her nails with great attention: they were black as though she had been digging up potatoes. All her emotions had been used up; the doctor's roaring did not move her. One thing was certain: she was not taking another step. If needs be she would take root on that bench, opposite his door, to remind him of her existence. 'Those poor women.' she heard the soldier complain, 'there are still some beds, why can't they sleep there? And they could get that ration of three potatoes too...' The doctor changed his tack; hearing out the soldier's plea was more exhausting than consenting. That night she lay in a real bed between smooth white sheets. Anna vaguely remembered the perception of unfamiliar luxury from long long ago, when she had arrived at her uncle's house in Cologne.

Although the chief doctor did not need anyone, on her rambles round the hospital the next day she had discovered a room with mattresses strewn on the floor. Young children were lying on them with a large bandage where an arm or leg had been lost, or with a bandaged head, eyes staring straight at the ceiling. Anna, who thought she had experienced the very worst with the dying soldiers in the night, who had intended to get rid of everything to do with children with her suitcase of baby clothes, walked in a daze between the mattresses, now and then kneeling down by a motionless child who looked at her with dejected resignation. No child was playing or laughing; an oppressive silence ruled as though they were all in a permanent state of shock and were waiting passively until their mother or father came to take the shock away with a kiss. But there were no mothers or fathers, no tellers of fairy-tales to distract them. They lay there, but overwhelmed by a collective resignation as though they were doing penance for something they had not done. An associated absurdity also struck Anna: they were light blonde without exception, they all had blue eyes. Well fed as they were, they looked like plump little cherubs who had been shot down from the fluffy clouds by a misanthrope whose hate extended to heaven. Although the chief doctor did not need anyone, Anna got down to work as usual.

'What had happened to the children?' Lotte looked at her nervously. There was a speck of foam on her upper lip, which made her look a bit ridiculous and so Anna found it easier to distance herself from the oppressive images that she had been recalling.

'They were living in a children's home on the Obersalzberg,' she said soberly, 'that had been bombed by the Americans. They were the Lebensbornkinder, pedigree children of the Nazi breeding farm. Specially selected blonde men and women were brought together – for insemination, as it were. A child then arrived and they donated it to the Führer.'

'And what did he want to do with it?'

'After he had tidily exterminated the Jews and the gypsies the noble Master Race had to be created instead, to rule the world. These children were being brought up on the Obersalzberg, well hidden from the outside world. After the bombing they were fetched down and taken to the emergency hospital on the Chiemsee – and then the chief doctor said he didn't need any sisters.'

It baffled Lotte. It was too much, too complex, too macabre. She disengaged. 'I think I'll ask for the bill, I'm so tired all of a sudden. It must be from all that eating, and the alcohol.' She pushed her half-full wine glass aside deliberately.

'At our age you can't take as much,' said Anna ambiguously, 'you are reminded of it over and over again in a painful way.'

Back at the hotel Lotte received a telephone call from her eldest daughter who enquired expectantly 'on behalf of the others too' about the progress of the cure. Lotte gave a flattering picture, full of false enthusiasm. I must tell her about it, hammered simultaneously in her head. But what should she say? I have found my sister, your aunt. And then? The incomprehensible, unbelievable, unsavory drama in X acts? How could she ever explain it? She let her daughter's counsels wash over her – take it quietly, enjoy it, relax, don't worry, have you already met nice people? – and said goodbye. I must stop all that talking, she said to herself angrily, the receiver still in her hand. It exhausts me – the children are expecting me to come home rejuvenated. They have a right to. It is their present, it has cost them plenty of money.

Nevertheless she left the bath house with Anna again the next day – at last the liberation was in view. Their whole meeting was a film she had failed to walk out of in good time; now she also wanted to know how it ended. The sun was shining, the world looked deceptively amiable. They dawdled around a little until they arrived at the Parc de Sept Heures and their nostrils were tickled by the aroma of *frites*. Anna sniffed with closed eyes. 'That's what I want!' she said from the bottom of her heart. Although Lotte had an aversion to doughnut and *frites* stalls 'because they make your clothes stink so', she walked behind her automatically. A little later they were sitting with paper cones on a bench in the park, surrounded by intrusive doves. The war, the vicissitudes of humanity, painful matters of conscience – all paled into insignificance compared with the adolescent enjoyment of a portion of *frites* in the winter cold – long, firm, crisp, golden yellow *frites*. Greasy, salty fingers. But the idea that life was actually very simple only lasted as long as the bag of *frites*. Then they wiped their mouths and their hands and the war resumed its rights.

Lotte's father ran out of flags to mark the Allied victories; his wife, who had read too many war novels in her time, shivered at the thought of the strategic and moral vacuum usually associated with the handover of power – a period in which the enemy reacted

blindly to the frustrations of its defeat with arson, rage, devasta-
tion, murder. What would happen to them if by chance they were
living in the line of fire? This was the first fear she had admitted
out loud since the start of the war. The situation had became
increasingly distressing. The tension was mounting and for Ernst
it was released in a clumsy proposal of marriage. Moved by his
awkwardness, Lotte did not play hard to get. Not only did she love
him for his frank vulnerability and unmasculine weaknesses, she
also nurtured a secret fear that life after the war would resume its
normal course again, even though it could never really be the same
as it had been before the war. The marriage would save her from
having to be involved in the disintegration of the enormous clan of
family and people in hiding – a priceless microcosm in a certain
sense, although it could be from addiction to anxiety – she hoped
to escape via the marriage from the emptiness that they would be
leaving behind, and the excess of time, suddenly, to pose yourself
difficult questions. She would also escape from her father whose
proximity would no longer be tolerable in peacetime.

A wedding they could not afford: everything they possessed
had been turned into provisions. They decided to marry before the
war was over – a good excuse to let the ceremony take place
quietly. Nevertheless that quiet was tactlessly disturbed at the critical moment by a squadron of low-flying Spitfires. On the way to
the town hall the discreet company – the betrothed couple, her parents and two improvised witnesses – continually had to dive into
the bracken. On account of the bridegroom's status as a person in
hiding they had chosen an inconspicuous route through the wood;
for the same reason the ceremony was performed by the stand-in
mayor, who was reliable: Lotte's father, always so charming outside
the house, had his contacts. The formalities were managed without
a glimmer of festive spirit, the stand-in mayor's words were lost in
the roar of aircraft. Lotte, picking sprigs of bracken here and there
from her brown suit, thought that never in the history of the world
had such a joyless wedding taken place. After it was over they

rushed back to the house taking the same route, where the lifetime contract acquired a little lustre in the dish of rye cakes and a bottle of gin – the very last one.

❧

As they crossed the Avenue Reine Astrid, their patience was tested by a military procession – the very one they had seen riding to the west a few days earlier was now returning to the east. Tanks with soldiers in battledress, jeeps, Red Cross lorries, all the colour of mustard.

Anna observed the procession with a stern expression. 'Da siehst du, it all goes on as usual,' she mused. 'As long as the economy is dependent on the arms industry there will continue to be new flashpoints and we will all be armed to the teeth.'

Lotte did not rise to the bait. It was such a generalization again, bending the question of guilt into a safe direction. If rearming was a worldwide pattern, then that saved Germany from responsibility for the economic revival in the 1930s – based on the arms industry – and everything that had flowed from it. But she was tired of refuting Anna's theories so she held her tongue and watched the mud-spattered column with mixed feelings. That was how the occupier, that was how the liberators, had entered the country.

Part 3

Peace

Après le déluge encore nous

I

The Führer was dead; it was a matter of days. The night before, the capitulation evaporated in general drunkenness. There were pre-war stocks of alcohol under shrouds of cobwebs in the cellars of the former hotel. Fearing that the Americans would start an orgy there and rape the sisters to the rhythm of their perverse jazz music, the hospital management divided the bottles up among the staff. Anna sat on the floor in one of the sisters' rooms and it gave her bitter satisfaction to undermine her sense of reality with red Martini. Humming, she took her tight nurse's cap from her head and combed her blonde hair. 'Take a look at this...' the others stared at her in surprise. 'Actually how lovely you look! Why stuff your hair under that cap, show yourself as you are!' Anna brought the bottle to her mouth again. She had no inclination to explain that 'to look lovely' was the last thing she aspired to. Everything to do with feminine coquetry and seductiveness – how perverse in relation to the dead – could count on her contempt. At the end of the evening she was led, laughing and giggling, past the reception to her dormitory.

The next day the brand-new peace made itself known right through her piercing headache: an endless procession of emaciated, exhausted soldiers dragging themselves along the autobahn, chased by well-fed Americans who blazed with conceitedness and disdain. Anna clambered up the slope and saw a disillusioned mass trudging past her on that sunny liberation day – grey faces, lips cracked from the dryness. She also became acquainted with the phenom-enon of the black American. Chewing gum, he turned to her on his thick rubber soles. 'Hello baby...' he grinned casually. She turned round offended and ran down the slope straight to the kitchen. She came inside breathlessly. 'Our soldiers are coming down from the alpine fortifications ... my God ... they can't go on any more...!'

All who could free themselves filled a jug with lemonade and hurried to the road with it. But as soon as three, four soldiers had drunk some, a Wild-West type appeared and pushed, knocked the sisters down off the slope. They quickly scrambled to their feet and climbed up once more to give out lemonade. The boys drank eagerly and stuffed letters into the pockets of their starched nurses' overalls. 'Please, please ... write to my wife that I am still alive,' they pleaded as they passed by, 'tell my mother that you have seen me...' Inside the hospital the sisters emptied their pockets and filled the jugs; tirelessly they held their positions. They were flung down, threatened with rifle butts, but obstinately kept coming back until the last soldier had passed. Back in the hospital they sorted out the post. Someone had thrown Anna a small parcel, without an address, without a letter. She opened it: inside was dark blue woollen material for an officer's uniform – a gift? When the postal service was working again she wrote dozens of letters: 'From Heinz, for my dear Hertha ... for Mutti from Gerold ... via Anna Grosalie.'

That same day the guard was changed. Jeeps arrived and the Americans quietly took over the military hospital. Soldiers who had recovered were taken prisoner and removed; doctors, orderlies and sisters had to continue their duties under guard. Huge revolving searchlights were installed in the grounds around the hospital to discourage daredevil dreams of escape. Among the wounded there were dedicated Nazis who had photographs of Hitler and other Nazi things on them. Just in time the sisters had collected these paraphernalia and, fearful of provoking the Americans, thrown them in the Chiemsee. One soldier, who could not be separated from his decorations, his Iron Cross and his photograph of Hitler, had withheld everything unnoticed. He buttonholed Anna a few days later. 'Would you do me a favour, Sister, and hide these things for me?' 'But where?' she said sceptically. 'In the wood behind here. Bury them, mark the spot and draw a map with it indicated precisely on it. I'll retrieve them when it's all over.'

Anna could not refuse him. In the evening, as soon as the beam had just passed, she ducked as she sneaked along the ground – continually looking round. She dug a hole between two birches, laughing quietly to herself: she saw herself rootling in the ground like a dog hiding a bone. After she had made a quick sketch of the location in the moonlight, with a cross on the spot where the Führer had been buried, she went back the way she had come, cursing the Americans for the ridiculous show of strength of their searchlights, as a result of which, in your own country in peacetime, you could not once move freely.

It did not take long for the Americans to discover the charms of the original hotel: you could swim and sail in the Chiemsee. They requisitioned it for their general staff. The military hospital was disbanded; the SS were sorted out and transported; the Red Cross sisters were taken as prisoners to a Wehrmacht barracks in neighbouring Traunstein, where little remained of the celebrated German orderliness. When the Americans were so close they could smell their fried bacon, the High Command had chosen to seal the Third Reich's downfall by carousing – the sisters were ordered to clean out the pigsty they had left behind. They felt degraded by their captivity, which conflicted with the neutrality of the Red Cross, and by the filthy work that was so remote from their calling. But all that very soon paled into insignificance in the light of the daily ration of one cup of black surrogate coffee, a slice of dry bread and a plate of watery soup. Light-headed from hunger, they scrubbed floors. After a week Anna could only carry buckets that were a quarter full.

One day one of the sisters broke the solidarity of the collective empty stomach and bartered herself to the Americans for a plate of food. Full of self-hate she returned; she wrung out her mop, crying about the irretrievable. They took it in turns to try to comfort her but she stubbornly refused to accept charity from those whose self-respect was still intact. Sister Ilse, who was friendly with her, knew that it was her birthday that week. 'We should do something for her,' she said to Anna, 'something nice.' Anna nodded gently – excessive movements of her head made her dizzy. 'There are marguerites growing on the other side of the road...' she suggested cautiously, 'but how could we ever get past the sentry by the gate?' 'Leave that to me,' said Ilse, 'I speak a little English.'

Ilse succeeded in softening the sentries after lengthy dealings in a charming gibberish mixing English and German. The gate opened – they had to restrain themselves not to run into the meadows like liberated calves, but rather to set foot with the absentminded detachment of privileged prisoners. Walking in blossoming grass, marguerites, buttercups, sorrel ... lying down in it and ceasing to exist! As Anna picked flowers the stalks of the grass on the banks of the Lippe scratched her legs again and she smelled once more that prickly green smell which was like nothing else. It did not bother her that there were American army tents further on, just as, long ago, she had ignored the proximity of the farm in which her step-aunt concocted new torments. From the constant bending she fell into a dizzy fuddle, a dazed sensation of almost fainting in the Arcadian meadow and forgetting everything.

All of a sudden a piece of chocolate landed at her feet, and another, and a piece of bread, and something else, and something else. She came back to the here and now with a bump. 'Verdammte Schweine...' she snapped. She wouldn't even think of touching it. Ilse was also carrying on as though she hadn't noticed that anonymous delicacies were flying at them from the tents. One of the sentries cried from the other side, 'Jesus, pick it up, they're only giving it to you!' Ilse wavered. 'If we take it with us,' she whispered, 'then we could all enjoy it ... then it will be a proper birthday party...' Anna had not yet seen it like that. She picked her Red Cross apron up by the corners, bent down and began to fill it. Eventually she stood up with a bulging apron and called haughtily:

'Danke schön!' The birthday girl would never in her life receive a bouquet to equal the exuberant bunch of wild marguerites. The sisters sat down in a circle. Each had a little heap of American benevolence in front of her. The birthday girl got the most and naturally shared it out again.

On the other side of Traunstein there was a military hospital. Since the brown sisters had been arrested and taken away there was a shortage of nurses there. One of the SS doctors, who worked under guard, drew the Americans' attention to the Red Cross sisters at the barracks – under an escort of two soldiers they were fetched and taken to the hospital. Anna was not in a state to carry her suitcase – someone put it in a cart. All she carried was the parcel of blue officer's material under her arm. Thus they walked in procession through Traunstein, stared at by the inhabitants. They were relieved: not only could they get on with their normal work in a hygienic environment where the reliable SS orderliness still prevailed, but they could also eat again. The head of bookkeeping, an SS sergeant-major born and brought up in Traunstein, had his connections in the hinterland. While the Americans stood in front at the gate, the farmers shoved smoked pork, sausage and potatoes through the rear windows and the Traunsteiners dug a tunnel to the cellar to bring the stocks up to the required standard. Anna stuffed herself for three days.

Even so, they still had prisoner status. It was high summer. The landscape of the alpine foothills spread out seductively, but they were not allowed beyond the gate. Anna leaned out of the window of her room with claustrophobic longing and stared at the Garden of Eden. Free citizens were walking on a country road that wound round a hill until it was swallowed up in a wood. Two anachronistic soldiers were patrolling on the same road and cried 'Hello baby' to each skirt that passed by – did they do that in the prairie too? She decided to take the law into her own hands. She took off her Red Cross uniform, and fished a crumpled two-piece out of the suitcase that had been through so much. Disguised as a citizen, she wormed her way out of the window; under cover of scattered bushes she managed to get to the wood unseen. It was an ordinary wood, in the simplicity of its multifaceted appearances. An oak was an oak, no more, no less – she greeted the beech, hugged the oak, ran from one tree to the next, inhaled the smell of humus, clambered onto a fallen pine tree and started a distracted song that turned into a fit of crying half-way through. The trunk bounced beneath her in time with the sobs – it was a fit of crying like a natural phenomenon, a cloudbreak that cleansed the dust from the leaves. It was not so much a question of heartache: her whole body was crying to the roots of her hair, everything contracted together and opened wide – the crying sang itself free from rationality until it became a free-standing form of more rarefied crying that slowly dissolved. When she came to herself dusk was falling. She picked sprigs out of her hair and went in search of the path. The way back was barred by two soldiers involved in conversation. She waited, crouching behind a tree. Eventually they strolled off together in the evening twilight and Anna could walk some way along the public road as a free citizen. She passed a farm – look at that, she thought in amazement, people are sitting there eating, no bombs are falling, the light is on! She realized that since 1939 she had not had an evening without black-out; she had got so used to the abnormal that she regarded the normal with astonishment.

From one day to the next the hospital at Traunstein too was disbanded. The patients were taken away, the guards disappeared, the doctors and nurses were left to their own devices – not one of them had thought of quitting. After two days a goods lorry drove up with an American at the wheel. They climbed into the back all together and sang at the top of their voices, 'I am a prisoner of war...' – a surgeon conducted the crew with his sensitive hands. The sun was shining, apples were hanging on the trees, there was no shooting, no vehicles jumped in the air, there were no swollen knee joints. Surprise and uncertainty were modified into fatalism, transformed into collective wantonness. The war was over, no matter how – slowly, slowly this awareness was trickling inside.

Singing, they entered captivity once more, this time at Aibling near Munich, a massive prisoner of war camp on a former airfield. The women, nurses and Blitzmädchen had been accommodated in hangars; the leaders of the Wehrmacht in the other buildings. Further on, under the open sky, separated from the rest, were thousands of SS soldiers, on the ground, in sun and rain, anxiously guarded by soldiers with machine guns. Anna and Ilse walked to the washroom to clean off the dirt from the journey. Women were jostling each other in front of the mirrors over the wash-basins. They were painting their lips and making themselves pretty. In the background popular music echoed through the hangar. Between two numbers a disc jockey sent greetings from Wolfgang to Sabine in a horrible accent, and congratulated Hans on his birthday on behalf of Uschi. 'What is this, in God's name?' Anna said. 'Have they gone mad?'

The purpose of the finery soon became clear. Outside, past the hangars, the heavyweights of the Wehrmacht mooched about in their uniforms with medals, decorations and pips – the tarted-up women at their sides, one lovelier than the next. The Americans, crazy about a show even thousands of miles from home, took care of the music and played the records they also played at home. Each day, from five to seven, it was a great courtship display for the top Wehrmacht, for those who had sent thousands and yet more thousands to their deaths, while beyond the reach of loudspeakers and pretty women, the SS soldiers who had survived it lay down in the fields like cattle. Anna and Ilse looked at the grotesque show with open mouths. The generals, the senior officers who had stayed out of range in the war, were parading round like honoured prisoners in time to the music of their conquerors. Anna stood there and watched and listened with clenched jaws to the inane native music of America's aboriginals and did not know what to do with the rage that flared up in her. Rage against all those self-important fops without whose orders the war would not have been waged, without whose co-operation Hitler's wings would have been broken. Rage against the conceited cowboy-stupidity of the Americans. Rage against her own powerlessness – all that was needed was for her to join in the applause or go and paint her lips too.

A week later the daily parade suddenly ended. No more music, no greetings, no generals, no more tarting up. The women lay on their beds sighing. For a time there was almost nothing to eat until the Bishop of Munich visited and negotiated an improvement in the daily ration as an intermediary between God and his sinners. Meanwhile the women were examined for venereal diseases and, irrespective of the outcome, gradually released from captivity. Ilse also left, in search of the authorities who could plead for the release of her fiancé, an SS soldier who was lying outside in the field. Anna was still detained on account of an inflammation that created confusion in the Americans' laboratories. When it appeared that she was mainly suffering from greatly reduced resistance, she too was put outside the gate.

❧❧

The stroller in the centre of Spa moves from health, via capital and faith, to the war – back and forth, depending on the buildings and memorials he passes: the bath house, casino, church, the monuments to the fallen. It is difficult to be there in the final decade of the twentieth century; everything breathes of the past.

The sisters landed in front of a shop window with a tempting display of items from the Second World War. Soldiers' jackets, helmets, kitbags, decoratively embroidered handkerchiefs of the American marine, tins of Emergency Drinking Water, an English parachutist's folding bicycle, an advertisement of a girl with a doll in her arms and the slogan, 'That she may never know the horrors of Dictatorship, let's all pull together for a victorious, prosperous America.'

'I hate that language,' said Anna from the bottom of her heart, 'I never wanted to learn it. That silly people, the one more stupid than the next. Hello baby ... And they came to us with their fat backsides and behaved as though they were bringing us culture. They felt they were the rulers of the world.'

'They were our liberators,' Lotte said drily.

Anna laughed huskily and pointed to the window with a gloved finger. 'Those idiots are still being honoured as heroes; yes, you see it, so many years after the war, all American and English things, no German ones of course. My feet hurt, can't we go and sit somewhere?'

They descended on the nearby café with the view onto the Pouhon Pierre-le-Grand. Lotte felt uneasy.

'I don't understand,' she said hesitantly, 'why you bear the Americans such a grudge. They didn't do anything to you.'

Anna sighed impatiently. 'Because they were mean dogs. Because they impressed us. You mustn't forget what we had behind us. Then those boys came over ... in many ways they weren't worth a shot of gunpowder, we could have blown them to bits if we had wanted to ... each one of us, every wounded soldier was worth more than them ... it was dreadful for us ...'

'I don't understand that,' maintained Lotte. 'They did bring the war to an end.'

'Come off it, those chewing-gum boys, straight out of the middle of Texas!'

'They could have been in Normandy ...' said Lotte sharply.

'Oh them? Those two or three Americans who had to perform there. They helped to win the war at the end. The English, the French, the Russians – just think what they have done.'

'But a lot of Americans were killed.'

'Ach God,' Anna leaned back sarcastically in her chair, 'here come the tears now. What do a couple of thousand Americans signify when millions have died?'

'It is not about numbers.'

'You Dutch have a different conception. We had this one. You have to accept that. They utterly disgusted us. We had six years of the war behind us, twelve years of dictatorship. Then those scallywags arrived, who knew nothing about it, those illiterates straight off their farms. Those arrogant, inflated, Wild-West boys, puffed up by gold. What sort of people are they really? They have been there for three hundred years – after they had evicted the Indians. That's all isn't it? Am I mistaken?'

'One people is no better or worse than another people,' Lotte said in a trembling voice. 'As a German you ought to know that by now.'

'But they simply are more stupid,' cried Anna. 'They are uncivilized!'

'There are intellectuals as well.'

'Only a thin veneer. Look at the masses.'

'That goes for our masses and yours too. Originally they were all English, Germans, Dutch, Italians . . .'

'But it was the real dregs who went over there. Look how they've turned out!'

'They were poor emigrants who had had no future in Europe.'

'Fine, fine, you're right . . .' Anna raised her hands in resignation, 'that puts my mind at ease . . .'

They were sitting opposite each other like badgered dogs at a pause in the fight. Lotte looked outside past Anna – suddenly she could not bear the view of her face any more. A furious, intolerant feeling of enmity inflamed her tongue. Her own criticism of the Americans – the communist witch-hunts by McCarthy, the Ku Klux Klan, the Vietnam adventure, the way they chose their presidents – changed chameleon-like into an absolute, sacred need to defend them by fire and sword. But she did not say another word. Weariness overcame her. Two different planets, she said to herself, two different planets.

It did not escape Anna that her ferocity had an off-putting effect. She abominated herself for her ardour. In an attempt at mitigation she said, 'You are a Dutch woman, that is quite different. I didn't want to have anything to do with the ones who were stuffed full of food. Our soldiers were emaciated, ill, they had no nation any more, nothing any more, they were my comrades. You don't understand that, you weren't in the military hospital with the German soldiers, in the squalor. If you had experienced it you would see it exactly like that.'

This was the *coup de grâce* – pre-emptively gagged, even Lotte could not protest any more. And it went on, Anna continued irrepressibly in the way that a teacher repeatedly explains the same thing with infinite patience to a backward pupil.

'But they did nevertheless liberate you from the Nazi dictatorship . . .' Lotte tossed in with a supreme effort.

'Ha . . .' Anna leaned across the table with a cynical laugh, 'you don't really think they came over to rescue us? They grabbed our scientists and took them back to America: chemists, biologists, atomic researchers, military professionals. Gestapo people like Barbie were brought in by the CIA. And then you say I must look on them as liberators. They made Adolf Hitler and his SS army the scapegoats – the Wehrmacht generals with their stripes, who have the deaths of millions of soldiers on their conscience, have never been punished. They were regarded as gentlemen. Whoever declares war decently and leads an army is a gentleman. And think about the judges who signed the death sentences, who sent the people to concentration camps – most of them have never been punished.'

'And what about Eichmann?'

'Wiesenthal did that. And the judge at the Nuremberg trials, he was an idealist, an exception.'

Lotte was listening and not listening. These arguments were familiar to her. A peculiar feeling of *déjà vu* distracted her. Where had she heard all that before, the same and yet different? She tried to hear that other voice behind Anna's voice. Suddenly she knew it: her father had blustered on about the Americans with the same heat. For years. It began immediately after the war, initially inspired by the charisma of Papa Stalin, after his demasking entirely under its own steam. The Yankees!

Liberation: not only from enemy armies but also from anxiety. The contrast made the continuous anxiety, day and night, almost tangible the moment it disappeared. In its place was a general euphoria that did not last long because anxiety still had a last fling from time to time.

A crowd had gathered in the centre of Hilversum to welcome the marching Canadian and English troops who were probably going straight to the radio station, where the Dutch tricolour waved wantonly. Although everyone had kept a close track of the Allies' advances and setbacks since the Normandy landings, their heroism had remained abstract – now people wanted to see them, embrace them, squeeze them with joy. Lotte and Ernst were standing on the edge of this force field and waited for the first tanks to appear round the corner. But shots sounded from a building on the other side instead, cutting right through the exuberance. The crowd scattered. Ernst pulled Lotte by the arm into a side street. The capitulation was definitely a fact, but had everyone capitulated? To be shot during the war would have been sad, but it would be a ridiculous, senseless tragedy to become the victim of a frustrated soldier after the war. They decided to go home and so missed out on the spectacle, shown in all the bioscopes, of the jubilantly welcomed liberators amid hordes of women and lanky boys clambering onto the tanks – symbolized by cigarettes and bars of chocolate.

A few days later Lotte saw a column of disarmed Germans filing past – her excitement was tempered by the dull sight they presented, the stuffing beaten out of them. They were jeered from the pavements, abuse exploded like grenades among the soldiers; five years of anxiety and hate were unloaded on the heads of the defeated. A vague feeling of sympathy flared up in her but she caught herself immediately and censured herself.

The Jews in hiding could not be restrained any more. They wanted to go home, they wanted to look for their families. Pent-up impatience and anxious premonitions drove them outside into the freedom that would never be as it had been before the war for anyone and certainly not for them. They had been warned: not all Germans have been disarmed yet, not all Dutch Nazis have been picked up. They stayed inside for ten long days of extreme self-restraint. Only Ruben could not stick it out. He wanted to see his parents' house, to surprise the neighbours: 'How glad they'll be to see me!' He set off despite all admonitions, ill at ease on a rickety bicycle, stared after anxiously.

Seemingly unharmed he returned. He sagged into a chair silently and sat still; only his eyes moved back and forth in bewilderment behind his glasses. Finally his head sank onto his chest and they realized that he was crying. That was unusual, alarming, after being robust and without shedding a tear for years. Without lifting his head he recounted how the reunion had gone. When the neighbour opened the door at his ring she recoiled with horror and dislike in her eyes. Her first reflex was to shut the door again but he had already stepped inside. He walked into the room as of old; his eye immediately fell on the chair where he had so often drunk a glass of lemonade or warm chocolate milk as a boy. But she did not invite him to sit; she paced up and down with agitation, flinging in his face that all that time she had been convinced the whole family had been taken off to Germany. 'Mother is still alive,' he told her, 'she will be delighted that you have looked after her things so well all those years.' He pointed absent-mindedly around at the Persian carpets and paintings that his parents had given to her for safe-keeping. 'Your father gave them to me,' she corrected sharply. 'I can still hear him saying: Liesbeth, have these things, we have no use for them any more, they are nothing but ballast to us.' Ruben stared at the portrait in oils of his grandfather, who looked at him disparagingly through a monocle. 'You had better discuss that with my mother,' he whispered diplomatically. 'I have nothing to discuss with your mother,' she said haughtily. The knuckles of her hands were white, gripping the edge of the table. 'Listen,' she blurted out, 'other people have already been living in your house for years. The world has changed and we have all had to adapt, and now you come here out of the blue thinking that everything will be the same as it was...' 'You're right...' Ruben went to the door as though in a dream. 'You're right ... excuse me for disturbing you...'

Little by little the community that had been founded on provisional strategies was being disbanded – one after the other they left Lotte's mother's ark. When the machinery for keeping everything going stopped and it had become silent all around her, her body went into cramp. She lay on her bed writhing – first she screwed her eyes closed in pain, then she opened them wide in astonishment. A bitter odour hung in the bedroom. Her soaking sheets had to be washed all the time. The family doctor called an ambulance after he had desperately sought a diagnosis. What an irony: those whom she had managed to keep alive all those years had simply walked out into the lane by the meadows on both feet, while she had to be carried away by orderlies. The cause was found at the neurology ward: an abrupt relaxation in the nerves, which had been giving out the 'danger' signal for years but had not been able to produce the associated 'flight' reflex.

For her husband the stresses were different. He grumbled about the English, the Canadians, the Americans; he lashed out against the new government; he opposed the rejoicing and glorification of the Western Allies while nothing was said about the grandiose exertions in the east. 'The western front would not have stood a chance,' he argued, 'without Stalingrad, without the eastern front, without the millions of losses in the Soviet army, without Stalin's indomitability and slyness,' he argued. 'The serious danger came from the east, Hitler knew that very well, all Germans knew that – why is everyone silent about it, why is it deliberately covered up in the press?' During his philippics he was generous enough to give himself the answer, 'From fear of the Bolsheviks! Ha! Because their actual enemy is Communism, not Fascism.' He added a further prediction without obligation: 'That fear will unite them all.' Shaking with indignation, he put a record on the turntable. Only the greatest composers could calm him – apart from Wagner who had to spend the rest of his life at the bottom of a deep drawer.

2

Long ago they used to sit in a bath-tub together, now they were lying in separate baths in pastel-coloured bathrooms and thinking about the bizarre, painful relationship that was attracting and repelling them. Every day they met in the deserted corridors on the way from the peat bath to the underwater massage or the carbonated bath. Overlooking the water flowing tirelessly from the fountains, they were driven together at the end of the morning by the longing for a cup of coffee in the Salle de Repos. Their penchant for coffee at least they had in common; could such a thing be built into the genes? They met beneath Leda and the Swan and drank their coffee in little gulps. Usually it was Anna who dispelled the heaviness and languor of the *après bain* by beginning on 'it' again.

⟡

Anna was outside the gate with her suitcase. It was the end of September, it was raining, it was peace. She had no one to go to. There was only one person she longed for; having decided to go and look for him, she had thought up a plan of campaign for getting as close as she could to his vicinity.

The first phase of it was Bad Neuheim in Hessen, where she would meet Ilse. She was allowed to ride in the back of an open freight lorry, crammed in with sixty released Wehrmacht soldiers. The wind went right through her drenched nurse's uniform. She clung on to the side of the lorry, shivering and teeth chattering. 'Go and sit inside, next to the driver, sister,' urged one of the soldiers. 'If he gets intimate, call us and we'll make quick work of him.' One of them knocked on the cab, the lorry stopped – he explained the reason in broken English. 'Of course,' nodded the black American, opening the door courteously for Anna. Inside it was warm and comfortable. He shared his lunch fraternally with her. Each communicated in their own double-Dutch on an unfamiliar wavelength. 'Where are you going to?' he asked. 'I have no one,' she explained, 'my husband is dead, my home has been bombed. I have a meeting in Bad Neuheim with someone who can perhaps help me with work.' Shocked by her own frankness, she looked at his supple brown fingers that held the steering wheel loosely. Who was he? Who was she herself? Where did they originate from? Where were they going to? A former slave from Africa come to Germany via America. A former maid from Cologne back in Germany via Austria, as an ex-prisoner, in the company of an ex-slave from Africa who had been regarded as a potential rapist until a few moments ago. As though he sensed her confusion he laughed with her in an amiable way.

At Bad Neuheim she went in search of the address Ilse had given her, lugging her suitcase. Dawdling Americans spoke to her. They looked at her, surprised to be ignored; most women put up no resistance to their lures, only too glad to saunter through the village on their arms and smoke their cigarettes. Anna was so focused on her unapproachability that it took a long time before she discovered that the street she was looking for was right there under her feet. The woman of the house let her in and pushed a letter from Ilse into her hand as though it concerned a state secret. She had already gone to her parents in Saarburg and requested Anna to follow her at her own convenience. 'How do I get there?' Anna asked. Saarburg was in the French zone; only the original inhabitants in possession of the correct papers had the right to return there. Anna, as a Viennese, had no ghost of a chance. 'We'll think of something,' whispered the woman, leaving her in a neat bedroom.

An American officer was billeted in the same house, a lawyer from Chicago. She was introduced to him the next morning and discovered that the enormous empire reaching from one ocean to the other, conquered by covered wagon, lasso and rifle, had for once brought forth a civilized citizen by chance who, above all, spoke her own language. 'I find it so awful, what the Nazis have done to the German people...' 'They haven't done anything to me,' said Anna dourly, 'American artillery shot my husband, American bombs destroyed my apartment, Americans took me prisoner.' But he would not be put off, patiently he dragged in his arguments so as to bring her another perspective. At the same time his lessons in politics and war studies were a veiled form of subtle seduction – Anna, not deaf to the erotic undertone, managed to keep her distance with polite objections during the days of enforced waiting. Bad Neuheim teemed with German soldiers who had lost an arm or a leg; they sat wearily on benches next to each other and stared silently at the passing Americans who had conquered their women as well as their country. Anna recognized Martin in their midst – it cut her to the quick to see them sitting there.

One evening the American invited her to a party. 'What's that?' she asked. 'Well...' he felt his clean-shaven jaw, 'there's a bit to eat, a bit to drink, a bit of being happy...' 'And then?' she asked suspiciously. 'Well, and then...? It would be good for you, you are young, you can't be sad for ever.' 'Danke, nein,' she shook her head, 'the end of the party is quite clear to me.' 'I can't help being a man,' he apologized. 'Nor I a woman,' she added, 'and my husband died a year ago. Excuse me but you didn't seriously think I would go to a party with you...' She uttered the word as though she had a bitter almond in her mouth. He bowed his head in acquiescence. He was no match for such intransigence, whether as a soldier or a man or a wordsmith. He was being re-posted the following day. An enormous bunch of red roses was delivered for Anna, proof of a frivolous extravagance in this time of shortages. A card was hanging among the leaves. 'For the first German woman to say No.'

Arrangements had meanwhile been made for her. A haulier from Bad Neuheim who had permission to cross the zone boundary was prepared to smuggle her to Koblenz. He drove up with his horse and wagon; she had to lie down with her suitcase on the floor that had been covered by a tarpaulin. Sacks with unknown contents were piled up over her, leaving an air hole. The relaxed Americans let them through but the French made spot checks, poking their bayonets into the sacks – just missing Anna, who was inhaling the smell of tarpaulin and waiting fearlessly. Perhaps she was only spared because secretly she longed for it and preferred the fate of struggling victims. The man on the box said his prayers, sweating, he admitted afterwards to her as he helped her out at Koblenz station.

No more trains were running that night. A herd of stranded travellers was sleeping in the station. Anna installed herself on the ground next to an old man in a patched-up army coat who put a bottle of wine to his lips and then generously allowed it to circulate in his immediate vicinity while he spread butter on chunks of white bread and distributed them at random. Anna declined his offer but he pushed his bottle into her hands with a gesture that would brook no opposition. 'I've got lots more,' he grinned, unconcerned, pointing to his bag with a shaking finger. She hesitated no longer; the ebullient atmosphere round the generous old man was infectious. The vineyards on the slopes of the Mosel were praised unanimously, the bottle went pragmatically from mouth to mouth. Anna stretched out on the floor, the suitcase beneath her head, and slowly dozed off. In the morning she was woken with wine – breakfast had the same ingredients as the previous evening's supper. They forgot their cares, there was singing, the autumn sun shone, even the train to Trier puffed into the station. Festivities continued in the compartment, the crumpled host at its beaming centre.

The train stopped half-way. The rails were missing for a distance of a few kilometres. They continued on foot, singing travelling songs, drinking. The sun glistened in the profuse tinsel of wild hops along the railway line. Another train was waiting further on. Nothing could suppress the jollity. 'What sort of company is this?' growled a priest sitting by the window. 'That boozing, that drunken talk.' Irritated, he took up his breviary and began to pray, to compensate for the immorality surrounding him. 'Will you have some?' Anna offered him the bottle, laughing. He shook his head with pursed lips. Everyone got out at Bernkastel, leaving her alone in the priest's company. She leaned out of the window to wave to the creased philanthropist who had spread so much happiness around him. He tottered along the platform, awaited by his wife who, with hawk eyes at a distance, had already put together the diagnosis for an empty bag. 'Where is the bread . . . ?' she let fly, 'where is the butter, where is . . . !' The shrivelled-up little man raised his arms to heaven. 'In paradise . . .' he moaned.

The train set off again. The feeling of happiness induced by the wine turned to sadness. Sentimental tears dribbled down the lowered window as she stared at his ever diminishing figure. She flopped back into her seat. The priest looked up flabbergasted from his breviary. Remembering his Christian duty he enquired haughtily why she was crying. She explained why the number of times she had been happy since October 1944 could be counted on the fingers of one hand. Moreover it was not an insouciant happiness as before but one that was rooted in despair. Familiar with this sort of paradox – suffering for the sake of salvation was another one – he nodded.

It was already dark and they were not yet in Trier. 'Have you got an address for the night?' he asked matter-of-factly. 'The station,' said Anna laconically. He looked disapprovingly at her. 'Why do you think I look like this . . . ?' she pointed to her dirty uniform. He was silent, pensive. 'If I took you to the nuns, in the convent? Would you come with me?' 'Good heavens!' she cried, 'does such a thing still exist?' 'Yes of course.' 'In these times?' 'Yes,' he said, ruffled. 'Of course I'll go with you.'

When they arrived at Trier, Anna was in the middle of the hangover-thirst phase. She got out, dead-beat. 'Follow me,' said the father sternly. He walked rapidly into the dark town. She dragged the heavy suitcase like a dog on a lead behind her over the bumpy cobbles. He walked ten paces ahead of her without looking round, for fear of compromising himself. She thought that he was not so much driven by Christian charity as by protecting his own place in heaven: 'Inasmuch as ye have done it unto one of the least of my brethren, ye have done it unto me.' She followed the black habit past the dark façades, panting. Every step was a step back in time, up to the Romans in the form of the Porta Nigra that towered threateningly above her in its sombre massiveness. The representative of the Church turned right and stopped at a heavy wooden door with iron studs. He knocked, muttered three words and was gone, without shaking hands, without saying goodbye; no sign of humanity whatsoever escaped from this servant of God.

God's female servants had quite a different attitude to their status as the chosen. They raised a hand to their mouth when they saw her and immediately began to put things in order. A bath-tub was filled with warm water, her dirty clothes were received; while she lay in the bath the convent filled with nocturnal activity. She was wrapped in a chaste towel and taken to a guest room where she slid between clean, smooth sheets and fell asleep with the picture of a heavenly smiling nun before her eyes. When she woke her light grey striped nurse's uniform was on the table, shining in the morning sun – washed, ironed and pressed.

She arrived at Saarburg as an impeccable Red Cross sister. History repeated itself. Ilse had already departed again, as advocate for her fiancé who was still in captivity, prompted to hurry by the disturbing prospect of the approaching winter. But there was work for Anna. A particularly unsavory chore had waited patiently for her all that time. In revenge for five years of war the Luxemburgers had crossed over the border and had given full vent to their feelings of displeasure in a hit-and-run raid on the villagers' property. The walls and windows of Ilse's parents' half-timbered house had been smeared with excrement. Linen had been pulled out of the cupboards and dirtied – they had sprawled on it, said the woman with a mouth taut from suppressed rage, and had manufactured the material of their revenge before her eyes. 'The tit-for-tat answer,

349

you understand. A disgusting people those Luxemburgers.' She was too sickly to take on the great cleaning herself, while her husband spent long days in his sawmill.

Anna rolled up her sleeves and began. She had gone away from a pigsty ten years ago, now she was back in it. What difference did it make? But when a lorry from the sawmill was able to take her some way in the right direction, she threw the mop and brush in a corner – she had made enough outflanking movements now. Ilse's mother, who knew what had brought her diligent cleaning woman to these parts, had to let her go. The lorry drove out of the town in a thick drizzle, to Daun in the Eifel. She continued on foot, through immense pine forests that dissolved in a mist of fine droplets. It was chilly, the damp penetrated through her soles, but the knowledge that she was getting closer all the time made her indifferent to discomfort. This deserted road, sauntering uphill, downhill between melancholy pines, was precisely what you could expect of a pilgrim's route to the underworld. She was not afraid. The end of the journey was coming into view, afterwards there would be nothing more to wish for, afterwards ... there was no afterwards. The cold crept up to her middle, she progressed more slowly, her soles were worn out, the patches hung loose and flapped with each step. All she could see was shiny black tree trunks and dripping branches – her spirit stubbornly insisted although her body was showing increasing signs of unwillingness. At a given moment he could not bear to look any longer and began to interfere. Listen, dearest, he said compassionately, do go home. What do you want? I'm not there at all ... Thus he chatted to her; initially she ignored him but when he – carefully as always – arranged an approaching driver who loomed up out of the mist, she capitulated. Today you win, she admitted, but come I shall ... at a more suitable moment ...

Back in Saarburg she continued the cleaning. The grousing about the Luxemburgers did not cease. It pursued her into all the rooms like a drill, driven on by revenge, which was overheard by

350

an old lady who lived in some rooms at the rear of the house. 'How can you stand it here?' she said, observing Anna cleaning. 'You're surely not going to stay on here doing that for ever.' 'What should I be doing then?' said Anna defensively, 'I'm waiting for Ilse.' 'My God, then you could be in for a long wait. Who knows when she'll find help. But listen, I've got a suggestion for you. I have an acquaintance in Trier, a retired teacher from the grammar school. She is looking for someone to do the housekeeping . . . not just any-one, you understand. Perhaps it's something for you.' Anna nodded slowly – her life ultimately hung together on improvisations.

She recognized Kaiserstrasse in Trier from her nocturnal journey in a priest's wake, and there she got to know a fascinating type of person full of incomprehensible contradictions: Thérèse Schmidt, a narrow, bony woman with thin grey hair held together by a clip, stingy in terms of material things but generous and helpful where the intellect was concerned. It was not apparent that she went to her brother's farm every day just outside the town, to stuff herself with bread, meat and dairy foods. Without shame she expatiated upon it. It never occurred to her to bring something back for Anna, who was trying to stay alive on two slices of bread a day, some potatoes and a cup of black coffee dregs – the rationing imposed by the French in retaliation for the hunger they had had to suffer. It was much harder to reconcile Frau Schmidt's rare stinginess with her daily visits to church, Bible study and fervent praying – never had Anna encountered close-up so much bigoted religious zeal. There were a lot of books in the house; her earlier appetite for read-ing returned between the housekeeping tasks. Surprised, the tea-cher drew up a chair when she returned from her daily visit and found her reading. 'You are not destined to spend your whole life between the stove and the kitchen sink, I could see that right away . . . What do you really want to do?' 'I have no idea . . .' Anna stam-mered, overwhelmed by the sudden interest. Her plans for the future extended no further than completing that one mission. 'Isn't there something you have always really wanted to do?' Anna frowned. Dante slid from her lap but was intercepted in his fall by Frau Schmidt's narrow hand. The idea of having the freedom to choose a career for oneself was so revolutionary that it paralysed her thinking. She had to let go of her picture of the world in which women were clearly divided into three categories: a broad lower layer containing farming women and servants, a small upper layer of privileged women who had the decorative function of being civilized, elegant wives, and the remaining category of unmarried women in teaching, nursing or convents. No one chose for herself, it was something they came straight into – through birth or circumstances. Frau Schmidt repeated her innocent question. 'Well...' Anna sighed. Her head was light, she did not know if it was from hunger or the thorny questioning. Her thoughts flitted criss-cross back in time, in search of examples for possible candidates to identify with, for someone who could say the word for her – thus she landed up in a dark, stuffy, small room where it smelled of sweating feet and a dead soldier hung on the wall who had been born to die for the fatherland (such an inevitable, obvious destination again). Opposite her stood a woman resolutely closing the door with her backside and lovingly opening her arms: come here...

'Child welfare...' Anna blurted out '...I believe I have always wanted to do that.' 'I see ... but why don't you then?' 'It would be quite impossible,' Anna said brusquely, 'I would have to do matriculation first...' Frau Schmidt laughed at her: 'Is that all!' From her past in the education system she ferreted out a teacher who was prepared to cram her ready for the state examination. Another woman attended his lessons; Anna could join her. From then on, every afternoon she walked to his house through the centuries-old streets between piles of debris and people collapsing from hunger, worn-out rubber overshoes over her worn-out shoes. 'Listen, you don't need to understand,' the teacher impressed upon her, 'all you have to do in the exam is to be able to give the precise answers. Read it out of your head.' Everyone had already been astounded by her memory when Anna recited 'The Song of the Bell' next to her proud father. Now it was the teacher who was breathless at the speed with which she acted on his advice. He rushed her through grammar, the foundations of mathematics, through history, geography, German literature. After fourteen days he said: 'I am working with two dissimilar racehorses here. You run ahead like a madcap, the other can't keep up. I shall have to separate you.'

Her head was entirely empty – she had hidden the war deeply away, deliberately lost the key. There was plenty of space for the dizzying quantities of information, so agreeably neutral in their capacity as cultural wares. She crammed and crammed, almost fainting away sometimes under the high revs. 'Are you dizzy?' the teacher enquired. 'Yes...' she said hazily. 'What have you eaten?' 'Two potatoes...' 'Good heavens, you should have said so earlier!' He made her a plate of oatmeal porridge. 'Don't be concerned, I get food parcels from the English zone.' Each day the lessons began with a plate of porridge: first the body, then the mind, was his view. He also pointed out that her overshoes had had it. It did not occur to her employer, who had at least ten pairs of shoes in the same size, to hand over one pair to her. The teacher bartered two bottles of gin for sound leather shoes. At home Anna showed them to her, elated. Frau Schmidt raised her eyebrows without interest: 'So...?'

On Christmas Eve she went to her brother as usual for an advance on the Christmas meal. She had said before her departure that she wanted a bath when she returned – to cleanse the body before she dealt with the soul during midnight mass. Anna had to get everything ready and heat a large cauldron of water on the coal stove in the kitchen. It was already dark when the bell went unexpectedly. A woman was standing at the door, clasping a crying baby wrapped in rags to her, threatening to collapse from exhaustion. Anna caught her, brought her to the kitchen and took the child from her, which smelled as though it had not been changed in weeks. She could see the steaming cauldron and the tub from the corner of her eye – everything was ready for the gnädige Frau.

Without thinking about it she filled the bath, unwrapped the child and threw the stinking rags in the passage. After she had washed the baby she wrapped him in a flannel towel. *En passant* she gave the mother a piece of bread and butter, a boiled potato and a cup of black coffee. Not a word was said, everything happened in a hurried sequence of self-evident actions – under the constant threat of the phantom Frau Schmidt, who might come home at any moment. What now, Anna asked herself feverishly, where should they go? The convent! The nuns, those angels of mercy! She slipped a coat on and took the mother and child to the Ursulines, who eagerly took pity on them. A comfortable feeling of synchronicity came over her on the way back: it was the eve of Christmas and there was no room at the inn! Above Trier's piles of rubble the sky was strewn with stars, she was walking beneath it in her new shoes. Everything was in equilibrium – for a little while.

She came home at the same time as her employer. When a tub full of dirty water was awaiting her there instead of a warm bath, the teacher was outraged. She raised her arms in a grotesque gesture; a torrent of accusations descended on Anna. 'Just a moment,' she squeezed past, 'I'll put a new cauldron on the fire, I'll clean everything up, it will be done in a moment.' Frau Schmidt only calmed down when order had been restored and the picture of the kitchen corresponded with the one she had had in mind as she walked home flushed and satisfied from the meal.

During the midnight mass she sat in the pew, smelling of soap and starch, singing, rejoicing, praying lustily. She ranted and raved like an angel of Our Lord with the same voice that was so good at torrents of abuse. Anna watched stoically. On the way home Frau Schmidt said, 'It escapes me how you could let such a dirty woman and dirty child into my house.' Anna stopped, looked her in the eye and quoted serenely what the pastor had said shortly before: '... because there was no room for them in the inn ... and Mary gave birth to her first-born son in a stable ... she wrapped him in swaddling clothes and laid him in the manger...' 'You are trying to get out of it by making a pun...' said the teacher, walking on gruffly. Nevertheless Anna received a Christmas present. No warm stockings, no vest, no milk or meat, but a Latin missal: the *Sacramentaria*, the *Lectionarum* and the *Graduale* – a silent hint that Anna still had a lot to learn when it came to Christianity.

Frau Schmidt's altruism lay more in the didactic sphere. Her search for an academy of social work had not been made easy. All training colleges indoctrinated by the Nazis had been shut down; what survived was a reliable Catholic institute in North Rhine Westphalia. The director responded immediately to her impeccable letter: she would be visiting the seminary at Trier in March, and would take that opportunity to assess Frau Schmidt's protégé herself.

As protection from the dust that blew out of the rubble heaps Anna wore a headscarf that flapped in the breeze. The closer she got to the seminary the stronger exam nerves took hold of her. The director, haughty and curt, did nothing to put her at her ease, but subjected her to a cross-examination. 'Why do you want to be a social worker?' she asked in a cynical tone, as though a plan so arrogant, brazen had never come to her notice before. 'I want to help people,' sounded weak. 'Why?' 'Because I want to help people!' Anna repeated, raising her voice, forgetting all ceremony and polite phrases. An uneasy silence fell. I've blown it, she thought, I saw to that in no time. But why does she treat me like a dog? But you stroke a dog's head, you say: you're a good dog. Finally she broke the silence penitently: 'I myself was a child who needed help.' Again that silence and the scornful, piercing look of the authority who was going to decide her fate. 'You can go,' said the woman abruptly. Anna came home dejected. Frau Schmidt dashed towards her. 'And how did it go?' 'I can forget it. It was nothing.' The teacher sniffed in disbelief. She had her own channels for getting objective information; some days later she reported with triumphant victory: 'You made a deep impression on her. At least that one knows what she wants, she said to the abbot...' Anna looked up wearily. She did not want to hear any more about it, the teacher was concocting it. But the post proved her right. A well-thumbed, damaged telegram was delivered: 'First semester starts: 1 September.'

Farewell Frau Schmidt, teacher! But before travelling to North Rhine Westphalia she had to make a second attempt. This time she had solid shoes, the sun was shining, she had a lift in a post office van up to the village itself. She got out in the centre; villagers told her where it was. With an armful of flowers plucked on the way she pushed open the squeaky wrought-iron gate. There was an aisle, as in the church, with rows of graves on either side. The oldest at the front: names from the district, mossy, worn away by rain and frost, on crooked headstones and cracked tombstones. Clipped yews and conifers in between and an impressive absence of noise, only interrupted by bird song. Further behind were the more recent graves. One stuck out immediately because it was square instead of rectangular, and three amateurish wooden crosses stood on it next to each other, as though seeking support from one another. As she began to walk intuitively towards it, a sudden irrational anxiety crept over her: the anxiety that he would still be proved right and would be all about there except in this one spot ... that he would laugh at her from all points of the compass for her naïvety. But there was no escape: she had been *en route* to this pathetic two-square-metre plot since her release from the American camp. So, step by step, she approached her disillusionment with diffidence. Each cross bore a name carved out in cuneiform letters – the middle one had his. The earth underneath had been covered with evergreen sprigs with white roses on top. From whom, whom were the flowers from? She knelt down, laid her bunch of wildflowers there and stared at his name in the hope that something of his presence would manifest itself, but the only thing she could see before her was the tanned soldier who waved to her in the tidy station at Nuremberg: '... this bloody hell will soon end anyway...' If he was living anywhere it was within her, there was no place on earth where that was as certain as here . . .

'What are you doing at my grave?' sounded behind her, straight through the silence, a female voice. Anna stiffened. She said carefully, not turning round, 'If there is anyone in the world whose grave this is then I am that person. My husband lies here, as it happens.' The indiscreet song of a blackbird came from a conifer; there were muffled sobs in between. Anna turned round. A young woman with swollen eyes was staring at her. Although the grave displayed the unpopular attribute of graves all over the world, by remaining proverbially silent, a suspicion arose in Anna that was too awful to be contemplated. There are two others, she reassured herself. 'Are you Frau Grosalie?' said the girl in a slurred voice. 'Yes, yes . . .' said Anna curtly, 'I am Frau Grosalie, but what have you got to do with my husband . . . ?' The other looked up to the sky as though she were expecting a sign. Anna could not think of anything to say to put it all into perspective. Their gazes crossed fleetingly.

'I will explain,' said the girl. She scratched her chin. 'He was billeted with our neighbours. We got to know him over the fence, my mother and I. Right away we found him sympathetic . . . both of us . . .' In this way she shyly introduced her story. Martin was making contact with Anna in an unorthodox manner via the last female being he had seen before his death – via her he was telling his wife the details. Only now did his abstract death – 'the heroic death of your husband' – become something that had happened to him at a specific moment in a specific place. At one moment he had still been alive and could see, hear, smell, talk, laugh – a moment later his mortal remains were being gathered up. In a dull voice the girl recalled the day concerned in September 1944. The office where she worked in Prüm had been closed because the whole district had become the front zone and all traffic was shut down. She was obliged to stay at home. She was sitting on the bench in the garden when the officer waved hallo to her and called out that he had

received an order to go to the Westwall with his men to take possession of a bunker full of signals equipment. She sprang up from
the bench: 'Could I have a lift with you to Prüm?' she asked on
spontaneous impulse. 'I've left a bag of things at the office.' He
shook his head: 'The roads are not safe, the Americans are shooting
at us from all sides.' But when she urged him and pleaded with
him to take her along he gave in. 'Well, if you absolutely insist.'

They set off; the lorry navigated a woodland path. Something
exploded in the distance now and then, leaves and berries trembled
in the air, then everything went quiet again. 'My goodness,' she
cried suddenly in a panic, 'I've forgotten the key!' Martin made
light of the mistake: 'You don't really need a key, you'll see, there
are no windows left in that house, you'll be able to climb in.' 'That
may very well be,' she said stubbornly, 'but I would rather fetch
the key.' She prepared to get out, he stopped her: 'It's perilous to
walk back alone.' But she would not be dissuaded. An immovable
belief in the indispensability of the key obliged her to go straight
back. She said goodbye, got out and walked back the way they had
come.

Half-way through the afternoon the signals technicians returned
to the village. Three of them wrapped in canvas like mummies, six
others unhurt. The villagers thronged together, the girl stood there
among them in confused desperation and asked the survivors in an
apologetic tone for an explanation, not suspecting that they were
already weighed down by heavy feelings of guilt. One of them gave
the account, with a hanging head. The lorry was approaching a
village. Martin was sitting up front – as she knew – between the
driver and a soldier. The others called from behind, 'Stop for a
moment, we want to pick a few apples.' There was an orchard on a
slope, red apples glistening defiantly in the sun. 'We can't stop,'
Martin had said, 'if we stop we will be an easy target for the
Americans.' But the men whined 'Just for a minute' and Martin,
good-natured as he was, did not persist. 'Hurry then!' he capitulated. Six soldiers jumped out of the lorry and ran into the orchard

like six rascals. They forgot the war, they shook the branches and collected apples until they were startled by an explosion below. The cab with the three who stayed behind blew up before their eyes, hit by shell fire.

The girl listened to him speechless, staring at the three prosaic parcels, and saw before her the men she had sat with fraternally a few hours earlier. Meanwhile the men's baggage had been assembled; in Martin's suitcase there were a pair of pale blue children's shoes and a silver evening purse among the books. Only the sight of his personal possessions now conveyed the full magnitude of the disaster to her. She turned her back on the scene in a flood of tears. Meanwhile someone took his chance in the commotion – when she had come to herself and turned round again the shoes and evening purse had disappeared.

Anna nodded slowly. 'The hero's death of your husband...' Killed for a handful of apples. It connected to that one apple that had brought disaster to mankind. Martin had trudged through the steppes of Russia and the fields of the Ukraine, he had survived the cold, an attack by partisans, a fatal illness, he had been spared throughout the whole war so that he could die on the outskirts of a farming village in the Eifel for a handful of apples. However absurd and senseless this death seemed, it was one that nevertheless suited him: he had died while giving others pleasure. She could recognize him as he had been in this. He had suddenly come close to her in the story of his death. 'Are the flowers from you?' she said gently. 'My mother and I,' the girl assented, 'bartered butter and eggs in Trier for those roses.' Anna turned round. The other graves were neglected; the square one with the three crosses was a lovingly maintained island amid overgrown tombstones.

The girl insisted on introducing Anna to her mother, who shook her hand emotionally. 'Your husband was such a good man...' she sighed, dabbing her nose. Then she prepared a reception for the widow as though she were a long-lost member of the family from America. Everything edible that could be found in the house and garden was put on the table, prepared with fragrant herbs. Anna understood that it was a celebration meal as well as a memorial meal. He was dead but she was alive – thanks to her paranormal obsession with the key. 'The thing that I don't understand...' said the mother at the departure, 'is that the SS buried them and put the crosses on top, but our pastor has refused to bless them because they are SS. Now is that Christian...?'

⸙

'At least you had a grave you could go to,' said Lotte coolly. She was disinclined to get carried away by the story of Anna's pilgrimage to the grave of her SS officer.

Lost in thought, Anna looked at her. 'How do you mean?'

'There was no cemetery at Mauthausen.'

Anna stroked her painful legs. For some days she had believed in the illusion that the pain had been diminishing through the soothing influence of the baths, but now it suddenly returned in all its ferocity. 'I went to Auschwitz a couple of years ago,' she said. 'Six thousand people were gassed there each day. I stood there, where all of them had gone, and remembered the beautiful summer of 1943. Martin came, we went swimming in the lake, we went over to the island, wonderful weekends for us alone. I did not know that it was my last supper. That millions of people had gone this way at that time when I had been experiencing a bit of good fortune in my life ... I could not cope with it, it was so dreadful...' She massaged her knees. 'But whether or not I was fortunate, they had not been helped...'

That was a truism. Lotte was silent.

'I did not believe it at first,' Anna continued. 'I saw the pictures on television for the first time in the fifties. Do you know what I thought? The Americans have collected the corpses out of the towns they themselves bombed and thrown them on a heap in a concentration camp. I could not believe it.'

'When did it finally get through?' said Lotte sharply.

'It began with a big exhibition, "The Jews in Cologne from

Roman Times". The truth slowly trickled inside there. You must understand: politics did not interest me. I was completely obsessed with my work, there was nothing else.'

'Wir haben es nicht gewusst, we had other things to do,' Lotte railed scornfully.

'Yes ... no...' said Anna irritated, 'you didn't hear anything about the Jews in everyday life. I don't recall anyone ever saying anything about it.'

Lotte stood up, overcome by a dull sense of futility. A nurse came in and requested them to get dressed. Closing time was approaching, the staff wanted to go home.

The inescapable family connection was continuing to claim its rights whether they wanted it to or not. Something was still forcing them to go on rowing against the current, towards each other – the one in active pursuit of conquest, the other as a passive victim of a maddening sort of affinity to which she could offer no resistance.

That evening they dined together in a small restaurant on the Avenue Astrid. It was Saturday; they did not have to be at the bath house at the crack of dawn the following morning. They went on to the Relais de la Poste in search of a little bit of Saturday night ambience and made themselves comfortable on the leather settees from the thirties, a time when they had still been young and did not know what was hanging over them. They drank coffee with Grand Marnier. The jukebox filled the space with velvet ever-greens from the fifties.

'Life goes on, they always say...' Anna sipped from her glass. 'When we have suffered a great loss, the other person gives us a clap on the back and says: chin up, life goes on. A cliché and at the same time a bitter universal truth. Our towns lay in rubble, our soldiers were dead, crippled, stripped of illusions. As a people we acquired the collective guilt for the greatest mass murder in the history of mankind. We were economically and morally bankrupt ... and yet, somehow or other, life went on. I threw myself into studying, my work. Everyone went to work, my God...' She emptied her glass in one gulp and laughed to herself. 'The whole reconstruction was one big occupational therapy!'

Lotte stared absently into her glass. Memories of the dreary peace drifted past. She did not want to think about it, and precisely because of that she thought about it.

◆◆

Ernst was working too. He was taken on by a violin-maker in The Hague who had rheumatism of the hands that obliged him increasingly to leave the work to him. They had moved into a small flat behind the workshop – Ernst earned a post-war pittance, like many others. Obsessed with his new responsibilities as husband and future head of a family, he stirred himself to ever greater productivity: five days a week he repaired violins, on the other two he made new ones that he sold. Seven days a week Lotte was alone with the thoughts marriage was supposed to have released her from. She paced about the room, wrenched from her family – a painful *déjà vu*. Where had she come to, had she wished for this? She dreamed of a large old house with high ceilings, a house that would reconcile her to the loneliness of the marriage, a house that she would recreate as a home. The dream drove her through a criss-cross of streets and canals. Autumn came, winter, the dark façades warded her off, the lit-up rooms shut her out – only the little match girl was missing. It was as though she were still doing penance, in the form of an eternal roaming, homeless, without relatives, the just deserts of someone who was neither one thing nor the other, a hybrid, treacherous on both sides.

Perhaps it was music that was missing. What had happened to Amelita Galli-Curci? The *Exsultate, jubilate*? The *St Matthew Passion*? She found a singing teacher, but already at the first lesson it seemed that not much was left of her voice. She wore herself out apologizing to the teacher – with great nostalgia she mentioned everything she had sung before, but when she saw the doubt in the other's eye she began to doubt it herself. What had happened to her voice, which had once effortlessly filled the water-tower from top to bottom? Her vocal chords were like dried out rubber bands that crumbled between the fingers.

If she wanted to hear music she had to visit her parents. But there the dislocation filtered through the façade of normal family life. Her mother, who held the thing together with an artificial cheerfulness, had developed an obsession with eating, to forget the hunger and everything else. She had lost almost all her children at the same time as the people in hiding left. Something seemed to have developed secretly between Jet and Ruben since she had lain in bed with concussion and he had read aloud to her for hours to kill time. Theo de Zwaan had long ago known how to melt Marie's Cinderella-heart. Mies had gone to live above the hat shop shortly before the war. They had all married and were living independently. Invited by Bram, Koen had gone to America, which had enjoyed almost mythical popularity since D-Day as a country of unlimited possibilities. The two youngest who were still at home could not concentrate at school and were boisterous and unruly.

Lotte also could not bear to watch her father being so cheerful, now that he had his wife almost to himself. He had been stopped in the street by an older gentleman who stared at him flabbergasted. 'You're still alive! Are you really Rockanje?' He nodded suspiciously. 'Once upon a time I gave you an injection...' cried the other enthusiastically, 'straight into the heart – a desperate act because I had already given you up!' Lotte's father, who remembered nothing about it and had heard everything about his sickbed second-hand, thanked him in bewilderment for his sturdy intervention and went home with a spring in his step. He felt as though life had been given to him for a second time and this time he decided he wasn't going to let anyone hold him back from really enjoying it. (The great disillusion was still awaiting him: Father Stalin was still a man of irreproachable behaviour.)

The war was regurgitated somewhat poisonously, for a moment, and an ugly crack would have appeared in his reputation if Sara Frinkel had not made a forceful appearance. A Jewish dinner had been organized. The Frinkel family, not yet departed for America, was also invited. Ed de Vries said during the meal, in that loud manner with which he had always known how to attract attention as a singer-entertainer, that the Rockanje family had swindled him out of a box he had given to them for safekeeping containing valuables worth half a million. Indignantly Sara Frinkel had cried, 'How dare you!' across the table. 'You take those words back immediately, old rat. How did you get that into your head? You didn't have a sou! Don't make me laugh, you with your half a million in a box, about which you said: I'm coming to bury a few knick-knacks. I've got your measure: you're trying to get it back on the insurance. That's your business but don't think of dragging the Rockanje family through the mud!'

Lotte sometimes looked at the film star photos Theo de Zwaan had taken of her and Jet before the war. With what self-assurance and defiance they looked into the lens, as though the world lay at their feet. What recklessness, what ignorance! She thought back to how life had been before the war with a sense of bitterness and nostalgia. Although they had been opposed to God and Colijn, under their mother's lead they had had a romantic belief in justice, humanity, beauty. While Beethoven flowed out of the open window on summer evenings and she looked at the stars and the dark edge of the wood with the others from their wicker chairs, they thought: if such splendid music can exist, life must be splendid too in the most profound ways. Now she was ashamed of those grand feelings. Beethoven was a German, Bach too, Mendelssohn was a Jew; the Nazis paraded with their German composers and prohibited the Jewish ones – never again would they be able to listen to music free from associations. To have to be silent about the *Kindertotenlieder*. Everything had been defiled.

⚜

They had not noticed it becoming busy around them. Older couples had settled at the tables, the men in suits with starched shirts and ties, their ladies – fresh from the coiffeur – in dresses with pleated skirts and patent belts. The age of jeans and T-shirts had not yet penetrated here. A popular song began to play; a few couples dared to make their way to the middle, now rearranged as a dance floor. A sweet-voiced Louis Prima led them on. They turned their snappy steps proficiently ... *Buona sera signorina ... buona sera ...*

'How lovely ...' Anna sighed, 'that they still have so much fun at their age.'

Lotte followed the greyheads with a disapproving expression round her mouth. 'Don't you find it a bit embarrassing,' she said demurely, 'that sentimental fuss, for such oldies.'

'Mensch, don't be so harsh ... for yourself. Did you never go dancing with your violin-maker ...?'

That 'with your violin-maker' offended Lotte and the idea that they would have danced together like these dolled-up old people was simply revolting. 'My violin-maker has been dead for years ...' she said sharply, hoping that Anna would be ashamed.

But it did not trouble her at all. A burly old man presented himself. He was buttoning up his jacket and bowing slightly ironically towards Anna. She stood up with an amused laugh, wormed past two tables and disappeared from view for a short while. 'Oh mon papa ...' warbled the jukebox.

Anna circled over the dance floor as though she had never been doing anything else since the nuns had taught her to dance in the shadow of the Von Zitsewitz castle. Chuckling, she thought back to the bother about 'Was machst du mit dem Knie, lieber Hans', but the Casanova in Spa behaved himself impeccably. He led her self-confidently, without suspecting that he was holding someone in his arms who had not allowed herself to be led for a long time, by no matter whom. Yes, he even made so bold as to dance his own version of the tango with her, with one arm stuck out straight and abrupt one-hundred-and-eighty-degree turns. Afterwards he brought her back to her seat chivalrously.

Anna was out of breath. 'Who would have thought it?' she

laughed hoarsely. 'A peat bath followed by dancing...'

They left the café late in the evening, after Anna had been tempted onto the dance floor twice more by her silent partner. The bath house cast its shadow over the road like a mastodon. They turned right, dizzy from the Grand Marnier.

'Those who dance keep death at a distance...' Anna giggled, bumping into Lotte. 'Just look what a clear sky! Tomorrow it will definitely be fine weather. We can go for a lovely walk. What do you say to that, Schwesterlein? The pain has gone, I'm telling you, disappeared ... ffft...' She put her arm through Lotte's.

She too had lost some of her reserve as a result of the alcohol and the unreal scenes that she had been absorbing all that time. 'Listen, Anna...' she said, 'just then, when I saw you whirling round on the dance floor, I remembered something from earlier, in a flash...'

'You mean from a very long time ago?'

'Yes ... You were dancing in the hall, wild, unruly, ungainly – or perhaps you weren't dancing but playing tag with ... there was a boy there...'

'The concierge's son,' Anna completed, intuitively.

'It could have been ... you were romping about up the stairs, your excited screaming echoed through the corridor ... Suddenly you were lying at the bottom of the stairs shrieking ... there was something wrong with your arm ... I was frightened and shrieking with you. I don't know what happened then ... although yes, wait a minute...' She spoke louder from the excitement. The memory was unstoppable once it had got going. 'You were taken to the hospital and came back with your arm in plaster in a sling. I was jealous ... I wanted everything that you had ... your pain, and also your bandage. They put my arm in a tea towel or something ... as consolation.'

'Now you say that...' Anna stopped, 'now you say it ... yes ... I had completely forgotten. It was broken, in two places even, I believe ... You still remember it! Now you see!'

She wanted to say something else but instead she embraced Lotte. The alcohol and the emotions were beginning to ferment dangerously. Their bodies swayed back and forth alarmingly above the asphalt, as though they were clinging tightly to each other on a ship in a storm. Before Anna's eyes the Athenae sailed with them in the background, before Lotte's the oranges and lemons in a greengrocer's window. They walked on step by step, the town of springs, Spa, came and went pleasantly, as though it had over-indulged itself on Grand Marnier. Anna stopped in the middle of the bridge over the railway. Leaning heavily on the balustrade, she made a grand gesture towards the stars, which were sparkling above the silhouette of roofs and surrounding hills, and recited in a pompous voice:

> 'For seeing begotten,
> My sight my employ,
> And sworn to the watch-tower,
> The world gives me joy.
>
> I gaze in the distance,
> I mark in the near,
> The moon and the planets,
> The woods and the deer . . .

'Er . . . how does it go on . . . ?' she cried plaintively. 'My God, I can't remember it any more . . .' Her arms were still raised to the stars, in an empty gesture now.

'Come,' said Lotte, tugging at her arm.

3

Lotte had chosen a route with the idyllic name 'Promenade des Artistes' with the help of a walking map. She regretted her sentimentality of the previous evening. A shared memory was no reason for fraternizing – strange that the word 'sisterizing' did not exist. She maintained a careful distance and placed her hands firmly in the pockets of her winter coat. A watery sun shimmered between the branches. A narrow brook meandered like silver beside the path.

With each step Anna rejoiced at the suppleness of her joints – the peat was beginning to take effect. She inhaled the tingling forest air and thought she could feel the oxygen penetrating deep into her lungs. Very soon her cheerfulness translated into communicativeness. She chuckled to herself, 'You'll never guess, Lotte, who came looking for me in Salzkotten.'

꧁꧂

The Institute for Social Work was located on the top floor of a Franciscan convent. Successful studying depended a good deal on the talent to improvise. There were no textbooks or exercise books. Those who managed to get hold of a roll of wallpaper or a sheet of wrapping paper could take notes. The lecturers, who had been scraped together from all over the country, arrived at the Institute from their ruined towns after an adventurous journey over a devastated railway network. They stayed at the convent and drove the students into the ground non-stop for fourteen days on psychology or sociology. Mindful of the Gospel of the Nazarene, the nuns shared their scarce provisions with the pupils, and when winter came they willingly sat in the cold so that the classroom could be warm.

There was an ironic coincidence – the village on the Lippe where her father had been born and her grandfather had died was within walking distance of Salzkotten, the village in the fairy-tale about the swineherd – but without the prince. She preferred not to assume that her peregrinations and destiny had calculated that she had to land up here, as an element in the inescapable course of nature. That that spot of calamities was so nearby she ignored; even the finest weather could not entice her to walk in that direction. But Salzkotten with its weekly market was the hub of the surrounding villages. One day she ran into someone from her village who had once sat next to her in class. They exchanged information, surprised at the reunion.

This chance meeting provoked one that was far less coincidental. Some days later there was a knock at her door. 'You have a visitor,' said a fellow student bashfully, 'if you would come to the parlour.' 'I have a visitor?' Anna exclaimed. 'That can't be so, I have no one in the whole world. Who is it, then?' 'Well, it's not a lady ... It is some woman or other who claims she is your family.' Anna walked downstairs unsuspecting. At the doorway she stiffened. The soberly furnished room was completely taken over by the figure awaiting her; the mere fact of her presence was itself a form of sacrilege. She was hefty and flabby, her skin gleamed, her eyes and hair were darker than ever, her vulgar self-importance contrasted stridently with the modest biblical subjects on the walls. 'Mein Gott,' she said in a whining, small voice adapted to the surroundings, 'what are you doing here, are you becoming a nun?'

Anna kept a suitable distance; an extreme self-control was required to resist the tortures and humiliations that emanated from her like a dark devil's aura. No ... oh no ... she thought, warding it off ... not this ... In a flat impersonal manner she explained what the purpose of her stay at the convent was. 'Ah, is that so ...' sighed the visitor, still insatiably curious. 'Listen, whatever you need – butter, cheese, eggs – you just have to say ...' Anna was forced into a dilemma by this reckless offer of hers. The threats of ten years ago buzzed in her head: 'You will come crawling to me begging for bread...' On the other hand there plainly was hunger, for everyone in the convent, and there was the settling of old scores: she plainly was entitled to all that this aunt owed her. 'Terrific,' she heard herself saying haughtily, 'we would all be glad of that, it can be left at the gate.' Her aunt nodded, not completely satisfied, and Anna thought that it was not something evil in her demeanour but a primitiveness in which every form of morality, of self-doubt, of intelligence, was alien: when there was no more to say. Aunt Martha left with her great breadth, having entirely fulfilled her role as amiable aunt who, concerned, had searched for her hungry niece with the nuns. Flabbergasted, Anna remained behind. What drove her to the convent? It could not be charity. Was she trying to bring inside the fencing the sheep that had escaped from her influence ten years ago? Did she still need a cheap source of labour, someone on whom she could indulge her destructive tendencies?

Nothing was delivered to the gate. Rather, Anna met people from the village more often, who brought her up to date, in fragments, with how her aunt had led her sordid, unpalatable life. While Uncle Heinrich had been fighting on the Russian front, his wife, it seemed, had to have turned out to be the most disreputable black marketeer in the whole area. Unhampered by sympathy, she had taken everything the refugees from the towns possessed – a jewel, table silver, a tobacco box, a portrait in a gilded frame – for an egg, a piece of bread. She made every piece of bread pay four times over. She was respected and admired in the wider district; hunger was stronger than fear. And the only one who could have put the brakes on her was now a prisoner of war in Russia.

The latest item of news that reached Anna was so bizarre that initially she burst out jeering. But her laughing very soon turned into an unchristian anger that contrasted painfully with the tranquillity within the convent walls. Aunt Martha was broadcasting it that she was financing her niece's studies at the Institute for Social

Work. If you thought you had seen everything after a fashion and had coped with it you were immediately punished for your naïvety. The squirms of a perfidious spirit – again it was succeeding in upsetting Anna's barely regained peace of mind; it was proceeding as usual, as though she had never been away.

But the influence of the intervening years did make itself felt. Anna crossed the meadow landscape of her youth at a brisk walking pace – no hills or mountains but fields as far as the eye could see. She was not burdened by melancholy or nostalgia – her resolution shut out all other feelings. She avoided the elder tree and the Mary chapel by the bridge over the river; encountering the farm again and the grown-up children did not disturb her equilibrium. She burst into the kitchen unannounced and seized her bewildered aunt by the blouse with both hands, at the height of her bosom, 'So, you are paying for my studies!'

'Please, please, what's the matter...' Aunt Martha's eyes narrowed with fear, like a vicious cat grabbed by the scruff of its neck. 'What are you paying, how much, since when? Well?' Her aunt's greedy mouth dropped open, closed and open again. No words emerged, only incoherent protesting. Anna continued unperturbed, without sympathy, without triumph. 'Do you really know how much you owe me? You owe me my youth, you owe me everything! I'll turn you in! I'm telling you. If you don't retract the lies you have been spreading all over the place, officially in the newspaper, I will set the police on you!' 'Please ... please...' She wriggled free, nervously looking for a way out. 'Paper!' Anna commanded, 'bring me a pen and paper.' With revolting servility, Aunt Martha brought her what she had asked for. Anna smoothed the paper flat on the kitchen table, pushed the pen into her hand and dictated in forceful High German: 'I, Martha Bamberg, withdraw the remarks made by me about the studies of my niece, Anna Grosalie-Bamberg, in Salzkotten. When I made out that I was paying for her studies I was not speaking the truth.' Anna checked the text, altered some writing mistakes and ordered her aunt to place the retraction in the local paper. Although in the corner of her eye she could see the draining board and the stove, two of the fixed reference points from her youth, from a time of serfdom, she did not deign to look over the whole mess. She closed the door behind her and walked across the yard without turning round.

With her hands clenched into fists she marched back across the fields. She would let nobody trifle with her any more, Anna Grosalie, war widow, Red Cross sister, training to be a social worker in child welfare. The pathetic creature that should have succumbed to tuberculosis, cancer or a bombing raid a long time ago would let nobody trifle with her any more – she was studying subjects the names of which Aunt Martha would not even have been able to pronounce.

But the fanfare of triumph became blurred, because above her head in the rustle of the poplars she could hear the hoarse lament of herself as a girl of twelve. She slowed down. She realized that, irrespective of the sweetness of revenge, irrespective of the number of children she would support in the future, she could not protect with retrospective strength the child she herself had been. That child had permanently, irrevocably been handed over to Aunt Martha's will, she would have free disposal of her until eternity. The idea of repayment was ridiculous in relation to a rudimentary soul that would never be able to think in terms of good and evil – the most she was capable of was to recognize that Anna was the stronger one now. A pyrrhic victory.

New teachers braved the obstacles of public transport to bring the group of chosen ones at the Institute into contact with such unfamiliar disciplines as the law of guardianship. Anna's thoughts went back involuntarily to the peddlers of the sterilization order and the guardianship declaration in which for years Uncle Heinrich had written that she was a bit simple-minded and frail. What kind of judge had he been in fact, if it had never occurred to him to send an inspector to the farm? To find that out she presented herself at the district court. The judge from that period seemed to have been replaced by a new one immediately after the war, a young man who presided there dejectedly as though he had been locked up in the heart of a pyramid with the job of finding the exit.

'How is it possible?' he sighed, when Anna had explained the story to him. 'That's what I am asking you,' she said, 'how is it possible? And why, please?' The judge played with his fountain pen for a moment. 'The law to which you allude...' he said thoughtfully, 'had at that time to prevent congenital disorders being passed on, by seeing to it that affected persons were sterilized. A judge in the Nazi period, sitting in this chair...' he faltered, '...had to prove that he was a Nazi by actively co-operating. If he said: there are no simple-minded cases in my district, then he put himself under suspicion. Whereas if he offered such a case, a poor child, moreover an orphan: there, thank God, he had something in black and white.' He laughed shamefacedly. 'Might I see that declaration?' said Anna. 'Of course,' he said, 'it must be somewhere in the archives. We will find it and send you a copy.'

But the declaration seemed to have disappeared without trace. She received a letter a fortnight later: the declaration preceding hers was still there, properly preserved, the declaration following it too – but hers was missing. Who had allowed her declaration to disappear, when, why, could not be found out. If Uncle Heinrich survived Russia she would not be able to go to him and push the declaration under his nose. The truth about her youth, including the lies, could only be found in the archive of her own parrot-memory now, where nothing ever disappeared for inexplicable reasons.

Aunt Martha's retraction did indeed appear, clearly legible in the newspaper. Anna's satisfaction about it quickly ebbed away in the middle of the metre-long roll of lining paper, the Dead Sea Scroll of social work, that had to be studied for the examination. She became acquainted with Freud and with the significance of the first six years of life. She thought about her father for the first time in a long while, in that context, about his cough, the tapping of his stick on the cobbles, his black coat, his hat, his pride when his daughters succeeded at something, his suppressed sadness when he could no longer take them onto his lap. The memories came in waves, that all-recording memory of hers did not spare her. She had to remember Lotte now too. Together in the bed, together in the bath. The self-evident inseparability, as though it would remain so in the years to come. Whispering in bed in the evenings, competing for their father's attention during the day – he could not simultaneously give both of them affection or reprimands. They had each developed their own talents and characteristic attributes in the competition for their father. Anna her legendary memory in the art of recitation, her empathy with a poor girl (a good exercise for later) on the stage in the casino, and her irrepressible vitality: running, jumping, falling, groaning, screaming. In contrast to all that commotion, Lotte presented her singing. With childlike veneration for her own voice she directed her songs up high to the round dome in the hall and listened to the reverberation with amazement. When she was not singing she was silent and compliant – her way of gaining her father's special protection, such that Anna, in her jealousy, ran, jumped, fell even harder. The more Anna remembered, the more her interest grew. These two people who had been her closest and most intimate family aroused an academic curiosity in her. Or was it longing, a profound, rash longing, now that she had been left alone more emphatically than ever before?

Old acquaintances spoke to her in the street to tell her that Uncle Heinrich was back and to describe, each in their own rhetoric, what sort of effect Russia had had on him. He was back, he was alive! An irrational, ambivalent excitement came over her: she did not want to see him, she wanted to see him. The image of Uncle Heinrich back from the event at Bückeberg came to mind: shocked, speechless, full of fear and loathing. He had seen visions of what was to come, in the perfectly recorded Great Germanic harvest festival, in the enthusiasm of the crowd, in the inflammatory, hyp-notic language of the Führer. He knew it but could not prevent himself being sent to Russia as part of the same stage directions. It was so poignant that her heart would have winced, if all the other things had not already existed in contrast. She did not want to see him, she wanted to see him. She wanted to ask him for clarification about the guardianship declaration. She wanted to say to him: my husband was in Russia too. She wanted Lotte's address, which she had lost, and her father's books, a row of bound German classics – the only thing he had bequeathed to her. She wanted to show: look, the simple-minded, frail child is still alive, she is a tough one – surely we did have a bond, once, or have I imagined that?

When she realized she would never be able to manage not to go, she borrowed a bicycle and went. She had carefully chosen Sunday morning. Her aunt, who ignored God's commandments, never missed a high mass. Anna had gambled well, the house was empty except for the small living-room, where she found her uncle by the stove in the chair where his father had slowly died, a little more each day, beneath the print of the dead soldier. She had pre-pared herself for this, that he would be thinner, but what she encountered in that history-laden, genetically determined spot was an emaciated old man who looked at her without seeing her, with a hollow, faded gaze. A thin neck poked out of his shirt collar, nar-row wrists emerged from the sleeves of his jacket, his fingers hung snapped on the arm rests. His stiff blonde hair had gone grey, a bony skull shone through it. Nowhere was the young uncle recog-nizable, the muscular farmer's son who parodied Christmas carols in Cologne. She greeted him shyly. Did she detect a reply in a very slight nodding of the top-heavy wrinkled face? The next obvious step would have been to ask him how he was – a question, she now understood, that would demonstrate obtuse lack of feel-ing. A sour air hung in the stuffy room, just as before she had sensed she could not breathe in there. But he sat in silence; it even looked as though he rather blamed her for something. The things

375

she had wanted to say died in her mouth. She moistened her lips. 'Uncle Heinrich...' she began. He did not react. How should she continue? To start with the declaration was impossible in these circumstances; Russia was a painful subject, Lotte taboo. The only one to occur to her as tangible, not dangerous, was the row of classics. 'My father's books...' she said hurriedly, 'you remember: Schiller, Goethe, Hofmannstahl ... I would like to take them with me.' A miracle happened: the head moved from one imaginary end of the horizon to the other. 'Why not...?' whispered Anna, but no further enlightenment followed. He looked at her, froze her out. She was suffocating beneath the low ceiling, between the oppressive walls, between two dead and one apparently dead. She turned to the door and fled.

She cycled back at a furious pace, oscillating between indignation and sympathy. You really would have thought that Russia had been an exercise in detachment – what did possessions matter if you were hungry, thirsty, in pain? But she corrected herself: don't you see that he is broken, a piece of ice from the tundra? Don't you see that all he can still say is a big square no to everyone and everything? This man, this shadow of a man, she would never again be able to call him to account, let alone ever be able to make peace with him.

A day later she was thinking differently about it. If everyone eluded her all that remained was the material. She decidedly wanted to have the books, her father's only tangible memorial. Once again she went to the district court. She got an official order, a written order to release the books. She made the pilgrimage to the farm for the last time. Nothing had changed inside. Although he did not speak he could still read. Respect for authority had been ingrained in him, first by his tyrannical wife, then by the army and after that by camp regime. He understood very well what the official document that he held between his fragile fingers contained. This time the top-heavy wrinkled head moved from the low beamed ceiling to the wooden floor and back. Anna lifted the books off the shelf above the sideboard. Clutching the pile to her chest she looked at him one more time, over the classics. *Faust* was on top. She looked at the desolate figure next to the stove and swallowed. Why was the Faust figure always masculine? Their Faust was in church with hands in prayer.

◆◆

They lost track of time and distance while Anna was doing the talking. They had already twice passed a crease in the map when Anna stopped in mid-sentence, clutched her heart with an almost pathetic gesture, and gasped for breath. Lotte stood next to her resigned. She recognized it. First running and jumping, then a broken arm or a tooth through the lip – first overwhelm the other under a torrent of words, then breathlessness.

'Let's . . . go back . . .' Anna uttered.

Lotte nodded. She actually gave her sister an arm; step by step they walked back on the winding paths to the rhythm of Anna's lumbering body and rasping breath. It struck Lotte that the return journey had taken an eternity, as she unloaded Anna in the lounge of her hotel. Coffee . . . Anna gesticulated, strong coffee. Coffee had brought her back to life before in the past. With a forced laugh she dropped into a chair, fanning herself with a waving hand. Her pale face was shining with sweat; she waited with closed eyes until her breathing calmed down. Lotte sat there sheepishly without worrying: Anna emerged from her own life story as indestructible, as someone who would make even death flee by telling it the frank truth, straight to its face. And sure enough, Anna slowly came to. Her eyes opened again. She was already looking at Lotte cheerfully and perceptively again.

'Entschuldigung, my body is a spoilsport from time to time . . . we're so comfortable here . . . please, order something yourself . . . Do you remember . . .' She made an effort to move closer to Lotte and lay a hand on hers. Stepping airily over her own body, which came to a halt now and then, as though over a fallen tree lying across the road, she said, 'Do you still remember, Lotte, when I came to look for you in The Hague?'

377

Lotte froze. But Anna waltzed on; it seemed as though she genuinely was in a hurry.

'But first I went to Cologne ... hoping that Uncle Franz was still alive, the only one who had your address ....'

Anna ordered a second cup of coffee. Two hotel guests went past looking at the noisy old lady with surprise. Lotte thought she could see aversion, yes, hostility in their gaze.

'Cologne...' Anna said dreamily, 'I shall never forget being on the east bank of the Rhine and looking right through the city to the west where the lignite factory chimneys stood out against the horizon. You could tell it was Cologne from the two spires of the Cathedral, which had miraculously been spared. There were still walls here and there, nothing in between. I was on the bank with some others – we looked at it but did not believe what we were seeing, because the city had always been there between the Rhine and the lignite factory. All the bridges had been destroyed. We were standing there and wanted to get over to the other side; a canoe paddled up to take us across as though it were a thousand years ago. Someone was waiting on the other bank with a cart for our suitcases and we began a journey along winding paths between the heaps of rubble and around the heaps of rubble, and people were living somewhere in a shelter or beneath the remains of a wall...'

Lotte listened uneasily. She felt a strong urge to go to her hotel. Not to have to hear, just for once, not to have to react to anything – to succumb to a languid Sunday afternoon feeling, no more.

'I wanted to see you, it had all begun there ... Of course I also wanted to know whether my uncle and aunt were still alive. They had been lucky, the hospital had been spared – they were not suffering from hunger, the English supplied the hospital plentifully with food. The only thing I could utter after the surprise of seeing them again was "I'm hungry". They made me a saucepan of rice pudding, I ate until I could eat no more. I got Aunt Elisabeth's address from them and thus eventually I came to you ... Gott im Himmel, I'll never forget that!'

While Anna was waiting for news from her great aunt in Amsterdam, of whom all she remembered was that she had separated Lotte from the symbiotic duality with surgical precision long ago, the anxiety suddenly crept into her that Lotte was no longer alive either. She remembered the successful bombing of Rotterdam at the start of the war – beyond that she had no idea what the war had brought about in Holland.

Some weeks later it appeared a little more rosy. Lotte was expecting her; in a cryptic letter she had assented to Anna's coming. From the train the destruction of the Netherlands turned out not to be as bad as expected. The meadows looked smooth and mown, the cattle looked well-fed in a picture postcard with bridges and church spires. The situation was less panoramic in the tram in The Hague. All seats were taken; the passengers were pushed against each other in the central gangway on each bend. A middle-aged man politely stood up for Anna. She flopped down with her inseparable stage prop, the leather suitcase, whispering 'Danke schön.' 'What . . . ?' cried the man in shock. 'You are a German! Stand up immediately!' Anna stood up, only half understanding what he was saying but understanding quite well what he meant. All faces turned accusingly in her direction. 'I understand you very well,' she apologized clumsily, 'I understand very well that you don't want to have anything to do with us. But I was not a Nazi, whether you want to believe me or not, I am an ordinary woman, my husband died in the war, I have no one else. I cannot say anything else to you . . .' There was a very telling silence around her. People turned away from her disapprovingly. Anna hung on tightly to the strap and sensed for the first time what it would mean to be a German from now on. To be found guilty by people who knew nothing about you. Not to be seen as an individual but as a specimen of a type, because you said *danke schön* instead of *dank u wel*.

But an unshakeable solidarity with her own history and the

lack of political awareness temporarily preserved her from the schizophrenia of collective guilt and individual innocence. For her, Anna Grosalie, this was a historic day. She was not so much a German as someone who, left alone in the world, was in search of the security of her first years of childhood. The ties of blood that were taken for granted by most people, that you could always fall back on, were for her something that had to be reconquered. She got out, stopped a passer-by and showed him the letter with the address, without saying a word. She would not let her own language cross her lips – perhaps he sent her in the wrong direction on purpose.

<hr />

'Those are the things you never forget in your whole life,' said Anna.

'You don't forget anything,' suggested Lotte sombrely.

'What a disillusion that was, my visit to you ... You refused to speak German, I could only communicate with you via your husband – in so far as there was contact at all. He translated everything I said, the brave soul, and the rare answers you gave.'

'No further word of German passed my lips. I had no more to do with that language. You might as well have spoken in Russian.'

'But surely that couldn't be so, your mother tongue! Even now you still speak it fluently.'

'Yet it was so.'

'It was psychological of course. You did not want to have to deal with me and you entrenched yourself behind Dutch ...' Now Anna became fierce. 'You have no idea how difficult it was for me. You were the only one I still had. I wanted to get to know you, I wanted to apologize for my behaviour when you came looking for me. I wanted to show that I had changed. But you were busy with your baby. A baby – that made it all the worse! You bathed the baby, fed the baby, combed the baby's hair ... You ignored me. I did everything to awaken your interest: I was thin air to you. Your husband was embarrassed with the situation. He tried to take care of it as well as possible ... Why didn't you rant and rave at me, call me everything under the sun, so I could have defended myself? But that evasiveness ... I did not exist to you.'

Lotte looked round with agitation to see if anyone was walking about whom she could pay for her coffee. She wanted to get away and as fast as possible. The longer it went on the crazier it got. She was even being called upon to justify herself now. The world was on its head. 'I hadn't asked for you to come, you didn't interest me.'

'That's true, I didn't interest you ... you had your baby ...'

'That child was my rescue,' she snapped at Anna. 'It reconciled me to my life ... my children are everything to me.'

Anna sighed despondently. Her sister was still unreachable behind the fortification of her progeny; she herself was still alone and childless, notwithstanding the hundreds of children she had helped in her life. She sensed a vague pain in her chest ... from the excitement ... stupid, stupid, stupid. Silly to have thought that she could still put anything right.

'Lotte, don't walk away,' she said remorsefully, 'it's all so long ago. Let's ... let's eat together, I'll treat you. It really is a miracle that we have found each other again, here in Spa, let's enjoy it as long as it can be ...'

Lotte allowed herself to be persuaded. What was she making a fuss about actually? It was Sunday evening, there was nothing she had to do. They transferred to the dining-room and ordered an aperitif.

'I've brought my sister with me,' Anna cried proudly. The waiter laughed formally. Lotte felt the irritation creeping up like an itch.

'When did your husband die in fact?' Anna asked, 'I liked him. He was serious, civilized ... refined, I would almost ...'

'Ten years ago,' Lotte interrupted her curtly.

'From what?'

'A heart attack ... overwork, all those years ...'

'Do you ever go to his grave? Or was he ...?'

'Sometimes...' Lotte refused any form of companionship here. She was not inclined to compete on this point – with an SS officer killed in action.

'I go twice a year, on All Saints' Day and in the spring, with a wreath and a candle.'

⊰⊱

Twice a year she was warmly welcomed by the mother and her daughter to commemorate the tragic death and the miracle of the survival. It gnawed away at her that the grave had not been blessed. She decided to speak to the unyielding pastor. She waited for him, straight after the mass, at which the holy commandment 'Love your enemies' had been the theme. He was still in full regalia. 'Father,' she buttonholed him, 'one of the three soldiers in the cemetery was my husband. We are Catholics, my husband and I, that is why I ask you to bless the grave.' He laughed scornfully. 'I do not care whether you are Catholics or not, they were in the SS.' 'But...' Anna reminded him, 'you have just been preaching: Love your enemies. He raised one of his heavy black eyebrows, which made him look rather mephistophelean himself, and sneered, 'I do not bless the grave of a member of the SS.' 'He had only been in the SS for a fortnight,' she cried, 'he had absolutely no choice!' In response to her emotional outburst the pastor cast her a dismissive look before leaving her where she stood and walking away down a dim aisle.

Blessed or not, from the first money she earned as an employee of the Cologne local authority she saved up for a headstone together with a sandstone cross with all three names chiselled on it. That was in place between the yews and conifers for a decade, well tended by the three women, until the end of the fifties, when the rumour was going round that the three soldiers were going to a newly laid-out military cemetery in a nearby village. In that case, thought Anna, I would rather take him to Cologne. She succeeded in getting a permit from the city council to have him interred in the soldiers' cemetery in Cologne. Thus armed she went to visit the pastor once again – the graveyard came under the church's jurisdiction. After she had informed him, formally and neutrally, of her intentions, and had shown him the permit, she left her address with him with the request to warn her when the grave was being emptied.

All Souls came round again and Anna made her ritual journey. A thick mist hung low over the earth; it smelled of wet leaves and chrysanthemums. Experienced, she pushed the squeaking gate open. She walked between graves with burning candles; the flames were motionless in the damp air. At the spot where her journey usually ended in wreath-laying and a prayer she found an impersonal square piece of grass with dry autumn leaves on it. Puzzled, she looked around. Had she walked the wrong way? My grave, she thought in panic, where is my grave? A procession was approaching along the mossy central path, enshrouded in the mist. The pastor was at the front in his chasuble followed by the villagers with their candles. It dawned on her. There he strode, the unbending representative of the mother church, in his solemn robes that were a harlequin costume on him. There went the uncharitable sanctimonious one, under whose direction people were going to pray for the salvation of the favoured dead. Perhaps he would be called to account one day, but she was not inclined to wait quietly for that. With large vengeful strides she walked up to him and stationed herself half-way along the path with her hands on her hips. The heavy eyebrows rose. 'Where is my grave,' she flung in his face, 'where is my husband, where is my headstone? After all, I gave you my address, you should have warned me!' The villagers stared at her in amazement. They knew precisely what Anna was talking about: she was their war widow. The pastor said nothing; he shifted his weight from one foot to the other and observed her disapprovingly, as though he had a hysteric in front of him. 'There's nothing there any more...' she cried, 'nothing...' She heard a ringing in her ears, the sound of her own voice disappeared into the background. She wobbled out of the way, overcome with dizziness, sinking down disrespectfully onto a slanting tombstone, her head in her hands, the wreath lost in the grass beside her. As the procession moved on an old woman knelt down by her and whispered: 'They were exhumed and taken to Gerolstein, to the memorial cemetery.'

Having come to her senses again, hours later in Gerolstein, she found no idyllic cemetery with mossy tombstones and crosses overgrown with ivy but a brand-new field divided into geometric squares. Parallel strips of white sand between vertical planks with numbers on them. She laid her wreath in the middle of the field of the dead. I am sorry Martin, she apologized, the wreath is for all of you now.

◆◆

'Crosses were erected later on there. The three soldiers are still next to each other.' Anna laughed. 'The fact that the three of them stayed behind instead of pinching apples has bound them to each other for eternity: It says "Unknown soldier" on many crosses. I still go there sometimes, mostly in the spring. The cemetery is high up on a hill, on the edge of the world, forgotten. It is quiet there. Sometimes mothers walk there with small children, because it is a peaceful spot. I sit on a little wall, right by the grave; they chat to me, ask me where I come from, why. Then I say: I am visiting my husband here. That terrifies them. They cannot place it any more, it was so long ago. Actually, nor can I either. In recent years I have asked myself: what am I doing here?'

Lotte nodded drowsily. She was drinking more wine than was good for her. The subject did not suit her. And Anna still went on with it, bringing yet more facts to light. That the death of a hero could have such consequences.

'Now I ask you,' Anna was imperturbable, 'why do we really believe that the spiritual existence of the deceased should still be connected to that one spot? Why do we go back there? Out of nostalgia? And whom does it benefit? The flower sellers, the groundsmen, the people who make headstones – there's a whole industry

connected with it. It's their livelihood, and that's why we still come
... Do you want to be buried?'

'Me?' Lotte started. 'Of ... of course,' she stuttered. With an
inappropriate frivolity provoked by resentment she said: 'I want a
grave full of wild flowers ... I have five children and eight grandchildren to care for them.'

'When I die there will be nothing left of me,' said Anna being
contrary, 'then there won't be any public garden you can go to and
where anyone has to spend money to put flowers there. Who
would do that for me? Who would interest themselves in it? After
all, I myself won't be there at all.'

Lotte pushed her empty coffee cup aside and stood up slowly.
'I really must go now,' she murmured. It seemed as though the
alcohol had shifted all her weight to her head. She left the dining-
room with a top-heavy feeling, Anna busy talking behind her.

She grabbed her by one shoulder, breathing heavily; 'Do you
remember the day that ... mother ... was buried?'

'No, absolutely not.' Lotte hazarded a grab for her coat. No
more cemeteries, she implored silently.

'They had placed her coffin on the sofa. We had climbed up
onto it, to look out from the bay, to see if she was coming yet. Our
feet were resting on the window sill. We drummed loudly on the
window with our patent leather shoes because the waiting went on
so long, hoping she would hear it and hurry up. Indignant members of the family lifted us off the coffin. Only now do I understand
that we were sitting on top of her ...'

'Well...' said Lotte unmoved. For her there was only one
mother: the other one. She buttoned her coat and looked round
wearily.

'I'll see you out,' said Anna. Beneath the harsh ceiling light she
could see an expression midway between resignation and irritation
on her sister's face. She remembered her father had looked exactly
like that in the latter days of his illness. That facial expressions
could have been inherited! She did not dare state her discovery out

loud. Lotte pushed off so swiftly, there could only be one reason for it: she had been too boisterous again.

With all the tipsy old lady's strength she could muster, Lotte pulled the heavy front door open. She hesitated on the doorstep. 'Sleep well,' she said weakly to the round figure who filled the doorway and still radiated an uncurbed vehemence.

'I am sorry I talked nineteen to the dozen today.' Anna put her arms round Lotte guiltily. 'Tomorrow, I promise, I will let my quieter side show. Sleep well, meine Liebe, schlaf gut und träum süss . . .'

That night Anna lacked the light-heartedness to fall asleep just like that. Images of funerals and cemeteries jostled each other. Her life had been punctuated by the dead, when she looked back over it, in the way that a cross-section of a glacier recalls the ice ages – how often it had given her life a brusque, harsh turn. She was full of a wonderful elation, as though something celebratory was going to happen. What else could it be but the apotheosis of the approaches she had been making for two weeks now? It was time for a proper reconciliation with her stubborn, squirming sister, discussed out loud. If the two of them, born simultaneously from the same mother, loved by the same father, would not succeed in stepping over silly obstacles tossed up by history, who on earth could do so? What was the prospect for the world if even the two of them, who were supposed to become milder in their old age, could not throw that one little stone?

She was oppressed, threw the blankets off and turned on her side. When it was almost morning she fell asleep despite herself. Her dream was populated with angels of diverse plumage. She recognized most of them at once, some only after thinking it over a little. With one exception they were operating together. The angels on either side of the steps to the Karlskirche left their plinths and flew, with strong beats of the wings and rustling robes over the green dome into the clouds, grasping the crosses to their breasts. The graceful female guards at the Thermal Institute stepped off the porch and flew after them. Up above, on a gold-fringed cloud, lay the two naked women who normally reclined on a shell-like decoration in the hall; the one strenuously tried to catch they eye of the other who was (deliberately?) looking past her pensively. The pink reflection of the setting sun touched all the faces. Behind, where the night announced itself in deep purple, a figure suddenly dived from a great height, gliding down in a broad, black coat. He held his hat down on his head with one hand, he clutched a walking stick in the other. Two plump children followed astride a fish, making use of the slipstream behind his wide flapping coat. Anna thought she vaguely remembered coming across them perfunctorily on a monument to the famous people who had visited Spa over the centuries: a cherub sat on a fish with a malevolent expression, on either side of a stone frame with the names.

After that it was night. Nothing flew past offering a distraction except by the light of the moon an unexpected angel, no, eagle, which cleaved like a thunderbolt through the blackness that was exactly as deep and absolute as the black-out nights had been in the war. Anna tossed onto her other side, which abruptly deprived her – released her from her dreams.

4

A cord hung above the decorative curved copper bath-tub with a handle that said 'Pull' in four languages. When the alarm clock gave the signal that the prescribed time was up, a short tug by the bath guest brought the arrival of a woman in a white overall, who helped with getting out and drying.

Lotte's final week had begun with a peat bath and a carbonated bath. She was resting, swathed in a towel; glasses of Spa-Reine were also cleansing her within. Silence reigned as in a padded cell. No sound whatsoever penetrated from the outside world, as though the complex of bathrooms lay in caves deep beneath the Hoge Venen, right at the source of the springs.

But the silence was rudely interrupted. Somewhere nearby somebody cursed: 'Mon Dieu!' Hurried footsteps in the corridor. A scream immediately suppressed. Her door was thrown open; the woman in the white overall stood on the threshold wringing her hands. 'Madame, madame ... since you were always together ... venez ... votre amie ...'

Lotte slid into her slippers and followed the woman to one of the adjoining bathrooms where the door was wide open. Inside, the doctor was being summoned. Someone ran out blindly and almost bumped into Lotte. She took two steps on the tiled floor. At first she could only see the broad back of the woman in front of her, who then stepped aside ostentatiously to allow her to see what had not passed her lips.

Anna was staring at her with glazed eyes out of a peat bath – it looked as though she had been decapitated, or her body had sunk for ever into the deep brown morass while her head had remained, forced up by the muddy mass. She was staring at Lotte with a gaze that lacked all the emotions: excitement, irritation, scorn, rage, sorrow ... a total absence of all those feelings that had alternated kaleidoscopically with each other for two weeks and together had formed the complexity called Anna. The most oppressive thing was that she was so obviously silent ... that she was not explaining what had happened to her, according to custom, talking energetically and gesticulating. Lotte looked around, orphaned. It was a bathroom like all the others, warm and damp. Had she become breathless? The light blue tiles ended at the top in a border with shell motifs – this was the last thing Anna had seen. Had it reminded her of the Baltic Sea where she had almost drowned, together with her husband ... where, subsequently, she would have preferred to have drowned ...? This was the last Anna had seen – just before then she had been alive and had got into the bath as vital as always. A macabre, tasteless joke was being played on her ... Next thing she would start to move again: Mein Gott, what a ridiculous situation this is ...!

A doctor rushed in followed by a rescue team. 'What is she doing here?' one of them protested. 'This is no time to let a guest in.'

'But she is her friend ...' stammered the nurse who had alerted Lotte.

Lotte moved back, away from that empty hollow gaze where only a heartbreaking nothing still came out, away out of all that unexpected, ultimate intimacy that Anna had involved her in without asking her.

The nurse came running after her. 'Excusez-moi madame ... I thought you ought to know immediately ... Perhaps ... perhaps they can still help her ... Sometimes wonders are done with resuscitation ... We have to wait ... Where are you going now?'

'To the Salle de Repos,' said Lotte hoarsely, 'I ... think I ought to lie down for a moment.'

'Of course ... je comprends ... I will keep you informed ...'

Apart from the busts of two professors who had contributed

much to the development of healing baths, and a solitary female figure who walked through a deserted landscape in a large painting that dominated the whole room, there was no one in the rest-room. Lotte flopped down on a bed at random. Too late, too late echoed in her head. She realized that she had constantly taken for granted the luxurious presumption that she still had all the time in the world. And now, all of a sudden, on a Monday morning, with one week still to go, Anna had taken herself off from that scenario. How was it possible . . . ? Anna, indestructible Anna, who never ran out of talk and not just because of that always seemed to have eternal life . . . Like Sam and Moos in the joke with which Max Frinkel kept morale up in the war: Sam and Moos, only survivors of a shipwreck, answered the question, 'How did you manage that?' with busy gesticulation reminiscent of a dog-paddle: 'We went on talking as usual.'

Outside the doves were cooing, as always. Everything was as it always was, only now something essential was missing. Fourteen days ago she did not yet exist for me, thought Lotte, and now will I miss her? Yes, roared the silence in the Salle de Repos, admit it! 'Tomorrow, I promise, I will let my quieter side show,' Anna had said. That airy promise was now coming about in a sour, ominous daylight. Whether she opened or closed her eyes, Lotte still saw that one frozen image before her. They had not been able to say goodbye. There was so much I still wanted to say to her, she thought, in a crescendoing feeling of remorse. Oh yes, what then, cried a cynical voice, what would you have said to her if you had known what was going to happen? Something nice, something that spoke of involvement, something consoling, perhaps? Would you ever have been able to say to her what she actually wanted to hear, which had come to mean everything to her? Would you ever have succeeded in squeezing out those two words: 'I understand . . . ?'

Those two words, apparently so simple, so revolutionary for Lotte, assembled in her throat as though she still wanted to propel them out – now that it was too late, too late, too late. Instead of that she began to cry, noiselessly and discreetly, entirely in keeping with the atmosphere in the Salle de Repos. Why had she remained stuck all that time in the resistant position she had adopted from the beginning? Although she had gradually acquired more and more understanding of Anna, and sympathy, she had remained fixed in unapproachability, intentionally obstinate. Out of misplaced revenge, not even intended for Anna? Out of solidarity with the dead, her dead? Or out of a deeply engraved mistrust: beware the apology 'We did not know', beware of understanding – you could even understand a hangman if you knew his background.

Her powerlessness flowed down her cheeks – too late, too late. The cooing of the doves sounded increasingly like mockery to her ears. Irrevocably too late. To escape from herself she raised the blinds and looked at the grey courtyard hiding behind them, the doves' domain. As she stared outside from behind the glass she recalled the memory Anna had wanted to share with her the previous evening, right at the very end. She saw herself, with an intensity as though it had happened the day before, sitting on a coffin on the sofa together with her sister and tapping on the window with her shoes – a tamtam to demand their mother to make haste. She saw two pairs of sturdy legs, white socks, shoes with bows. They pattered exactly in time, as though together they had one pair of legs – not only to warn their mother but also to drown out the din of the strange voices behind them and in order to keep an unbearable reality at a distance. She looked sideways at Anna's blonde head, her tightly closed lips were pursed and fierce eyes cast her a conspiratorial look.

Too late! Lotte let go of the blind. The door opened at that moment and the woman in the white overall, her personal angel of death, tiptoed in.

'Alas...' she clasped her hands together, 'they could not do any more for her. The heart, ah. We knew ... it was in her dossier that she had a weak heart and that we should not make her bath too hot ... Do you know if she had family? Someone must organize

her transport to Cologne and the funeral ... We don't know ...
After all you were her friend ...'

'No ...' said Lotte, straightening up. Her gaze fell on the bottles
of mineral water and the stack of plastic beakers. Again she heard
Anna asking in school French, 'C'est permis ... for us ... to drink
this water?' And again she heard herself replying, from an intuition
the consequences of which she only now accepted: 'Yes, das
Wassser können Sie trinken.'

'No ...' she repeated, looking at the woman defiantly, 'I am ...
she is my sister.'